John Bowles, Richard Hooker Wilmer

The Stormy Petrel

An Historical Romance

John Bowles, Richard Hooker Wilmer

The Stormy Petrel
An Historical Romance

ISBN/EAN: 9783337347819

Printed in Europe, USA, Canada, Australia, Japan

Cover: Foto ©Andreas Hilbeck / pixelio.de

More available books at **www.hansebooks.com**

THE

STORMY PETREL

AN

Historical Romance

BY

COL. JOHN BOWLES

NEW YORK
A. LOVELL & CO.

LONDON
WALTER SCOTT

DEDICATION.

TO
AN INTELLIGENT
AND UNITED PEOPLE, NORTH
AND SOUTH, WITH ONE COUNTRY, ONE
FLAG AND ONE COMMON DESTINY, THIS LITTLE
VOLUME IS IN THE UTMOST FRATERNITY
AND WITH THE GREATEST
PLEASURE, SINCERELY
DEDICATED.

PREFACE.

On looking backward from the present time it is difficult to realize that almost half a century has passed since the events related in the opening chapter of this little volume occurred, and what wonders have been wrought by that master-magician—Time!

On the banks of that great river where the little Petrel, bound by law to a merciless master, was cast, before the wondering gaze of the author, upon the troubled waters of a stormy life, there now waves the flag of freedom for all men, white and black alike, encompassing within its sacred folds the lowly and the lofty, the rich and the poor, from the Gulf of Mexico to the St. Lawrence, and from the Atlantic to the Pacific.

The angry passions of the border strife, then just awakening into fury, have well-nigh burned out, after a terrific contest of four years and the more than twenty-five of recuperation and repose.

The North and South are better acquainted, and hence better friends, with juster estimate of each other's attributes. The South no longer accuses the North of cold, commercial "cowardice," nor does the North speak sneeringly of Southern "bluster and braggadocio." How far from the truth were these epithets recent history recounts. If love of country and determination to defend with life and fortune cherished and sacred rights, as understood by each, if these be patriotism and heroism, then was this country, North and South, filled with patriots and heroes of the highest order.

The contents of this story are in a great measure reminiscent, and the impelling motive in writing, or rather in publishing it, has been to do justice to characters whose acts and motives have been too long and widely misunderstood.

Since the passions of the hour, together with many of the chief actors have passed away, the author feels at liberty to do this act of justice to the memory of the innocent, without harm to the guilty or fear of giving pain to the misguided of either section. In dealing with historical events, the author has been careful to state only what he knows personally or has upon reliable testimony; while in that which relates to the Southern people, he has quite naturally, being himself a Southerner, earnestly striven to be fair and just. Having but few friends to reward, and no enemies to punish, there has been nothing extenuated, nor aught set down in malice.

J. B.

THE STORMY PETREL.

CHAPTER I.

ONE stormy day in November, 185–, at a point not far from the confluence of the Mississippi and Missouri, a man could have been seen walking with rapid, swinging gait down the steep bluff of the western bank of the river. His tall form was enveloped in a capacious fur-trimmed overcoat and top-boots, while a soft felt hat was drawn well down over a handsome face, the cleanly-cut lines of which were only partially veiled by a brown beard and mustache.

He paused for a moment, and gazed intently upon the scene. Ragged islands of floating ice, of every imaginable shape, covered the surface of the great river, which glided serpent-like on its devious way, with these great, glistening scales upon its back, as if eager to meet its mighty rival, the Mississippi, which, clad in like polar coat-of-mail, was waiting only a few miles beyond. There these giants would meet and grapple, rush on and on in fierce struggle for the mastery, each maintaining its separate and distinct life until melted and forced to mingle under the burning sun of the Gulf of Mexico.

After pausing for a moment to enjoy the wild spectacle, Frank Clayton walked on rapidly, as if to keep pace with some great section or continent of ice, that now stood on end, and again on one side, till at last, with a thundering swash, it was merged into the mass of its fellows.

The table-land extending along the opposite bank of the Missouri shut out the view beyond, until circumscribed to the limits of the little county town of St. Charles, with

its red brick court-house, its modest church-spires, a few
pretentious stores and dwellings, and the country inn, dig-
nified by the name Palace Hotel, while near it was the
ferry-boat, lying at the water's edge, now crowded by the
ice-gorge out upon the bank. There was no smoke-stack
to this wonderful craft, and only the semblance of a cabin,
with pilot-house perched on top. From the window of the
cabin stood peering out the motor-power of this nonde-
script boat, a mule, his long ears moving back and forth,
in defiance of, or opposition to, the war of elements, and
his sonorous voice at this moment raised to its highest
pitch, as if in protest at some new injustice.

As Clayton approached the dock, his attention was attracted to a strange group just embarking in a skiff, evidently intent on forcing their way across to the St. Louis
shore. He observed a large man standing in the stern of
the boat, which was still fast to the land, and holding
what seemed to be a bundle of some kind in his hands,
raised as if to cast it into the surging torrents of ice and
water that went roaring by. He heard distinctly the wail
of a babe and the angry oath of the man, calling out to a
few persons who were standing on the shore: "Here,
some of you take this damned brat, or by God, I'll throw
it in the river!"

Clayton saw that the brute was in earnest; and, springing
with a bound down the cliff, holding out his arms, he said
fiercely: "What are you doing, man! Are you a murderer?"

With a savage laugh, the trader, for such he was, tossed
the babe, which came spinning through the air, directly
into Clayton's arms, while from the stern of the boat came
a piercing cry, as of a broken heart; and he saw a woman's
form sink down, holding out her manacled arms in speechless agony. "Push off!" said the trader. "And some
of you look to that wench that she doesn't get overboard."

"No danger ob dat, massa. She done fainted, I 'spec,"
said one of the negroes.

"Throw water in her face, and she'll be all right,"
shouted the driver, as the boat pushed out from the bank,
the boatmen busy with pikes and poles, parting the ice to
prevent its crushing the frail craft.

All upon the wharf stood breathless, expecting to see

the boat and its contents swallowed up by the mad torrent, as they made toward the opposite shore. The shouts of the boatmen, the oaths of the trader, the cries of the frightened slaves, the shrieking of the wind, and the roar of the ice-floe, made confusion worse confounded.

Clayton stood spell-bound, watching the scene, and holding in his arms the little waif, while the frightened cries of the slaves became fainter and fainter as the boat receded, and the crowd which had gathered, dispersed.

The child seemed to feel the magnetism of Clayton's sheltering arms, for it lay perfectly quiet while he opened the wraps to look at the little creature so strangely cast upon his mercy. A pair of soft brown eyes looked confidingly into his, and he felt a strange thrill of tenderness as a tiny, warm hand closed trustfully over his finger.

"Poor little waif," said he; "poor little bird, which stress of weather has sent fluttering into my arms, like the little stormy petrel. I shall not disappoint you, my little Petrel! I shall protect you always." And somehow Clayton's eyes did not see quite as clearly as before.

And now, what was to be done? He thought at once of the motherly woman at the inn near by, and had soon placed his strange charge in the capacious lap of Tabitha Handy.

"Well, I never!" that good woman said when she had heard the story. "Well, I never!" she said again and again. "Why, it's as white as a snowflake!" And she adjusted her spectacles and critically examined the little one. "And she ain't no white trash, neither! Look at them hands and them ears, Mr. Clayton," said she, with warming interest. "Now, for the Lord's sake, what was it doin with them niggers and that tradin feller? Mr. Clayton," said she solemnly, "that child is stole! Sure as you're a born man, that child is stole!"

"It may be," said Clayton, thoughtfully. "And yet— no, that cry from the boat—such a cry as that could only have been wrung from a mother's heart."

Clayton stepped outside the door for a moment, to ask a question of some one who had observed these people, and might be able to give information concerning them, leaving Tabitha crooning in delight over the child.

"Mr. Clayton! *O* Mr. Clayton!" she called, with the

peculiar falling inflection of that phrase in southern lati-
tudes. "*O* Mr. Clayton!"

"What is it?" said Clayton, returning.

"What's her name? What will you call her?"

"Well, I don't know," said he, hesitating. "Petrel
will do," said he, after a moment. "Yes, call her Petrel."

"Petrel?" said Tabitha, "Petrel? Well, of all hea-
thenish names! But it's of a piece with the whole out-
landish business. There's been some powerful queer
things in my life, but this beats all I ever seen! Only
to think! She might er been floatin round under one of
them big cakes of ice,"—and at this point Tabitha addressed herself to the baby;—"stid er bein here so warm
and comfortable. And it's a beauty, so it is!"

There is, as everybody knows, a universal language—a
sort of baby-Volapuk—which is supposed to be adapted
to the infant understanding in all lands; and Aunt Tabitha was mistress of the resources of this language. She
chirruped and chuckled, and grew red in the face making
grimaces and sounds impossible to be represented here,
but which were supposed to be vastly entertaining to
Miss Petrel, who gazed in mild, unwinking wonder at
this new scene in a new world, with a calm superiority, as
if she might be saying, "What fools these mortals be!"

"Poor little dear, poor little dear!" And the warm-
hearted woman busied herself making a soft nest for the
storm-tossed bird, and clucked over her in as much delight as a hen over its one little downy chicken.

Clayton was impressed with the idea that the child had
been stolen; and yet the swooning of the slave and her
imploring words seemed to come from the pleading of a
mother's heart.

Every effort was made during the day to induce some
of the boatmen to ferry him over the river, but to no
purpose; for the ice was running thicker and faster than
during the morning. The captain of the ferry-boat, run
by mule-power, was a man of large river experience, and
advised against an attempt to cross with such a run of
ice. He said the night would be cold, and by morning
the river would bridge over. Then reckless men who
were willing to risk their lives were at liberty to do so,
"but he warn't goin to help em kill themselves."

So Clayton waited impatiently, till, on the following

morning, from his hotel window, he observed that the ice stood still in the river, and resolved upon the effort to cross and make his way to St. Louis as rapidly as possible, to learn the fate of the mother of the little waif who was snatched from the jaws of death.

"Stranger," said the captain, "hold that ere pole eggz-actly in the middle, and pick your way carefully along, so if you step through one of them infernal slush-holes atween them cakes of ice, your pole will hold you up, if you'll only stick to it, which I advise you to do closer an death to a dead nigger. It's your only salvation in a place like that. Don't try to go straight across, but kinder lean down to our dock, an I guess you'll come over all right."

Clayton made the perilous passage as a group of boat-men stood watching him from shore; and when safely landed found a conveyance, and set out for St. Louis. He met parties who had seen the slave-driver and the gang of negroes, and also the men who had ferried them over the river. One of them volunteered the information that the woman had been loaded into a wagon and hauled away, "talking like wild" about the baby, and "actin like she was boun ter kill herself."

"What color was she?" said Clayton. "Very light?"

"Kinder lightish copper-colored; I should say a mu-latto or about 'alf and 'alf," shouted one of the crew, who was evidently an Englishman.

CHAPTER II.

We will leave the Petrel safe in the care of Mrs. Handy, and Clayton on his search for the proper guardians of the child, while we briefly review the circumstances which led up to the dramatic incident related in the last chapter.

Frank Clayton's earliest home was a plantation upon the Rapid River in the Blue-Grass Region, where Nature seems to have lavished her richest treasures.

Major Lucas, his grandfather, was a gentleman of the old school, whose ancestors came over from England with Lord Baltimore and settled in Maryland. A son of the third generation emigrated to Kentucky and built the substantial Queen Anne house, with its antique gables, which was known as the Lucas Homestead. This stately old home contained relics, which were priceless heirlooms in the family, rich and rare enough to turn the head of the modern collector.

The tall clock upon the stairs, which had tolled out the happy hours of Frank's childhood, was of fabulous age, and the silver tankard and goblets upon the massive side-board, had been used upon festive occasions in the days of Queen Elizabeth.

In this home, the early days of Frank Clayton were passed with his widowed mother; and looking back to his idyllic childhood from the troubled days that followed, it seemed like a dream of Arcadia.

The Cherokee rose that climbed over the piazza, framed a living picture of mother and son—a picture always fresh and new. After two years of happy married life, Fanny Clayton was left a widow, but also a mother. The boy, who bore his father's name, seemed a treasure left to her care, for which she was to give an account; and so it happened that for the first ten years of Frank's life, he had for companion, play-mate, teacher and lover, this young mother, who left the strong impress of her own mind and character upon her son.

There is an insidious disease, which sometimes even in the genial climate of Kentucky, seeks its victims. Fanny Clayton may have inherited her ethereal loveliness from some remote ancestor, quite unlike the queenly daughters of her own State. Her fragile form became more and more slight, and the dark eyes larger, while a hectic flush deepened the color; and, in due time, consumption claimed its victim.

After the funeral, the house seemed so desolate, Judge Stanley, who was judge of the Supreme Court of Kentucky, took the little boy home with him to "Beechwood," where he shared with his cousin, Kate, Judge Stanley's only child, lessons from her governess.

With his dog and pony, he was Kate's escort and companion in exploring the beautiful woods that border "Rapid River," for "Beechwood" was only three miles from "The Glen," his former home.

It seemed hard to exchange these childish pleasures for the training of the military school. "But you must prepare, my dear boy," said Judge Stanley, "for the rough and tumble of life, as—who knows?—you may have to scale a fortress or lead a forlorn hope."

But instead of a soldier, Frank Clayton became a lawyer. He was naturally a student, and adopted the scholarly profession of his uncle, attending law lectures at Louisville, and entering the office of Mr. Wyckliffe, a distinguished member of the bar of that city.

The marriage of his cousin, Kate, to Bernard Fletcher, summoned Frank to "Beechwood."

Judge Stanley, who loved and greatly admired his nephew, had long and secretly entertained the hope that in time, a marriage between the two cousins would unite the plantations of "Beechwood" and "The Glen." But Frank, with no slightest thought of sentiment for his charming cousin, excepting that of brother and protector, had observed what her father had not—that is, her growing interest in the handsome young Kentuckian, Bernard Fletcher. The two men were by nature thoroughly antagonistic—Frank, tall and slight, with deep-blue eyes, brown beard, and straight, Greek profile. His quick perceptions, strong sympathies, and keen sense of justice finding their soil in the temperment of a poet and an artist—to which was added a dash of the philosopher,

just sufficient to serve as an amalgam, to fuse the whole.
But Bernard Fletcher, dark-eyed and broad-shouldered,
who could ride like a Comanche, bring down with his
rifle anything that can fly, and could woo as well as he
could ride or shoot—picturesque—heroic—he it was who
had won Kate's heart.

And to tell the truth, that gentleman was not surprised,
nor did he consider it more than his due. He was in
love with Kate Stanley after his fashion, but was not at
all insensible to the fact that she was an only child, and
prospective owner of a splendid estate. In fact, he told
himself quite in confidence, that he had never met so
nice a combination of personal charms, broad acres, fine
intelligence, quick, warm sensibilities, perfect manners,
and most important of all—the bluest blood in Kentucky.
For be it known, this benedict was a patrician of the
patricians; and would have thrown over the woman he
loved, broad acres and all, and broken her heart into the
bargain, rather than abate one jot his ideas of caste.

"I tell you, my dear fellow," he would say, as he
watched the blue rings of smoke interlacing in delicious
curves over his handsome head, "I tell you, blood will
tell."

Frank had fixed his keen blue eyes upon him many a
time, as he delivered himself of this and other views of
life; but had said nothing, nor intimated to Kate that
he had small respect for the man who was to be her
husband. And so, the thin surface of decent amity was
never broken, although both men were perfectly aware of
the antagonisms and repulsions it covered. And so it
was that Frank made the best of things, and came on to
the wedding, which happened to be appointed for the
day commemorating also his twenty-first birthday.

The wedding festivities had passed away as they are
wont to do, with flowers, and laughter, and smiles, and
tears, and congratulations, and rice, and slippers; hearts
heavy, and hearts glad—and it was all over.

The last carriage had rolled away; Kate had lifted her
bright, though tear-stained face to be kissed by her father
and Frank, and the handkerchief which fluttered from
the carriage window had disappeared at the turn of the
road.

Judge Stanley and his nephew came back into the now

deserted house, both silent and oppressed with its still-ness. Each tried to hide the gloom he felt at sight of the scattered flowers and confused traces of the recent scene.

When the lamps were lighted, and they sat in the library, things seemed rather better. Judge Stanley said : " Well, my boy, I have not forgotten that this day is an impor-tant one for you, as well as for the rest of us. Twenty-one years old to-day," said he, musingly. " How time does steal upon us ! Why, it seems only yesterday that your mother—ah, well," and his voice trembled as he spoke, " well, well, Frank, now to business," and he put on his briskest tone. " Now, here," said he, opening a locked drawer, " here, Frank, is your grandfather's will, and the papers that secure to you the inheritance of his estate. I have done my duty as executor, and you now come into possession of the plantation of The Glen, and forty negroes. This makes you independent of any pro-fession. I suppose you'll keep Sparks as overseer ? "

" No, sir ! " said Clayton, flushing, and showing much feeling. " Uncle, Sparks is a coarse, unfeeling man, utterly unfit to hold power over these helpless creatures. Old Ned tells me——"

"Frank," interrupted his uncle, with some severity, " you are very inexperienced and have much to learn on this subject. If you want to spoil your negroes utterly, consult with them in this manner, and allow them to crit-icise white people. It is all wrong, my dear boy," he added, more gently. " Sparks is not a bad man, and he can get more work out of them, twice over, than you or I could."

" I have long been looking forward to this responsibil-ity, my dear uncle," said Frank, very steadily and very respectfully, " and I have resolved to manage my own hands for this year, if you will give me advice as I need it. I will organize matters at The Glen, and leave Uncle Ned in charge while I go to Louisville and make my ar-rangements for the change."

" Well, my boy, you will find these fine-spun theories do not work well ; but experience will be the best teacher. I will give you the benefit of my ten years on the plantation, if you are bent on trying this foolish experiment." And the old gentleman sighed as he went up-stairs in the great empty house. Kate's marriage was not the only thing which lay heavily on his heart.

"Foolish boy, foolish boy," he said to himself. "He has a good heart, though I am sorry to see it run away with his head in this matter. But he will grow wiser. I cannot control him any longer, but time and experience will."

CHAPTER III.

THE old routine of life at " Beechwood," was restored after the wedding, "and still the days rolled on," as they will, be they good or be they ill.

Kate and her husband were abroad and would not return until late in the fall; so Frank spent much of his time at " Beechwood," and more and more entrusted Ned with the affairs at " The Glen."

Kate's letters were the chief events in their quiet life, and one was read and discussed until its successor arrived.

Frank had had many misgivings concerning this marriage, and scanned these letters very closely " between the lines," at first, to discover any incipient signs of disappointment or disenchantment; but no, Kate was happy. There could be no doubt of that, and she was deeply in love with her husband, too—that was equally clear.

Her choice had seemed to him a miserable mistake; but he tried to believe it was going to turn out for the dear girl's happiness after all, and was careful to speak of Bernard always with the greatest consideration to his uncle.

It would not be very long now before they would be at home, and then Frank would have more time for his own affairs, which began to press more and more seriously upon his thoughts and attention. He sat, one afternoon, upon the piazza, as was his custom after their early dinner, but his eyes were wandering from the book he held, down the road, with more and more frequency. At last he said to his uncle, " I cannot understand what detains Ned. He was to have returned at one, and now it's three," said he, consulting his watch. " Two hours behind time. I think I'll ride down and see what's the matter."

A few moments later his handsome black mare " Stella," enchanted to exchange the dull dim monotony of the stable for the road, the wind, and the sunshine, was speeding her master toward the ferry, in quest of the missing servant and team. She seemed to think she was out for a race with the wind.

"Steady, steady, my girl," said Clayton, reining her in gently, and laughing at her exuberance.

To be riding such an animal on such a day, through one's own broad acres, and with splendid youth in the veins, was it not enough to make one feel mere existence a joy? and Clayton was conscious of a kind of elation in sympathy with the mare, as she sped swiftly through the cool afternoon air.

Things were going very smoothly with him. He did not miss Sparks at all. His uncle had looked in vain for the trouble and insubordination he had prophesied. No one could wish troubles for those they love, and yet, one does not like to lose all *prestige* as forecaster of the future! And never had the affairs of the plantation run as smoothly as under this new *régime*.

Upon arriving at the ferry, Clayton learned that Ned had loaded up his grist and then started for home a little after twelve o'clock, intending to stop at the blacksmith's by the way.

So there Clayton followed him. To his surprise he found his team tied to a post in front of the shop, but no Ned, and upon inquiry was still more astonished to learn that his servant "had done got into trouble with Sandy Guiton," and was now under arrest and in charge of a constable "up to the Squire's house."

"Who is this Sandy Guiton," said Clayton, "a negro?"

"No, sir," said the smith, with a good deal of spirit. "No, sir, he's a gentleman, and if you——"

"Where can I find him?" said Clayton, impatiently.

"At the shooting-match, I reckon, seeing as how he's the best shot in the county."

And sure enough, there Clayton found him, a few minutes later but too busily engaged in getting his number of shots in for the beef to have anything to say about this matter until the match was over; and all Frank was able to ascertain was, that there was to be a hearing of the case at the conclusion of the match "up to the Squire's house."

While these researches were being made, Clayton observed a whispered conference going on between Sparks, his discharged overseer, and Ben Baugh, who seemed to be master of ceremonies at the match ; and it was easy to see, from sundry glances and gestures, that he, Clayton, was the subject of the conference.

A few moments later Ben lounged up to him, with an air intended to be very casual, and said, " Stranger, we are going to shoot for them ere turkeys soon. Wouldn't you like to take a chance ? "

" Thank you," said Clayton. " I am not here to take part in the match. I am on more important business."

" Ah ! More important business, eh ! Wall, we kinder think this is right peart and interesting business itself. Howsomever, what is it ? Maybe I kin help yer."

" I came to see about my negro man, who seems to have gotten into a difficulty with one of your party down at the blacksmith-shop."

" I see, I see. Then that's your sassy nigger what struck Sandy, is it ? Wall, I reckon yer'd better leave him in the hands of the Squire, till he gives him a lesson in perliteness, an teaches him how to treat white folks. Pears to me, yer'd better give him some lessons of the kind at home, an' then p'raps twouldn't be necessary to rub em in under his shirt."

" My man is esteemed a very well-behaved and respectful servant, and I want no suggestions or insinuations from you as to how I should teach my slaves their duty to any one."

" Yer seem d—n techy bout this sassy nigger. If yer take my advice and know when yer in good health, yer'd go home, and let the law have its course. 'Twill do him a world of good and save trouble."

" I told you before, sir, that I did not need or desire any advice or suggestions in this matter. I would like to know, however, who saw this difficulty and what it was about."

" I seed it," said he, with rising temper. " And Jim Sneed, he see it too. He was standin by, and'll swar that the nigger struck at Sandy moren a dozen times, and hit him on the face oncet."

" Pardon me, sir, I should have to see that myself, before I would believe it."

" Makes a d—n little difference to me what yer believe,

sir, an I'd like ter know if yer mean to say you doubt my word.   Maybe yer'd better call me a liar, yer d—n abolitionist!   I'll war yer out on the yearth if yer say two words more to me."   This was in a *crescendo*, ending in that tone of rage and defiance so dear to the hearts of such assemblies, and succeeded in making the two men, at once, the central figures in an eager crowd just as Ben had intended it should; and then, turning to the spectators, who were pressing in upon them he said: "What der yer think, this d———d abolitioner has come down yer to defen and stop the whippin of that sassy nigger what struck Sandy down to the shop."

"Can't save that nigger's bacon, stranger; his shirt's gotter come off; and tain't healthy for yer to try and prevent it," spoke up promptly one of the crowd; and a dozen voices cried out: "That's so; them's my sentiments."

Encouraged by this Ben Baugh advanced to Clayton in a very menacing manner, and said:

"Now, stranger, yer got to leave here; we'r goin to take care of that nigger and sen him to yer to-night in pickle."

Frank looked the fellow square in the face, and calmly answered:

"I will wait until after the trial before I go."

It was growing more and more interesting to the men peering over each others' shoulders, and when Ben made a thrust with his great fist directly toward Clayton's white, set face, the "match" was forgotten.

But the attempt was neatly parried, and with his left hand Clayton swiftly dealt his burly adversary a fearful blow under the chin, which seemed to lift him from the ground, and he fell heavily, as if he had been shot.

There was a general rush, Ben was on his feet in an instant.   Blind with anger and the effects of the blow, he struck wildly at Clayton, who warded the attack with the skill of a professional boxer.   Soon another opportunity offered, and he dealt the ruffian a blow in the temple which brought him down a second time.

"Knock the d———d scoundrel in the head," shouted some of the friends of Ben, and a rush was made for Frank, who had been giving ground to the crowd.   Just at this moment a horseman dashed into their midst, and shouted:

"Stop! in the name of the law, I command peace! Another blow at your peril!" Then, dismounting, Judge Stanley stepped through the crowd of disappointed onlookers, and for the first time beheld his nephew.

"Frank Clayton!" said he, in utter astonishment, "you engaged in a rough and tumble fight with these men! What does it mean?"

"It does look rather disgraceful, sir," said Clayton, wiping his now flushed face with his handkerchief, and looking about for his hat. "But that ruffian attacked me, and I had to defend myself." Then, first looking around to assure himself that they were quite alone, the crowd having returned to the match, he told his uncle hurriedly about Ned.

"We will go right up to the Squire's office," said Judge Stanley, "and talk it over on the way."

They found Ned a sorry looking object. A deep cut over his eye and the blood still unwashed on his ebony skin.

"Why, Ned, what's the matter?" said the judge, kindly. "How did you get that cut over your eye?"

"Why. sah, hit was jes dis way. I was hurryin back to Mars Frank, coz he tole me he was mighty pusht for time ter day, an I jest stopt a minnit at the blacksmith's, when a white gentleman I never seen befo come in, an tole me, I musn't onhitch my team til after de match done be over—coz why, he wanted to drive home. Well, sah, of cose I couldn do dat, and so I said Mars Frank was waitin an I muss go right back wid de hosses, an when I stept up to ontie em, he up and struck me with his stick over de eye. Den, I was rested. Fo God, dat's de whole story, massa,"—and the old man, whose voice had been steady enough throughout the narration, had some difficulty now in saying these last words, and was evidently overwhelmed by the injustice of his position.

"On what complaint is he arrested, Squire?" inquired Judge Stanley, after a moment's silence.

"On the affidavit of Sandy Guiton that this man assaulted him and struck him twice."

"Bless de Lord, Massa Frank, I neber teched him; I tried to keep him from hittin me, but I didn't hit at him; no, sah, dey can't make dat out ginst me."

"Yes, Ned; but Sandy and Ben Baugh both say they will swear you struck Sandy, and he has a mark on his nose and chin."

"Must ave scratched hissef for sartin; I didn't do it."

"Squire Barker, I wish you would continue this case until Monday, and I will go this man's bail for his appearance at one o'clock that day."

"Certainly, Judge Stanley; I will do that to accommodate you, but don't you think it is a very aggravated case which ought to be punished promptly?"

"No, sir. There is some foul play in this case, and I know it. This is one of the most respectful, humble negroes in all Kentucky, and I want to protect him if I can from the lash." So it was that Judge Stanley with his nephew and the unfortunate Ned, returned to "The Glen."

The Judge and Frank sat till late that night conferring over the trouble.

"Uncle," said Frank, excitedly, "they must not, and *shall* not, whip Ned. It would be monstrous to add that to the injustice with which he has already been treated."

Frank had many times paced the length of that library since dinner, and more than once made his uncle repeat his reasons for thinking that Ned had no chance in the trial on Monday.

"But, uncle, several negroes stood by and corroborate every word Ned says."

"My dear boy, how often must I tell you, that goes for nothing. A negro cannot testify, and the blow you gave that ruffian Ben Baugh, will be returned with accumulated interest on poor Ned's shoulders. No, there's no way out of it. He's got to stand it."

"Well, it's damnable injustice," said Frank, fiercely, "and I, for one, am ready to cast my all into the pile which shall burn up such a cruel system."

"Tut, tut," said Judge Stanley; "Frank, my boy, you are intemperate in your language, and you will keep yourself in hot water all the time if you do not bridle your tongue. Of course, you do not mean——"

"I mean just what I say, uncle, that when I see such injustice as this, I am more than ever sure that a system which makes such things possible is iniquitous, and should not exist."

The old gentleman gathered himself to his fullest height as he rose to retire, and said, with a great deal of dignity, "Of course, sir, in this matter of Ned's, you will have my entire sympathy and co-operation; but, when your utterances become revolutionary, and subversive of social order, we must part company," and not waiting for a reply, he left his nephew to his reflections.

CHAPTER IV.

PROMPTLY at one o'clock on Monday, all were assembled at Squire Barker's house.

Sandy Guiton was first put on the stand.

He said, "he come by the blacksmith-shop on his way to the shootin-match, in company with Ben Baugh, and seeing the team driven by the nigger Ned hitched at the shop, he asked the driver how late he was goin ter stay."

At this point, Frank asked the court to exclude the other witness from the room, which request was complied with.

Sandy resumed and said the nigger answered him and said: "I'm goin home when I git ready. What d'you want to know my business for?"

"I told him," continued Sandy, "that if he was goin ter stay till after the shootin was over, we'd like to ride as far as he went our way. He give me some more of his sass, and I called him a d——d black nigger, and said he better mind, or I'd have him peeled."

"He said," resumed Sandy, 'no white trash in this country could do dat thing for him.' An he struck me a kinder glancin lick on the cheek here. He tried to hit me agin, an I struck him one blow on the head and brought him down."

"Is that all you have to say in this case?" asked the Squire.

"That's about all there was to it, Squire."

"Do you wish to cross-examine the witness, Judge?" inquired Squire Barker.

After a few minutes' consultation between Judge Stanley and Frank, the latter asked the witness if there were any other persons present when this difficulty occurred, and was answered in the negative.

"Are you quite sure there was no other person than yourself and companion?"

"I'm quite sure there was no one present, cept some niggers."

" You say you are quite sure there was no white person present during the controversy with the defendant ? "

" Yes, I said so."

" Now, tell us how you know the fact ? "

" Well, yer see, Ben, he looked all round and so did I, and we seed no one but these niggers I spoke of before."

" Why were you looking to see if there were' any white people around ? "

" Cause, if they'd been bout, I wouldn't er—er said anything to the nigger."

" Why not ? He would have been less likely to be impudent to you in the presence of several white people, than where there were only two ? "

" Oh, well, yer see every white man who seed it could swar to it an be a witness, and we didn't want but two witnesses to the row."

" Did you know there was going to be a difficulty ? "

" Not xactly; but we knowed Ned was a sassy nigger an would say something back."

" Then, we understand, you wanted to get into a difficulty with the driver."

" No, not xactly."

" We have no further questions to ask the witness, your honor," remarked Judge Stanley to the court.

Ben Baugh corroborated Sandy's story in the main, but was too shrewd to admit, as Sandy had actually done, that it was a preconcerted plan to get into a row with Ned.

After the evidence had been finished, Frank asked the court to hear the statement of the prisoner at the bar.

To this, the squire could not listen for a moment; it was not evidence, and was inadmissible.

" I want your honor to come to a proper understanding of the case before judgment is rendered ; and I am sure you could not listen to his plain, simple story without the conviction that he was telling the truth and that these two men have perjured themselves for a purpose."

" Whatever impressions I might receive outside of the lawful testimony could not influence the decision of this Court, which I am sworn to render in accordance with the law and the facts in the case," said the squire, loftily. " If the defence has no testimony, I will proceed to render the judgment in the case."

" We have no witnesses," said Frank, with a sigh.

"I will read the law upon this subject, if the defence desire it, before judgment is rendered."

"I think it is hardly necessary," said Judge Stanley. "I presume you will feel bound to enforce the law by the lash, as provided in the Code, which leaves no discretion except in the selection of the person who is to inflict the punishment."

These last words seemed to strike Sandy Guiton at once. He sprang to his feet. "I say Squire, why can't I do that? I'd like mighty well to be pinted to do that little job, and I'd do it mighty neat, too."

Frank Clayton's eyes flashed fire as he interposed.

"If the negro must be punished under an inhuman law, I trust your honor will, at least, designate a human being and not a brute to execute it. I would suggest that the constable who has the prisoner in charge, be designated to carry your sentence into execution."

"Don't you call me a brute," muttered Sandy, "or I'll go through you like——"

"Be silent," said the squire. "Constable Sampson, you will take the prisoner, and give him thirty-nine lashes on the bare back, in accordance with the law and the finding of this Court."

"God hab mercy on me," said Ned, bowing his gray head in his hands. "Oh, Massa Stanley," and he turned in agonized appeal to the judge. "Oh, Massa Stanley, you won't let dem do dis ting, I know you won't. You's a judge. *Can't* you sabe you ole serbant from sich disgrace? How kin I eber hole up my head agin?

"Massa Frank," and he turned to his young master in his extremity; but Frank was gone. Perhaps he could not bear to look on as the old man, with bowed head and reluctant feet, followed the constable to the barn where he was to receive the punishment.

There was a brief pause after they had disappeared within. It did not require much imagination to picture the scene, Sampson arranging the preliminaries, while the old man's trembling fingers were taking off his homespun shirt.

Judge Stanley, sick at heart, had walked away. Sparks was modestly in the background, while Sandy and Ben were in high glee over whispered jokes, of which Frank was evidently the subject,

But there was a look in Clayton's eye as he stood there with arms folded, face white and set, every nerve and muscle at the highest tension; there was something in his eye, which even these men did not like to meet, and which kept them from more than furtive glances at his motionless figure.

The nearer man comes to the brute, the more readily does he quail under this strange power of the human eye.

But they had not pictured *all* that was going on within that barn.

Frank had found an opportunity in the thirty seconds during Ned's appeal to Judge Stanley to say just these words to the constable:

"Sampson, don't be hard on the old man. He is innocent, and those scoundrels know it. This is only done to make *me* suffer. Make it light as you can, there's a good fellow."

There was no time for a word of reply; Frank had gone, and Sampson was pondering over the hurried, whispered words as he took the trembling negro to the barn.

"Now, Ned, off with yer shirt," and then, in a whisper, "and every time I bring the lash down on this ere bag o' wheat, you holler like you'd take the roof off."

Stupefied with wonder, Ned never moved. "Do as I tell you," roared Sampson, and then in a whisper: "Mr. Clayton asked me to make it light, an by —— I'll do it if it costs me my office. He done me a good turn last year when the sheriff was goin ter sell me out, and I ain't a man ter forgit such er kindness. If them durned fellers want somebody to hurt Frank Clayton over *your* shoulders they've come to the wrong place, that's all there is about it; I ain't their man for that job.

"Now, holler, jest as loud as yer can,"—bringing down the lash on the bag; "louder, *louder*, LOUDER! There now, kinder faint an tired out; now, like you was all worn out. There, that'll do." And then, laying the lash lightly thirty-nine times on Ned's broad ebony shoulders, just to keep within the letter of the law, the constable's official conscience was appeased.

"Now, put on yer shirt," said he, panting and puffing from the exercise. "But, for the Lord's sake, don't look like that. Why, you must pear like you was all cut up;

so there, that'll do. Now, if you ever let this git out,
I'll——"

The awful threat was not finished, for they were out in
the sunshine again and in full view of the group awaiting
them with such diverse feelings.

Frank's face flushed, and he looked eagerly at his servant. The crying in the barn was so well done he felt
afraid his appeal had done no good, but a curious twinkle
in the eye over Ned's old handkerchief reassured him.

They rode home, much of the way in silence, Frank
driving, with his uncle on the seat beside him, and Ned
sitting behind.

"The poor old fellow bore it very well," said the judge
at last, in a low tone.

"Yes," said Frank, drily, "he did;" and they lapsed
again into another long silence.

Frank was thinking unutterable things. These events
were hastening the growth of thoughts which had been
long germinating in his mind.

"Uncle," he said at last, "what can be done to prevent such injustice as we have seen to-day?"

"Well, I don't know. It's a hard case, but the law
must be respected and enforced."

"A law," said Frank, impatiently, "which permits such
things should be repealed. Why are there no legal en-
actments to protect these helpless beings from such
vicious creatures as Sandy Guiton and Ben Baugh?"

"What kind of a law would you enact for that purpose, Frank?" the old gentleman asked, a little scornfully.

"Why, I would make them competent witnesses in
courts of justice, for one thing."

"And so they are now as against a negro."

"Well, I should make them competent witnesses
against white as well as black."

"But, my dear boy," said the judge, striving to be
patient, "don't you see to what complications that would
lead? Don't you see that if a man's slave could bring
him into court and testify against him, there would be
continual litigation and end virtually the absolute control
of the slaves by the master? It would be recognizing his
rights as a man, and would be an entering wedge that
would end in the utter overthrow of slavery. There can
be no half-hearted, half-way measures in this. My dear

boy, your theories are impracticable, and however pleasant it may be for you to indulge in them, I advise you by no means, give expression to them in the presence of any person hereabouts. Your motives will be misconstrued, and get you into trouble. For instance, if those men we have seen to-day, even though they had no interest directly in slavery, were to hear you talk, as you have to me, they would get up a mob and run you out of the State as an abolitionist."

Frank realized they were drifting into the endless mazes of argument so often explored before, and which lead nowhere. His ideas must lead to *action*, not words. That was more and more forcing itself into recognition in his mind, and he did not speak again except of matters about which he felt quite indifferent.

As Ned climbed down from the seat behind, Judge Stanley put his hand kindly on his shoulder and slipping a crisp bank-note in to his hand, said, "There is something to buy a present for the old woman and the children."

"Oh, Massa, I can't—" But Frank unceremoniously sent him off with his scruples, saying to him as he went, in an undertone: "Remember, not a word."

"You may pen on me for dat for suah," said Ned. "I'll neber open my mouf on dat pint."

But the news of the flogging had sped swiftly to the plantation and there was awful wailing and lamentation in Ned's cabin, and when he opened the door his wife said: "Oh! My pore ole man, my pore ole man."

"Don't cry, honey, I aint hurt a mite," said Ned, soothingly.

"You ain't?" said she, looking at him with incredulous eyes.

"No, not a mite. Massa Sampson he gib me de lashes for suah, Liza, but de good Lord, he sent a angel what kep him from hurtin me. Ceptin de disgrace," said he, with a quaver in his voice, ceptin de disgrace!" and he hung his head.

"Was it a sure enuf angel, Ned?" said she, in a scared undertone. "*Did* de Lord do dat for true?"

"Yes, for true," and Ned nodded solemnly.

"How did de angel look, Ned?" said she, in awe-stricken whisper.

"For all de worl jes like Massa Frank, honey."

CHAPTER V.

KATE had returned to "Beechwood," and the radiance of her happy face had illuminated every corner of the solitary old house.

"How different everything looks since you came back!" said her father. "I declare, Kate, it was such a dismal place without you I really considered whether we had not better close the house and go to Louisville for the winter."

Kate laughed at the idea of anything being as pleasant as "Beechwood," in winter or summer.

"I really don't know how I should have stood it, if Frank hadn't helped me through.".

"Dear Frank," said Kate, "how good it was of him to come here. But then, Frank always does the right thing."

"I am not so sure of that," said the judge, laughing. "He is a splendid fellow, indeed, an extraordinary fellow, Kate. I admire and love the boy, but he is erratic—very erratic and headstrong; and we had some pretty stormy times while you were gone."

"Did you really, papa?"

"Yes. That is, he expressed himself imprudently on two or three occasions, and I felt obliged to rebuke him pretty sharply. You know he took an aversion to Sparks, and got it into his head that he would run the plantation alone, and I found——"

"Oh, Massa," said Sam, bursting unceremoniously into the room; then recovering himself—"Excuse, Massa, but dars trouble over to de Glen!"

"What's the matter?" said the judge, in alarm.

"It's about Uncle Ned, sah. De boy what brought de news is jist outside. Shall I call him in, sah?"

"Yes, at once!" Then turning to Kate—"Just as I told you—Frank is in Louisville, and now there'll be the devil to pay, and no one to look after——"

At that moment Sam returned with the ebony messenger from "The Glen."

"Well, what is it?" said Judge Stanley, a little fretfully.

The boy fumbled with his cap, while he scraped his right foot backward in the most approved fashion.

"It's about Uncle Ned," stammered he.

"Well, I heard that before. What about him?"

"Why, they've done cut him all up, sah."

"Who? What do you mean?"

"I donno who dey was, sah, but four men comd and took him outer his bed last night and carried him to de woods back er der house. Den dey fassened a corn-cob in his mouf,"—the boy was getting warmed up with the narrative and his round eyes looked as if they were about to be projected from his head—" and dey jes cut his back all ter pieces, and den dey trow salt water all ober him and go away an leab him."

"Monstrous!" said the judge, "those fiends ought to be——"

"He's in er awful bad way, no mistake, sah—wid a great gash in his head, too."

"Great heavens!" said Kate, trembling. "Papa, what's to be done?"

"Aunt Liza and de childen's nigh bout crazy," went on the boy, "an it seems like nobody knows what to do fus."

"Dick, send at once for Doctor Barnes, and here—this message," said he, writing on a slip of paper with the pencil attached to his watch-chain. "Send this to the telegraph office instantly, and have the horse harnessed for me to go to The Glen.

"I think I'll write to Frank, too; he'll get it in time, and the despatch is not explicit enough," and the old gentleman sat down to his desk.

"Papa, dear," said his daughter, laying her hand on his shoulder, "I am going with you to The Glen."

He nodded and went on with his letter, while Kate rang the bell for her maid.

In an instant the summons was answered by a tall, olive-skinned girl, with an air almost patrician.

"Do you want me, Miss Kate?" said she, with the soft, rich intonation of that latitude.

"Yes," said her mistress. "I'm going to The Glen; bring my wraps and—wait—tell Dick to fill a hamper with things for Liza and the children—a bottle of brandy, too," she called, in a louder tone, the girl being swiftly on her way to obey her instructions.

" Oh, how terrible ! " and she paced the floor, wringing her hands in distress.

Martha returned with the things, and stooping to put the overshoes on her mistress' feet, said : " It's a mighty bad day, Miss Kate, for you to be out.   I brought this for you to wear under your waterproof," said she, wrapping a fur-lined cloak about her shoulders."

" There, that'll do," said Kate, impatiently.

" Martha, tell Mr. Fletcher when he comes, that I've gone to The Glen ; and—don't forget to see that the fire burns brightly in his dressing-room."

Martha was fastening the waterproof at the neck as she said this, and Kate was surprised by a curiously pained look in the face opposite her, as a flush of deep red crept under the olive skin.   She did not speak.   Kate looked at her, puzzled at her silence.

" Did you hear me, Martha ? "

" Oh, yes, Miss Kate, I will see to it ; and Sam has the hamper in the carriage," said she, handing her mistress her fur-lined gloves.

" Papa," said Kate, as they were driving through the dreary fog and rain, " I'm afraid something is the matter with Martha."

" Why ? " said he, absently.

" I don't think she's happy."

" Nonsense."

" No," she said, very positively, " she is in trouble, I'm sure."

" Some falling out with Dick, I suppose," said he, indifferently.

" Yes," mused Kate, " that is it."   What could touch *her* so deeply as " falling out " with Bernard ?   And she thought compassionately of her maid's unhappiness from similar cause and determined to help her.

A dusky crowd was hanging around Ned's cabin, which silently drew back to make way for Judge Stanley and his daughter.

The moans they heard as they stood on the porch outside, were not from Ned.   He was still enough, not having yet come back to consciousness of his suffering.

But poor Liza rocked back and forth in piteous anguish, which made her almost unconscious of the presence of Kate and her father.

"Oh, my pore ole man—de Lord dun forgot him dis time. If he could sen a angel one time, why couldn he anoder? Dat's what I can't understan. Pears like his arm was shorten dat he couldn sav! If he *could* an he *didn't*—what sort a Lord is dat?" said she, in a kind of passion of grief. "No, Aunt Jemima, don't you hinder me. If I tought de Lord he hear dose cries and looked on and wouldn help his ole faithful serbant—I wouldn *love* him;" and she paced the floor, gesticulating wildly.

"No, don talk to me bout sech a Lord as dat," said she, pushing aside her would-be comforters. "I'se gwinter have my say, I is."

Kate could think of nothing comforting to say, so she wiped her own tears and silently took the things out of the hamper. This suggested the best thing she could have done. That is, to mix a little brandy and water and sugar, to calm the poor old creature's nerves.

"Tank you, Miss Kate," said she, gratefully.

Dr. Barnes found nothing serious in the case, unless the concussion should give trouble, but "I reckon not," he said, with a facetious glance at the judge. "The race is pretty well protected there," said he, tapping the unconscious Ned on the skull. "He is suffering now chiefly from nervous shock." He did all he could to make the old man more comfortable, and promised to call again before night.

CHAPTER VI.

The following day Kate sat before the mirror in dainty dressing sacque. The hair which Martha was combing fell in rich, waving, auburn masses, which, soon as released from the comb in Martha's hand, spread out as if electrified.

They had been talking of Ned.

"It seems like there was nothing but trouble, Miss Kate," the girl said, in a tone of wearied hopelessness.

Kate looked at her very steadily in the glass.

"Martha," said she, after a moment ; "is Dick kind to you?"

"Dick?—kind?"—she almost gasped. "Why, Miss Kate, I think Dick would die for me."

"And you are sure you have no trouble with him?"

"Oh, no—no. If you could only know how good he is to me!" Big tears gathered in her eyes, which her busy hands let fall as they would.

"Well, then, Martha, what is it? I have observed ever since I came home, you are not happy."

"Oh, Miss Kate, Miss Kate," said the girl, dropping the comb, and burying her face in both hands, "don't, don't!"

Kate was shocked.

"Why, Martha, what is it? What can I do for you?" And she put her hand kindly on the girl's shoulder.

"There's nothing—nothing," said she, sobbing hysterically. "Oh, it breaks my heart to have you so good to me!"

"There, there," said Kate, who heard Bernard's step on the stairs. "There, I'll do my own hair—you go and lie down," and she pushed her gently toward the door. As Bernard entered, he looked at the retreating figure of the girl, and then, swiftly, at Kate.

"Well, what is it now?"

The tone was not pleasant, neither was the frown which accompanied it. But Kate perceived neither,

"Why, I do not know, Bernard, what it is. Martha does not seem happy—something troubles her. She was so light-hearted before she married Dick, and now——"

"Will you spare me any more of these details," said her husband, in a not very engaging voice. "For Heaven's sake, can we not find something pleasanter to talk of than the servants' troubles!"

"Bernard," said Kate, shocked and surprised.

"Well, dear, I can't help it. It bores me—you are not vexed, are you?" said he, leaning over her coaxingly.

"No," said she, refusing to look at him. "I'm not vexed, but I am disappointed."

"Well, it's a little too much to expect of a man, you know," and, with his hands in his pockets, he lazily paced the floor, while Kate brushed her hair in silence.

"Last night, it was Uncle Ned: you could't talk, play billiards, sing, or even think of anything but Uncle Ned; and now I come home, and, by George, it's Martha."

Kate said not a word, as she gathered the auburn mass together and then coiled it upon the top of her stately head.

"By Jove, she's handsome," Bernard was saying to himself.

Kate furtively glanced at her husband as he stood at the window, his profile in strong relief against the light. She had taken great delight in studying that profile; but now, somehow, in the silence that had fallen between them, its perfect lines irritated her.

But before she had placed the high shell comb at the right angle in her hair, the old feeling had asserted itself.

What was she doing? Trouble with Bernard! The thought was insupportable.

She was at his side in another moment, looking wistfully into his face.

"Bernard, I was unreasonable," and she slipped her hand into his.

"Of course, dear," she went on, "I cannot expect you to feel as I do about these servants. Why, I have loved Martha all my life—we played together in the nursery, and then grew up together, and——"

Something warned her that she was boring him again.

"And, Bernard, you must be patient with me if I am hasty sometimes. It's the Lucas blood, that you think so much of," said she, smiling archly. "We are all so—papa, Frank and I, all alike; but we get over it in a moment, unless it's a *real* injury, you know."

"Ah, well," said he, "I suppose we must have our little misunderstandings sometimes, like other people. But we will avoid many of these if you will give up expecting me to be like your-priggish cousin Frank."

Kate looked hurt. "I'm sorry you dislike Frank"

"Oh, I don't dislike him. But we go different ways, that's all. He likes this sort of thing, and I don't.

"Now, dear, we understand each other, don't we?" and he drew her to him and kissed her.

She was silent, but there was a strange misgiving in her heart. What if they did not, and *could never* understand each other.

The evening was long to Kate. Bernard was especially agreeable, but somehow her spirits would not rally; and finally, when her father and husband became interested in a game of billiards, she slipped quietly up-stairs, took off her dress, braided her hair in two long strands down her back, and then, in soft dressing-gown, sat in the flickering light of the open fire. She was fond of this, and in that girlhood she was fast leaving behind her, had built many castles out of those changing lights and shadows. But there was no castle-building to-night. She was only trying to comprehend the strangeness of the *now*. A veil seemed to be dropping from life. Could it be that its poetry and romance would vanish? She sat long, gazing silently, and in differrent ways asking over the same question.

She started at hearing Bernard's step. "Alone, dearest?" said he. "Kate, I'm afraid you think I was unsympathetic to-day—I am not, and if Martha——"

"O Bernard, she is not in trouble; that is, it was all a stupid mistake of mine. She is not very well, that is all."

"Oh, well," said he, "give her that, it will make her better, or else you buy her something with it. You know what would please her."

Kate flushed rosy red with pleasure and surprise as she saw a ten-dollar bill lying in her lap.

"My darling, how kind you are!" said she, impulsively.

"Oh, there are worse fellows than I," said he, laughing, as he replaced his pocket-book.

She laid her head on his breast. How unjust she had been! how exacting! how absurd! and he—was so generous, so tender!

CHAPTER VII.

Upon receiving the dispatch, Frank immediately arranged to return, and before the steamer started that night, his uncle's letter had given the details of the affair.

Too excited to sleep, he paced the deck far into the night, his mind revolving plans of swift vengeance upon the men whom he suspected of being the perpetrators of this outrage, whom he correctly surmised had discovered the thwarting of their first attempt. It was aimed, as he well knew, not at Ned, but himself.

"But what good will it do?" he asked himself, despairingly. "What security is there against future and endless troubles of a similar sort, in a State where the laws are framed, not to protect the helpless, but rather to secure immunity for the strong and vicious!"

The problem to be solved was, How should he administer justice to these human beings committed to his care by his grandfather's will! He had been powerless to do it thus far, even with the aid of Judge Stanley.

"But it must be done," said he, setting his teeth together with a sort of fierce resolve. "By Heaven! if justice cannot be found for them *within* the system, why, by all that's sacred, I'll put them *outside* of it. It's got to come to that," said he, more quietly; "I see there is no other way out of it."

The moon rose above the hills, and a pathway of glory stretched before him through the dark waters of the Ohio. To his excited fancy it seemed a type. Here was the path of duty illumined by divine light, which seemed to cleave its way straight through the darkness which environed him. He recalled his mother—his beautiful, sainted mother—and could hear her voice, as of old, urging the simple, yet ah! so difficult precept: "My son, do unto others as you would have others do unto you."

And if ministering angels do visit the earth, there was an angel who imparted strength and courage to a human soul that night. He felt the soft touch of a hand upon his brow, and sprang to his feet. Was he dreaming? The moon had disappeared; the rosy light of dawn was in the east, and the cool morning air gave freshness and vigor to the duties of the day. The night's vigil, though it left no trace of fatigue, had been an era in the life of Clayton, and during its anxious hours he had passed from youth to manhood. His resolve was taken; there was no more uncertainty as to what was to be done.

His carriage was awaiting him at the landing and took him at once to his own home, where his whole thought for some hours was given to consoling his old servant, and, so far as he could, bringing comfort and cheer into Ned's forlorn cabin.

Not till evening did he set his face toward "Beech-wood," and then, reining in Stella's impatience, he tried to prolong the ride thither. The approaching interview with his uncle must be a painful, and probably would be a stormy one. He would have preferred never to array himself in opposition to his more than father—but the time had come sooner than he intended; the hands on the dial could not be set back now.

They had just finished dinner when he entered. Judge Stanley and his son-in-law had lighted their cigars. Kate knew well the ring of Stella's hoofs on the gravel road, and had flown to meet him at the door, with the old-time welcome, which quite atoned for Bernard's listless greeting.

"Well, Frank," said his uncle, we've had a pretty bad time here since you went away. I wrote you most of—"

Bernard, looking terribly bored, said in an aside to Kate, "Let's have some music, dear; your father and cousin have so much to discuss." So Frank and his uncle were left alone.

The butler, who went in later, to remove the cloth, was told impatiently by his master to leave things as they were, he could not be disturbed; and the rise and fall of voices within the closed doors gave indication of an interview more than usually grave and important.

Kate was puzzled and anxious, for it sounded at times almost as if they were angry. But that *could* not be !— and she waited, restrained by an indefinable feeling from confiding her disquietude to her husband.

Ten o'clock—and, at last—eleven o'clock; and still the

doors remained closed and the voices were no less earnest and continuous.

"Your cousin and the old gentleman are holding a long session," said Bernard, lazily stretching. "Don't you wait, dear; if anyone need do so, I will."

"Oh, not at all," said Kate; "it's not necessary for anyone to sit up; Frank is one of us, you know."

But there could be no sleep for Kate, as long as she heard the distant murmur of voices down-stairs. It must be something very serious—and what *could* it be? Twelve o'clock—one—and, at last, two! Then the voices grew more distinct, although speaking very quietly now, as the dining-room door opened. She heard Frank say:

"Good-night, uncle." Then the front door closed heavily.

"Has there been some misfortune? some trouble of which I do not know? Is Frank in difficulty?" And she asked herself these fruitless questions till the clatter of Stella's hoofs was lost in the distance. Then, the tension removed, she dropped into the restful sleep of youth and health.

There was little conversation at breakfast next morning. Judge Stanley looked careworn and aged, as he silently took his coffee and buttered toast. It was not until Bernard had gone, and the old gentleman had settled into his easy-chair, with his newspaper, that Kate ventured to broach the subject uppermost in her mind.

"Papa, dear, you were up late last night; I hope Frank is not in any trouble."

"Kate," said he, laying down his paper, "your cousin is a fool; he is going to free his negroes."

"Well, I'm glad it's nothing worse than that," she said, with an expression of relief.

"Nothing worse," said he, vehemently, "nothing worse than committing such an act of folly? I hope *you* are not going to uphold him." He seemed almost angry with her.

"Why, no; not exactly that, papa," said she; "but if he thinks it his duty, I must say I think it is heroic."

"Well, *I* think it is madness to throw away fifty thousand dollars on a piece of mistaken philanthropy. Why, it is an act of cruelty to turn those negroes adrift. What do they know about earning a living? They will die off like sheep. But, I've nothing more to say about it; he thinks he knows better than I; now let him go and throw away his inheritance, let him pull down his grandfather's house about his head if he wants to—I shall say nothing more. He is of age and has a right to do what he will with his own. I've done my duty in pointing out the dangers and folly of this course; now if he persists—as he will—I shall acquiesce without another word. But don't talk to me of its being *heroic,*" he said, as he returned to his paper, which Kate well knew he was in no mood to read.

Perhaps her father was right in his view of the unfitness of the negroes to take care of themselves; but she was none the less strongly impressed with Frank's fidelity to his ideals, and, so far from striving to make him waver, she would have strengthened him in his resolution. All day her thoughts dwelt upon these things, feeling instinctively the while that she could not speak to Bernard about it and invite the scornful comment which she was sure would follow.

CHAPTER VIII.

A few days later there were assembled in the old library at "The Glen' one morning four men, seated round a large oaken table, with its quaintly carved legs and mouldings in keeping with thé bookcases which lined the walls, containing richly bound volumes and rare old books, which had been the pride of Colonel Lucas, who had bequeathed these treasures to his grandson.

One of the persons at the table was a heavily built man, with an intellectual head, slightly bald, and with an air of authority, which plainly said : " 'This must be so, because I say it." He stood at one end of the table, resting his hand upon an elaborately prepared legal document, and said :

"You see, Judge Stanley, the will of Colonel Lucas provides that if his grandson, Frank Clayton, shall desire to dispose of the estate, he shall first offer it to his cousin, Kate Stanley, or to her father for her."

"Mr. Blackstone," said the judge, "he has complied with that clause in full."

"Pardon me, Judge. I believe not in the spirit nor yet in the letter of the clause ; for you will observe, in every case, reference is made to this property as a whole, and the negroes are enumerated as part and parcel of the estate so bequeathed and provided for in the clause as an entirety. Evidently, Colonel Lucas did not intend to have the estate divided up into parcels, but to be kept intact and in the family. It would be a sacrilege to allow this young visionary to thwart so noble a purpose ; and if you take our view of the case, and refuse to buy except he conform to this view, mark my word, the money consideration will bring him round."

"No," said Judge Stanley. "He will find another purchaser for The Glen, and hold that the conditions of the will have been complied with , and besides. I shall not be a party to such a forced construction of the will. He refuses to sell either the library here or the family pictures, which were a part of his inheritance. As well insist on his selling these as any other particular portion."

"And so I should, your honor," resumed Mr. Blackstone. " The estate should be kept intact ; and if you will allow my client, Captain Fletcher, and his son Bernard here, to arrange this conveyance with my help, I am sure this instrument," holding up the voluminous document, " will make a sure bind."

" Mr. Blackstone is right," said Captain Fletcher, as he rose from his seat and approached Judge Stanley, who sat in deep thought. " Mr. Clayton is not the man to oppose our united opinions and demands, if you support our views."

" I, for one," said Bernard, " am not in favor of allowing him to carry these slaves away for any such purpose as he has avowed ; and if he will not listen to reason, he must yield to force, and abandon the wild scheme."

" If you knew Frank as I do," said the judge, looking rather contemptuously at his son-in-law, " you would not expect to control him, by subterfuge nor yet by force. He is a determined, brave, clear-headed fellow. I don't approve of this business—far from it—but I will say this much for him, if——"

What more he might have said, we know not, for at that moment his nephew, accompanied by Kate, entered the apartment. Frank apologized for his delay in appearing; while Kate, furtively reading the lines in her husband's face, moved to his side and rested her hand upon his arm. She was uncomfortably conscious of an impending storm, which she meant, if possible, to avert.

Mr. Blackstone, in pompous, consequential fashion, now called attention to the business of executing the papers, transferring the estate to Kate Fletcher ; and then, stepping up to Clayton and handing him a carefully prepared document, said :

" Here, Mr. Clayton, is a deed, prepared by myself in strict compliance with the provisions of Colonel Lucas' will ; and I will ask you to be so kind as to examine it."

Clayton took the paper from the lawyer without comment. Running his eye down the first page, he caught the name of " Uncle Ned." Then followed an inventory of all the negroes, horses, cattle and stock of various kinds ; and as he read, the hot blood surged to his cheeks and temples. He repressed his heart, which had come unbidden into his throat, and calmed its wild beatings.

Kate watched him as he read, and observed the struggle with secret sympathy, but dared not leave her husband's side.

A look of ominous determination was creeping over Frank's face, which was now quite pallid and set. There was a moment's pause, all eyes fixed upon him, as they waited for him to speak; then, looking Mr. Blackstone steadily in the face, he tore the paper from end to end and then into shreds, saying calmly as he did so: "Uncle Stanley, where is the deed we prepared yesterday?"

Judge Stanley turned from the window just in time to interpose. Mr. Blackstone had fairly bounded toward Clayton, in order to save his pet conveyance, saying, "How dare you destroy my paper, sir?"

Bernard, with clinched fist, tore away from his almost frantic wife to second Blackstone in his attack on Clayton. Judge Stanley's tall form stood between them in a moment. "Gentlemen, you forget yourselves, Bernard, I am astonished at you," he said, turning sharply upon his son-in-law.

Clayton stood calmly looking on. "I suppose you will be making out a bill of sale of my soul next," he said, "and expect me to submit to its being retained by you as though I had thought of such a sale. Now, Mr. Blackstone, if you want your papers to be respected by me, keep my name out of all such nefarious transactions. I know my grandfather's will better than you or your client," glancing toward Bernard, who was standing by the side of his wife.

At this point Judge Stanley handed to Clayton the deed he had prepared and for which his nephew had asked.

"Here, Kate," said Frank, "you and I are the two interested parties in this transaction. Look at this deed, and see if it suits you. If not, then I will find a purchaser whom it does."

Bernard's eyes were fastened upon his wife, as she, with great dignity and deliberation, took the deed and read it through. What would she say? The issue all rested upon her now. Having finished reading the paper, she returned it, with a quiet smile, and a look of determination not unlike her cousin's.

"I see no objection to that, none whatever." Her eyes kindled, and a flush crept up into her cheek as she added, taking Frank's hand : "If you desire to free your slaves, if you feel it to be your duty to do so, I shall not interpose one technicality to prevent it ; it would be most ungenerous and unfair. You have my best wishes in the fulfilment of your purpose."

It was bravely said. Judge Stanley's eyes looked very dim as they rested upon his daughter, but they held admiration as well as tears. There was nothing more to be done. Kate and Frank, the two contracting parties, were fully in accord. So the battle was lost, and it only remained for the various actors in the scene to retire with such grace as they could command.

Without one word to his wife, Bernard Fletcher strode out of the room, muttering something through his closed teeth which sounded very much like an oath ; but of course, that could not be—for was he not a gentleman, with the most chivalric blood in Kentucky flowing in azure stream through his veins ?

He and his lawyer mounted their horses and rode away, and their discourse was known only to themselves.

Frank Clayton had a tremendous task before him, but he addressed himself to it with an intensity of purpose which swept away all obstacles. Sparks, with his miserable company of followers, was doing all in his power to thwart and overthrow his plans. The laws of the State made it impracticable for the freed slaves to remain within its borders, and the removal of the little band, furthermore, had to be accomplished with the utmost secrecy and even diplomacy. But it was done ; and the new year dawned upon the colony of dusky freedmen, settled in Illinois, each family in its own comfortable cabin, in all the dignity of proprietorship, their benefactor having given to each, as a New Year's gift, manumission papers and the deed of a farm. The details of the scheme were carefully worked out, and Frank spared no pains in trying to make them understand the responsibilities of their new position and to stimulate them to their highest and best endeavor.

The last week of the old year was a wonderful holiday week, and enthusiasm ran high in the new colony. There was feasting and singing and dancing; Ned laughed and cried at the same time, and Eliza would have knelt at the feet of the deliverer if he would have let her, as she poured out her gratitude. "O Marsa Frank, de Lor bress you for takin my ol man to saf place whar dem wicked men can't fin im. Honey, you do grow mo and mo like yo modder, Miss Fannie, der sainted young Missus, when she cum home from de big city wid de dearest little baby boy. Now you's dat same pickanniny, an I spose yer done forgot all bout it. When you got bigger, Marsa Lucas, your grampa, would take de ol hos and put the saddle an bridle on, den to see dat little spec o a boy what was one ob desc days to grow up to be such a fin hansom man—I can see yer now, wid de white fedder in yer hat, and wid top boots on, whip in yer han an ol Marsa Lucas put his little man on de hos and gib yer de reins all to yersef. I kin see de proud blood ob de Lucasses mount up in de cheeks as you make de ol hos go under de trees an roun de yard and de orchard, an finly, you brung im up jis under de big apple tree, when you pull hard on dem reins, and say 'who;' and dar you was all mixed up wid de apple blossoms. De boy an' de bees after de honey in de blossoms, an I clare to you, Marsa Frank, an no mistake, it was de putties pictur you eber coud see. Ole Mars Lucas, jis call de young missus ter see de young man an de hos an de blossoms, all so mixed till yer could hardly tell which was toder. Marsa Frank, I'd jus like a big picture ob dat in a big frame, and set an mire it all day long."

CHAPTER IX.

THERE was one person at "Beechwood" to whom Frank's absence brought unmixed satisfaction. Mordecai no longer sat at Bernard Fletcher's gate. "Confound his impudence," he said, grinding his teeth, "I wish it was the South Sea Islands, instead of Illinois, and with six feet of solid earth over him, too."

Bernard realized, fully, the unpleasant impression his conduct had left at that ill-starred conference in the library, and would have given a good deal to have effaced it, and to have felt entirely reinstated in Kate's and her father's esteem. He knew well how to charm, and made it his study during the ensuing months to try and make his wife in love with him afresh, and to knit up anew the tie he had so nearly sundered between her father and himself.

A great peace and happiness came into Kate's heart. She began to feel an absolute trust, and a sense of security which had been lacking in the first months of her marriage.

As the winter advanced, she was far from well; but as Dr. Barnes assured them there was no cause for uneasiness, the physical *malaise*, so new and strange, became almost a happiness, so strangely did it bring out the wonderful tenderness of her husband.

At last there came a day when Dr. Barnes' carriage stood all the day, and far into the night, in front of the house at "Beechwood," the servants going about on their errands silently and swiftly and with scared faces. The gloom of a frightful uncertainty hung over the house. Would it be life or death?

"My God, how could I bear it?" asked her father, when he was told of the possible event of Kate's death; and something like a muttered prayer came from Bernard's white lips, as he paced the hall outside of his wife's door. If she could only be spared, what would he not do to make her future happy. Poor, shallow, sterile, though his nature was, he loved her, and this desperate crisis revealed to him how much.

But God was merciful, and an hour later Judge Stanley's grateful heart was full as he looked down upon a soft little package which he was told was his grandchild.

The strain of anxiety being over, Bernard was himself again. "Pshaw!" he said, impatiently, "a girl; only a girl!"

The convalescence was slow, but Kate felt as if she could have had it last forever, so delicious was it to lie and watch that marvel of Nature's delicate handiwork— her little girl. She was denied the privilege of nourishing her child; but most fortunately, Martha's baby being only a few weeks older than hers, she was enabled to perform that office in Kate's stead, and the young mother would lie and watch in a kind of rapture the dressing and the undressing, the warming and the comforting of her darling.

"Isn't she a beauty, Martha?"

"Deed she is, Miss Kate," answered the mellow voice of the maid.

"Is your little girl pretty?"

"Yes, Miss; *I* think so." But Martha was too busy adjusting the little Katie's wraps to look up.

"Martha, you must bring her for me to see her," persisted Katie.

Martha's face wore a very strange expression as she suddenly rose, saying as she did so: "Miss Kate, you mustn't forget the doctor's orders; no talkin', you know, Miss Kate." And laying the sleeping child by its mother, she found plenty to do in folding and putting away dainty little bits of lace-trimmed garments.

CHAPTER X.

About a fortnight later, Judge Stanley sat in his library reading a letter just received from his nephew Frank, when he was startled by a message from Kate that she wished to see him. There was something in the tone of the message, or perhaps it was a vague premonition of evil, that made him go towards Kate's room with strange foreboding. After the lapse of a half-hour or more, the old gentleman, very pale, and looking as if he had received a blow, came out of his daughter's room. He ordered a servant to go at once for Dr. Barnes; then returned and the door was once more closed upon father and child.

When Dr. Barnes's carriage drove up the gravel road to the house, Judge Stanley went down and met him at the door. Drawing him at once into the library and closing the door, he said, in a broken voice:

"Doctor, we are in trouble, great trouble : that scoundrel Bernard will break my child's heart before he gets through."

"Why, my dear old friend, what is it ? What has happened."

"Oh, there's no time to tell you now; go up and see Kate, and give her something sedative. She has had a shock, a terrible shock, and she feels that there is nothing to live for, now that she has lost trust in her husband. You will see how it is; she scarcely knows what she is saying, poor thing."

The doctor went up-stairs, and Judge Stanley, with hands clasped behind him and head bent, paced back and forth, trying to see the best way out of this for all concerned.

Martha must go—yes, that is settled—she and her child must go. Kate demanded that, and it must be done. Should he send her to Frank's colony ? or where ? Give her her freedom as a reward for her conduct ? No ; that would scarcely do. And yet he had a conviction that she was a good girl, after all. "More sinned against than sinning," said he, nodding his head. "More sinned against than sinning," he said again, even more positively than before. "I'd stake a great deal on that."

At this moment the doctor returned. Looking at him anxiously, the judge said: "Well, how is she?"

"Oh, very quiet; I have given her a soothing powder, and I think she'll get through the night comfortably. But, by Jove, it is a shame! I'd like to wring that man's neck! I'd——"

"Well, he is her husband, and she is *my* child, and we've got to make it as smooth and easy for her as we can. The girl must go away, that's clear; she and her child must go somewhere, and at once."

"I have it," said the doctor; "just the very thing. My sister-in-law, in Louisville, has been a long time looking for just such a maid as Martha. Now, let me suggest that, as in law you are her real owner, you allow Kate to execute the manumission papers, and you can make a bill-of-sale to my sister. With these, we can send Martha and her child to Louisville. The free papers can be destroyed and the name left blank in the bill-of-sale, to be filled in after my sister consents to the purchase, as I have no doubt she will. Harry Barnes, her son, will stop to see me on his way home from New Orleans. I expect him daily, and he can take the mother and child and deliver them safely to his mother."

Dr. Barnes' suggestions were adopted, and the papers were made accordingly.

CHAPTER XI.

On a beautiful afternoon in June, as the magnificent steamer "Aleck Scott" was cutting the bright waters of the Ohio River, making good speed against a swift current, two men were sitting on the hurricane deck smoking and talking of the events of the trip thus far from New Orleans. One, a young man of about twenty-five, with dark hair and eyes, a clean-shaven face, except the conspicuous mustache. He evidently belonged to some one of the professions, and was, although young, quite a man of the world.

His companion, who was somewhat his senior, wore a large brilliant in his scarlet necktie. He was regretting with loud voice the approach to Lucaston, where they must separate, and said :

"Come, Barnes, make the trip to Louisville with us, my boy. The old uncle will wait till your return for his visit."

"No, Hawks, I can't afford to take any chances on the old man. He kind o' dotes on me, and he is without an heir ; has lots o' niggers and land, and but one poor relation. You see, he wrote me just before we left the city to be sure and stop on my way up, as he had important matters for me to attend to ; you'd better stop off with me and perhaps you may be able to gather up some negroes there to fill your orders."

"I have no orders, Barnes, for anything but for some fancy articles. I reckon you don't keep that kind of cattle there in your small town. Come down, and let us have another game before you leave us anyway."

"No, Hawks, I won't play another game. You already have my spare cash, and I must not ask favors first thing when I see my uncle."

"Tell you what I'll do, Barnes. I'll play you $200 against your watch and chain. Come, now, if you dare. I'll give you a chance for your life ; and if you win, I'll agree to stop over a day or two, and we'll go up to Louisville together."

"Damn it, Hawks you know my weakness, and that I can't take a dare. Come on, I'll give you a trial even if I am out of luck to-day."

When the "Scott" blew her whistle for Lucaston, Barnes and Hawks came out of the saloon wiping their mustaches, Barnes looking flushed and smiling.

"You are going to stay over with me in accordance with your promise, eh?"

"Yes. Porter, bring down my baggage," said Hawks.

"I'll take you to the hotel, as I know nothing of my uncle's household arrangements," said Barnes.

"All right, my boy; we can have a good time there, I reckon."

At the wharf, Dr. Barnes was waiting with his carriage for his nephew; and after their greeting was over, young Barnes introduced, "My friend, Mr. Hawks" to his uncle.

The doctor drove to the hotel, and on the way home he said: "By the way, Harry, who was that flashy looking fellow you introduced to me?"

Harry colored, and said hastily: "Oh, he's an entertaining sort of a fellow I picked up on the road; his name is Hawks."

"Humph!" said the doctor. "Well, if you were so indiscreet as to 'pick him up,' I advise you to lose no time in dropping him."

The doctor had been fond and proud of his handsome young nephew, but there was something now which made him put on his glasses and give a long, scrutinizing glance at his young face. What he saw there, we do not know, but he said to himself, "I must go down and talk with Lucy about this boy; he needs looking after. Why, it would break her heart if he went wrong."

When young Barnes was made acquainted with the nature of the business his uncle desired to entrust him with he seemed greatly puzzled.

"I am at a loss, uncle, to understand why Miss Kate, or rather Mrs. Fletcher, wishes to part with such a valuable servant. And it occurs to me, uncle, that the baby Martha was carrying this morning, which, I take it, was hers, is about as white as Mrs. Fletcher's. How does it strike you?"

"Yes; and I suppose this is the cause of selling or sending away this valuable woman. It looks as much

like Bernard Fletcher as his own child does; and yet it may
be unjust suspicion, for, by the laws of physiology, the
sins of the fathers are visited upon the children to the
third and fourth generation; and some white ancestor
may reappear in this poor little waif, who, with her
mother, is turned adrift, like Hagar in the wilderness."

"Yes, uncle, it is the old story repeated; so the world
has not changed much in the last four thousand years."

So it was settled, that when the old steamer "Clermont"
came on her way from St. Louis to Louisville, Harry
Barnes was to take to his mother Martha and her child.

When all were safely stowed on the steamer, and Martha
and her baby turned over to the chambermaid for care,
Hawks took the arm of Harry Barnes, and said:

"Let us have something to drink. You have done
little else than attend to that uncle of yours. Are you so
fond of him?"

"Well, I am as much as a poor nephew can be of a
rich uncle who is likely to make him his heir; and then,
you see, he has been giving me instructions in regard to
a piece of important business I am to transact for him at
Louisville."

"Has that handsome wench and baby anything to do
with it? How is it you never mentioned to me there was
such a piece of furniture to be had in your little burgh?"

"Well, you see, Hawks, I had no idea that woman could
have been bought for love or money."

Then Barnes detailed to his companion the troubles at
"The Glen" as he understood them; not omitting the
transfer of Martha and the blank bill-of-sale which he had
in his possession. Hawks's eyes twinkled with delight as
he heard this latter bit of news, and giving his companion a
thrust in the ribs with his cane, he good-humoredly said:

"Barnes, you are a lucky dog. I'd give you a clear
thousand for that article; but damn the brat—what could
be done with that? I don't suppose anything would tempt
the mother to part with it."

During this time, they had taken their drinks, and returned to the upper deck and were now seated at the
stern of the steamer, looking back at Lucaston, which
was beautifully located on a commanding point of the
river bank.

"I want revenge on you, Barnes, for the last game you

beat me the other day. Come, let us step into 'Texas,' here, and have a game to while away the time."

"No," said Barnes, "I don't feel in any mood for playing this afternoon."

Hawks knew his man too well to press the matter further, and said:

"Well, join me in a bottle of wine. I have had nothing at your country tavern but whiskey straight."

"Then, I conclude you found the whiskey good."

"Nectar; fit for a pirate king; but come in, and let us have the wine."

So saying, they sauntered into the room under the pilot-house, usually denominated "Texas" on Southern steamers. The wine was called for and drunk. Barnes also called for a bottle, and under the generous influence of potations, the subject of cards was renewed, and they were soon playing for small stakes. The fickle goddess seemed to favor Barnes, who won nearly every game. Hawks declared the stakes were so small as not to tempt him; and the game was soon discontinued for the night.

Toward midnight of the second day, Hawks and Barnes were again playing, when Hawks called on the bartender for some brandy and sugar for two, saying as he looked up to his companion:

"I presume I may order for you?"

Barnes nodded assent, as, with an abstracted air, he only half saw Hawks shuffle the cards, adding:

"I want to retire soon, Hawks. I can't bear to have my mother see me to-morrow, after such a night as I see you have laid out for us."

"Never you mind about to-morrow; you'll look as fresh as a daisy after an hour's sleep."

The bartender himself brought the brandy; and, while Barnes was eying intently the cards dealt him, Hawks took one of the glasses and, turning around as if to examine it, emptied a white powder into the liquid; then taking the other glass, he said:

"Here's to Fortune: may she ever favor the fair!"

Wiping his mustache with deliberation, and watching his companion as he examined his cards, with a perceptible smile upon his face, before drinking his brandy, he inquired:

"Well, how do you like them? Not a bad hand, I judge by the way you smile, Barnes."

"Ah, did I smile? Well, to be candid, you gave me a pretty fair hand, Hawks."

As Hawks examined his cards, a scowl was plainly visible on his face; and he said:

"What do you do, Barnes?"

"Since you complain of the small stakes, I am in for that 'pot'—$50."

Hawks mused a moment; looked at his cards again; then, as if speaking to himself, said:

"'Faint heart never won fair lady,' or anything else worth winning," and he covered the $50, and then hesitated a little. "I'll go you $50 better, just to try your mettle," he added, in a half-sneering tone.

Barnes looked up quickly and the blood rushed to his face as if an insult had been offered him, and excitedly put down a $50 bill, saying as he did so:

"Well, I'll call—no, I'll risk the pile; here is $300 better. Now, we will see *your* mettle."

His companion smiled as he had not done before.

"I like your grit, Barnes, but I am in now, and 'the longest pole knocks the persimmons.' There is $300 to see yours, and a cool thousand that says mine's the best hand."

Barnes bit his lip, and the blood surged again to his face and back to his heart, as he sat speechless, gazing at his cards. Finally he said:

"You know I have no more money, and you must give me a show for my life."

"You have other valuables that will enable you to come in if you have confidence in your hand. Can't admit this pleading the baby-act here. 'Put up or shut up' is my motto."

Barnes felt goaded by each of these taunts. He replied:

"I only have my watch; that is not enough to call. You make it $200 instead of a thousand, or—lend the $800 to me, and I'll call."

"Oh, no; I don't care, my boy, to lend you a stick to break my head with. You are too modest by half in enumerating your worldly goods. He leaned forward, a curious expression coming into his beady black eyes. I think, if you will examine the packet sent to your mother, you will find there the wherewith to call me."

" No, you are mistaken, sir," said Barnes, at the same time drawing out the package of papers referred to and handing them across the table to his companion, saying :

" Examine for yourself."

Hawks did as he was requested; and after carefully reading the bill-of-sale and the private letter of Dr. Barnes to his sister-in-law, which was unsealed, he coolly handed the bill-of-sale back, saying : " Put my name in the blank there (indicating), and "$1,000" in this blank (indicating), and you can call me for that pot. Otherwise, I shall be under the necessity of raking it down."

Barnes looked at him with scorn and contempt; his lip curled as he said : "Do you take me for a thief? Here is a trust I don't propose to betray." A look of honest indignation blazed for a moment in his face, and then faded out, as he added :

" Make the stake $200 and I'll call it with my watch. You must give me a chance for my life. You know I have the best hand and you propose to bluff me out ! "

" If you are so sure your hand is the best, Barnes, you run no risk in filling in my name there, and it can easily be erased. Come, I am tired of this; either play the game or quit ! " and with that, he put his hand upon the money and sat looking at his companion, his cold glittering eyes freezing the blood.

Barnes looked again at his hand and then at the paper that had been handed to him. Finally he said :

" It is impossible. My uncle will know it whether I should win or lose."

" Not unless you have a mind to tell him, Barnes. The letter there to your mother treats the matter as of so great secrecy that she is not to mention it in her correspondence, and he will conclude you have carried out his orders, unless, as I said, you choose to tell him."

" Damnation, Hawks, did you read the private letter ? "

" Of course ; you handed me the papers and told me to satisfy myself, and I did so. You're all right with that paper in your possession ; all that ails you, Barnes, is lack of sand. I see you are going to back," and Hawks began to " haul down " the money.

"Hold!" exclaimed Barnes, stung to the quick by this last taunt. "Where is the pen? By ——, I'll see that hand if I die for it!"

He put his hands to his head; his brain seemed on fire; and there was a strange sensation there that made him falter.

"Don't give out, Barnesy boy," said his companion, producing the pen and ink. "There's pen and ink, if you are not too much excited to write. Come, come—quiet down. You are not going to die for this, nor anything like it," he added, in a conciliatory manner.

When young Barnes returned the paper Hawks looked over it, remarking: "What now?"

"Place it on that pile, and I call you!" exclaimed Barnes.

"Very well," said Hawks. "I have two pairs," as he placed the bill-of-sale on the pile of money."

"And I," said Barnes, laconically—"how big? Let's see? Can you overtop those?" exposing a pair of kings and a pair of aces; and so sure was he of winning, that he put forth his hand for the prize, when Hawks, by a quick movement, placed his hand on the "pot," saying as he did so:

"Look at these!" laying four jacks on the table. "You see my two pairs are all alike."

Barnes sprang to his feet and stood gazing at his companion, half bewildered, as Hawks carefully folded the bill-of-sale, placing it in his breast-pocket, stuffing in also the roll of bills. He counted out five $50 bills and said, as he threw them to Barnes:

"There; you may return this at any time it may suit you to do so. Now, let me see: we will soon meet the 'Scott' on her return trip. I must have things in readiness to go back to St. Louis on her, as there will be pressing need for me in Jefferson City on Saturday. Barnes, my boy, I wish you would arrange with that girl to be ready when we meet the 'Scott.' In order to save a scene, you'd better pretend to go on board and leave me to make arrangements for the change of destination as well as ownership."

Thus Hawks ran on, as though only an ordinary event had occurred.

Harry Barnes sank down, with his head bowed in his

hands, resting upon the table, paying no heed to what was said or the money which had been flung upon the table.

Leaving him, Hawks stepped up to the pilot and inquired where they should meet the "Scott."

"Just around the bend—that is her light you see there now. She is a little late."

"Hail her, Mr. Pilot, and run alongside; I want to board her. Where is the captain? Is he on watch to-night?"

"No, Mr. Hawks, not since eleven o'clock. He turned in then, and the first mate is on duty since."

"Call him through the trumpet, and have a line passed to the 'Scott' and a plank for some passengers," said Hawks, authoritatively.

He next went to the chambermaid, whom he found nodding in her chair.

"Kitty," he said, "I want the woman and baby that got on at Lucaston yesterday, gotten ready immediately. Tell her Mr. Barnes, her young master, and myself are going to return on the 'Scott' when we meet her, which will be in a few minutes. "Take that" (slipping a silver dollar in her hand), "and see that you have her ready in time."

"All right, Mr. Hawks, rely on me for that. We are sorry to lose you so soon."

While the chambermaid was getting Martha in readiness, and the mate below arranging his gang-plank and line, Hawks looked in upon Harry, who remained in the same position he left him at the card table in "Texas." Touching him upon the shoulder and calling him by name, he continued:

"Cheer up, old boy. Here, put this money away," at the same time stuffing the bills into the breast-pocket of the miserable man's coat, adding in soliloquy: "I'll take all these papers that have reference to the nigger; now that she's mine, I may need them." So saying, he gathered up the letter of Dr. Barnes, and the other papers lying upon the table.

"Come, Barnes, rouse up, old fellow; you're not drunk are you?" and he gave his companion a rousing shake; but still no sign of consciousness. "Damn it! I don't want to leave you in this condition. Can it be that I have overdosed him? Oh, I guess he'll be all right by morning."

He then went quickly to the clerk's office and told that worthy to have Barnes put to bed, adding : "He has taken too much, and must sleep it off. Are we nearing the 'Scott'? I suppose the mate told you I want to return on her."

"Yes; we'll run alongside."

"I have some papers for Captain Swan, and instructions to deliver them on meeting him anywhere, as they are of importance; so his agent in St. Louis said."

Soon, the steamers shrieked out their signals and ran alongside.

Martha with her child was hurried across the plank, in the light of glowing furnace fires of both steamers and she seemed going to a fiery region.

Hawks followed soon after; and Captain Swan cried out :

"All aboard! Let her go down there! Give her a turn ahead, Mr. Pilot," and ahead she went.

Martha stood upon the lower deck. her haggard eyes looking piteously about for Harry Barnes, her young master. When Hawks came near her, she said to him, in soft, timid voice :

"I saw you with Mars Harry Barnes yesterday. He has sent word to me to get on this boat ; can you tell me where he is, sir?

"Oh, yes; I guess that's all right. He'll be 'round soon. However, I'll see to you. Come to the chambermaid and wait until I find him for you."

He returned soon to the clerk ; gave orders concerning Martha's care, and instructions that if she inquired about her young master Harry Barnes, she was to be told he was all right.

"That's something fancy you've been buying, I reckon," said the clerk, with a wink at Hawks. who seemed to know all river men.

"Well, you see I have a sister up in Jefferson City who wanted a good maid, and gave me an order some months ago to find one for her; so I am taking her up, and hope she will suit."

So saying, he placed a package of papers upon the counter, remarking :

"Jim, take good care of these ; put them in your safe. I am going as far as St. Louis with you. Now, the next thing is, to have that girl there stowed away; then you may dispose of me. Got any place, eh ? "

"Oh, yes, your old room. I'll look after the other matter and you can turn in whenever you are ready. Here's the key."

On the following day, Martha sat, with her babe in her arms, upon deck, motionless, silent, despairing. If she could only summon courage to end it all, by one leap with her child into those dark, rushing waters ! She could have done it gladly had she been alone. But how could she drag that warm, clinging little creature down into those cold depths ? She shuddered to think of it, and clasped the sleeping child convulsively.

Hawks had been watching her from a distance, and sauntered carelessly by where she sat.

"I suppose you found your young master all right ?" said he.

The desperate impulse faded away, and with languid submission, she answered: "No, sir; I haven't seen him. What am I to do ? "

The pathos of the helpless question would have touched any but a heart of stone.

"Well, you had better come along with me," answered Hawks ; "I'll see that you get to him all right. He must have got left on the other boat, and he'll be along in a day or two. I'll look after you."

"Thank you, sir," she murmured, timidly.

CHAPTER XII

WHEN Hawks arrived at Jefferson City, he informed his sister, Mrs. Hunter, that this was a woman and child he had bought, and wanted them to remain with her for a short time until he returned to New Orleans; and that he had to play a little deception in order to get her quietly away from her former master and home, by telling her she was sold to Mrs. Barnes.

"Humor the thing," he said, a few days later, on taking leave; "and see if you can't bribe her to sell or give you her baby."

"No, Tom," said Mrs. Hunter; "I would not have that child at any price or on any conditions. If she is the mother, it is too white to be a slave. I am somehow led to suspect it is a stolen white child, for I can see no trace of the negro in its features."

"There's no doubt about her being the mother of the child, d—n it; she wouldn't cling to anybody else's baby as she does to that. Why, she glares at me like a tigress if I talk of separating it from her, and I reckon its white complexion is what made the trouble and led to my getting hold of as pretty a piece of property as there is in the South. By Jove, what eyes, and what a carriage of the head, and what shoulders! Egad, I'm fortunate!" And Mr. Hawks gave one of his pleasant, suggestive laughs.

"By the way," said he, turning to his sister, "see that she is kept out of sight and that she keeps her mouth shut."

So saying, he passed out by way of the servants' quarters, and soon found Martha, the object of his search.

Martha listened impassively as he told her that Harry Barnes had been left by the boat just as he supposed, and was ill now, but would come or send for her in a day or two.

What difference did it make to her where she was or with whom! Such was her thought as Hawks stood examining her points with scrutinizing gaze.

"You are to stay right here for the present," said he.

"Now, Martha," he added, in gentler tone, "if you will consent to part with that child of yours *I* will buy you, and give you a home where work will be a stranger to your hands. Think of what I have told you, and on my return, I'll see what Mrs. Barnes will take for you."

Martha looked after him as he walked away, hate, loathing, reckless despair in her eyes. "If you take away my child, I will kill myself." She said it with deliberate, determined emphasis. A memory of past kindness, of Miss Kate, of Dick, swept over her, and, for the first time, tears—blessed tears—came to her relief; and as she sobbed, the awful passion of her grief seemed assuaged.

Some time elapsed before Hawks succeeded in obtaining the number of slaves he desired, to fill the orders he had received. He decided to concentrate them at Booneville, where Martha could see and know what he was going to do, and she could then choose her position as *among* the slaves or *above* them.

Mrs. Barnes, of course, did not appear to claim her; and upon Hawks' return to Jefferson City, Martha was informed that she belonged to him; that young Barnes had been taken violently ill, and been sent to his mother, in Louisville, where he had died of brain fever; that Mrs. Barnes had offered to sell Martha to him for $1200, which sum he had paid for her.

That portion of his story relating to Barnes' illness and death was too true. Soon after the steamers parted company, in mid-river, on the Ohio, during that night in June, the clerk sought to arouse young Barnes, but was unsuccessful; and he was finally carried to his state-room in an unconscious stupor, evidently the result of the drug that had been administered to him in his last draught of brandy.

On the following day, he awoke with great pain in his head; and after several ineffectual efforts to rise or to recall the events of the last few hours, he finally remembered the trust his uncle had given him, and at last came the memory of the game of cards and the stake for which he had played and—lost! His mind could only grasp the dim outlines of the events of his companion's departure from the state-room, and some injunctions about silence regarding the fate of Martha.

In despair, with a moan, he attempted to rise again from his pillow only to see the state-room and its furniture spin around, and finally to dissolve into space, and he fell heavily back in a swoon!

Upon the arrival of the "Clermont" at her dock at Louisville, Harry Barnes was found in his berth in a comatose state with high fever, and continued mutterings about the "betrayal of a trust." When the captain learned his condition, he sent a messenger to his mother and had him conveyed to her home.

For days, incoherent words were all that he uttered; and what was supposed to be brain fever dragged its weary and painful length over the sufferer. The fearful agony endured upon the steamer in that last game of cards, now came surging over him with every increase of the fever, and the face of Hawks appeared like a mocking demon luring him on to destruction.

Upon his return to consciousness, Harry Barnes made an effort to explain to his mother something of the circumstances that had befallen him. The effort brought on a relapse, and he never recovered consciousness afterwards, dying with the secret locked in his bosom and only known to Tom Hawks, who had returned to Louisville and kept himself informed as to young Barnes' condition while he remained at a safe distance from his victim.

The warm weather had passed, and autumn with its brief Indian summer was waning rapidly, when Hawks returned to Jefferson City. He had drank deeply since the death of Harry Barnes, and his usual prompt business habits seemed to have deserted him. He had seen the funeral procession of the widow's son at Louisville, and in a debauch that night, had tried to escape from the avenging angel that followed him.

The brutal nature of the man was now fully aroused; and when he became convinced that Martha would resist any attempt at separation from her child, he determined to resort to the harshest measures in his power on the trip and at Booneville.

A month later, when preparing to start south, he bound his human chattels, Martha with the rest, in couples, and placed them on board a steamer for St. Louis. It was late in November, and he had received an urgent summons from parties in New Orleans to reach that place at an early day.

On the second night, there came up a fearful storm, compelling the steamer to lie-to where she had stopped to discharge freight. The wind shifted suddenly to the north and the weather became intensely cold. The gale prevented the steamer from attempting to move on the following day, and the floating ice gave warning that there was danger that the steamer might have to winter in the unlooked-for quarters.

On the third day, the wind abated, and the captain made an effort to proceed on his voyage. After a night of battle with the ice, about daylight on the following morning an alarm was given that the boat was leaking badly from a large rent in the hull, cut by the ice.

The wildest confusion prevailed on board, especially on the after-deck, where the slaves were bound together in hopeless bondage. Hawks rushed from his state-room, and with pistol in hand, commanded silence and obedience from his slaves.

The pilot headed the boat for the shore and succeeded in reaching it, when she careened to one side and settled down so that the floating ice almost swept the lower deck. Hawks hastily marched his slaves to the upper deck, where a staging was rigged and passengers were transferred to the shore.

Martha was encumbered with her child; and in crossing the staging she fell, and but for the main strength and presence of mind of the woman to whom she was tied, would have fallen into the angry waters that were howling like so many demons between the sunken vessel and the shore.

The command of Hawks to, "Let the d——d brat go and save yourself," was unheeded; and as soon as the slaves were on shore, he said in an angry tone:

"Your devilish obstinacy in hanging on to that child has come near costing me two thousand dollars; and now I warn you, I shall dispose of it at the first opportunity, in my own way. I have tried kindness and coaxing with you; now we'll see how another tack will answer, with your infernal fuss about that baby."

"If you want to please me, you will kill us both," said

she, with a reckless defiance, looking straight into his cruel eyes.

"Not another word, d——n you," and he turned away to superintend his luggage, which was now being transferred ashore.

The morning was very cold and the wind blew violently. Some cabins of the wood-choppers were taken possession of and a fire kindled in the old deserted and tumble-down fire-places. This being a wood-yard, the steamer's whistle, that was blown violently as soon as she was in distress, brought the men who lived near by. Hawks made arrangements with one of them to carry him to the next town where he could get conveyance for his slaves to St. Charles, from which place he hoped to be able to reach St. Louis before the close of lower navigation on the Mississippi. After three days' tedious travel, he succeeded in reaching St. Charles, and obtaining some venturesome boatmen, under heavy bribes, to attempt crossing the Missouri River, filled with floating ice of wonderful shapes and sizes that the current was bearing rapidly down, so as to effectually prevent the usual ferry boat from crossing.

The boatmen said they could force their way over, so that the party embarked on what seemed like a frail skiff for such a voyage. On stepping into the boat, Martha missed her footing and would have fallen into the water had not Hawks seized her, snatched the baby from her trembling grasp and hurled it through the air, as related in the opening chapter.

CHAPTER XIII.

AFTER crossing the river at St. Charles, with his gang of slaves, Hawks procured teams and arrived in St. Louis that night. He drove to one of his well-known haunts, where Martha and the other slaves were placed in a back portion of the building, by means of a private way through a narrow alley; and though delirious and burning with fever, Martha walked along, caressing a bundle of clothes as her baby, sometimes talking soothingly to it and again raving and trying to rescue it from drowning in the most piteous tones.

Medical aid was at once summoned, as Hawks felt alarmed for the result of his inhuman act in taking the child from the mother in such a brutal way.

The physician pronounced the case brain fever, caused by cold and some great mental shock. After leaving medicine and giving instructions to keep the patient as quiet as possible, he took his leave, promising to look in on the morrow.

"That is a valuable woman," said he, as he walked downstairs with Hawks, who had been present and witnessed the diagnosis of the case. "She must have cost you a round sum. Where did you get her? Up country, I suppose? But you may lose her. She is desperately ill."

Hawks answered or evaded the questions of Dr. Elmore as suited his purpose.

On the following day, Martha's condition was worse, and day after day the doctor called. He shook his head when Hawks inquired if there was any hope, saying only :

"'As long as there is life, there is hope.'"

"I must go on the steamer to-morrow," said Hawks. "It may be her last trip for the season."

"As for taking that woman on board, Hawks, that's out of the question. You may as well put a bullet through her head at once."

"Let me have your bill in the morning, Doctor. How much is it?"

"All told, two hundred dollars."

"Indeed ? So much ? I had not expected it," said Hawks, dryly."

"You told me to spare no pains, time or money. I have called in two of our best physicians in consultation, and for the last few days, I have almost lived in this sick room ! "

"I'll have to sell a nigger to get the money to pay you." Hawks reflected a moment, then said, "Doctor, if you will pay the consulting physicians and give me a receipted bill for your services, I'll give you a bill-of-sale of this woman and let you cure her, if you can."

"That's a bad bargain, " responded the doctor, "but if you are hard up, I'll do it and take my chances."

So the necessary papers were made out and exchanged on the following morning, Hawks going south on the steamer, and Dr. Elmore redoubling his efforts to save his property, as well as patient.

The ninth day had come, and Dr. Elmore sat watching Martha, expecting a change, and hoping for a favorable one. A more quiet state of mind and body had set in ; the wandering eyes were closed, and sleep was now the last hope.

"Keep her perfectly still," said the doctor to the nurse. "If she wakes again, she will be saved ; answer no questions, and she may pull through."

At the expiration of three hours, the eyes of the sick woman opened wearily, and the faint light in the room disclosed the strange nurse.

"Where am I ?" whispered the patient.

"Be quiet, child, yous bery sick, and the doctor says you don mus talk any ; so be quiet, honey."

"Where is my baby ? Bring her quick or I'll get up and find her myself. Oh, I had such a dream about her. I thought she was lost in a river of ragin ice ! "

The nurse handed her the old bundle that had deluded and quieted her during her illness, but it failed of its purpose now. In great excitement. she cast it from her and with an effort to rise, fell back unconscious.

Upon the doctor's return, he gave her a soothing draught, and again she slept quietly.

In the morning, she said to her nurse in a natural voice :

"Where is my baby, and where am I?"

"Deed, honey, I can't tell you anyting. Marsa doctor done gib me one scorcher for lowin yer ter talk yistidy."

"But, Auntie, I must know about my baby," said Martha. "Tell me, is she safe and well?"

Dr. Elmore came lightly into the room just at that moment.

"She's woke up all right, Doctor," said the nurse.

"Doctor, where is my baby? I shall die if you don't tell me."

"You are too weak to talk now, Martha."

Martha shuddered and put up her hands to her head.

"O my God!" she said, in great agitation; "I remember all, now. How he tossed my baby into the water."

"Now take some of this broth," said the doctor. "I will talk this over by-and-by."

She did not seem to hear or see him; her eyes were fixed upon some imagined scene. "Oh, it all comes back now—the river—the floating ice—my baby whirled through the air. Somebody on the shore calling and holding out his arms—and then, all is blank—oh, my God! my God!" And she sank back, with dry, despairing eyes.

"Now, Martha," said the doctor, "I see how it was. You fainted and thought you saw your baby fall into the water. I warrant it is safe, and I will make an effort to get it for you. Take this broth and be quiet, so you may get well."

"Doctor, I don't want to get well; I want to die," said the girl, closing her eyes, but taking the broth, in obedience to the doctor's request.

Dr. Elmore was a kind-hearted man, and thought very seriously of making further inquiries into the story Martha had told him; but second thought prevailed. "She is likely to live, and I won't bother with the business; I may get into trouble, so I'll let events work themselves out," he thought to himself.

"How is your white elephant, your new purchase?" said the doctor's brother at dinner that day.

Chester Elmore was less inclined to the sentimental side of life than his elder brother, the doctor. He had been to see Martha, to satisfy himself as to what kind of an investment his brother had made in buying "a half-dead nigger," as the transaction was termed.

Seeing the woman with a fair chance of recovery, he was now feeling his way to a purchase if he could get a bargain. He was a bachelor, living with his mother and sister, at Independence Missouri, and was visiting St. Louis on business.

"Oh," said the doctor, "I think she'll pull through and in that event, I have made a thousand dollars."

"How much did you pay, Doc," persisted the brother.

"Let me see, Chet. My bill was one hundred and fifty dollars: I was to pay consulting physicians, which was fifty dollars extra."

"When Hawks left here," said his brother, you thought the case a desperate one; and I am mistaken if you wouldn't have preferred your doctor's bill to the nigger."

"Be that as it may, I would not take two or three such bills to-day for her. Now get her well, and she will bring in New Orleans fifteen hundred, easy."

"Provided," said Chet, "you could find a fool for a customer; one who had more money than brains."

"Well," said the doctor, "New Orleans has a double portion of such fools."

"However that may be, her talk about the lost baby shows there is something crooked in this matter. You may get into trouble yet. You know Hawks—not so well as I, perhaps, but well enough to be on your guard. I'll tell you what I'll do;—pay the charges and give you a hundred dollar bill and take my chances."

"No, Chet, I won't do that: but if you'll make it two hundred it's a bargain, for she would suit your family better than mine."

So the bargain was struck, and Martha was transferred to Chester Elmore by a bill-of-sale; and in the course of two weeks was declared well enough to go to Independence, where she was received by Miss Gertrude Elmore as a present from her brother Chester.

Miss Gertrude was a highly nervous sentimental young woman, very romantic, and though a spoiled child, had never been indulged in a waiting-maid; and when "Brother Chet," as she called him, made the announcement that Martha's duties were to wait on her, she was profuse in her thanks, and ordered her servant at once to place flowers upon the mantel-piece, with the air of a young princess.

Martha entered upon the discharge of her new duties with a heavy heart, for though she had told Dr. Elmore the particulars concerning the loss of her baby, she could give him no names of places, nor form any idea of how far they had travelled. The world had been a blank to her since swooning on the river, when the angry ice flood had risen up and (as she thought) engulfed her child.

Her new master had bid her abandon the foolish hope inspired by his brother of tracing the child. So, weak from sickness, with a hopeless yearning in her heart, she performed the rounds of duty like an automaton.

Miss Gertrude was informed of the occurrences of the few preceding weeks and thought it "perfectly horrid " that a human being could be so hard-hearted and cruel; and she repeated the story to Sally May, her dearest friend and companion.

"Wouldn't it make a splendid subject for a novel, Sally?" said Gertrude; and taking her pen, she wrote the headings of Martha's narrative down as nearly as possible.

CHAPTER XIV.

THE death of Harry Barnes very nearly proved fatal to his mother. He was her adored and only son, and every circumstance attending his last illness was so terrible, so mysterious, that it seemed as if her life, or else her reason, must succumb to the blow. She had not even the support of her brother's presence at this awful time, as Dr. Barnes, the day after his nephew had left him, was thrown from his carriage, and for weary months afterwards was laid up with a broken leg.

Owing to this combination of circumstances, a long time elapsed before the brother and sister met, and he could only administer such consolation and help as could be conveyed in letters.

At last she yielded to his earnest solicitation to come to Lucaston. He was cut to the heart when he saw the deep lines which suffering had left on her gentle face. Her heart was indeed broken, and he knew not how to comfort her. He tried to talk to her of indifferent things, and lead her mind away from the one absorbing subject.

"I forgot to inquire," said the doctor, "about Martha; do you find her useful?"

Mrs. Barnes looked at her brother in astonishment, and said: "I know nothing about Martha."

"Not know? Did not Harry explain?"

His sister looked at him in a bewildered way. "I do not know what you mean," she said. "You know my poor boy never said anything coherent: there were only strange, disconnected words. But, O William," said she, in an agony of recollection, "they will ring in my ears forever. He was in such distress about something. What was it? What had happened to my poor boy?" And convulsive sobs shook her frame.

"There, there, dear Lucy; don't think about it," said her brother, soothingly.

"But I *must* think about it; I can never forget it for

one moment. William," she said, catching her brother's hand eagerly, "you must help me to find out what it was that killed Harry; for I tell you he was *killed*," she said, with awful emphasis, "murdered."

"Did you find nothing of my letter, with the bill-of-sale to you?"

"Bill-of-sale!" said she, bewildered. "I have had no letter, and do not know what you mean by a bill-of-sale."

"My God!" said the doctor, "what does all this mean?"

Dr. Barnes then related all the circumstances attending the sending of Martha and her child with a bill-of-sale to be filled out with his sister's name if she consented to take the slave.

"I remember," said he, "how well Harry was looking when he boarded the steamer. Let me see—was it the 'Scott'? I must lose no time in learning from the captain all we can relative to the disappearance of the woman. There is something wrong about the matter, and I shall leave no stone unturned until the mystery is solved."

At the next trip of the steamer "Scott," Dr. Barnes called at the office and inquired for Captain Swan. The clerk was summoned, and the passenger record, upon careful search showed that, on a certain night of that year, there were transferred from the Clermont to the "Scott" by running alongside, a woman and child and one cabin passenger named Thomas Hawks from New Orleans.

"I know Hawks well," said Captain Swan. "A bold, vicious man."

"Yes," said Dr. Barnes, "this man Hawks came to Lucaston with Harry on his last visit, and they took the same boat for Louisville. I will go to New Orleans and search for him. I'll go down with you, Captain Swan, on your return trip, and in the mean time, we will think over the best plan of procedure."

A few days later, Dr. Barnes stepped on board the steamer "Scott" on her down trip to New Orleans and was welcomed by the captain.

"Then you have decided to go down and search for Hawks?" said the latter.

" Yes, Captain, and I shall need your services if we find him."

Arrived at New Orleans, both men made diligent inquiry in every quarter that Hawks frequented, but no trace could be found of him. The detectives were put to work, but with no better success, so that after an absence of two weeks, Dr. Barnes returned to Lucaston, disheartened, but feeling impelled forward in this search, that must not stop short of success.

CHAPTER XV.

Upon Tom Hawks' arrival at New Orleans, he disposed of his slaves to Colonel Ray, one of his old customers, who said finally:

"Well, Hawks, you have disappointed me in not bringing that woman you wrote me of; and from your description, I had expected to see something extra nice. How did it happen, anyway?"

"Oh, d—n it, I didn't write you anything about the baby she had; and in getting rid of that, I lost both. After the child had gone, the woman, like a fool, raved, took fever, and I suppose is dead before now." Then Hawks gave his own brutal version of the story of Martha, and how he had disposed of the child and its mother.

After he had concluded, Colonel Ray remarked rather dryly:

"I think you acted like a d——d fool, in giving away both mother and child. Take my advice, now, retrace your steps, and try to recover both."

"No need of immediate action in regard to the woman. Doctor Elmore is an old acquaintance, and if she's alive, I can reclaim her at a fair price any time. And as for the child, I don't think, Colonel, the game is worth the powder."

"A girl did you say? Take my advice and go back to St. Charles and pick up those dropped stitches in your work, so that you may at least make a finished job of it."

"You attach too much importance to this matter, Colonel, but I'll think of it. Now, let's have something to drink," and the two men strolled away to the spacious and elegant bar-room of the St. Charles Hotel.

Hawks had been drinking very heavily ever since Harry Barnes' death, and now celebrated his meeting with Ray with double quantity in his potations. His tongue began to feel the loosening effects of the stimulants.

"By G—d!" he said, "Ray, that was the sharpest game I've played yet." And then he gave his friend the particulars of the whole transaction on board the "Clermont."

Ray's face grew dark as he listened. "Hawks," said he, at last, "you must take care; you are talking very imprudently, and if you have done all you say, why, I advise you to skip."

Hawks was sobered in a moment. "What do you mean?" said he.

"Why, just this: Now,—suppose inquiry was made for the woman and child; they are known to have been on the steamer in the custody of your friend Barnes and yourself. He returns home in delirium: dies, I think you said, without recovering consciousness. Suspicion of foul play will rest on you, to whom they can be traced, and an ugly trial may ensue."

"But, d—n it, Ray, you must remember the bill-of-sale is regularly executed, and if Harry Barnes saw fit to gamble, lose, and I win them, there is nothing wrong, or at least criminal in that."

"But the transfer is illegal if the owners chose to question the transaction; besides, the drug you used will leave a trace, that is, if search were made. To be sure, I understand that in moderate quantities there is no danger, yet in larger doses, it is attended with fatal results; and how do you know that an overdose was not administered? I also notice that your name and the amount here are filled in with a different handwriting," and he pointed to the paper Hawks held in his hand. "No, by Jove, if it isn't your own hand! Why, man, what are you thinking of? That, in connection with Harry Barnes' suspicious death, would make an ugly case for you."

Hawks sat with lips compressed, silent for a moment. Then he said, angrily: "Look here, we've had enough of this now. In the first place, Barnes wrote there what you ascribe to me, and you convict me of murder and theft by your suppositions."

"No, no, Hawks; I am not trying to convict you of anything; I only want you to see the thing in its true light. Of course inquiries will be made about this woman and child. They can easily be traced to you.

Coupled with Barnes' death, it has an unpleasant look to me, and my motive is to have you see it in its true light. I'm your friend, old fellow," said he, putting his hand on Hawks' arm. "You may count on me every time."

"Well, what would you do?" asked Hawks, quite humbled and subdued.

"Well, I'll tell you what I'd do: I'd keep shady in these parts while you must be here; put on a planter's disguise, go to Missouri and get trace of the woman and baby, and you may also get information of your own case, for you will certainly be searched for here."

"Well, I'll think of it," said Hawks, indifferently. But he had secretly resolved he would do it, and from that night, the haunts he was wont to frequent knew him no more for a long time.

CHAPTER XVI.

"My Dear Kate:

"Anticipating your surprise at the above, I will try to tell you briefly how it is that I am here.

"While visiting my Colonists, a few weeks ago, Sam, whom, of course, you remember, was kidnapped in open day, by some ruffians, and forcibly carried away. I was able to trace them as far as Booneville, where I learned the poor fellow had been sold to a gentleman owning a large stock-farm. Of course misleading clues were plentifully scattered upon the trail by the miscreants, so that I lost much time in my pursuit; but, through the aid of an extraordinarily clever fellow it has been my good fortune to meet and impress into my service, I think we are now on the right road and not far from the object of our search, that the gentleman who purchased him is, in fact, a resident of Missouri, and, through the aid of Mr. Duvall, I hope soon to find him. What we are to do *then*, I cannot yet see very clearly, as I suppose there is no place on this planet where justice is so difficult to obtain to-day as in this perturbed border State. It would be impossible to imagine a more strangely disordered condition of society than exists here now.

"Colonel Gordon, a Southern gentleman of swelling pretensions, who is here on a singular and questionable mission, has taken me under his distinguished protection because of my Kentucky birth, forsooth! In fact, but for his intervention, I doubt if his followers would have permitted Duvall and me to land at all. It is surprising that a gentleman, such as he unquestionably is, can have gathered about him such a band of miscreants as the fellows who actually took possession of the steamer on which I came to this city. They inspected the baggage, and if they found arms in the possession of Northerners, they were confiscated, and the owners told they would be shot if they attempted to land on Kansas soil. The method of inspection was, to say the least, original. After being saturated with bad whiskey, they fired pistols into suspicious packages, then broke them open, and threw their contents into the river, or appropriated them as suited them. Colonel Gordon, when appealed to, frankly confessed his inability to hold in check the pandemonium he had invoked, which was about at its height when we approached Kansas City, and Captain Jim, Colonel Gordon's lieutenant, ordered four men with revolvers to stand at the gang-plank, and prevent any one from landing who was not vouched for by himself.

"You may imagine that Duvall and I were challenged, and I cannot tell how it might have ended had not Colonel Gordon interposed; and after a whispered conference we were permitted to pass with our luggage. For the sake of the success of my own mission here, I submit to this 'protection,' and have not let the colonel find out what a political renegade I am, from his standpoint, nor in what contempt and loathing I hold the methods he and his band of followers are using to capture this territory of Kansas for their iniquitous system.

"Duvall has to hold me in check all the time to prevent me from, exploding with wrath and indignation; and nothing but the thought of poor Sam restrains me. But this matter once settled, I shall soon tear off my mask, and cast 'my lot where my inclinations and my convictions lead me.

"I have met a singular and most impressive man,—a man with a mingled suggestion of priest, prophet and king. If these were heroic times, I should expect him to fill a great *rôle*; but the age is prosaic, as is his name, —John Brown. Yes, I confess it is not easy to invest that name with sublimity.

"I must not forget to tell you something about my friend Claude Duvall, to whom I have so frequently alluded. He is a foreigner, Italian, but thoroughly at home and conversant with things in America. He is accomplished, brilliant, versatile, vivacious, with wonderful charm of manner and person, and better than all, with a heart ardent as a child's. I think he is especially delightful to me because he possesses all the qualities I lack; and I am most fortunate in having so sympathetic and congenial a friend and co-operator in this search. Although the soul of truth, his tact, skill, fertility in resource are unfailing. He does not carry his heart upon his sleeve; has, in fact, a talent for diplomacy, which, perhaps you remember, is *not* my forte. He sympathizes with my feeling about human freedom and such kindred subjects, but naturally does not take it so much to heart as I do, and, I think, perhaps, is more impelled by a feeling personal to me than by any sentiment more abstract.

"Regarding himself, he is reticent; so that I do not understand at all his mission in America, nor why he has been willing to follow my fortunes (or rather misfortunes) during all these past four years. Chance threw us together shortly after that strange and still unexplained incident, the finding of Petrel. He has shown great adroitness in his efforts to unearth the mystery, and is much chagrined that he has not yet been successful; and we are as far as ever from knowing the fate of the woman, presumably her mother. It is a strange story— but, in the mean time, the little girl is happy and well cared for at the Colony, which seems the best place for her at present.

"Will you present my compliments to the fair little maid who bears your name, and who, I hope, will inherit at least a portion of her mother's virtues? I have not yet become accustomed to thinking of you in this new *rôle*, my sweet cousin; but I am sure you fill it, as you have all others, with rare perfection. At least, such is the belief of

"Your admiring and very affectionate cousin,

"FRANK."

Frank was not mistaken. He was near the object of his search. A camp-meeting was held at Big Springs Camp Ground, and, knowing the custom of Southern people to carry their servants to these meetings, and the habits of the slaves on Sunday to congregate in large numbers about the grounds, he suggested to Duvall that they should ride over there from Kansas City.

In strolling about, they came upon a group of three persons conversing, in a small grove, some distance from the central grounds. Clayton felt strongly impressed by the vicious-looking trio, and was observing them closely when Duvall said,

"Did you notice the old negro the young men were talking to there? He sits bowed over, with his head on his hands."

After the men left him, Clayton approached the bowed figure, and said,

"Are you sick, old man?"

The man sprung up as if struck by an electric shock.

"Bless de Lor'! Dat bin Mars Frank's voice. Whar is yer, Mars Frank, whar is yer? Let dese eyes behol' yer once mo'!" And, standing almost as tall as his young master, he grasped the extended hand of Clayton and covered it with kisses. At the same time falling on his knees, he bowed his head to the very earth, saying, "Tank de Lor'! Tank de Lor'! He done foun' dis poor slave to libber him outer bondage."

Clayton, who was nearly as much moved as his old slave, lifted him up, and said soothingly:

"Come, come, Sam, rise up. I am glad at last to find you, as I have sought you faithfully for months."

"Dar, Mars Frank, I knowed you was a lookin' in ebery hole and corner for dis ole nigger; dat war de star ob hope I hung onto when eberyting else looked dark. I jis said to mysef, 'Mars Frank he knowed dese foxes what steals niggers, an' he's gwineter foller der tracks.'"

"Tell me, Sam, how you came here, and whom you are living with?"

Clayton learned from his old servant that he had been bought by a man named Skinner, living near Big Springs in Missouri. Sam told the story of his being kidnapped at the Landing, and being knocked down and taken into a boat by four men, one of whom seemed to be the leader, and was Sam Sly, of Lucaston. He had mistaken Sam for Uncle Ned.

"Yes," said Clayton. "He and Sparks consider themselves revenged now. But this is not ended yet; they will hear from me again."

Clayton had seated himself upon the rustic bench beside his old servant, but Duvall's quick eye detected danger in a sinister-looking man who was watching them.

"Dat is young Mars Skinner hissef," said Sam.

Clayton gave a parting injunction to Sam to keep quiet about their meeting, and if questioned, to say only that he was an old acquaintance.

Poor Sam's face fell in disappointment, as he saw his master leave him.

"Dar now, de sun done set again. Does seem as do Mars Frank oughter took Sam 'long wid him." But he rightly suspected that he would not be deserted by him.

After arriving at home that night, Sam was questioned by his new master as to whom he was talking with so earnestly down near the Springs.

"Dat was Mars Clayton. He comes from de same part ob ole Kaintuck what Sam did. Bress yer life, Mars William, 'twould do yer eyes good ter see dem folks what lib in ole Kaintucky!"

"Well, never mind about that, now, Sam; I am going to my claim in Kansas to-morrow, and I want my horse in readiness early, as Mr. Livingstone and Bill Hart are going also. Look to my pistols and shot-gun. I notice they're rusting. Is there one of the loose horses up from the pasture, Sam?"

"Yes, sah, dar's Charley and Wil' Injin."

"Well, you see that both horses are fed early, and taken good care of."

"Yes, sah, I'se gwinter do dat."

Sam stood looking after his master, and saying to himself:

"I hope Mars William's not gwinter ax me to go out dar to dat dar place what he call 'claim' whar dey all meets ter drink whiskey and kill ablition yankees. I done had 'nough ob dat; an' I wants ter see what Mars Frank gwinter do ter take Sam back."

"Sam," said William Skinner, on the following morning, while inspecting his pistol, "I want you to saddle Charley and go with me out to the claim directly after breakfast. You need not say where you are going. Mend that girth to my saddle, and see that my bridle is all right, for I'm not ready to go to heaven by a somersault over Wild Indian's head."

Sam's worst fears were now being confirmed; and it was with a heavy heart that he completed the preparation.

"I doe like ter know, Sam, what makes yo face so much longer dan usual dis mawnin'?" inquired the old cook, as Sam's appetite, hitherto excellent, seemed entirely to fail him at breakfast. He had previously told Aunt Hannah his story, and now an idea occurred to him that she would be sure to see any one who came to see the young master on business. So he confided to her his meeting his former master and friend at camp-meeting the day before, and his belief that an effort was to be made to recover his liberty. He described his young master; and told her if he should come to the house, she was to tell him privately where Sam had gone, and where young Skinner's claim was located.

In the afternoon, three gentlemen rode up to the house of Mr. Skinner, dismounted and walked in. Aunt Hannah was on the lookout, and recognized Clayton at a glance. As they were about to enter, she said to him:

"Young Mars looks as do he's tired, an' like he wants dis good drink ob nice cool water," holding it toward him from the bucket. He stepped to where she was, and as he took the gourd she told him in an undertone, where Sam had been taken and how he could reach the claim.

On inquiring of the elder Skinner, he could give no information of his son Bill's movements. He might be at Independence, or down to the camp-meeting. Skinner recognized the officer with Clayton, and said:

"I hope Bill hasn't been getting into trouble down at the Springs?"

"Oh, no," said Duvall, "our business can wait until he returns," and they took their leave.

Skinner, attended by Sam, and accompanied by two visiting friends, Hart and Livingstone, started for the claim or settlement. He related to them what he had seen at the camp-meeting; and ended by saying that as a precautionary measure, he was bringing Sam where no legal process could reach him.

"He would have to make a mighty strong case out there to get his man," said Hart, significantly pointing to the revolver. "He would have to beat, not only two 'pairs,' but three of them; eh, Tom?"

"Damn the law!" said Livingstone. "There oughtn't to be any law. The weak are made to serve the strong in the same manner that the little fish serve the big ones,

the bugs the birds, the birds the hawks, and they in turn
serve us. I'd like to keep outside the law and its
restraints."

Thus the trio chatted during their ride, keeping Sam at
a safe distance in their rear.

After leaving the house of Mr. Skinner, the officer said,
" Mr. Clayton, my functions end at the state line of Missouri. Any time you come within this jurisdiction, I'll
serve the process, or a new one, if this expires."

" I must find the man," said Clayton, " and trust to circumstances to get him within jurisdiction of the law. I
will ask that this matter have as little notoriety as
possible."

So they separated, the officer going to Independence
and Clayton to Kansas City. He now felt assured that
young Skinner knew or suspected Sam's status, and in
that lay his danger.

After consultation, it was decided that Clayton and
Duvall should each buy a butternut disguise and an outfit
for camp life or "taking a claim," and follow, as nearly
as possible, the fortunes of Sam, led as he was, by the trio
of reckless men, Skinner, Bill Hart and Livingstone.

The following day they left Kansas City with a covered
wagon, two good horses attached, a negro driver, and each
mounted, armed and equipped in appropriate style.

A week later found them located on a high plateau of
ground near the now thriving city of Lawrence, overlooking the valley of the Waurarusa and the Kansas River for
some miles away to the south and to the east, and about
ten miles from Lecompton, near which was then Camp
Gordon, in honor of our steamboat acquaintance, Colonel
Gordon.

To this latter point had Clayton traced William Skinner and his companions with Sam. The staking off of
their claims was done in the usual way, which was only a
loose formality; for very few of the men who came from
Missouri ever expected to return to these claims after the
vexed question of slavery in Kansas was settled under
squatter sovereignty.

CHAPTER XVII.

The election which was to be held in November, 185-, was an important event not only in Kansas and Missouri, but for the whole country, North and South, East and West, being interested; for it was not only to select a Territorial legislature and local officers, but to determine directly the question of slavery or freedom on the soil now neutral.

If slavery, by such means as we have seen at Kansas City and Camp Gordon, can extend and occupy Kansas, then Nebraska, Minnesota, and the western territories would be an easy prey.

In great contrast to those at Camp Gordon were the settlements at Lawrence, Topeka, and other points in that section. In these latter places were seen women and children, cattle, farming implements, and all the paraphernalia pertaining to agricultural life, none of which were noticeable in the other settlements. Most of the settlers were Northern or Eastern people, as distinctly sectional and as outspoken against slavery as the others were its advocates, but with much more of the permanency of citizenship, which gave the right of voice in controlling the question.

A few days later there rode up to the rude shanty Clayton and his companions had erected, five men, and, without ceremony or parley, the leader proceeded to inform the gentlemen that there now remained but a few days before the election and it had been determined to make quick work in driving away from the settlement, any and every man who was going to vote against the institution of slavery in Kansas, and all must come forward and bear a part, as there was considerable territory to be visited.

"We are expected," he said, "to clean out two d——d Yankee settlements just below, and all will be needed, for they have already defied the written notice served several days ago."

Clayton arose from his seat, evidently to enter his indignant protest, when Claude said:

"Allow me to speak first. I intend to vote for Kansas to be a slave State. I shall vote in good faith. I am a Southern man, in favor of extending the institution, but not by such means."

"You then decline to join us in preventing these Yankee paupers from stealing Kansas?" said Livingstone, fiercely.

"Yes," said Clayton, stepping forward, "we most respectfully decline to engage in this business, either before or at the elections, as I understand the game is to prevent any one from voting who will not vote your ticket."

"Sir," said Livingstone, eying him with ill-suppressed rage, "I hope you mean no disrespect in referring to this matter with such accent on 'game.'"

"Nothing more, sir, than to call things by their right names."

"Oh, sir, we understand each other. I expected nothing more of you, but we are disappointed in your companion. Now we would not be surprised to find you in the Yankee camp when the conflict comes, as it seems likely to."

"They are our neighbors here, and we would be hardly deserving the name if we should refuse to help them defend their homes against such a wanton outrage as you propose. Yes, I think you may calculate on find ing us standing shoulder to shoulder with them in defence of our common rights as American citizens."

"I have a damn big notion to take you prisoners to Colonel Gordon, and thus prevent you from going to the enemy."

"It might be well to count the cost before you under take such a task, sir." And at the same time Clayton imitated Claude in buckling on his revolvers and picking up his rifle. Both had observed Livingstone nod to his men, who turned their horses and came to his side.

"Now, gentlemen," said Livingstone, "you can see the utter folly of two of you contending against five of us. I have only to say the word and you either surrender or die."

Clayton and Claude, as if with one thought, sprang

inside the log cabin and barred the door. Then, thrusting the muzzles of their rifles out of the cracks, they said :

"Give the order, and take the consequences!"

"Hold on!" yelled Livingstone, dumfounded by the unexpected turn affairs had taken ; and with a sickly smile, which was meant to be conciliatory, he added, " I was only joking with you and trying a little bluff. Come, come, let us talk the thing over in a friendly spirit. Open your hospitable doors and come out."

Clayton said, " Now, sir, you and your squad have just five minutes to get out of range of these Sharp's rifles."

" I be dogone if 'tain't one of 'em, Cap'n. Yes, Cap'n, it's one of them damnation ' Beecher Bibles,' sure as fallin' off a log. We'd better git," said two of the men, almost in the same voice ; and, without waiting for further orders, both of them wheeled their horses, and were soon out of sight.

Clayton now unfastened the door, and stepped out, saying :

"Our numbers are more equal now. I guess we don't need the blockhouse." At the same time taking out his watch, he continued: "You have only two minutes of your allotted five in which to get out of range of this rifle."

"You don't mean to execute that threat made in anger ? "

" If you are not out of sight within five minutes, you will find we did mean it," said Clayton, with an unmistakable determination in his eye.

The two men who had stood by Livingstone, like their companions, put spurs to their horses, while Livingstone moved off sullenly, swearing loudly for revenge.

"Now," said Clayton to his servant, " bring my horse quickly!" And turning to his friend, " You get everything in readiness to move down to Lawrence. This is no safe place for us over-night. Livingstone had murder in his eye when he left here. I am going to ride up to the trail on the bluff, and see where those fellows are."

Two hours later, when he returned, the wagon was loaded with everything, in readiness to move. Clayton and his companion mounted their horses, and were followed by the wagon.

"I am really attached to this spot," said Clayton, "and I intend to have that claim, which was only staked off as a matter of form, to be my abiding-place. Our reception of Gordon's men now cuts us off from Sam and any means of information of his master's movements. That is my chief regret."

Clayton and Duvall soon reached the little settlement of Lawrence, on the bank of the Kansas River.

They rode into the town, dismounted, and as their team drove up, several of the settlers crowded curiously about them.

A large man, with piercing, deep-set eyes, severe brow and commanding presence, approached them.

"I hope you are not leaving us, Mr. Clayton?" said he, extending his hand to Frank.

"No, indeed. Mr. Brown," replied Frank, flushing with gratification at the warmth of this welcome; "no, indeed; so far from that, I have come to stay with you, if you will permit."

The large hand grasped his with a stronger pressure. "You are most welcome, sir; it is such men as you that we want here."

"Well," said Frank, laughing, "they were not especially desirous of keeping us at the place we came from, so we are here to cast in our lot with the people in Lawrence."

In the few hours that followed, Frank found a willing and deeply interested listener in Mr. Brown, as he recounted to him all the circumstances which had led up to the manumission of his slaves, their successful colonization in Illinois, the kidnapping of Sam, and subsequent search for him, ending with the adventure of the day with Livingstone and his band.

All these things were vividly told by the narrator and listened to with rapt, eager interest by his visitor.

The old man looked in silence at Frank for a few moments, after he had finished, and then said: "It is strange, we see sometimes a man like you come out of such unnatural surroundings. How do you suppose you came by all these splended impulses? I will tell you." said he, answering his own question, in impressive tone, "they are God dwelling in you. It is a good thing to have freed your slaves; you have done well; but," he added, with a sigh, "that is not the way this thing is to be done. That is not the way," he added, musingly—and then, with sudden fervor: "It will require a convulsion —a *convulsion*, I tell you," said he, with suppressed passion in his voice, "to rid us of this iniquity. But it is working: the leaven is working."

Frank looked with a kind of fascination upon the strange light in the face before him. They walked together out under the stars; although it was midnight, he was reluctant to part from his new friend. As his eye swept the horizon, in the direction of his "claim," he saw something which startled him.

A light! It increased, wavered, then grew brighter and brighter. "The scoundrels!" he exclaimed. "Mr. Brown, look there! see, they are burning my cabin, just as I expected," said he, with a grim laugh. "I knew they would come back to-night for revenge, and finding we have gone, they wreak their vengeance on the cabin."

He was not mistaken. In the morning, when Clayton rode over to the claim, he found nothing but a pile of ashes to distinguish the spot where the friendly shelter from the storm and savage violence had stood on the previous day. Posted on a board, driven in the ground near by, were these words, written in a bold hand:

"So we treat all traitors to the South."

CHAPTER XVIII.

In a few days followed the election—and to attempt a description of the disgraceful scenes which were enacted would be a difficult task.

The ruffians marched from poll to poll and paraded around, firing pistols, and voting as often as they could think of a name under which to cast a ballot, and in many cases, openly putting in two or three tickets in utter disregard of law.

A protest was an invitation to be shot; and few indulged in the expensive luxury.

The election over, and the result announced, thousands of those who came only to vote returned to their old homes in Missouri. Among the number were our friends from Camp Gordon, Livingstone, Hart and Skinner.

Claude Duvall and Clayton followed closely on the heels of the returning party, and when they reached Kansas City, a new process was issued and served on Mr. Skinner, calling on him to bring his servant Sam into court and show title.

On the day of the trial, Livingstone and Hart were seen in earnest conversation near the door of the courtroom. Hart was evidently protesting against his friend's threat to lynch Clayton as "a d——d traitor to the South and the meanest kind of abolitionist."

"Even if the justice holds that the nigger is a free man and that Jim's bill-of-sale is not valid," said Hart, "we can take him from the officers and shove him out in Kansas, where no process from court will have any effect. No need to be in a hurry. Let us hear the case and *act* afterwards."

So he prevailed, and when the case was called, Sam was brought in, accompanied by Wm. Skinner, who produced a regular bill-of-sale, signed by Samuel Sly for the valuable consideration of $700.

"Now, Mr. Skinner, have you any witnesses to this purchase and bill of sale?" demanded the Court.

"I have, your honor. Mr. Livingstone here was with me on the day of purchase, and heard the representation of Sly and his neighbor, Mr. Smith, as to the ownership of this man ; and to the fact that he had been recently captured in an effort to escape from him and was sold for no other fault."

Livingstone's testimony corroborated Skinner. Clayton was asked if he had any further testimony to offer other than was set forth in his affidavit, on which the process was issued.

"I have, your honor, a witness whom I should like sworn."

When the oath was administered to Claude Duvall, the justice asked :

" Do you know this man Sam ? "

"Only since I saw him some weeks ago in the service of Mr. Skinner."

"How did you come to know him ? "

" I was employed by Mr. Clayton to aid him in recovering a negro who he said had been kidnapped and we have been on the trail some months."

"So you do not know whether this is a slave or a free man ? "

" I do not."

" Where do you live ?"

" St. Louis, Missouri."

" Have you known Mr. Clayton long ? "

" Only since employed in this case, except a casual meeting some time before."

" Mr. Clayton, would you like to question the witness further ? " asked the justice.

" I would like, your honor, to ask if he was present when I found Sam at Big Springs ? "

" Yes, your honor, and I should judge by the manner of the nigger that they were in the relation of master and slave."

"There ! you simply judge this man belongs to Mr. Clayton. You know nothing about it absolutely," roared Livingstone. " I object to the witness answering the question, your honor. This is an unwarrantable interference of an outside party."

" The witness need not answer the question."

Clayton himself was then sworn. He testified to having

known the man since his boyhood, and that he had inherited him from his grandfather Lucas' estate, and was absolutely sure this was the same man so inherited and removed from Kentucky to Illinois, from which place he was kidnapped.

During this time, there was a whispered conversation between the trio and Claude in one corner of the courtroom. Then Mr. Skinner stepped forward, and said:

" Your honor, I would like to ask the witness a few questions before he leaves the stand. I wish to know if he claims this man as his slave, or as merely held illegally as a slave by myself as set forth in his affidavit ? "

" Oh, of course, as a slave," answered the Court.

Skinner remarked: " I would like to have the witness answer the question."

" I claim as set forth in my affidavit, that he is illegally held as a slave by Mr. Skinner ; and as his friend and attorney, I demand his release."

" Then this man is not your slave ? "

" He is not."

" Is he a slave at all ? "

" He is, in law and equity, a free man, kidnapped from his home and family, and as his friend and former master, I demand his release."

" Has he his free papers, Mr. Clayton ? "

" I have them here, sir," taking from his pocket Sam's manumission papers ; " there they are, for your honor's inspection."

While the justice was examining the papers, a further whispered conference ensued between Skinner and Duvall, and Skinner said aloud :

" The man cannot be set at liberty as a freeman in this State without first giving a good and satisfactory bond in the sum of two thousand dollars for his good behavior. Am I not right, your honor ? "

" Such is the law," answered the justice.

" I think we will have no trouble in giving any bond your honor may exact," responded Clayton.

" We will see about that," answered Livingstone, with a hiss like a viper.

" We will," said Clayton, turning upon him with a look of defiance.

Sam had been anxiously watching the proceedings from

the corner where he sat, and judging from the pallid face and earnest manner of his young master that the case was going against him, could restrain himself no longer, as he burst out with great feeling :

"Bless de Lor', massa jedge might jis so well say Sam don' know he head nor his own han's as ter say dat Mars Frank dar don't know and own dis nigger. Ebber since he was little pickaninny, I done bin call him Mars Frank, long afore Mars Lucas or Miss Fannie died."

During the delivery of this speech, the Court had ordered silence. Clayton told him to sit down ; that he was not allowed to say anything. The judge ordered the bailiff to "silence that nigger," and Clayton had gone over to compel obedience, when Livingstone strode forward and in a threatening manner, said :

" I'll silence the d—n scoundrel."

" No, you'll not," said Clayton, interposing to stop the mad bull. " The officer of the court will do that without your assistance." And the two men glared at each other, as if each were taking the full measure of his adversary.

"Order in court," shouted the bailiff, as he forced Sam to sit down ; and, stepping between the two angry men, he said :

" Be seated, gentlemen."

" Is there any further testimony to be offered in the case ? " inquired the justice.

" None," answered the plaintiff and defendant alike.

" Then the Court will render judgment. The testimony is conflicting as to ownership of Mr. Skinner, and in opposition to his bill-of-sale, is offered in evidence the free papers of this man, and his discharge is asked on the ground that he is a free man by virtue of such manumission. If we admit the genuineness of the papers, the Court could not release this man in absence of the required bond."

" That bond we stand prepared to give, whatever the amount or conditions," responded Clayton."

" I believe, if your honor will permit, the law requires two or more property-holders in the county where such manumitted slave shall reside, to be bound each in double the penal sum of the bond," interposed Skinner.

" We can meet that objection," said Clayton, "by depositing the money in the hands of the Court."

"That does not meet the requirements of the law. Two property-holders who shall reside in the county where the nigger lives," persisted Skinner.

"Then," continued Clayton, "we will deposit the money with some property-holders who can go on the bond."

"Yes," put in Livingstone, "'can go on the bond.' I'd smile to see any man in this county go on that bond. Not much, Mr. Clayton. You can't give that bond here."

Clayton stood speechless, as the Court continued:

"Gentlemen, the case does not turn altogether on the validity of a bond. The preponderance of evidence is in favor of the bill-of-sale ; and in view of this fact, and, as I take it, the impossibility to give the bond as required by law, judgment is rendered in favor of the defendant."

The case was lost. "What else could I have expected?" Clayton was saying to himself, as he left the court-room, trying not to see the vulgar jeers and laughter of the three victors, nor, what hurt him most of all, the disappointment and distress of Sam.

Clayton returned the following day to Lawrence. There he was a witness to the farce of the installation of officers recently elected, who, in many cases, were absolutely residents of Missouri ; and to the meeting of the Territorial legislature, composed of the same class of people.

Sam went back to slavery with a heavy heart after the trial, when he thought himself under the double protection of his young master and the law. There was one hope left him, and to this he clung with all the tenacity of a drowning man, and that was he knew "Mars Frank neber would quit tryin' ter get Sam outer der clutches ob dese heah nigger-stealin' white trash till de day of judgment done come, suah nuff."

CHAPTER XIX.

THE flowers had blossomed five successive summers upon poor Harry Barnes' grave. And since that interview with his comrade and patron, Colonel Ray, Hawks had been seen no more by his friends. The sad episode had ceased to be talked about. Dr. Barnes had apparently relinquished his purpose of unearthing the mystery of his nephew's death, and time seemed to have covered this with the decent mantle she spreads over so many other unsightly things.

Hawks believed he might now safely emerge from his long retirement (or perhaps it was exile); and one bright May morning there appeared in the little town of St. Charles a sedate-looking, dark-complexioned gentleman, with a broad-brimmed hat and a closely buttoned coat, which left one in doubt as to whether he were planter or Quaker.

It will be interesting to read the thoughts which were at work under that broad-brimmed hat, and the purposes in the heart buttoned so respectably under that drab coat. This gentleman was saying to himself, " Five years is a good while, and people are not likely to busy themselves about all that now. It'll be a mighty nice thing to get hold o' that kid. I was a —— fool to throw her away, and I managed the whole business like a —— fool. Kinder lost my head for once in my life. But I'll catch up with 'em yet. This old boy hasn't been thinkin' and thinkin' this five years for nothin'. I'll find 'em both, sure's my name's Tom Hawks."

Such were the unpleasant thoughts of the respectable stranger as he wandered carelessly down by the riverside, and entered into conversation with whomsoever chance threw in his path.

One man in answer to his question, said :

" Why, yas ; I do remember hearin' my old friend Si Jones tellin' suthin' like that happenin' to him. 'Twas in his own boat not fur from where we now are. How he did cuss that trader, though ! I hearn him tell as how he was nigh to knockin' him overboard when the wench screamed and fell down in a faint as her baby was throw'd on shore."

"Do you know where Si Jones is?" queried Hawks, as he saw the old fisherman shifting his quid of tobacco for a fresh start.

"Well, stranger, there an't many folks, I reckon, as knows much about Si durin' summer. I hearn some say as he follows the geese and ducks and wild fowl way up 'bout the North Pole, where he has a kind of knack for fishin' and huntin' in the open sea. P'raps you know what that is, an' whar' 'tis. They do say that Si Jones has owned up to having actually found that North Pole, and to have fished with it for whales, using a two-inch cable for a line and a ship's anchor for a hook."

"You're a jolly fellow," broke in Hawks to the garrulous fisherman. "There, take that," tossing him a silver dollar. "Make further inquiries about Si Jones or any of his crew who ferried over the drove of slaves."

Turning to leave the crowd of fishermen who had been listening to Gulliver, or "Gull," as he was known among his companions because of his wonderful stories he never tired of telling :

"Stranger," said a small man, ill-clad, with one leg six inches shorter than the other, an oar in one hand and a slouched hat in the other, "I was here when that boat-load of niggers was set across the ice, and I seed the man ketch the baby. I b'lieve you's mistaken 'bout its being a nigger baby ; 'twas jis' as white as any of us, and that are fine gentleman which caught it, jis' like a trab-ball, he declared it were a white baby some one had stole. He follered nex' day over to St. Louis to kinder find out about the thing. But he didn't, all the same,—leastwise, I hearn him tell the lan'lady up to the hotel that no soundin' could be had of 'em ; and so he finally kinder took to the chile an' carried it off with him. Stranger, I sells fish to the hotel an' the lan'lady knows what I tell you is all true ; an' if yer wanter know mor' 'an this, she kin tell it to yer."

Hawks had listened attentively to this story, walking slowly away from the crowd.

"Now," said he, putting some silver in the man's hand,

"say nothing of what you have told me, but meet me here to-morrow at this hour."

At the hotel Hawks heard from Tabitha's own lips all the details of that dramatic incident, which, indeed, she had told, at least a thousand times since, and with which she invariably entertained a new guest.

"What became of the child?" said Hawks.

"Well, I tried to get it myself and offered to adopt it if Mr. Clayton would——"

"What did you say was his name?" interrupted Hawks, impetuously.

"Clayton—Mister Clayton—and as fine a gen——"

"Where from?" said Hawks.

"Kentucky," said Tabitha, rather stiffly. She was not used to such lack of respect in her listeners, and began to look at this Quaker gentleman through her spectacles with a fresh scrutiny.

Hawks was quick to perceive that he was losing ground, and very graciously praised the fried fish he was eating before resuming.

"Did I understand you that Mr. Clayton was from Kentucky?" in his blandest tone.

Tabitha melted at once.

"Why, yes, I think so, or was it from Illinois? No, it was Kentucky—from Louisville or Lucaston. I have heard him speak of that little town often."

At the name "Lucaston," Hawks gave a start, as though the ghost of some recollection had thrust a dagger into his hardened conscience, and, pushing away his plate, he left the room.

When old Crank was met according to appointment, he was plied with questions as to where Clayton lived.

"Well, stranger, I think it is in Illinoy, somewhar; but Si Jones knows all about that ere man, and can go an' put his hand on him. You see Si, he claims to be a Kentuckian and that kinder makes him and the fine gentleman take to each other. You know Kentuckians are worse 'an a bird of a feather."

"But damnation, Crank, where is Si?" said Hawks, losing all patience with the old man's loquacity.

"He's gone north with the wild fowl, but, stranger, he comes back in cold weather an' you kin git all you want

out of him by givin' him a drink of likor and startin' him
on the subject."

Failing to get more information, Hawks decided to employ Crank to work for him in this business, and to aid
him in making a search at the river towns. Hawks and
Crank searched the towns on the Illinois side of the Mississippi River, Hawks making Alton his headquarters.

"If we succeed in finding this child," said Hawks one
day to Crank, "there will have to be a trial in court, and
I am going to claim it as my own slave."

"The devil you are! it's no nigger," said the astonished Crank; "it's white'n 'n you an' me put together.
That won't go down nowhere, stranger; no, sir, that won't
go down—leas'wise, I don't think so," he added, as he
looked up and saw his employer's scowling face glaring at
his own diminutive figure.

"Well, that is no concern of yours. You remember that
the child was handed to the man on shore by the gentleman in the boat."

"No, stranger, I said it was throw'd to him like a trab-
ball."

"Damnation, Crank, here's what I want you to say
when you are asked, and it's the truth too:—that the
baby was put in this man's hands to hold while we were
fixing the niggers in the boat, and pushed off, leaving the
child in his custody. I am going to swear to that state
of facts; do you understand?"

"Yes, stranger, but they are not all facts, for you was
agoin' to throw the kid under the ice, that's jis' what you
said when you——"

"*I* said? You say *I* was goin' to throw?" thundered
Hawks, glowering at Crank's diminutive figure. "What
in h—l do you mean by that?"

"Come now, stranger," said Crank, with a queer laugh,
"that won't go down. Why, I know'd you from the fust
word you spoke about that."

"Oh, well," said Hawks, more quietly, "that's all right.
You and I are going to be sort of partners," said he, slap-
ping his friend good-naturedly on the shoulder. "But—
mum's the word," he added, with a warning gesture,
"don't forget."

"No; I won't forgit." But there was something in
the tone which was not quite satisfactory to Hawks.

"Crank," said he, fixing his eye upon him so that it seemed to hold him, "I pay well for work; I think you know that. How does that suit of clothes compare with the one I found you in?"

"Yes, stranger," said Crank, meekly; "I only kinder thought you was mistaken about some of the fax. That's all."

"Well, now, you just bear in mind you've got to remember things as *I* do. Do you hear?"

CHAPTER XX.

Spring had blossomed into summer, and Hawks was still searching for his prey. He and Crank were on a steamer, passengers to St. Louis, when a slight accident detained them at Perkins' Landing on the Illinois side of the Mississippi River. Strolling up to the warehouse—store and saloon combined—Hawks inquired of Mr. Perkins the price of land, and the character of the settlers.

"Have you many Southern people here?"

"Some few, mostly from across the river. Mr. Stanley, or Mr. Clayton's team has just left the door. They are from Kentucky. Mr. Clayton, I think, owns the settlement and his cousin, John Stanley, superintends the niggers that work for him. Clayton is away from home, and is absent a good deal."

"What is Mr. Clayton's first name?" inquired Hawks, ordering a drink of whiskey and inviting the proprietor to join him. Perkins looked up and observed the eager expression of his questioner.

"Frank Clayton is his name, sir."

"I think I know or used to know this Mr. Clayton. Can you tell me, has he any family?"

"About five years ago, he brought a small child to the settlement; some say it might be his, though the old nigger woman who tends to it, says it is a stolen baby that he found somewhere. But I don't know anything about it. None of my business you know."

On leaving the warehouse, Hawks said:

"I believe I'll stop over and see my old friend and visit his place. How far is it from here?"

"Only a few miles back, sir."

So Hawks had his baggage removed from the steamer to a small hotel or boarding-house, and he sent Crank to a different place, after rehearsing the testimony the latter was to give when occasion required.

On the day following there was a great commotion at the colony. Little Petrel had been seized by an officer on a process issued by the justice. John Stanley had been summoned from a distant part of the settlement when the officer executed the writ, and, on arriving, found his room occupied by two men—one the officer, whom he knew casually at the landing, holding by the hand the child who had cried herself hoarse, nay, speechless. In her effort to escape from her captor, she had exhausted herself, and was lying back in the chair by his side sobbing. The other, a tall, dark man, sat tapping the floor with his cane. On the outside stood old Aunt Liza and Aunt Dorcas, both in tears and lamentations, surrounded by half a dozen negro children.

The officer had only waited out of courtesy for Mr. Stanley's return, before taking the prisoner before the Court. On seeing her protector, whom she had been instructed to call "Cousin John," enter the door, the child sprang forward with a cry of joy.

"Oh, 'Tousin John, take me away—take me away."

Her movement was so like a flash of lightning that she freed herself from the officer and was in the arms of John Stanley in an instant, with her little curly head nestled on his broad chest, as he stood glaring like a lion at the two intruders.

The officer made an effort to intercept the child and to gain possession of her, but was waved back with a hand brown with honest toil, herculean in size and strength, and in a commanding tone, that there was no mistaking, Stanley said :

"Back, sir, back, I say, or, by the Eternal, I will not be answerable for the broken bones in your body. By what authority do you come here and seize this child? Under what pretext do you do it?"

Recovering his presence of mind, and prompted by Hawks, the officer produced the warrant issued by the justice. Holding the paper in one hand, with little Petrel clinging tightly about his neck with both her little arms, her head still bowed on his shoulder, John Stanley read it over, and then said with deep deliberation :

"And you, Thomas Hawks, claim this child as your slave?" and John Stanley's eyes blazed with light like two planets as he looked at the complainant.

Hawks nervously averted his face, arose from his seat, and walked to the door, where he turned and said :

"Officer, do your duty. I am tired of the dumb show—bring along your prisoner."

"Ah, it is well for you, villain as I know you are, that I am a law-abiding man, else I would take you in these hands of mine and literally pulverize and return you to mother earth as fertilizer, all you are good for."

Then he sat down more calmly, and bade the officer be seated while he made inquiry as to the mode of procedure,—when the trial would occur: if it could be postponed until Mr. Clayton could be present, not only as protector of the child, but as an important witness in the case.

"I can only say," replied the officer, "that I am commanded by this writ, as you see, to bring this child before the justice who issued it with all possible dispatch, and there my duty ends, and your inquiries must be made of the Court."

"So I see," said Stanley, as Hawks looked in at the door and said : "Officer, when are you coming? I am growing tired of this nonsense."

John Stanley ordered the old carriage that had been brought with them from Kentucky, and the officer was invited to take a seat with him and his little charge, whose arms were still clinging about his neck, and who could not be induced to raise her head or speak but in a whisper to her protector. All this was done with such quiet power as left no room for question or dissent. Hawks followed sullenly, occasionally muttering threats of vengeance.

Arrived at the court-house, the justice was notified of the return of the officer with his prisoner, and the writ executed.

In opening the case, Hawks demanded that the officer should take charge of the prisoner, and not leave her in the custody of an irresponsible party.

John Stanley spoke to the officer who sat at his side, and they arose and walked to the dock, where both sat down.

Hawks evidently expected to see Stanley resist the taking of the child from him ; but now the law was satisfied without commotion.

Hawks, being sworn, proceeded to state his case.

He said he had bought the mother and child, and then

recounted the difficulties of getting to New Orleans with his slaves.

When he came to that part of his statement touching the crossing of the river at St. Charles, he glanced around the room at the motley crowd assembled, and then, with a satisfied air, continued :

"And in arranging the slaves in a boat, this child, then a young baby, was handed to a tall man to hold for a moment while the mother, with the other negroes, were getting seated; the crush of ice was very great, and, in the confusion, the boat was pushed off, and we only made the discovery that the child had been left when too late, for we were in the current and could not return, and it was impossible to recross the river that day. Instead of the man leaving the child at St. Charles in the custody of some one, where it might have been easily found and reclaimed by the real owner, he secreted her here. Important business has compelled me to be absent for the last five years, or I should have looked up this negro-thieving Yankee before." And he threw an insolent look of defiance at John Stanley, with the child gathered close in his arms.

"What evidence have you in support of your statement?" inquired the judge, as Hawks took his seat.

"I don't know, your honor, that more should be required. I am sure there are none to gainsay what I have testified to ; but since your honor has suggested it, I will say that the wharf at the time was crowded with boatmen and fishermen, and I see quite a number here. Some one of them might know of this affair. If any one present knows anything of the matter, I wish he would come forward."

After this request was made, there was a stir in the crowd and an insignificant figure emerged therefrom, and limped up to the witness-box. Stopping there, he was interrogated by the judge.

"Do you know this man?" pointing to Hawks.

"Well, Jedge, can't say I know his name. I've seed him afore this."

"Where did you see him?"

"In St. Charles, Missouri, nigh on to five year ago?"

"Have you heard his testimony?"

"Well, Jedge, I have, some of it."

"Do you know anything about the case?"

"Yes, Jedge, I seed somethin' o' what was done at the ice flood he's been tellin' about."

"The witness may be sworn," instructed the judge. "What is your name?"

"My name is Crank, sir."

"Crank, indeed?" inquired the clerk. "You seem well-named. Have you no other?"

"They called me Tom Smith when I was a boy. I got my leg broke, and the man what sot it said he was a good surgeon, but he made a bad job outen it, and lef' one leg shorter'n the other. So people called me Crank Smith, and at last they drapped the Smith and it is only Crank now."

"Well, Smith, take this book" (extending the Bible), "and I will swear you."

"I'll take this ere book, but that was never my way of swearin'."

Crank was then sworn, and related the story of the preparation for crossing the river substantially as Hawks had done, but getting excited as he went along, he said:

"This man heah cussed the fellows on shore, and said if some of 'em didn't catch the d——d brat, he'd——"

Hawks sprang to his feet. "I beg pardon, your honor, I did not hear what the witness said. Now, my good man, if you will repeat the last part of your testimony, I will be obliged to you," saying which he gave Crank a look of rage which made the witness quail.

He cleared his throat in confusion, and was about to begin again, when John Stanley, in turning around, brought the little head that rested on his shoulder near to the witness, and the breeze lifted the soft, dark hair which fell upon the old man's hand, resting on the railing, revealing a portion of the distressed little face, so appealing and helpless, that Crank involuntarily extended his hand, and stroked back the curls. She felt the touch and turned her face to see who it was. Their eyes met, and the little girl smiled; she recognized a kindly face; and the small hand that had clasped John Stanley so tightly was timidly extended to her new friend.

All this happened in a moment: but the chord that makes the whole world akin had been touched.

Crank bowed his head on the dimpled little hand resting in his own, and, perhaps, gave the first kiss that memory had recorded; and like the sacred rod that smote the rock, a fountain was loosed in his heart, and down the hardened and bronzed cheek stole a tear, while in a choking voice, he said :

"No, Jedge, I can't change that ere evidence, if it killed me. That man there, he swore worse'n the fiends that he'd heave the brat into the ice ef somebody didn't take it; and he tossed the little thing high into the air, an' a tall man on shore ketched it on the fly."

All this time, Hawks was glaring ferociously, at the witness who deserted his cause and clung to the desperate fortunes of little Petrel.

"Then the child was literally thrown away?" inquired John Stanley.

"That's it, stranger," said Crank, "an' he throwed it mighty hard, too."

"How came you to be present here?" continued Stanley, seeing his advantage in the old man's emotion.

"He brought me here," nodding his head towards Hawks, who had not removed his eyes from the witness ; but Crank was looking at the little face peering out of the dark night of soft hair, like the silver lining of a sombre cloud, and sparkling from its depths were two eyes like the star of hope.

"Did he pay your way here ? "

"Yes, sir ; paid my fare and paid me, too."

"Did he ever instruct you how you should testify in this case when it should come up for trial ? "

"I object, may it please your honor, to such questions," shouted Hawks, in a towering rage, as he arose from his seat and approached the witness, "and I trust the Court will not permit the witness to answer them."

"I want to show by his own witness, your honor," remarked John Stanley, "that the complainant employed this man to come here to testify in his favor."

"And what if I did ? " asked Hawks, breaking in with an oath.

"Sir, you will be fined for contempt of court if you repeat that offence," said the justice, as the two men stood savagely staring at each other.

"I desire to show," continued Stanley, "that the com

plainant attempted to corrupt the witness to give false testimony."

"Be seated, gentlemen," said the constable. "Order in court."

"The witness may answer the question," said the justice.

"Well," continued Crank, "he tole me he was gwine ter testify fust, and then I was to foller his lead."

"That he should be the next witness, your honor," interposed Hawks.

"Follow him how?" asked Stanley, "by saying just what he had previously sworn to?"

"I object to putting words in the witness's mouth," shouted Hawks again; but all too late, for Crank responded:

"Jis' so, stranger. He said I mus' swar to jis' what he did; an' when I kinder objected, he said, 'Da'n yer, don' I pay yer well, an' I want yer to earn yer money.' Well, Jedge, I war kinder unsartin 'bout jis' what ter do, till I saw that little thing thar so pitiful-like; then I seed my way cl'ar. A fellows may kinder warp the truth 'roun' to suit circumstances when thar ain't anybody gwinter git hurt by it. But if I was to say anything that warn't true, ter help him git that ar' baby, I'd expect my tongue ter cleave through my mouth an' my ha'r to stan' on en' like the quills of a freckle porc'pine.'

When Crank left the witness-stand, all eyes were turned on Stanley, seated in the dock holding the little prisoner.

"Have you any testimony to offer in defence, Mr. Stanley?" inquired the judge.

"I desire, your honor," said Stanley, rising and approaching the justice, "the postponement or continuance of the case until Mr. Clayton, the real protector and guardian of the child, can be present: I am sure your honor will hesitate to commit this babe, born, I verily believe, of white parents, to the mercy of that human vulture who, from some diabolical plot, has cast the net in which to ensnare an innocent soul. That there is some foul wrong hidden under this proceeding, I feel assured. That this child is no slave, I can convince your honor by a single glance at her features. Raise your head, little pet, so that the gentleman may see you.

Don't you want to know the kind judge who will protect you from that rough, bad man ? Don't be afraid. Let the gentleman see your face, and then you can go back home to old Aunt Liza."

Slowly the little head was lifted up, up until she sat erect.

"Open your eyes, my little girl," said the judge, coaxingly.

The lids that had been closed tightly, fringed with their long, dark lashes, relaxed a little, and by degrees, like the breaking of dawn in the east, the full-orbed day was revealed. Her large, dark eyes, soft and almost black, with a tinge of amber, looked timidly at the judge.

Hawks arose and stepped in front to look again and gloat over his victim.

At sight of his face, the child screamed and buried her head on John Stanley's breast. For the first time Hawks had looked full into the innocent face of the child. What was there in that to make this hardened scoundrel blanch, tremble, and gaze with distended eyes as if he looked upon a ghost ? Perhaps it was the shadow of some victim of long, long ago, whose memory started into life as he caught an expression in this child's luminous eyes. But this was no time to think of " the shadowy past," and he said, falteringly :

" I have a bill-of-sale, your honor, of this child and her mother, which I offer for the inspection of the Court, and which, for private reasons, I prefer should not be shown to others. The evidence in this case is for the court and not for the public. This paper shows conclusively that the child is a slave and is my property, and I demand her under the laws of our country. As for the delay or postponement of the case until Mr Clayton can respond as defendant, it is out of the question, as your honor will see. As near as I can learn, he is somewhere in Kansas, and it may require three or four weeks to have him here. I have a large estate in Louisiana ; am now going direct to New Orleans where I live, and where the child's mother is anxiously awaiting the result of this trial. After five years' separation from her child, it would be inhuman to keep her a day longer in suspense than is necessary. I will leave your honor my address, where any process the court may choose to issue, will reach me."

The judge took the bill-of-sale obtained from Harry Barnes by Hawks on the steamer, and after examination, said :

"This seems all regular ; and if you have no testimony to offer, Mr. Stanley, I will render my decision."

John Stanley bowed his head until his chin rested upon the little shoulder of Petrel, and thus in silence, heard the decision which the Court proceeded to render.

The judge held that, while it was evident from the testimony of the principal witness in the case that the plaintiff intended to desert and abandon his ownership in the child, yet he nevertheless could reclaim his property "for lack of consideration and legal conveyance, by proof of ownership and payment of costs, upon the doing of which he shall have possession of the child."

When the decision had been rendered, Crank stole quietly from the room, vowing in his own heart never to lose sight or trace of Petrel until she was rescued from Hawks.

When the Court had concluded, the necessary order was prepared, directing John Stanley to surrender possession of the child to its rightful owner.

Totally oblivious to all surroundings, the two stood, like the sturdy oak and the clinging vine after the woodman's axe had severed the support.

The officer approached and placing his hand on Stanley's shoulder, said :

" 'Tis the order of the Court that you surrender the child to the custody of the law to be delivered to the rightful owner. Stanley released his hold and both arms fell to his side. There was a perceptible shudder and tightening of the arms as little Petrel clung to the neck of her guardian. Without raising his head, Stanley said :

" I am a law-abiding man. Do your duty."

" Yes, but you must release her."

" That, I have done."

" Then you must make her release you."

" The law does not require it, and I only conform to the commands of its letter. It is like having my heart-strings torn when done by other hands; and I shall not dip mine in human blood. "

At this juncture, Hawks approached and said to the officer, as he took one of the little arms roughly in his grasp and tore it from Stanley's neck :

"Now loose the other," and the child was borne screaming, almost in spasms, from the room with extended arms and streaming eyes, crying :

"Tousin John. Tousin John."

As John Stanley raised his eyes to behold that helpless little one, his first impulse was to fly to her aid ; and with one great stride, he bounded to the side of Hawks, but immediately three rough men interposed, as if by a preconcerted arrangement, and the foremost of the trio laid a heavy hand upon his shoulder. Stanley freed himself from the grasp of the man, but in doing so, lost his sleeve and thus revealed an arm that would have graced well an Ajax. The three men surrounded him, each striving to strike him down, but Stanley's wonderful strength and superior skill in boxing (for he and Clayton had made the manly art one of their regular course of exercises and amusements) soon succeeded in flooring the three.

By this time, Hawks and the officer had disappeared with Petrel ; and as Stanley saw the angry roughs preparing to assault him anew, he walked to where the judge and clerk of the court were standing, the judge having rapped and commanded the peace to no purpose. As he approached, he said :

"Judge, I shall be charged with a breach of the peace, and perhaps resisting an officer in the discharge of his duty, though God knows I had no such intention. To avoid further trouble, which I see impending, I surrender myself as prisoner to answer the charge when made."

The judge placed his hand upon Stanley's shoulder and commanded the crowd to disperse, as the offender had surrendered and was under arrest ; and at this moment the bailiff, having returned from his duties, was directed to disperse the crowd, which he did.

The judge, turning to Stanley, said :

"Now, take my advice and go home at once. I will take your personal recognizance and will notify you when you are wanted."

CHAPTER XXI.

LATE in the afternoon of an October day, Clayton sat in the door of his cabin, rebuilt upon the site of that which had been destroyed by fire, gazing at the western sky as the golden tints of the setting sun illumined the masses of lazily drifting clouds, looking like great icebergs on fire, afloat in an ocean of blue.

He had sent his servant to the post-office at Lawrence, and was now awaiting his arrival with the mail. The horse and rider soon appeared on the Indian trail leading to his cabin, and impatient to get the news, he walked to the brow of the hill to meet Aleck, who delivered to him two well-worn letters, which bore the post-mark of Perkins' Landing and were both in John Stanley's handwriting.

Breaking the seal of the one with the earliest date, he read as follows :—

" Aug. —, 185-.

" DEAR FRANK :—

"Our crops are now assured. The rain came in time to avert the threatened drought. I am really proud of the season's achievements. All of the hands have done well, with one or two exceptions ;—you know who the 'old soldiers' are—but under the rules that I have enforced, 'those that sow shall reap, and those only.' Tom and Bob are doing better. Ned's example is good, and Aunt Liza works their little garden, which is a model for the others, and a great success."

After some further details concerning farm work, Stanley wrote :—

" This is Sunday, and I wish you could see all the people assembled as they are now, under the old canvas church, where Uncle Ned is preaching a sermon upon the duties of life from the text : ' Be diligent in business, fervent in spirit, serving the Lord.' Little Pearl, as I call her, is near me, kneeling upon the rug, with pencil and paper on a chair, 'writing to Uncle Frank.' I shall enclose the hieroglyphics, which you must decipher. She is a winning creature. I am not sure I should be so contented here if her bright little face did not welcome me at the door every day.

"There seems to be a lull in Kansas affairs now; why not come home and see for yourself how things progress at the settlement?

"Do you get any news from Sam?

"Sincerely your friend,

"JOHN STANLEY."

Clayton sat musing for awhile upon the possibility of returning to Illinois. This vagrant life was becoming tiresome, and he longed to see his little ward, who had found refuge from the storms of life in such a harbor.

With his thoughts still in a reverie, he abstractedly broke the seal of the remaining letter and continued to read, when suddenly he sprang to his feet, exclaiming, "My God! Petrel kidnapped by Tom Hawks, the notorious gambler and dealer in human flesh! Heaven protect her! Let me see—since August—two months she has been in the hands of that human fiend!"

Maddened at the thought of the child's peril and possible fate, Frank strode up and down the floor in an agony of agitation, trying to compose his thoughts, that he might determine what to do first—for reclaim her he would—and grasping his Colt's revolver, he said:

"Let me set eyes on the villain, and I'll make him bite the dust, if he does not give her back to me safe."

At this moment, he heard a firm, heavy footstep approaching, and, looking up, saw the benign face and massive form of John Brown standing in the doorway.

"Oh, my friend," said Clayton, impetuously, seizing his hand, "the fiends have been at work again."

"Why, what is it, my boy?" said the old man, kindly, putting his hand on Frank's shoulder. "What has happened?"

Then he listened with earnest, kindling eyes as the outrage was recited to him, saying not a word, but slowly nodding his head as the details were read by his young friend in a choking voice. But the deep fires did not blaze, they only smouldered, as he said, " The same old story—wrong, cruelty, suffering ! As is natural, *you* are thinking of the child who is so dear to you, but *I* am thinking of this hideous upas tree, which poisons the blood of the nation, converting men into monsters." Now the fires began to blaze, as he strode to and fro.

" Yes, monsters, Clayton," and he paused, his eyes shining with a strange light and fixed upon Frank's. " Now listen ; and remember what I say. Kansas is merely the skirmish ground ; the battle will rage through all the land ; the soil of every State will be stained with blood ; the nation will be shrouded in mourning and covered with ashes ; dead men's bones will bleach upon the field of carnage. But out of this desolation, blood, and ashes, shall arise, Phœnix-like, a republic in which justice and mercy shall rule and all men shall be free and equal. But," he added, in a softened tone, and taking Frank's hand in his, "do not think I am unsympathetic, my dear boy; but I see so much in all this—so much more than others seem to see—that I feel as if a great burden was laid upon me which I must bear for the rest —but let it go, let it go," and he passed his hand through the halo of gray hair which glistened in the sunlight.

" Now let us think what's to be done," and with a sort of practical determination he sat down by the table, and drawing paper and pen before him, said : " You must go, of course, at once ; and if your clever young friend, Duvall, can go with you, so much the better. I will look after your matters here ; so just tell me briefly what I can do about Sam, and I will make a memorandum of it."

" Oh, Mr. Brown, how kind ! With all you have to do here, I could not ask you——"

John Brown waved his hand in reply to this protest.

" No time to be lost ; go on," said he.

So Frank speedily gave him all the clues and their plan of procedure regarding Sam, and left everything in his hands. " Duvall will remain where he is and be in communication with you. I think it is better so, as emergencies may arise here which would impose too much upon you. Thank you, my dear friend, for all that you have done."

He hastened to Kansas City, and after a hurried interview with Claude, confiding to him the new and dreadful trouble, charged him to confer with Mr. Brown as with himself. "Trust him as you would the Apostle Paul," were his last words.

The steamer's whistle blew; he hurried on board and was borne down the river at a rapid rate, though slow indeed compared with his desires. As a precautionary measure, he stopped at St. Charles and made inquiries at the hotel, where he learned of Hawks' previous visit there and of his efforts to obtain Clayton's address. He also learned that Crank had disappeared with Hawks, and it was reported that he was in his employ. The landlady was distressed at the fate of little Petrel, and described to Frank the Quaker gentleman who seemed so interested in the story.

"The scroundel," said he, through his closed teeth. "We'll run him down; we'll corner him like a rat."

He concluded it would be well to see John Stanley before doing anything, so directed his steps to the Colony, where his arrival produced great rejoicing, mingled with lamentations over the loss of Petrel.

Aunt Eliza seemed to feel that she was responsible for the loss of her charge, and was overwhelmed with distress.

"I'se been bery misfortent old nigger, Mars Frank. I done try to do all I promise. 'Twould done yer heart good to a seen dat chil' afore dey took her away f'om dese yer han's. Bress de Lor', I warn't gwine ter gib her up till dat officer, he took out he pistol and say dat he gwinter shoot dis nigger, an' dat big tall debel gemmen, he kep' sayin' to the officer, 'Why don' you shoot de d——d ol' nigger ef she don' leg go de chile?' an' all dis time I had dese two arms wrap' roun' her, an' if you believe me, dat chil' nearly goed inter spasms, she was so scart. Well, Mars Frank, 'twould a broke yer heart to a seed what I seed. Mars John clare broke down, but Laws, dey had all de officers an' de jedge on dey side an' dey took her 'way f'om him."

Clayton was deeply moved, and at the particulars of the outrage from Stanley, he decided to leave at once for New Orleans and search for the villain who had done this deed. So, after giving a few necessary orders, he took the steamer at Perkins' Landing for St. Louis, thence to New Orleans.

After registering his name at the St. Charles Hotel,

New Orleans, Frank heard a genial voice say : " Hello ! is that you, Clayton ? One—two—why, I believe it's more than three years since I saw you—and, by the way," and Captain Swan drew him confidentially one side, " you know Doctor Barnes and your uncle have been lying low for that man Hawks."

" Hawks ? " said Frank, with a start. " What in Heaven's name do they want of him ? "

" Oh ! You don't know about it ? Well, they've been mighty close about it, because, you see, they knew if they kept quiet he'd come back."

" Captain, I don't know what you're talking about," said Frank, puzzled and bewildered

" Well," said the captain, " now I've told so much, you may as well know the rest."

Frank gave his hand reassuringly. " Depend on me for discretion. And I'll tell you, by the way, that my business here is to find that scoundrel Hawks and bring him to justice on my own account."

" No ! " said the captain, astonished. " Well, then, we'll just join forces. That's pretty good, pretty good," and he laughed with satisfaction.

" Well, you see, it's this way. When Harry Barnes died, his uncle, the doctor, was laid up with a broken leg, and it was some time before he began to suspect that there had been some sort of foul play with the boy. So, soon as he was able, he went and talked to his lawyer, and mighty carefully they worked up the case. Sure enough, when they had the remains exhumed and analyzed there was poison in his stomach, enough to kill him and to convict his murderer. Hawks had disappeared ; so they concluded to wait and to throw them all off the scent by not seeming to care a —— what had become of him. Why, bless your soul, it was the clearest case— but to go on. Last week I had a letter from the doctor, saying the old fox was back—had been up the river some-where and would walk straight into the trap if we'd set it ; and, by George, if I haven't got the warrant for his arrest this minute in my pocket, and three or four men watching around town ; for he'll come here, sure's my name's Swan. They're keeping an eye on that man Ray, Colonel Ray, for they're great chums and will turn up to-gether somewhere."

As he was speaking, a boy came up and placed in the captain's hand a telegram, which read thus :

"Booneville. Come at once; game here." Signed, " B."

He handed it to Frank, and it required only five minutes to have the recently arrived trunk brought downstairs again and once more placed on the up-going steamer, where he had ample leisure to relate to his companion his own reasons for desiring to find Mr. Thomas Hawks.

After Dr. Barnes' recovery, he had, as related by Captain Swan, had the body of his unfortunate nephew disinterred and the stomach and liver analyzed. The result showed the presence of a poisonous substance sufficient to produce death. The facts were laid before a grand jury, together with the testimony of the clerk and bartender of the steamer upon which Hawks and the deceased were passengers on that fatal trip. The bar-tender was very explicit as to the game of cards, the high stakes played for, and the several drinks taken and their character; also, as to Barnes' rational condition about eleven o'clock, and that an hour later, with but one drink intervening, he was found senseless at the card-table after Hawks had left on the down steamer, taking the woman and her baby with him. The bar-tender remembered distinctly the order for the two brandies and sugar,—one weak and sweet, with a litle port for coloring. The bar-tender himself took the drinks to the private room where the men were playing. He further swore that Hawks took the dark glass and turned his back to them to drink, when he suddenly wheeled about, and said ;

" Hold on, Barnes, you like yours stronger, and this is yours," and exchanged glasses.

He thought at the time there was something put from a paper in his pocket in the glass, but could not say positively.

On this testimony, the grand jury found a true bill against Thomas Hawks for the murder, by poison, of Harry Barnes, on the steamer " Clermont " on the night of ——, 18—.

On this indictment, the governor of the State issued a requisition on the governor of Missouri for the said Thomas Hawks, as information had been given the parties concerned that Hawks had been seen in St. Louis. A fruitless search for the criminal there resulted in tracing him to Jefferson City; but on arriving there, the bird had flown. It was said that he made his home at one of the river towns below. The governor of Missouri had complied with the requisition of the governor of Kentucky, and issued the writ for Hawks' arrest and empowered the officers to serve it anywhere in the State.

It soon became evident that Hawks had eluded them, and after consultation with the prosecuting officer, it was decided to let the matter drop, and, giving the impression that the prosecution had been abandoned, quietly to wait till such time as the miscreant should return of his own accord, as he would be sure to do, believing the thing had blown over and he would be safe.

CHAPTER XXII.

On the following Saturday night there were assembled in a well-furnished and lighted room in the rear of a somewhat pretentious-looking brick building just opposite the Booneville Hotel, three men, talking and smoking, each with a glass freshly poured, when a smart rap was heard upon the door, followed by three more, equally loud and sharp.

"Who in thunder can that be!" said the one who seemed to be the host,—a tall, well-dressed, dark man with long black mustache, who may be readily recognized as Tom Hawks. As he spoke, his eye glanced across the table to two men, each in rank and station far below the speaker, but having the appearance of sporting men. These two men also arose, and one of them remarked :

"Colonel, I guess Sly has forgotten his cue, or else he's got excited and hit the knocks too hard. Shall I open the door?"

"No, Mr. Sparks, not by a d—n sight. If he can't remember enough to give one moderate knock followed by three lighter ones, and not make such a h—l of a fuss, he can stay out, d—n him."

Just then, the knock was repeated, followed by three light taps, and the door was opened to Sam Sly.

An expression of anxiety and fear was visible on his face as he came to the table, and said :

"I be d———d, Colonel, if there is not something wrong in the cards to-night. As sure as we are here, something is up."

Every man was again on his feet in an instant, leaving his whiskey untouched.

"Tell us quickly, man!" said Hawks, walking to where Sly stood, and putting his hand on his shoulder with the grip of a vise. "What's the matter that has turned your liver white to-night ?"

"Who says I have a white liver?" replied Sam, trying to shake off the hand.

"I say you look like a frightened girl. Now tell me what you saw, and that d——d quick. I am getting tired of this d——d nonsense. Now to the point at once."

"Since you are in such a hurry, I'll tell you there are three men over at the hotel just arrived, and two of them are officers with warrants, for I heard them talking of probable resistance; something about a requisition from some governor, I think he said of Kentucky; and I'm pretty sure your name was mentioned in the conversation as well as my own. They have been making inquiries and learned our association together, and may be, our location as well!"

"How do you know these men are officers of the law?" anxiously inquired Hawks.

"I saw their papers through the key-hole. I happened to be in an adjoining room and heard them comparing notes."

"And who was the third party? You say there were three of them."

"Well, Colonel, I couldn't say positively who the third party is; but I have my suspicions, from seeing his long stride as he walked across the room giving directions as though he were the commander of the expedition, whatever it is. I think I recognized the voice of the man too, but I hope I am mistaken. We shall see all too soon, perhaps."

"Tell me who you suspect?" said Hawks, impatiently, "and let us drink the whiskey waiting for us. Here, Ben, pour out a drink for this man to give him courage to tell his fears."

"If my suspicions are well-founded, Colonel, neither you nor I can find much ground for rejoicing."

"You be d——d, Sly, there is no man living or dead that I am afraid of: so here's to the new-comers, whoever they are, and we will give them a warm reception; eh, boys?"

"That we will, Colonel," was the response of all, as they drained the glasses.

"Well," said Sly, "we can give them about as good as they send,—seeing there are four of us."

"I am glad to hear you say so much, Sly. Now tell us the name of this Ogre, who has frozen your courage and manhood up in your boots."

"Colonel Hawks, I am not more easily frightened than

you are, but let me tell you, Mr. Frank Clayton isn't one to be hunting for us with two officers of the law on a child's errand. He is in terrible earnest, and told the officers to look well to their arms before attempting to serve their warrants, and then he added : ' Don't hesitate to use them, if any resistance is offered.' "

At the mention of Clayton's name, Sparks quailed perceptibly, and a slight shade passed over Hawks' brow as he involuntarily put his hand on his pistol ; and when Sly had ceased speaking, he dryly remarked :

" We all mean business, and I, for one, don't propose to be taken alive. Here, fill up the glasses, and we'll keep our spirits up by pouring spirits down."

Just then, the tramp of feet was heard outside the door, and a heavy knock sounded through the room. The brimming glasses were set down hastily, and each man's hand reached for his pistol.

" Who's there ? " demanded Hawks, gruffly.

" An officer of the law, with a warrant for the arrest of Thomas Hawks," responded the officer outside, " and in the name of the law and by the authority of the governor of Missouri, I demand admittance."

" And suppose we tell you he is not here and that you can't have admittance."

" Then it becomes our duty to break down the door and make a thorough search of the premises."

" I think you had better do your duty then, sir ; but before you begin, let me warn you there are four of us in here, well-armed, and we propose to kill the first man who enters the room."

" Yes, and yer can bet I'll git the second one," roared Ben Baugh, so as to be heard through the hall.

Then stillness reigned for a moment ; and the officer said in a firm, loud voice :

" Mr. Clayton, and you, good citizens, I command you, in the name of the law, to aid in the execution of this writ."

Then, after trying the locks which were found secure, there was a whispered conference and it was arranged that the three men draw their pistols, step back a few paces, and run full force against the door, breaking it down, and land, all at once, in the room, taking the enemy by surprise.

Inside, the men were ranged, Hawks and Sly in front

of the door ; on one side of the table stood Ben Baugh, and upon the other was Sparks, all with pistols drawn ; and upon the table were two large bowie knives unsheathed, with their blades glittering ominously in the light.

On the outside, the three men ranged themselves side by side in the wide hall, and at the words, "One,—two,—three,"—they went thundering against the door, which, as they had calculated, gave way with a crash, and the three men rushed into the room pell-mell and were met by a volley of shots and bitter oaths ; but above the din was heard : "In the name of law. I command you all to surrender," to which there was no answer save from the mouths of the pistols. Then came groans and shrieks of anguish out of total darkness, for the table had been overturned and the lights extinguished. Out of the inky background now and then there shot forth a lurid flame of fire and sulphurous smoke, laden with a messenger of death aimed only at a voice or the sound of footsteps.

"Cease firing, I command you in the name of the law," shouted the officer, "if you expect mercy."

"I neither receive nor show it," said a man in a harsh, unnatural voice, from the floor in one corner of the room, and, at the same time, a flash of the pistol revealed Tom Hawks lying on the floor, resting upon one elbow, firing as best he could to the last.

"Shoot the scoundrel," shouted the officer, as he leveled his pistol and fired in the direction where Hawks lay.

A scream of anguish came back like an echo, and all was still.

"I surrender, Mr. Clayton, I surrender," said one of the desperate men.

"Who are you?" asked the officer, as a light was brought, revealing Sparks crouched on the floor in one corner of the room, still holding his smoking pistol.

"Lay down your arms, then, if you surrender," replied the officer, stepping forward and placing his hand upon the crouching man's shoulder.

Then, looking around, Hawks was found covered with blood, lying upon the floor, with a wound in the left breast and one in the hip, with blood flowing from his mouth freely.

"This is the man we are seeking," said Clayton, approaching, with his left hand pressed tightly to his side,

"In God's name, I hope he is not dying; at least, that he may live to speak. Bring water, quickly! Let us revive him, if possible. HE MUST SPEAK!"

"Wash out his mouth, and give him a little of that brandy I see upon the side table," said the officer.

After repeated applications of brandy and water, Hawks opened his eyes as Clayton bent over him with spoon and glass. A strange light shone in his eyes, which were sunken under a threatening black brow, such as Lucifer, son of the morning, may have flashed back upon the battlements of heaven when cast in the pit. The lips moved as though he would speak, but no words came.

"Take this," said Clayton, "it will revive you," placing the spoon in his mouth, when the teeth were shut like a vise, fairly crushing the spoon.

"Tell me where you have put that child. Come, tell— and undo, as much as you can, the great wrong you have done."

Again the lips moved convulsively as if to speak.

Clayton put his ear down, and said:

"Do try and tell me before it is too late, and may God have mercy upon your soul."

In a broken, choked whisper, there hissed, as if from the iron jaws of death, the words:

"I wish I could spit in your damned face before I die!"

It seemed as though his whole remaining strength and life had been concentrated and exhausted in the ferocious message. The fire faded from the eye, the lips were compressed, and with a slight convulsion of his frame, death claimed another victim.

As Clayton leaned over the dying wretch, the glass and spoon slipped from his hand to the floor; everything grew dark, and he fell forward across the prostrate form of his deadly enemy.

On lifting the fainting man, his left hand fell from his side followed by a stream of blood, the first intimation of his wound. The surgeon who had been summoned for Hawks arrived in good season for a different patient, as the other had gone beyond his reach.

Restoratives were applied to the wounded man, and he was removed to a quiet room at the hotel, borne upon the

door which he had so recently and bravely helped to
break down.

Upon lifting the table, the body of Sam Sly was found
with a bullet-hole in the temple. He was still grasping
his revolver, which had but one empty chamber, showing
he fell at the first fire.

Ben Baugh and Sparks were both taken into custody,
charged with resisting an officer in the discharge of his
duty, and assault "with intent to kill."

The coroner held an inquest upon the dead bodies, and
a verdict was rendered by the jury that "death ensued
from pistol-shot wounds inflicted by officers of the law
·in the proper discharge of their duty."

Sparks, who was no longer employed by Judge Stanley, confessed to having aided Sly in the kidnapping of
Sam, but didn't know to whom he had been sold.

The sentences in the case of each man were made as
light as the law permitted.

In a darkened chamber in the hotel, Frank Clayton
was lying, the pulse of life feebly fluttering at its centre.

The wound in his side had been probed, and it was
found that the ball had passed out without striking any
vital part or fracture of the bones ; but there had been
great loss of blood. The first night the patient appeared
to be sinking ; the effect, the physicians stated, of pros-
tration of the nervous system ; but in twenty-four hours
there was a change ; nature seemed to rally all her
forces and in the morning the doctor found instead of
fever having set in as he expected, the pulse was weak
but regular, and sleep brought renewed strength to the
sufferer.

Youth and a constituion that had never been taxed or
broken by excesses now came to the aid of the physician.

Temperance and kindred virtues brought their reward
to the life that had trembled in the balance and now gave
fresh light in the eye and color to the pallid cheek. Convalescence seemed like the magic transformation that
nature repeats every spring, clothing the fields and for-
ests in beauty. The excitement and mental distress of
the last few weeks, which had culminated in that night of
bloodshed and the curses of the dying criminal, were followed by what seemed a Rip Van Winkle-like nap to

Clayton, and he awoke with a more quiet pulse to a new
lease of life. It was happiness to live and breathe and
look at the blue sky and drifting clouds from his window.
The past was a dream; a night-mare he would not
recall.

The doctor was proud of his patient's recovery, without
fever or the many ills that wounded flesh is heir to, and
he ascribed Clayton's restoration to his own skill. One
morning he was surprised at finding his patient up and
dressed, ready for a walk, but he compromised with a
drive, and soon the day was fixed for his departure.

The duties of life must be taken up and search made
for little Petrel, whose captor had died and made no sign
that would lead to her recovery.

CHAPTER XXIII.

THREE weeks from the day of Clayton's arrival at
Booneville, he went down to take the steamer for St.
Louis. Standing upon the wharf, his attention was
attracted by a man limping badly, making his way toward
the boat, holding by the hand a little girl, apparently one
of the poor whites, with bare feet and a sun-bonnet drawn
over her head. Something about the child, and the manner of the man, caused Clayton's eye to follow, and, like
a flash, it occurred to him that it could be none other
than Crank, the lame fisherman of St. Charles, who had
testified against Hawks at the trial. With his eye
fixed on the halting figure as he was jostled here and
there, nearing the gang-plank, he tried to overtake him.
The din and cursing of the draymen and boat hands, all
crowding to and fro, were at that moment joined by the
steamer's whistle blowing her last call for ' all aboard.'
He saw the man start on the gang-plank just as the men
were rushing on shore for the last freight, and the passing
throng jostling him, he lost his balance and went with a
loud splash into the water, bearing with him the little
girl.

Then went up a shout : " Man overboard ! Man overboard ! Boat ahoy."

All was confusion, and Clayton was just in time to see
the sun-bonnet floating away down stream. He forgot
all medical advice as to remaining " quiet and avoiding
excitement," and with one bound plunged into the river
and grasped the child as she came up after disappearing
under the water. With a few strokes, he reached the
shore, and to his joy and the surprise of all, the old man
still held the other hand of the child. Both were drawn
out and placed on board the steamer and soon
revived. Clayton was taken up in a greatly exhausted
and almost unconscious condition, and placed in a state-
room ; a physician was sent for, who gave him medical
attention. After an hour's rest, he said he wished to see

the man whom he had rescued. Crank was found near the room door, waiting anxiously to hear from his benefactor.

"Well, stranger," said Crank, as they were left alone, "you've give me a helpin' han' out o' the water; now what can I do for you?"

"Crank," said Clayton, "don't you know me?"

"Bless my eyes, if it ain't Mr. Clayton; an' I've been studyin' how ter fin' you."

"What child was that?—tell me," said Clayton eagerly.

Without a word the man limped out of the room, and then returned, leading by the hand a little girl, in a coarse, homespun gown which the chambermaid had put on her in place of the wet garments. Her feet were bare, and her hair still wet.

"God be thanked!" said Clayton, as he saw the little creature actually before him. The soft eyes were timidly averted, as if she knew not what dreadful thing might be in store for her. Her pathetic docility almost unmanned him.

"Petrel, darling, said he, "come to Uncle Frank."

Swift as lightning the face turned to his, and with a cry and a bound, she was in his arms.

Crank limped away and wiped his eyes with his sleeve, looking out of the window to recover himself.

"Wall," he said, I s'pose it's nat'ral; she's knowed him longer'n me; but I *did* think p'r'aps she'd kinder like to stay with me some."

"Crank," said Clayton, from the sofa, "come here and give me your hand. You have brought me what I most longed to see in this world. Now sit down there and tell me all about it. I have heard how you tried to upset that scoundrel at the trial, but I want to hear your account of it."

"Well, you see," he answered, uneasily, "I ain't bin altogether what ye'd call a good sort of a man; but p'r'aps that's my bringin' up, p'r'aps I ain't so very far from the averidge."

"Very likely," said Clayton, smiling reassuringly.

"Well, yer see, I needed money pretty bad, and I thort if Hawks wanted to git back his nigger, which was his own property, I was willin' to lend er hand— and so—yer see—he gave me considerable money, an I didn't take all the wickedness of it in till I seed this ere little un's piterful face in the court-room, an' I jis broke down? Why, Mr Clayton, when she put that little sof' han' in mine an' loked so 'pealin' like, I just vowed in my heart that this little chicken should never git in the clutches of that-are 'hawk' an' so, I out with the truth. How he swore that he'd 'throw her in ther ice ef some one didn't kotch her, an' how he heaved her high in ther air, an' a tall man on shore kotched her on the fly.' That feller Hawks looked as though he'd murder me when I sed this, but he smoothed it over to the jedge by takin' a paper outer his pocket. 'There,' said he 'is the bill-of-sale of the mother and chile.'

"Are you sure he said the mother and child, Crank?"

"Yes, sir, he said jis them words. 'It seems to be all reg'lar,' said the jedge, 'an' you had a right ter do what yer pleased with the young un.' Well, when I seed how things was a goin' and heerd the screams of that baby as she was kerried off, I jis' slunk away and got on the steamer, down with the boxes and bar'ls in the hold and got my passage as a stow-away on the same steamer with that nigger trader and child. I kep well out o' his way, for I knowed he'd murder me, but I went on shore at Jefferson City after dark and tracked 'im to Mrs Hunter's, his sister's, house. He lef' the young un thar, an' I watched her sittin' so sorrowful in ther yard with the little niggers, an' the little thing 'membered me bein' in ther court house that day and knowed I was her friend, and she jist clung to me in a way to make yer heart ache. So when news come that Tom Hawks was shot I told the young un' ef she'd creep thro' the fence we'd try an' fin' Mr. Clayton down to St. Charles. So she picked up an ol' sun-bonnet an' put it on her head an' then we went down to the steamer. At Booneville I went on shore with the child to buy her a pair o' shoes, but some-how we got pushed off by the crowd in gittin' aboard agin, an' the new shoes an ol' sun-bonnet was lost in the water. An' that's jest all ther' is about it. An' of course it's nat'ral for her to like you bet-ter'n me, of course—but she kinder took ter me, an'

it was pleasant ter think somebody cared, yer no—an'
I—" Here Crank's feelings got the better of his rhet-
oric; and Clayton said:

"Cheer up, old fellow; you've been faithful to this
innocent child, and you will never have reason to be
sorry for it."

"But, Mr. Clayton, please don't sen' me 'way f'om her.
She's the only livin' crittur that's fon' o' me, an' when
she holds onter my finger with her little sof' han' I could
go throo fire for ter serve her if 'twas necessary."

"By George, I believe you would. And we'll see what
can be done." And Frank tried to move the head of the
now sleeping child into a more comfortable position.
She was exhausted with the excitements of the day, and
the pretty, unconscious face bore pitiful traces of the
rough usage of the last few months.

"Poor darling," said her protector. "Where can she
go; where will she be safe?"

He thought of Kate, and was inclined to make the
proposition that Petrel should share the nursery of her
own little girl, Katrina Fletcher, so nearly the same age.
But then, he thought,— "Bernard is such a bear, and "—
he wanted to use a stronger term—"he would be sure
to object." He was quite aware of the tragic sorrows which had so altered the course of his cousin's
life, but had no suspicion of Petrel's association with
that sad story, and did not suspect that in entertaining this project he was venturing on a very thin crust
over volcanic fires!

"Kate would be just the one," he thought, "to love
and train this gentle creature," And his hands fondly
caressed the clustering curls.

Finally his decision was taken; it seemed as if
the Catholic Mission, in Kansas, would, all considered, be the best and safest refuge. He decided that
Petrel must receive the care and education befitting
the position he intended to give her. Those kind
sisters would spare no pains, he knew, to make her
happy; and perhaps he could manage to have Crank
employed in some capacity and thus reward the fellow's fidelity and devotion to Petrel.

All was arranged happily. The late "Crank" was
now "Tom Smith," gardener and man-of-all-work at

the Convent. Clayton gave instructions that no expense must be spared in the little girl's education and that she must be surrounded by everything that would develop love for the beautiful, the good and the true.

Of course the parting with "Uncle Frank" was another strain on the little heart; but an atmosphere of love and tender care soon healed the wound, and a romp in the garden every day, where Tom filled her little basket with flowers, was not without its consolations. Sister Agnes, to whose special care she was consigned, soon occupied a large place in the loving nature of the child.

CHAPTER XXIV.

It was with a thankful heart that Clayton recited to Duvall, on the day of his return to Lawrence, the strange and exciting events which led up to the rescue of Petrel.

"You did well," said his friend with approval; "you were very wise to place the leetle maid with those good ladies. Ah! what a refuge has our Church for all kinds of deestress!"

"Yes, I knew *you* would approve of that," said Frank, laughing. "You know, Duvall, although I am something of a heretic myself, I like to encourage right belief and faith in others. I think it is a blessed thing and, God knows, I do not wish to implant a germ of doubt in the soul of another, when it has been such a tormenting guest in my own."

"That ees ze trouble wiz your Protestantism," said Duvall, impetuously. "When one wanders from the faith Catholique, the door ees left open and what you call vagarees come to rush een. Philosophique—scientifique—all verra well, verra interesting" (*eentaresting* he said) "I like them myself—these speculations—but not like ze consolations of religion."

"You are right, quite right," said Frank smiling; "and I like to hear you defend your own faith, which no doubt you love quite as much as you do your country."

"Ah! my countree! my beautiful countree!" said Claude, rapturously. "Mr Clayton, do you know the longing which sometimes envelopes my soul to see it? But you cannot. How can you understand unless you know all!"

Claude had never before spoken so freely of himself. Frank watched him as he paced the floor, with intense desire to ask him why he was here—what circumstances had made him exile himself from what he so loved.

"Duvall," he said earnestly, placing his hand affectionately on the handsome youth's shoulder, "Claude, you are very dear to me, and whenever you can trust me with this I shall be glad."

The dark eyes were moist now. "You make me play the woman, Frank. My heart would many times break in this strange land—all so different from my own—did I not have your friendship. Yes, my friend, some day I will tell you. But it ees a dark story—to make you weep, not to amuse; and you have your own troubles and need not more."

Frank pressed his hand in unspoken sympathy; and the entrance of Mr. Brown changed the current of conversation.

Capt. Brown listened with eager interest to the story Frank had to tell, and at the conclusion uttered a heartfelt "God be thanked!"

"The hand of Providence is apparent in finding the child; you were led—evidently led—to that spot, at that very moment. Do you not see it!"

"It did seem almost a miracle," said Frank, evasively.

The eyes look into his with a sad earnestness from under the heavy overhanging brows, as John Brown said: "My dear young man, why do you not recognize this over-ruling care? I am grieved to see you, so admirable in most respects, yet lacking this one thing."

· "What can I do?" said Frank.

"Cease groping in the light of human reason and open your heart to this illumination of the spirit which is here," said he, with a sweep of his arm, "here all about you. Abandon that cold philosophy of yours."

"But, my dear friend," said Frank, "I cannot *compel* belief. I can utter the last part of the Publican's prayer: 'Help Thou my *un*-belief;' but not the first. If I said "Lord, I believe," I would lie; and if He is a God of truth, He would be sorry to hear me say it." Then he added earnestly: "Mr. Brown, I am not indifferent to this subject. If what you believe is true, I want to believe it. He knows better than I can tell Him how earnestly I seek the truth. I once had your simple faith and was happy in it. I had been taught that the Heavenly Father was to man as his earthly parent to his infant state. Then when I learned the awful weight of human misery I asked myself, 'Can this be a loving father, who has the power to prevent this suffering, and does not? One of two things must be : either he is *not* all-powerful, or he is *not* a loving father.'   Then the belief grew within me that the Creator is like His creatures and like them subject to law. Our infant minds once conceived the earthly parent to be all you ascribe to the Heavenly Father, but in after-life learned that the parents were only a little wiser and more powerful than ourselves and were subject to the same laws which govern us.   The God of law says, ' I am not above the law, but of the law and subject to its operations, and obey its mandates.   Seek thou me through the law, and come thou to me nearer and nearer, upward and ever onward.'   I know well that good comes from working and waiting, holding yourself ready to move forward in the path where duty points."

"No, Mr. Clayton, your cold reasoning only obscures the face of the Heavenly Father from your vision.   His eye is ever on you, His loving hand guides and directs your steps, and He smiles at your doubts, and will, in His own good time, bring you to see His love, power and glory, in some great work that could not be brought about by law and philosophy."

"May I be permitted ?" said Duvall.   "*Pardon, monsieurs, mais c'est vrai.*   That is so true,—to believe, that is the only rest for the soul.   As your beautiful poet has said, 'Our's not to reason why.' "

"Well," said Frank laughing, "with you, Mr. Brown, and Tennyson against me, I suppose I must surrender."

"*Ah, mon cher, si vous etiez——*"

"Now, Claude," interrupted Clayton, "you are not a Frenchman.   Why will you insist upon speaking French rather than English ? "

"Because, monsieur, in Europe it is the common medium in which all the educated people exchange ideas. Are you not just a leetle narrow—prejudiced ? You find the English language, the English people, the best in the world, eh ? "

"Well, my dear fellow, with all due respect for the antiquity of the Latin races, I confess the Anglo-Saxon does seem to me the one destined to rule the earth in the future. You Latins ought to be satisfied," said he, laying his hand caressingly on his friend's shoulder, " you have had your turn ; now it is ours. And it seems to me that the

English-speaking races will hold a peculiar ascendancy in the ages to come."

If Claude had felt any irritation, it melted beneath the magnetism of Frank's touch, and he did not dispute the claim for Anglo-Saxon supremacy.

After the little diversion, there was a pause, which was at length broken by Capt. Brown, who said:

"And this is the second time you have snatched that child from drowning."

"Yes," said Frank. "It would seem as if some malignant fates were luring her down into the dark waters. I have a dread a sort of premonition that she will perish in that way."

The old man looked at him silently a moment and then said, impressively:

"Premonitions are strange things, strange, very strange things. I have had them myself—but—our business is with the present, not the future. Things here are assuming a very serious shape, Clayton. Several prominent citizens have been indicted for offenses, and warrants are out for their arrest. Anticipating resistance, the United States troops and the militia have been ordered to aid the civil authorities in the execution of the legal processes. Bands of Missourians are camped about ready to pounce upon us the moment this crew of thieves and scoundrels, brought here by Sheriff Jones and Governor Shannon, shall sound the charge."

"Well, from what I have seen of the defences in preparation, I fancy they will not be in a hurry to storm the town."

"The danger is not from the militia so much as the United States troops," answered the captain. "You see they obey orders, as well against the right as the wrong. Friends and foes are unknown to machines like the United States soldiers."

"Yes," said Frank, thoughtfully, "that is the danger; the United States troops will be the Trojan horse, under cover of which this mob of border ruffians will gain access to and then destroy this inoffensive town."

"That's precisely it," said Brown. "Only to-day the Committee of Safety decided to allow the United States marshal and the sheriff, with posses of United States soldiers, to enter the town and arrest any citizens for whom he has warrants.   I protested against such a course, believing, as you suggest, that the mob will follow the army, and once safely in possession and power, God knows what they will do."

"Yet, Captain, you must not forget that Governor Robinson and his committee of citizens, as you tell me, must either pursue this course, or else resist the United States troops and civil authorities, which is no light responsibility, and would entail dire consequences to the Free State cause in Kansas.   I think they have acted wisely."

"Mr. Clayton, in the sight of God wrong always is wrong, and He is quite able to take care of consequences if His children shall bravely do their duty."

"But what course would you advise?"

"I would have the sheriff present his writs of arrest, and make demand for the offenders named therein. Then I would call upon these citizens to come forward and surrender, even to the demands of unjust laws.   Thus would the semblance of legal right of entrance be destroyed, and if the mob persisted after this in forcing ingress, I should resist to the last drop of blood; and I believe in my heart, in such a cause God can and would give victory to the right, in the face of ten times the odds that now exist."

"Now, you will pardon me for saying that I think some things impossible to God, and that it is a well-established principle in war, that ' He gives victory to the heaviest ordnance,' and that we must not hazard all on the justice of our cause."

"God commands us, Mr. Clayton, ' to resist evil and it shall flee from us.'   If I obey this command in the face of all danger, He will, in His own good way, give the victory to the right."

"Begging your pardon again, Captain, I think as I stated before, that God is a God of LAW, and He commands us to know the law, and we know Him in proportion as we learn the law."

"My dear Captain," added Frank, rising, and laughing good-naturedly, "I'm afraid you think, as my friend Duvall here does, that I'm a sad renegade."

Duvall, always awed into silence by the presence of Captain Brown, only waved his hand deprecatingly, a gesture which, if translated, would have meant, "Whatever you believe, you are the best of men and dearest of friends."

After taking leave of the old man, the two younger men sauntered to the hotel.

"That is one grand figure heroique," said Claude, enthusiastically.

"Some people do not so describe him," said Frank, dryly.

Duvall always took refuge in French when his feelings overflowed the limits of his English.

"Bah! *Que sont-ils? Bêtes!* I see always around his head a shining aureola—like a saint."

"Then you do not consider him a crank?" Frank said, with apparent seriousness.

"*Excusez-moi, monsieur; mais* I hear often this word, 'crank.' I look for it in my dictionnaire, and I find it not. Please have the goodness to tell me what means this word 'crank.'"

Frank's laugh rang out loud and merrily on the silent street. His friend's grave question was so comical.

"Well, I'll tell you what it means, Claude. A man who does not think as other people do is a crank."

"Ah, yes, I see," said his friend. "Well, this Meester Brown he certainement does not think the same like other people; so they are quite right—he is a crank. And you, monsieur," said he, with a droll twinkle, "*n'est-ce pas que vous aussi*—are you not also a leetle bit of a crank?"

Frank laughed more heartily than before, and confessed that he might be so considered, and was not sorry to be so classified, inasmuch as the mechanical world was moved by cranks, and the moral and religious world was in a semi-stagnant and almost decomposing state in refusing to be so turned forward.

CHAPTER XXV.

Frank and the captain had arranged to leave the town early the next morning, neither feeling that he could witness the scenes which would probably accompany the *entrée* of the troops. Accordingly, at an early hour the two men might have been seen walking up the bank of the Kansas River, until they reached a raised plateau some few miles above Lawrence, where they halted and turned about to take a look at that devoted city which both felt to be doomed. Gazing intently, the captain pointed his finger in the direction of Mount Oread and asked in a deep tone of his companion :

"Tell me what you see there with your glass?"

After careful scrutiny, the young man replied :

"A motley crowd, half soldiers; the rest look like bandits. There seem to be flags of all colors and clans, and—no—not one—not one of the United States in sight."

"Clayton," said the captain, "I came all the way from my home at Ossawatomie and brought with with me three of my boys and several of my neighbors to aid the people of Lawrence in averting this humiliation, and, as I believe, this impending disaster, and they have denied me the pleasure of performing this duty. The responsibility rests with them. I have done my part."

All day long these two men walked and talked in sight of this hateful band and its helpless victims in the valley below.

Late in the afternoon, when like a serpent it began to wend its way down the hill and encircle with its venomous coil this quiet hamlet, Captain Brown rose from the commanding seat he and his companion had long occupied in silence.

"Come, Clayton, I can not be further witness to this desecration."

And the two men walked as before in silence, to a point where the city was obscured, and yet the house of Gov.

Robinson as well as the humble cabin of Clayton were plainly discernible against the southern sky, off beyond Mount Oread and the green fringe of timber skirting the Waukarusa River.

Late in the afternoon, Clayton observed the sky assume a lurid hue over and about Lawrence, and said :

" Captain, I see our worst fears are being realized, as yonder blood-stained sky is ample and cruel proof."

" Hark, do you hear that cannon ? " inquired Captain Brown, springing to his feet. " Can it be there is at last, when too late, resistance to the fiendish mob by the citizens ? " And again the thunder of the distant cannon shook the ledge of rocks upon which the two listening men stood.

" Run, Clayton, with your glass, scan the situation, and see if there is aught that looks like defence ; for God knows I would rather perish with them in a hopeless resistance than share this shameful humiliation without a blow at its wicked authors ! "

Soon, Clayton was upon the eminence from which they had so recently retreated, sweeping the valley with his glass to ascertain the source of the strife.

Before him lay the once prosperous town of Lawrence and the peaceful valley about it, now in the coils of a drunken and debased mob who, with hearts full of hate and brains on fire with drink, were burning houses and robbing the people. Helpless women with babes in their arms were fleeing from the minions of slavery, maddened to deeds of desperation. The cannon could be seen planted in front and aimed at the Free State Hotel, manned by men too drunk even to hit so large a mark, making merry over each discharge of ordnance.

" O God, what a sight ! " exclaimed Clayton, lowering his glass, and slowly retracing his steps to where Captain Brown stood watching him with eager eyes. Looking in the direction of Mt. Oread, he observed the red tongue of fire shootimg up from Governor Robinson's house, and thought, " Yes, I expected that ; and mine too," as his eye took in his own cabin in flames.

The conflagration grew brighter as the shades of approaching night set in and scores of fires sprang up in every direction, as the enemy, like a serpent, unwound its folds from the ashes and ruins of the fallen city, and retreated from its work of devastation, leaving a fiery track behind.

"Yes, yes, I see," said the old man, rising and stretching himself to the full height of his heroic manhood. With his right hand resting upon the sword-hilt, he shaded his eyes with the left; gazing intently in all directions upon the illumined sky, he burst forth into what seemed a prayer of consecration : "May God strengthen my arm to avenge this dastardly act of desecration, as He did that of David and of Joshua !"

On the following morning Captain Brown joined his sons and neighbors at Palmyra, and with a single companion returned to Ossawatomie in all haste, in answer to a special messenger from home, while the people of Lawrence proceeded to repair as well as possible the devastation of the preceding day.

The Free State Hotel was pillaged and then burned. The offices of the two newspapers, *Herald of Freedom* and *Free Press*," were looted, presses broken and type thrown into the street. Many of the most prominent business houses and dwellings were robbed and some destroyed by fire. Men and women moved about as in a city of the dead.

On his arrival at home that afternoon, the captain was visited by a negro man, and the following conversation ensued :

"Yer see, Mars Cap'n, I done heah dem mighty bad men down in Missouri whar I come from callin' on yo name, an' I said to myself, dey doan got any lub for de old Cap'n, an' Jim, you can jis well listen ter what dey gwinter say. Well, bress yer life, dey tell how dey make all deir 'rangement to hab a messenger man wat would bring dem to yer house an' to de oder Yankees' house in de middle ob de night; an' den dey gwinter to kill de las' one o' you. Now, Mars Cap'n, yer better not be ter home when dey comes, case dey gwine to hurt you suah nuff now. Jim knows dem men mighty sight better'n yo' does.

Captain Brown sat, an attentive listener to what Jim was relating, and finally asked :

"Did you learn, Jim, when the men propose to make this visit ?"

"Yes, sah, Mars Cap'n. I done got all de 'ticlars ob dem fellers ; but dey an't gwine ter pay yer no visit.

No, sah. Dey is gwine to come wid big knives and deir guns all loaded with buckshot to kill yer suah nuff. An' dey is comin' dis berry night; case I heerd dem say dey gwinter git a letter from de man what is ter meet dem at de ribber crossin' 'cisely at dark, an' he's gwine ter p'int out der Yankees dat's got ter be killed. All deir frien's 'bout heah gwine ter stay close ter home on dat night. I tell yer. Case dey say dey can't do de killin' an' be to home bofe at de same time. So dey got suah, what dey call er Albi.

"You are sure, Jim, the place of meeting was at the crossing?"

"Yes, sah, on dis side de ribber an' 'cisely at dusk."

After some further conversation, Jim rose to leave, and as he did so, the captain took his hand cordially and said :

"God bless and reward you, Jim for your noble deed. as I am not able to do. And if it were not for your family that, you say, compels your return, I could show and aid you to freedom. Remember this, Jim, if ever you need a friend and I can be that one, call on me. All that I have is at your service, for you have saved my life and that of my friends.

"Thanks, Mars Cap'n, Jim done got he pay already in 'lowin' dese eyes ter see yer and dis heah han' ter tuck yourn, an' to heah de voice what scare so many ob dem bad men in talkin' 'bout de freedom ob de niggers as dey says. Now, Mars Cap'n, yer gwinter be on de look-out fer dem men what's comin' ter kill yer?"

"Oh, yes, Jim, they will not find us asleep; be assured of that."

An old-fashioned clock struck three as Jim closed the door to hurry back to slavery.

John Brown sat thinking for some time, tired as he was from his long day's ride. Finally he said to his faithful companion, who had been a silent spectator and auditor during Jim's wonderful story :

"Hal, what shall we do in this matter?"

Hal, who was one of those mercurial men who think and act with the rapidity of lightning, said :

"Captain, if you will trust me with this affair, I'll promise to turn it to good account for all of us. Can you do it?"

"Yes, Hal, I have trusted you before and you never failed me; I will leave all to your management."

On this same evening, as the sun sank below the western horizon, a solitary horseman rode up to the crossing of the Osage River and, after making a careful examination of the surroundings, he turned his horse's head in the direction of the dense forest that skirted the stream, and rode out of sight.

Soon emerging on foot at the edge of the clearing, called the crossing, he carefully concealed himself in a clump of bushes that surrounded the base of a large walnut-tree. Half an hour passed, and the shades of night were beginning to gather, as another horseman rode boldly up to the river's edge. He gave a shrill whistle and then sat listening to the echo that sounded and resounded through the still forest.

After some moments, an immense owl overhead, hooted long and loud, and the horseman involuntarily put his hand to his hat as if to keep it in place.

"D——n that owl!" he ejaculated. "I always did hate them. They make me think of graveyards and ghosts. I hope his note is not one of warning to turn back from this accursed business. I could kill the old captain in a hand-to-hand affair, but to steal on him like a thief and murder him in bed or at the door with wife and children round—I detest it. However, I'm in for it, now—only as guide, though; their blood is not on my head or hands either," as he held them up, scanning them by the dim light, and then dismounted.

He had little more than touched the ground, when a stern voice from behind him said :

"Surrender, you are my prisoner! Move a hand, and you die."

"My God, is that you, Hal?"—"Yes, Bob, I am here."

Bob looked over his shoulder to see a heavy dragoon revolver in the hands of his worst enemy, cocked and pointed directly at him.

"Hal, what do you want with me?"

"I want the letter you have, and d——d quick, for it grows late."

"That letter?" asked Bob, with a start. "What do you mean? I have no letter."

"Yes, you have, Bob, and you are now trifling with time when death hangs trembling in the balance at your threshold. Give me that letter without turning around, or I'll put a ball through you on the spot. Come now, this minute," and Hal's voice fairly vibrated with deep desperation. Bob saw that the moment had come when a decisive blow must be struck ; and he said with a feeble effort to laugh :

"Well, Hal, you may have the damn thing. I see our secret is given away. Only spare my life, and I'll tell you all."

Then raising his hand as if to produce the letter, he grasped his revolver, and with a spring like a cat, he leaped to the right and turned about-face, drawing his revolver as he did so.

Two loud reports, so near together as almost seemed one, broke the dusky stillness, while the owl flapped his wings and flew hooting and screaming away.

The aim of Bob had been wild, and the ball from his revolver merely grazed the coat of Hal, who, on the alert for his man, had sent a bullet through his heart, and Bob fell forward, a lifeless corpse.

Hastily possessing himself of the coveted letter, Hal dragged the body into the thick woods, leading his horse after him, as he kicked the dust and sand over the fresh blood.

Hal soon returned and sat upon his horse, waiting events. He had not long to wait, for by the dim light of the rapidly expiring day, six men were soon descried riding down the opposite bank. As soon as they were across, Hal rode up to them and said :

"Were you expecting to meet a guide here ?"

"Well, yes, we were expecting a messenger from some friend in Kansas," replied the leader. "Did you bring a letter ?"

"Oh, yes, here is a letter from Henry——"

"Never mind who it's from, partner, give me the letter."

After reading it, by the dim light, he turned to his companions and said :

"It's all right, boys, and this is Bob, our guide."

Noiselessly the men took up their march of death ; and on the way, Hal rode up to the leader, and said :

"Captain, I am instructed to say 'Allow no parleying.

Least said, soonest mended. Short, sharp work, and return '—you understand ? "

"I think I do, young man," responded the captain,
laconically.

Shortly after twelve o'clock that night, the men surrounded the house of ————. One, a tall, powerful man,
knocked at the door, and then withdrew a few feet. Soon
the door was opened by a man, holding in his hand a
lighted candle, which he raised so as to shade his eyes,
and asked :

"Who is there ? "

A low, soft whistle from Hal was the signal for a volley that riddled the victim, extinguishing the light and
spark of life at one blow.

Hastily remounting, the men rode silently to the house
of ————, not far away, where the knock was repeated
and answered as before. Hal's signal whistle sounded
ere the man could ask if friend or foe had called.

In quick succession three more charges of buckshot
were sent hurtling through the darkness, scoring one
more victim, fallen in his own trap.

Another and another followed, until the plotters, with
Bob, their tool, slept the long sleep that knows no waking;
the last two victims being literally hacked to pieces with
knives, instead of being shot like their neighbors.

Thus was buried in the graves of the dead men, and
the bosoms of two of the living, the secret of the " Potawa-
tomie Massacre."

The assassins rode at great speed back to Missouri,
and only learned two days later how they had murdered
their friends at the instance of their enemies.

The body of Bob, the messenger, though found, was
never recognized, and his horse and pistol enlisted in the
Free State cause.

The enemies of Captain Brown boldly asserted that he
was the perpetrator of the outrage, to which he deigned
no response. His friends could make, therefore, no de-
nial. But there was a fearful warning in this ghostly
spectacle that seemed to say:

" *It is a two-edged sword you men of the South have been
using. Beware !* ""

CHAPTER XXVI.

When the convention of the people of Kansas was called to meet at Topeka on the same day that the Free State Legislature was to convene, Clayton, with a large number of his neighbors, was present. Some went armed with rifles, revolvers and swords; others with their simple faith in the protecting care of the United States government.

Rumor was current that Colonel Sumner, of the United States army, had said that the soldiers would disperse the Legislature at all hazards, in accordance with acting-Governor Woodson's proclamation. Some advised resistance to the usurpation, even unto death; and insisted that if resistance were shown, the soldiers would not fire, or Sumner go beyond the show of executing such a vile scheme.

So when the people met in Topeka on that memorable day, each man looked into his neighbor's face and sought to measure by some intuitive power, the length and breadth of his purpose.

Captain Brown was there, boys and neighbors, prepared as before at Lawrence, for resistance, and determined to act in concert with those to whom leadership had been accorded; but he said to Clayton:

"I came armed, ready for the worst if it should come."

When the convention was quietly convened and proceeded to business, the rattle and clanking of sabers and spurs broke in upon the scene, and Colonel Sumner strode to the desk of the secretary, accompanied by an officer of his staff and a deputy United States marshal, and read, with some hesitation and embarrassment, the acting-governor's proclamation commanding the Legislature to disperse, and his own order to enforce this instrument, which "it was his painful and imperative duty to obey."

When profound silence was his only answer he became embarrassed, and asked if obedience or resistance were contemplated.

Colonel Sumner was soon informed of his mistake. This was not the Legislature, but a convention of the people of Kansas, and he and his officers at once withdrew.

As soon as he had left the hall, Captain Brown, and a few of his followers, were busy in the crowd, counseling the members of the Legislature to make at least a show of resistance. Some few sympathized with this view, but the majority hesitated, and timidly urged submission rather than violence in resisting law.

Captain Brown and his party were to display in the button-hole of the coat a red string, indicating their purpose to resist, even to the shedding of blood.

When the hour had arrived for the meeting of the Legislature, Captain Brown, Frank Clayton, and one or two others, were mingling with the crowd, counting and consulting those who displayed the red badge of resistance to oppression.

"How are we to know what to do? Who is to determine our strength?" said one of the timid.

"I will," said Captain Brown, "if you will give me two hundred strings with men attached to them. Colonel Sumner will be informed by the Free State Legislature, that we propose to remain in quiet possession of these halls, and peaceably transact the business that brought us here, as the representatives of the people, until we are outnumbered, overpowered, and destroyed by any hostile force that may be brought against us. If we timidly submit, all is lost; if we heroically resist, we secure Kansas to freemen and freedom."

A careful count showed less than half the number required for successful resistance, and, added to this, was the influence of the members of the Legislature, counseling submission rather than bloodshed.

In answer, Captain Brown said:

"Yes. Submit; and if our fathers had been made of such pliant stuff, we would to-day be paying England duty on tea, and taxes to support a foreign army in our midst."

Slowly wending their way out of the humiliating scene, John Brown and his followers dispersed to their several homes.

The days following this were very dark to the lovers of freedom. Many in discouragement, gave up the conflict and returned to the East; while others resolutely prepared to fight it out; and new temporary structures rose out of the ashes of the old, at Lawrence and elsewhere, to meet the rigors of the coming winter.

On the 14th of August, a detachment of Free State men, took up the line of march from Lawrence for Fort Saunders, where Colonel Gordon was intrenched with his adherents and a large force of Missourians.

Reinforcements from Topeka met them by the way and the whole command moved on under General Lane, and surrounded the fort on all sides except where a deep and almost impassable ravine protected the flank. Then at a signal for attack Captain Brown gave the order "forward," and as soon as within firing distance with Sharpe's rifles, the command went ringing along the line, "Lie down," and the line of battle disappeared into the prairie grass, while with body concealed, the soldier could take good aim with his rifle.

Clayton, thinking the order to lie down also the signal for battle, took deliberate aim and sent a ball crashing through the door of the log fort now only about three hundred yards distant.

The premature shot caused some merriment in the line, and some other desultory firing ensued without any response from the fort.

Soon it was discovered that the enemy had evacuated the fort and retreated down a deep rugged ravine in the angle of which the fort was situated, well protected on two sides.

Then a charge was ordered and a running fire kept up between the advance of one force and the rear guard of the retreating one, over rough ground, and under cover of rocky bluffs, brush and thick trees. This lasted until late in the day when a halt was called; and at this point, a messenger from Captain Walker stated that a very large force of men under Colonel Titus, who was strongly fortified near Lecompton, had been down near Lawrence on a raid among the Free State settlers on the night previous.

At a council of war it was decided to make a rapid march that night and attack Fort Titus early on the following day.

Midnight found the Free State forces bivouacked on the road from Lawrence to Lecompton and within easy striking distance of Fort Titus. During the night, the pickets of the two forces fired upon each other, and the border ruffians chased the others into their camp, being much the stronger; and there received a volley from the men who had been sleeping under arms in true soldier style.

Several horses of the enemy were killed, and some prisoners were taken. The remainder retreated to Fort Titus and gave the alarm, so that, on the following morning, the 16th of August, when the assault was made, the enemy were found in full force and prepared for extraordinary defence. But when Captain Bickerton brought his twelve-pound field-piece into position, it spoke in thunder tones to these defiant men with ball made of type from the Free State presses of Lawrence.

"Thunder on, thou Free State Press, Herald of Freedom, as thou truly art!" exclaimed Clayton. "Remove from the face of the earth the stronghold of slavery with the double-leaded editorials!" adding as the cannon boomed again, "There is an extra issued for your special benefit, Colonel Titus!"

Boom! went Captain Bickerton's fourth issue.

Then he turned to Clayton, who was using the Sharpe's rifle with telling effect, and nodded with a significant wink as he stooped and sighted the piece for the "fifth issue."

"A little further to the right, Captain," said Clayton. "Hit him between the two centre-ports."

The captain made no response, but carefully adjusted his piece, and commanded "fire." Instantly the very crest of the hill was obscured by a volume of smoke.

"A bull's-eye, by the Eternal!" shouted Clayton.

A breach in the fort was made, which Clayton and his comrades endeavored to fill with rifle-balls. Titus and several of his men were wounded with splinters from the cannon-shots or the Sharpe's rifle-balls that flew thick and fast against his crumbling stronghold.

The smoke and din of battle, the dust of rapidly moving cavalry and infantry, the crash of cannon-shot, the bray of the trumpet, the neigh of horses, and the ringing notes of command,—"Right wheel!" "Forward!" "Steady!" "Charge!" with the echo and re-echo of the strife combined to make the little valley around Fort Titus a scene of fearful contrast to the beauty of its surroundings of but a few hours before.

Soon there fluttered out of one of the port-holes a white

flag, a shirt torn from the bleeding body of Colonel Titus and suspended from a bayonet amid the shouts of the soldiery. This was the origin of "waving the bloody shirt."

Just then a messenger arrived saying that the United States troops were coming out from Lecompton to prevent further bloodshed. In great haste, the prisoners were secured, and the Free State men returned to Lawrence in triumph.

The 17th of August was a proud day for that little city when messengers came from Lecompton asking for a council and an exchange of prisoners. John Brown, although participating in that council, allowed no word of triumph to escape him at the humiliation of the enemy, nor even at the liberation of the Free State prisoners at Lecompton. All these he accepted with a profound silence.

Men went back to their homes hoping the battle had been fought and Kansas would be left unmolested. John Brown shared this hope of a regenerated territory, but returned to Ossawatomie to "watch as well as pray."

CHAPTER XXVII.

The watching and praying were unavailing, for not many weeks later Ossawatomie was attacked by a band of ruffians, and although stoutly defended by Brown with a little band of forty men, of whom three were his own sons, was burned to the ground, and his son Frederick killed and brutally mutilated.

Governor Geary who had recently been appointed, was active in trying. to prevent further collisions between the contending factions, and attended by United States troops, he was visiting, urging and commanding both parties to disband and return to their several homes and occupations.

Under pretence of obedience to the governor's orders several bands of the border ruffians marched away and attacked unsuspecting settlers, killing and burning as they went.

Some of these men entrenched themselves at Hickory Point, from which place they made predatory attacks upon the surrounding country, and defied the governor's orders.

Two detachments of Free State men, mostly of the Stubb's company and Cabbott Guard of Lawrence, under Major Harvey, on the the 13th of September, marched from Lawrence to the fort and took the whole force prisoners after two hours, hard fighting. On his march back to Lawrence, Harvey was surprised by Captain Cook's command of United States cavalry, and all were made prisoners. Captain Cook liberated the border ruffian prisoners held by Harvey and retained the Free State men in custody and turned them over to Colonel Titus, who now was in command of the militia at Lecompton.

Early on Sunday morning, the 14th of September, Captain Brown and six men rode into Lawrence and startled the citizens by informing them that a large force of Missourians were marching on that town with the avowed purpose of destroying it, and that every available man ought at once be armed to meet and resist them.

Great was the commotion at the news among old and young, women and children. Captain Brown was asked to take, and accepted, command of the forces. Clayton with ten men was placed in the rocky walls or breast-works crowning the heights of Mount Oread, with strict orders to surrender only with his own life and the lives of his men ; others were placed at different points on the out-skirts of the town in squads of ten. Permission was given Clayton to take such of the men as had Sharpe's rifles and join the force on the plain south of the town, but not to be drawn too far from the fort.

Thus stood the beleaguered little town when the sun began its western descent to the horizon. Then a faint line of haze was discovered, forming a gray streak on the blue sky beyond Franklin in the direction of the Missouri border, from whence the attack was expected.

Captain Brown rode rapidly along his line of battle in the grass (though his whole force amounted to only a line of pickets) encouraged each man to stand firm and only to fall back to the town as a last resort.

Approaching Clayton he said :

" From the length of that gray streak of dust, it looks as though they were coming in force. You must not be led too far from your support there, for that breast-work may become a very important point."

Captain Sam Walker, Murat-like, with all the mounted men, had dashed out to meet the enemy's advance and were now engaged at long range near Franklin, and the ringing reports of the Sharpe's rifles could be distinctly heard in the distance, answered occasionally by the louder and fuller response of the shot-gun or musket with which the border ruffians were armed.

Soon, the advance guard of the enemy consisting of five hundred cavalry, came down the slopes in line of bat-tle with their skirmishers thrown well in front, driving Captain Walker's little band before them and the ominous and increasing nearness of these shots horrified the women and children in the seemingly doomed little town.

A volley from a cornfield where Captain Brown had posted some of his men, threw the enemy into great confu-sion, dismounting and wounding several of them. They had evidently not calculated well the range of the Sharpe's rifles, and the rapidity with which the bullets came, gave evidence of a much larger force than really existed.

The enemy's cavalry, though in great confusion, kept advancing. The firing all along the line was now general; riderless horses were running wildly about, throwing everything in disorder. It soon became evident to the enemy that these horsemen could never break through that line of fire and smoke impelling its swift and deadly messengers. Casting their glances backward for the expected reinforcements that came not, the whole force in a helter-skelter retreat got over the brow of the hill and back to Franklin.

So, for some unexplained reason, this handful of brave men kept twenty-seven hundred Missourians quite at bay until midnight; when the United States troops from Lecompton reached Mount Oread, and were welcomed by Clayton and his men who held the fort.

These troops had been fifteen hours marching twelve miles, under the most urgent request that could be framed by unprotected citizens! Was this delay for the benefit of the border ruffians or the people of Lawrence? inquiring minds will ask.

Captain Brown rode up and turned the command of the defence of Lawrence over to the United States officer in charge.

"Where is the enemy we are brought here to check on his road to carnage?" asked the officer, sneeringly.

"Sir," said Captain Brown, "if you look over there (pointing to the hundreds of camp-fires plainly visible from where they stood,) you will find answer to your question. And now will you be kind enough to detail a guard and relieve the citizens who have been on duty since early morning?"

Captain Brown then pointed out the strong places he had guarded, and the men on duty were relieved.

CHAPTER XXVIII.

Claude Duvall was compelled to go to the East and South upon important private business of his own; but Frank's frequent letters kept him fully informed of the flow of events in Kansas; and Claude felt almost like a deserter at leaving his friend alone in such troublous times—the whole Territory in a condition of tumult and alarm—collisions, and even victories, seeming to accomplish little. Winter was approaching, and thousands of brave fellows had not resources even to fight its rigors, and hence must bear the present ills until Spring had recruited their forces, and then renew the conflict.

John Brown's domestic sorrows, added to the other trouble, had broken him sadly. His home and his family were wrecked. Fire, sword and the plowshare of grief had left little of a once happy circle. All the energy of his mind now seemed turned upon one object, upon which he pondered night and day—that was, aiding slaves to escape into freedom. It was a perilous undertaking to get off one of these parties of fugitives; but he engaged in it with a kind of reckless energy.

Just at this time a negro came to him, introducing himself as Jim.

"You disremember me, Mars Captain," said the fellow with a curious twinkle, "don't yer reklect Jim what come to tole you bout de men what wuz comin' to kill yer dat night?"

"Why, Jim!" exclaimed the captain, much moved and clasping his hand.

"Yes, sah; it is me for sartain. I dun heard about you over in Missouri, an I sez 'I know Mars Brown ain't gwinter let dem take me down to Texas.' We all ob us, mo'n a dozen, belongs ter de young missus, an' she's berry sick an' gwinter die; an' if she do, she say we're all a gwinter be free. Now, de young mars, he gwinter sen' us off ter Texas 'fo she die, so dat nobody can fin' us to gib us freedom. Nigh as I can l'arn, deys gwinter start us off sometime nex' week an' w'at we's gwinter do mus be did mighty quick, Cap'n. Well, Mars Cap'n, I ses to my ole 'oman, I sez: 'Don cry, honey; Mars Brown h'ell come and car us off to Kansas—suah—case he sed as how he would help dis yer nigger ef ebber he need it ; and we do need it now mighty bad, an' no mistake. '"

The next day Frank received a message asking him to come at once to Captain Brown's rooms.

"Clayton," said he impressively, " I have heard a voice from Heaven. When I was revolving plans for Jim's rescue the whole thing opened up to me as clear as noonday." And fixing his eyes on Frank as if he expected to electrify him with his words : "We will open a highway right through the State of Missouri ; have organized bands to protect it all along the way; and the slaves will rush through it in an an irresistible torrent toward freedom. Nothing can withstand them !"

"But, my dear friend," said Frank, amazed, "this is madness. I implore you to reflect that——"

"Reflect ? I have reflected. Do the waters pause when a breach is made in the dam? I tell you we can empty the South of suffering humanity by opening up these points of egress—for there must be others. I have thought of Harper's Ferry; that is one point that must be looked after. In a half-hour we could possess ourselves of the United States Arsenal there—and then "—and there was a gleam of strange triumph in his eye—"nothing on earth could stay that flood which would pour through to Canada."

"My God ! You are not serious ?" said Frank, in agitation.

John Brown looked at Clayton in silence for a moment, then said : " Clayton, I am disappointed in you. I thought *you*, at least, I might depend upon ; but I see I must lean upon no human arm. God and justice are all I shall have to help me. But it will be done, sure as the Red Sea opened for the Israelites."

"A Red Sea, yes," said Frank, gloomily ; " but a sea red with blood !—and now——"

"Pardon me, my dear friend," he added more gently, " but I see danger in all this—danger to you and to the people you would serve. My reason revolts, I must candidly tell you, *revolts* at the whole plan as illegal and impracticable."

"*You* have no scruples against aiding *one* fugitive to liberty, which is equally illegal; yet you hesitate to send a thousand on the high road. I do not understand your reasoning," said the old man with bitterness. "In other words, you think it right to retail freedom, while it 'revolts your reason' to give it broadly to the whole race."

Frank was overwhelmed when he found how impossible it was to avert the impassioned old man from this plan. He paced the floor in silence a few times, and then said very earnestly:

"Abandon this, I implore you—or at least, wait. Wait, be patient, and time will avenge the wrongs we have all suffered. And though I confess yours have been most grievous and hard, and Jim's full of injustice and cruelty, yet would I bid you wait until action shall *mend*, not *mar* the situation."

John Brown arose, and said impressively:

"Let me paint a picture for your contemplation, Clayton, and then you may answer me. On the banks of a small river was an humble cottage, under the roof of which lived an aged couple and their four sons. Contentment, peace and happiness were written on all parts of this quiet picture, animate and inanimate.

"Lo! a change! Look again! In the short space of two summers the hand of the destroyer, Slavery, has been at work. There under the scorched boughs of a spreading oak that formed almost a part of the cottage itself, lies the swollen, distorted and mutilated body of one son, and kneeling near by is the wreck of another. Hovering about this group is a woman whose fifty recurring autumns have sprinkled their frosts upon her dishevelled hair, and down her furrowed cheeks flow a mother's tears; while with raised hands she cries in agony: 'Can such things be, with a God still in Israel!'"

Then approaching his companion almost fiercely, Captain Brown added: "Now, sir, in the presence of this picture can you ask the father and husband to be patient? 'Be patient!' Yes, I'll be patient and tarry with the thunder-bolts of an avenging God!" and he walked on, saying to himself: "Yes, I'll wait for the slow process of Ages, perhaps, when these black men shall be aroused and made to stand upright before God."

Then, stopping suddenly before Clayton, who sat watching this storm of human woe, he continued:

"No, it's false and impossible. I'll not be patient nor passive. I will rush forth and arouse these men from their slumber of centuries and bid them in the name of God, our common Father, to claim their heritage of freedom! Yes; though I had a thousand lives instead of one to answer for this act!"

"Listen!" he added, with a solemn gesture. "Only last night I was pondering on these things, weighing all prudent objections, when suddenly the room became illumined by a soft light, and, as from a cloud, a human form dimly appeared, until finally it stood as in life, and I started forward to embrace my son; but, with a wave of his hand, he bade me desist. His eyes were full of tender light and sympathy; yet he spake not. Then I said: 'In the name of God, my son, what can I—what *must* I do in this great duty that lies before me?' As if I had anticipated his wish, he smiled, saying: 'Father, I come in the name and in behalf of the wronged—look there!' and he pointed to the opposite wall; and there, written in blood-red letters, I saw 'Fear not to do thy appointed work.'"

John Brown seated himself and remained bowed for some moments. Lifting his head finally, he said:

"Can I—ought I to wait?"

Clayton arose and clasped the outstretched hands, as he said, with much feeling:

"Captain, compose yourself. I think you did but dream; and to act is to rush madly—— "

"Stay, stay, Clayton!" he interposed. "I am the prophet, the priest and the sacrifice. If I dreamed *then*, so do I dream *now;* your task is silence—assent, or aid, but no opposition. As well try to stay the bolt after the electric flash. No, no; the die is cast—I go to answer the call of duty and my God!"

CHAPTER XXIX.

"LAWRENCE, Oct. 10th, 1858.

"MY DEAR DUVALL :

"I told you in my last brief letter of my painful interview with our old friend, Capt. Brown ; but I did not tell you the distress it cost me even for a moment to differ from and almost rebuke him. And yet, I cannot follow him in this mad enterprise upon which he is fully bent. I am dismayed when I think to what it may lead. I sometimes think long brooding over wrong has partly dethroned reason. Had he ten lives, he would gladly lay them down for the end he wishes to accomplish. But he will *not* accomplish it, and so the sacrifice will be vain ; that my reason assures me. But what use to tell him this ? Does the wind turn Mt. Oread, as she sits there facing the sun ?

" He is not of *our* world. Its code of laws, its prejudices and conventions are nothing to him, because he recognizes only a *Divine* Code and defies human courts and penalties. So—I can only leave him to work out his own problem alone. I have consented, however, under certain conditions, to lend my aid in his attempt to gather the band of slaves in Missouri. He promises the thing shall be accomplished without bloodshed ? and, of course, I anticipate that Sam will by this means escape from his captors and *pseudo* owner.

" This reminds me to tell you of an unexpected visitor from my old home, in none other than Dick, the husband of the poor girl who was, with her child, so mysteriously spirited away from that misguided boy, Harry Barnes. God only knows what became of the poor creature ; but it seems that Mr. Fletcher has given him his freedom, that he may go in search of her. As that gentleman never did a good act in his life, (that I am aware of) I naturally see my cousin Kate's hand in this. She is the dearest and the best of women—and—well, if *she* is satisfied with her fate, I suppose I should be !   And she seemed very fond of that underserving fellow, although I thought in my last visit home, some two years ago, I discovered signs of disenchantment. At all events, she had lost her vivacity and there were lines of pain in her face which troubled me.

"My dear fellow, how I do pour my heart out to you ! It has become my habit to tell you everything. Oh, how I miss your sympathetic smile, your magnetic presence and your musical halting English ! Now, don't be vain, old fellow ; but really, I have found your friendship so congenial and so comforting, I want you to know it.

"You have listened so patiently to my troubles and so bravely concealed your own ! And, frankly, I have no sorrows but those of others, which I take upon myself.

"The one sorrow of which I told you—the loss of my early love—seems a dream now ! and since my uncle Stanley is gone, there is no one nearer than my cousin Kate. I have an ample fortune, life and the world before me, I am heart free ; what right have I to ask for sympathy? So to this confession I will add one more— that I am,

"Ever most faithfully yours,
"FRANK CLAYTON."

CHAPTER XXX.

Upon the banks of the Osage River, near the line of Vernon County, just as the sun was sinking in the west, a group of men stood looking across the small stream, which ran swift and muddy from recent rain.

"I wonder what is the matter?" said a tall, muscular man, in whom we recognize Kagi, Capt. Brown's trusted friend and lieutenant. "The captain is usually so prompt, and we have only a few hours now in which to do our work."

"Perhaps some trouble in obtaining a wagon," suggested Charles Partridge; then he exclaimed, "There! I see him coming."

And soon the tall, erect form of Capt. Brown stood upon the opposite shore.

The two men with their companion, Frank Clayton, bounded into their saddles and forded the narrow stream which they observed was rising.

"We will have hard work, Kagi," said Clayton, "to recross this creek five or six hours from now; and if the ferry-boat cannot be found up at the crossing, we may have to swim. No telling what kind of a following we may have." Then, tnrning in his saddle, he said :

"Partridge, do you know on which side of the river the ferry is kept below here?"

"I am unable to say, for it is used now by those dare-devil boys about here.

"I have information that Livingstone and Hart are both down at Skinner's ranch ; and some kind of deviltry is on foot, for the trio never come together unless mischief is brooding. I have made arrangements to have the ferry-boat on this side ; and if those devils don't discover it, we will be all right," said Kagi, as they ascended the bank where Capt. Brown stood looking at the four trusted men who were coming over for a final council before action.

All of the horsemen dismounted, and after shaking

hands with their leader, stood about him, waiting for his commands. It was finally agreed, after some discussion, that the ferry should be the rendezvous instead of the ford, in view of the rapidly rising river.

When all arrangements were made, Clayton and his friends mounted, to recross the stream where their field of action lay, leaving the other horsemen watching them until they had ascended the opposite bank.

After several hours' swift but noiseless travel, Partridge said :

"Now, we are near Skinner's ranch; and if you will remain here, I will reconnoitre and report to you."

Clayton's servant, Dick, had joined the party, and was by his master's side.

Soon, Partridge returned, saying :

"I see Sam has a light burning in his cabin, which means there is danger. I will go and warn him and his fellow servants and then have them quietly saddle the horses, and you can keep watch on the house where the master and, perhaps, his guests are sleeping."

The force was disposed of, and Duvall had Sam and three other men engaged in saddling horses and gathering together such articles as were needful for the flight.

Dick observed a dark figure approaching from the house, and gave a low whistle as a warning to the man on guard. When this figure was quite near, he said :

"Halt! If you raise a hand, you're a dead man!"

Skinner, for it was he, looked around to find himself face to face with Dick who had him covered with a pistol not ten feet away; and though he carried a navy revolver in his hand, he hesitated a moment; then turned suddenly and fired; another report followed his closely, and Skinner fell to the ground.

"Whar's Mars Frank? asked Sam, running up. "Dem debils 'll be on us now, suah. Dem shots was de sign for dem to come tarin'—I mean Mars Livingstone and Mars Hart."

Hastily mounting their horses, the party put spurs and were soon on their way to the ferry. Livingstone, Hart and four others from an all-night debauch they had been attending, arrived on the ground well filled with whiskey, and in no condition for hostilities requiring cool, deliberate action. They found Skinner dead, and leaving him with one of their number, then followed a hasty consultation; in which they decided that John Brown and his "jay-hawkers" were the perpetrators, and that they had probably returned to the ferry as the river was too high to cross at the ford.

With a yell of rage, the party of madmen set out by the most direct route for that point.

"There's hell to pay now!" said Livingstone, as shouting and firing pistols like drunken savages, they started for the ferry.

Clayton and his party heard the shots in the distance, but they had a good start, were better mounted, and all sober. Arrived at the ferry just before daylight, they found the boat had been taken to the opposite shore, while the river had risen, and froth and foam covered the surface of the roaring stream. No time was to be lost. In order to swim over to get the ferry-boat, it was necessary that the swimmer start from above. and go down with the current.

Claude plunged into the mad, muddy water, but soon became entangled in the underbrush.

"Come back, Claude," shouted Clayton, "and make a fresh start. Now," said he, "I am a more amphibious animal than you; let me take the lead in this." And, stripping himself for the perilous swim, he was soon out beyond the brush and in the angry water. All held their breath in suspense until they should hear some signal of success.

Out, out into the darkness, the swimmer pulled carefully, reserving his strength for the final struggle on the opposite side. In the middle of the stream where the long rope stretched from shore to shore upon which the ferry-boat clung as she glided back and forth, Clayton caught hold and rested a moment. As he clung, almost breathless, there came a drift of logs and brushwood, striking the rope and lifting him partly out of the water. Releasing his hold, he sank beneath the surface, but soon reappeared and struck out for the shore, where he could just see the dim outlines of the boat and landing.

Too much exhausted to make any signal of victory, he clung to the end of the boat to regain his breath before raising himself in. Then he sent on the wings of the wind a shrill note over the turbulent water; "T'ank God! He done cross de dark ribber suah 'an' sartin!" cried Sam.

Soon, the staple was forced out by Clayton and the bow of the boat turned toward the opposite shore. As he was approaching it, there came on the chill morning air, the shout of pursuers and the ominous report of pistols.

Partridge and Dick were now called in from picket duty, and all were soon on board the frail boat, almost too heavily laden for safety.

The voice of Livingstone was first heard as the pursuing party came thundering to the landing, only to see, by opposite light of the early dawn, the boat nearing the the shore.

"Cut that d——d rope, quick, boys! Kill or drown the d——d jayhawkers!" he commanded.

Meantime, Kagi had posted his men in the stern of the boat with orders to return the first fire.

Soon, the flash came, and revealed the pursuers in a confused mass; and Kagi sent a bullet from his rifle in response to their challenge. Then another and another was sent in quick succession, as the bow of the boat under Sam's careful management ran with a slight shock against the bank.

A flash and a volley from just over their heads revealed that John Brown had arrived, and was paying his compliments to Livingstone across the river, while yells of rage and defiance came over the roaring water, with occasional shots from the baffled pursuers.

On ascending the bank, Captain Brown was the first to grasp Clayton's hand, saying, as he did so:

"I am glad to see you unharmed. I trust all the others are safe."

"We are all right, Captain, and we have rescued our man and three others in safety, to say nothing of four good horses; and we left Skinner wounded on the ground near his door-sill."

"I had hoped," said the captain, "we could make this expedition a success without shedding a drop of blood. I am glad to say we have brought out our entire party without pulling a trigger until we came here."

By this time the team with Captain Brown's party

came up, composed of men, women, and children. The sun had risen, and the old friends, Sam and Dick, met for the first time face to face, and embraced in their demonstrative fashion.

And now again the party was put in motion, keeping the edge of the timber that skirted the river bank.

When a place of safety had been reached on Kansas soil, Captain Brown and Clayton, accompanied by Dick, rode by night to Lawrence, leaving Kagi in command, with instructions to use all possible care to avoid surprise and to move with great care and secrecy through to Nebraska and thence northward.

CLAYTON had returned to Lawrence. One evening, a week later, as he sat watching the unusual glory of the setting sun, he saw a horseman covered with dust, ride at full speed to the Eldridge Hotel, dismount, throw the reins to a servant, and hastily ascend the steps. Clayton saw all this, but his thoughts were far away at the moment with Captain Brown, whose crayon portrait was standing upon a rustic easel in the room. Lost in revery, he hardly heard the light tap at his door some moments later, until it was repeated, and he said, "Come in," without observing who entered.

"Is Mr. Clayton in?" was demanded, in a youthful voice, the sound of which brought Clayton back to the world and duty.

"I am he. What can I do for you?" he said, advancing toward his visitor, a youth of some eighteen years, rather below the medium stature, with dark eyes and hair, clean-cut features, a fair oval face which was flushed from riding.

The messenger drew from the inner pocket of his coat a letter, which he handed to Clayton, saying:

"I beg pardon for intruding upon you, Mr. Clayton, but my business would admit of no delay, as you will learn from the contents of this despatch—which I hope you will lose no time in reading," he added, seeing Clayton stood gazing, as if trying to read the messenger instead of the message.

"I beg you will sit down," said Clayton kindly—"you look fatigued, and now may I ask the name of the messenger to whom I am indebted for this despatch?"

"My name is Roland Priest," said the youth, with downcast eyes, as though he dared not encounter the earnest ones of the questioner.

"Roland Priest," said Clayton, "I am very thankful for your promptness in the delivery of the message, since I see it left my old friend Captain Brown only last night. Do you know anything of the contents?" he inquired, looking up from the paper and thinking how unwise it was in Captain Brown to select such an inexperienced youth to bear so important a despatch.

"I only know, sir, that Captain Brown and his party are in great danger, and that after writing and delivering this letter, he said not to come with less than twenty men and to come without delay, by way of Topeka."

"I see Captain Brown says they are surrounded;—did you come through without adventure or discovery?"

"Yes—I mean no, sir. There was discovery, and some adventure in getting beyond the enemy's lines which are drawn pretty close around Captain Brown's party."

"I notice on this envelope, Mr. Priest——"

"Please call me Roland, Mr. Clayton; I am not used to being called 'Mister;' and—and—it confuses me," interrupted the young man, blushing like a girl.

"Well, 'Roland' then; I observe blood-stains upon this envelope; and I trust Captain Brown's messenger was not hurt seriously in bearing his despatch?"

"Yes, sir—I think—I mean, the other messenger is hurt quite badly."

"Then, you are not the same person into whose hands Captain Brown delivered this paper?"

"No, sir; I took the despatch when the other messenger fainted from loss of blood, and I brought it as soon as possible——"

"Pardon me: I was only wondering how my old friend came to select such a young and, perhaps, inexperienced——"

"Yes, I understand, but the messenger who started with the despatch was one of the swiftest and most daring riders in all Kansas; but you see, there were unforeseen difficulties, and you ought to be——"

"Thankful, you would justly say, for the delivery of the message," interjected Clayton. "And so I am. You are a brave young man, and will make your mark in life. But now, you must have rest and something to eat, if you are to accompany us, as you say."

"What time will you start, Mr. Clayton?"

"I think we can be ready by twelve o'clock to-night, and by hard riding, we can be within striking distance of Captain Brown's position by the same hour to-morrow night."

After registering his name in the hotel, Roland was shown to his room to rest; and Clayton sallied forth to find the requisite twenty men who could be mounted and ready for the hard ride and prospective fight.

The first persons he met, were Partridge and Parker; the former of whom was of John Brown's liberating party which had recently returned from Missouri, and they had their own horses. Both would be ready and meet on Mount Oread at the hour designated, armed and equipped.

Several others were found who would gladly go, only they were not provided with horses. Colonel Eldridge, the proprietor of the Eldridge House, came up where a group of three men were discussing the matter, and said promptly:

"I have twenty horses at your command, Clayton, if so many are needed. No man need stay who wants to go on such a mission?"

So, through this patriotic and generous offer, in less than two hours the party was made up under promise to report on Mount Oread at midnight.

On returning to the hotel, Clayton found that Roland had supped and retired, asking to be excused to Mr. Clayton, and to be called at half-past eleven o'clock.

In order to understand the preceding, we must rejoin John Brown in the preliminary movements of his undertaking.

CHAPTER XXXII.

Captain Brown had determined to move quietly through Kansas and Nebraska, when he took up the line of march for freedom, making no demonstration in Iowa or elsewhere, which would tend to excite opposition, as the rewards offered by the Governor of Missouri and the President of the United States, were likely to make new and additional incentive to the excited and embittered spirit in the South and some parts of the North as well.

Evidence was furnished of parties being organized for the purpose of interrupting his march, with headquarters both at Lecompton and Atchison.

About a day's journey beyond Topeka, he had unmistakable evidence of the enemy's spies and pickets hanging on the flanks of the little band, carefully keeping out of range of his Sharpe's rifles, but rarely out of sight.

Riding thoughtfully in advance of his train, it occurred to him that a messenger ought to be sent to Lawrence for the promised reinforcement. As night drew near, he decided to go into camp beside a narrow stream bordered by a thick growth of timber. On the western bank, overlooking the country, stood a double log cabin with strong doors chinked between the logs with stones, over which was plastered a coat of red clay.

Before unharnessing the teams, Captain Brown rode up to this comfortable log cabin and, in response to his call, a young man, dressed in a hunting-suit of buckskin, came out. His quick elastic step, dark eyes, waving hair and open brow, bespoke a youth in whom border life and its attendant dangers had brought out the full vigor of his not more than twenty years. He wore at his belt a navy revolver and large hunting-knife.

"Come in, Captain ?" said the young man, in a pleasant voice, as he came promptly forward and took the extended hand of Captain Brown, who had dismounted as he also advanced.

"Why, Roland Priest. I am rejoiced to see you; and is this your cabin?"

"Yes, Captain, these are my bachelor quarters. My mother lives up the creek a few miles, and I am down here to look after my claim. Are these your teams down at the creek, Captain?"

"Yes, those are my wards on the road to freedom, of whom you perhaps have heard."

"Yes, I have heard, and I warn you that others also have heard of your undertaking. You had better stop here to-night, and bring your wagons up to the house;—you will be more comfortable as well as safe. I have noticed here to-day, more than a dozen men, mounted and armed, passing and repassing. They are evidently on the lookout for your train, and you may expect an attack before you go much further."

The teams were driven up in the yard and unhitched; the negroes were safely housed, and preparations made for supper, when Roland Priest and Captain Brown walked out, talking of their old home in York State, where they were neighbors.

"How did your mother ever consent to come out to this wild country, Roland?" asked the captain.

"I tell you, Captain, I acquired a taste for this western life, as you know, and I couldn't stay there contentedly; and mother finally decided that she would rather live here with me than there without me, so we are all here now, safe and sound."

"What of your sister, Isabel. How does she like this life?"

"Admirably, Captain. She often hunts with me, and is a captial shot and horsewoman. You must go up with me and see my mother. She'll be so glad to see you."

"Ah, my boy, much as I would like to see my old friends, I dare not leave my post of duty, now. And that reminds me—there must be posted a picket guard at once. Ride out with me and let us select a good point. You are familiar with the location?"

The two men mounted and rode out a half-mile beyond the cabin to an elevated point from which the picket could command a good view of the surrounding country. As they were sitting in their saddles enjoying the beautiful prospect, looking westward, two men rode up a ravine and stood in the path several hundred yards away. Seeing Captain Brown and Roland, they moved off in the opposite direction, paying no heed to the command to halt, but answered by two ringing shots from their rifles, as they put spurs to their horses and rode away.

"There is a challenge for you, Captain. They are in force, with ways guarded; for they never would have made such an assault if they had not been sure of their game. Now, what is to be done? I'll warrant the road from here to Topeka, as well as Grasshopper Falls, is guarded."

"Yes, perhaps," said Captian Brown; "But let us go inside and talk the matter over. We must act with deliberation."

"Roland, my boy," said the captain, when they were seated in the cabin, "can you carry a despatch to Lawrence for me, and start immediately?"

"I'll go to the ends of the earth to serve you; only I should be glad to go home, a distance of only a few miles, and inform mother and Isabel of my absence and my mission. They are looking for me at this moment, and I never disappoint them when I can help it."

"How much out of your way is it?"

"Very little. My horse Thunderbolt carries me as if I were a feather, and thus there will be little time lost."

In half an hour Roland Priest stood before the captain in boots and spurs, ready for the ride.

"Roland," said the old captain, "do you appreciate the danger as well as the importance of this ride?"

"I think I do, Captain; and you may depend upon my seeing your friend Mr. Clayton and carrying out your instructions."

"Read them first, so you will understand the situation," said the captain.

Roland read aloud.

"Danger Creek Crossing.

"My Dear Clayton:—

"We are here surrounded by the enemy. We are fortified in the two cabins on the bank, and can hold out against a hundred until succored. Come at once with double the force agreed upon. Messenger has verbal instructions to avoid mishap, and you can trust him.

"Yours truly,

"J. B."

"Now for verbal instructions," said the captain, when the young man had finished reading. "I want Clayton to bring not less than twenty men and to come via Topeka, and co-operate with any force he may find there, but on no condition to wait a moment, but come at once. Let him move so as to reach here, if all works well, by Sunday morning, and make the attack about daylight. You, of course, will return with him. You will find him at the Eldridge House on Massachusetts Street, Lawrence."

Roland Priest led his horse down the bank of the creek, and was soon hidden in darkness from Captain Brown, who stood in the door watching the messenger upon whom so much now depended.

Skirting the creek was a narrow strip of bottom-land, which Roland followed for some distance, where a high plateau formed the bank to the creek, compelling him to emerge, since he could not cross on account of the treacherous bottom.

As he came to the top, he stood for a moment, peering in every direction for the enemy's pickets, which he had no doubt were posted not far from this point. Not seeing or hearing anything suspicious, he remounted Thunderbolt and rode carefully for a short distance, when his horse swerved to one side as a voice with an oath called out:

"HALT! OR YOU ARE A DEAD MAN!"

Roland, without obeying the command or stopping to think of the consequences, threw himself forward and to the opposite side of his horse, at the same time firing his revolver at the dark outline of a man and horse but a few rods away, saying as he did so:

"Now, Thunderbolt, go!"

He saw a flash from his antagonist's pistol, and felt a sharp twinge in his shoulder that warned him he was hit, but he hoped not seriously, as he found the use of his arm not impaired. Riding directly home, he dismounted and staggered, faint and exhausted, into his mother's presence.

"O my son!" was the greeting that met him at the threshold. "Roland, what has happened?"

"Oh, he is dying!" exclaimed Isabel, in terror.

Dr. Russell was most fortunately at a neighboring house and in five minutes was with the distressed family.

"Do you feel any internal pain?" inquired the doctor. "Take a long breath?"

Roland did as requested, and found considerable pain from breathing, and spat blood.

"Now," said the physician, "you must lie down and remain as quiet as possible."

"Doctor," said the wounded boy, "I cannot. I am intrusted with an important dispatch from Captain Brown."

"No matter," said the doctor, "from whom the dispatch is, nor for whom, you can go no further."

"Dear Roland," said Isabel, "give yourself no anxiety about this dispatch. I know of a messenger who will take your place."

In a whispered tone, Roland gave his sister the verbal instructions he had received from Captain Brown, and handed her the letter, then fell back fainting.

For a few minutes, the house was in a state of alarm, then Roland wearily opened his eyes and inquired what had happened?

Isabel knelt by the side of the couch and kissed the pallid face.

"What a likeness!" said Dr. Russell, "even for twin brother and sister it is remarkable!"

"Rolla, the doctor says you are not too much hurt for me to leave you for a while, and he will remain with you ; so good-bye, my darling." Then stopping at the door with her mother, she said a few words in an inaudible tone, and Isabel Priest vanished with John Brown's dispatch.

CHAPTER XXXIII

At precisely half-past eleven o'clock Clayton rapped at the door of Roland Priest's room in the Free State Hotel, and the response came promptly.

"Rolla—oh, Mr. Clayton. Yes, I remember. I will soon be down."

Clayton paced the floor impatiently, wondering who the "Rolla" could be for whom this young man, in his first waking moments, mistook him.

Soon Roland appeared in person, somewhat pale, but refreshed.

"I hope I have not delayed you. I was tired, and slept soundly, but I am at your service now."

The coffee was brought, and while partaking of it Roland's face deepened in color under the intense gaze of his companion, who saw in the boy an unexplained mystery, that one seemingly so young, refined and educated, should be leading such a wild, adventurous life, and yet changing color like a girl under his scrutinizing gaze.

But there was no time for pondering over these problems, and the two were soon in their saddles, wending their way to Mt. Oread, where were assembled the relief party, eighteen in number.

Only a few minutes after twelve o'clock they were joined by Clayton and his young companion on Mount Oread.

"Gentlemen," said the strong, manly voice of Henry Parker, "I suggest that Mr. Clayton shall command this expedition."

"I endorse what friend Parker has said," responded Partridge, "and hope that Mr. Clayton will be unanimously chosen to command our relief party."

"Ay! Ay!" responded every voice.

Clayton thanked them for their confidence in him, and accepted the responsibility.

Then, in line, counted off by "twos," they wheeled into

column, and the command "Forward!" was given as Clayton and Roland Priest rode at their head.

Sunrise found the party dismounting at the hotel at Topeka, where man and beast were refreshed, after which, the day's march was resumed, and a beautiful day it proved. Though winter, it was a spring day in temperature. The news of Capt. Brown's perilous situation created excitement in Topeka, and a party was to be organized to co-operate with the Lawrence force at once, and follow to the rescue.

The day's march was drawing near its close, as Frank Clayton and Roland Priest rode side by side.

"Observe, Roland, what a peculiar haze of a rich pinkish hue the heavens have in the west; not only at the horizon, but far above. What can it mean? See there. It runs in broad feathery lines, as of falling rain."

"I also have observed a chill in the atmosphere, Mr. Clayton. That augurs a radical change in the weather. It looks very like a snow-storm."

The wind sprang up from the northwest; the sun sank lower and lower, and finally disappeared in a dark bank of clouds.

The pinkish color of the heavens gradually merged into the more sombre hue of the storm cloud; then the whole panorama was illuminated by fiery zigzag lines as the lightning cleft for an instant these masses of cloud, followed by the sharp report of thunder.

Others of the party looked in dismay at the phenomenon as they rode under whip and spur by order of their commander, hastening to reach the timber before the storm overtook them.

In half an hour the storm burst upon the travellers, who were little prepared for its approach.

"We cannot be far from that skirt of timber on our right, can we?" asked Clayton of young Priest.

"No, I think not; but had we not better keep on, at least to the crossing, where we will find shelter?" replied Roland, as the blinding wind and snow obscured all objects.

"Halt! Who comes there!" exclaimed Clayton as the column came upon a number of dark objects driven with the fury of the snow-storm which had now burst upon them in full force.

To the command and inquiry, given in quick succession, there was a loud " Mooah, mooah," from the deep throats of a large herd of cattle, and the response was taken up and repeated all the way down the line of terror-stricken animals, as they continued their course with the wind and snow, in the direction of the timber on the right of the line of march.

The episode was so absurd that despite the peril there was a shout of laughter in which all joined, though they realized the danger of a snow-storm on a western prairie.

Keeping the wind to their backs, and joining the herd of cattle, they soon reached the timber skirting the small stream whose high banks and some fallen trees with over-lapping cedars, furnished temporary shelter for the little party.   Soon, a roaring fire was crackling in the branches of a fallen oak ; horses secured, and arrangements made for spending the night in this wild and desolate region.

Details of men were made to keep guard and others to bring wood for the fire, which had no sooner shed its bright and cheering rays through the clouds of drifting snow, than the herd which had preceded the horsemen, began to crowd around and almost contest the space about it with the men who were busily piling on the broken boughs.

Through the long and seemingly interminable night these beasts at short intervals would indulge in lowing plaintively, which, interspersed with the shrieking wind and the occasional sharp click of their horns as they crowded around the fire, sounded not unlike the snapping of hungry wolves accompanied by low rumbling as of dis-tant thunder, as one after another of the vast herd shook from his shaggy coat the fast accumulating burden of snow. Their eyes gleamed in the dim light like so many phosphorescent lamps, and the falling snow-flakes seemed like myriad moths diving into unearthly fires.   These weird sights and sounds, in addition to the storm of wind, roaring and howling among the groaning trees, made a deep impression upon even the stoutest of the party.

Sheltered under the boughs of a spreading cedar, Clayton and Roland sat, looking into the fire in silence ; and ever and anon, the pale face of the youth was upturned to the other inquiringly, as if to ask if all were well.

Clayton was not unmindful of what was passing in his companion's mind, who drew instinctively closer to him, and he answered reassuringly:

"We are all safe, my boy, have no fear."

About midnight, as the fury of the storm abated somewhat, and the cattle became more quite, Clayton said:

"Come, Roland, you must lie down and have your rest. No soldier can do his whole duty who goes into battle cold, worn, and without sleep. If you are, as you say, afraid for both of us to sleep at once, I will keep watch while you get a few hours' sleep; and then you may take your turn in the vigils."

"I will lie down on the condition that you call me in two or three hours,—which is all the sleep I want."

"Indeed, Master Roland, after your two days' ride and only a half night's rest, I am sure you need sound sleep; so now, wrap yourself in this blanket, and lie down."

And without further parley, Roland pulled the felt hat down over head and face, and was soon asleep.

Hour after hour, as each relief came on, the fires were renewed, and still Roland Priest slept on and Frank Clayton kept his watch. Tired and sleepy, he said to himself: "Why should I not lie down and get some rest? This youngster has no right to dictate such terms." And putting his hand upon the blanket to turn it aside, Roland started up and took his post as officer of the guard while sleep brought refreshing rest to Clayton.

At daylight, the relief party mounted and ascended the bluff, now covered with snow, leaving the cattle in possession of the camp and crowding into the vacant space around the fire.

The dim outline of Danger Creek Forest was discerned some miles away, to which Clayton and party marched across the trackless expanse.

Soon the cruling smoke that issued from the chimney of a cabin in the distance, was discernible; and Roland. pointing to it, said: "There—that is Danger Creek Crossing, and there is the cabin in which Captain Brown is lodged."

Keeping well under cover of the bank and skirt of timber, Clayton led his men unobserved, within striking distance; then halting the column, Mr. Partridge was given command of a detachment with instructions to remain quiet until Clayton, with the remainder of the men, had made a short detour under cover of an angle of the creek bank, whereby he could strike the besieging force from another quarter, whose pickets and smoke from their camp-fires could be seen. A single shot was to be the signal for a simultaneous charge with a loud shout "to follow the enemy as far as you can see him, and meet at the cabin."

Turning to Roland, Clayton said:

"Will you go with us, or remain here? Perhaps you will be less exposed here."

"No, Mr. Clayton, I am familiar with the country, and can give you the benefit of my knowledge. I'll go with you."

Winding around the hill for a half mile or so, a favorable position was obtained from which the single picket on duty could be seen on this side of the creek. The cabin was in full view. Captain Brown and party were all astir, and a move was evidently contemplated.

Carefully stealing to the top of the bank, in line, Clayton raised his rifle and fired at the picket; then gave the command to charge, and away went the pursued and pursuers, and almost instantly, Partridge and his party came shouting and firing over the hill.

Taken entirely by surprise, the border ruffian relief mounted and rode helter skelter in different directions.

"Every man for himself," said the last of the pickets, "and the devil take the hindmost!"

It was an odd spectacle, as the men rode pell-mell into the deep snow, the plunging steeds throwing the light feathery snow in clouds about them. The ringing reports of rifles broke upon the clear cold atmosphere, mingled with the shouting of both sides.

A small party of the enemy, in attempting to escape in the direction of Lecompton, were cut off by Clayton's detachment and driven back upon Captain Brown, who took them prisoners.

Clayton and Roland rode side by side in hot pursuit of the enemy. Commanding one of the pickets to halt and not being obeyed, Clayton looked in astonishment to see that Roland had not drawn his pistol, but was pale and agitated.

"Why Roland, you don't show fight!" exclaimed Clayton, as he took aim with his own pistol.

"Oh, don't shoot, Mr. Clayton!" pleaded his companion.

Continuing the chase, Clayton shouted, "Halt!" and quickly fired over the head of the fleeing horseman. The shot had the desired effect, for he halted, turned round, and held up his hands in token of surrender.

"Ah, Livingstone, again I have the drop on you!" exclaimed Clayton, as he covered him with his pistol. "You are a foolhardy fellow, and owe your life to this young man." Observing another body of men, Clayton said, "Here, Roland, you and Dick" (who came up at this juncture) "disarm and take this prisoner, and turn him over to Captain Brown with my compliments. Tell the captain I'll see him later."

Putting spurs to his horse, Clayton rode away with the rest of the detachment in pursuit of the fleeing horsemen, leaving the prisoner to be conducted toward the cabin, some two miles distant, by Dick and Roland.

Captain Brown demanded the surrender of the four men who had been driven back on his camp. Their fine horses were given to Jim and Sam and to two others of the party of negroes who were not mounted. Against this order the prisoners protested and swore loudly. Captain Brown ordered them to desist, at which they redoubled their blasphemy.

"Now," said Captain Brown, drawing his pistol and approaching one prisoner, who was fairly melting the snow with his red-hot oaths, "you shall kneel down here, and ask God to forgive you for blaspheming His sacred name. Come, sir, kneel down!"

The prisoner looked sullenly into the captain's face as the latter continued, with pistol levelled at his head:

"I'll give you just two minutes in which to determine whether you will kneel down, or be shot down."

In the face of the old man who held the revolver with its leaden messenger of death, there was written in unmistakable lines of determination the decree, If you will not do right and serve God while living, then you shall die at the hands of His agent. Without waiting for two minutes to expire, he knelt in the snow, in the presence of his friends and enemies, and prayed God to "be merciful to me a sinner."

When he was about to rise, Captain Brown forbade, and, with uncovered head, prayed God to grant this now penitent child of sin the forgiveness he sought for his many transgressions, "and turn him, O heavenly Father, turn him from the persecution of thine own children as thou didst Saul of Tarsus, and make him one of thy powerful instruments for the establishment of the truth and of freedom."

Just as the kneeling man had risen, Roland and Dick, who had arrived during this episode, came forward with their prisoner.

Captain Brown welcomed the messenger with extended hands.

"Roland, my boy, I am proud of you!"

The youth dismounted and put up his pistol. Captain Brown shook both hands of the young soldier, who had received the first lesson in war or the "baptism by fire." Looking intently in the youthful face, he suddenly released the hands, and said, stepping back a pace:

"What? Oh, my God! My child, what does this mean?"

Putting his finger to his lip and shaking his head, Roland ran into the open arms of Captain Brown, and whispered in his ear what the reader already knows.

"God will bless you, my child,—yes, abundantly bless you for your heroic act! Tell me of Clayton. Where is he?"

"He sent this prisoner," said Roland, turning to Livingstone, who, under Dick's watchful eye had dismounted, "and he was in pursuit of the enemy when last seen."

Capt. Brown ordered the train to move forward, and Roland to ride by his side and relate as they rode the horrors of the past night.

"I suppose you were frightened, my dear, when the storm struck you," said Captain Brown.

"Oh, it was terrible! What with the roaring of the storm and the unearthly noises of the cattle, I believe I should have died of fright had not Mr. Clayton kept alive my courage."

"Then you like Mr. Clayton?"

"Oh, I admire bravery. I know him so slightly, you see, I cannot say."

"Does he suspect——"

"Nothing," added the youth, turning quickly, "and I would not have him know for the world. Leave him where he is, in bewilderment and doubt as to who the first messenger, or Roland Priest, or both of them, are. And now here is the road that leads to our cabin, and I must leave you, Captain."

"My child, how can I sufficiently thank you or express my gratitude? I wish I could make you believe it were best that I should inform Mr. Clayton of this service and to whom the honor is due."

"No, no, Captain. You must allow me to manage this myself. The gratitude and appreciation you have expressed is payment a thousand-fold."

Tears were on the youthful face, and the strong lines in the war-worn visage of John Brown relaxed and softened into womanly sympathy and tenderness as with a mutual "God bless you!" the two parted.

Turning abruptly to the right over the pathless snow, the youthful rider gave rein to the steed, which flew as on the wings of the wind. And yet the pace was not equal to thoughts which pictured the joyous return to her mother and Roland. She trembled at the thought of what might have happened in her absence.

CHAPTER XXXIV.

THE afternoon was well-advanced when Partridge and Parker, with some of their companions, arrived at the cabin where Dick was found in possession, with a roaring fire, to give a warm welcome in the name and by the authority of Roland Priest.

"Dick, where is Mr. Clayton?" inquired Partridge.

"Bless yer life, Mars Partridge, 'deed I don't know. I saw him flyin' cross de kuntry lookin' fur all de worl' like a snow-bird."

"Why didn't you go with him, Dick?"

"Case he sent me heah wid dat young Mars Rolan' wid a pris'ner w'at he took, an tol' us to gib him ober ter Cap'n Brown, an we done done it, an' Mars Rolan' an' de Cap'n done gone 'way on de road rejoicin', an' Mars Rolan' say fer me ter stay heah an ter keep de fire agoin' till you all come."

Then Dick continuing told of the prayer-meeting; how "de man kneel down on de snow an' de Cap'n prayed der Lord ter turn dis heah sinner inter postle like Paul ob Sarsus, an' ter gib him power to stop prosecutin' ob de chillen ob de Lor', an' dat de good Lor' would gib ter de Cap'n hisself de wise strength an' grace ter swaller up de sinners in de Red Sea like de sons ob men done de chillen ob Israel under de faithful sarbint Moses, who did lead dem a long time ago from a lan ob freedom ter a lan' ob bondage." Here Dick became hopelessly confused in his narrative upon observing his young Mars Frank and his companion, who had entered unnoticed, and were listening with much amusement.

Night was fast approaching, and still Roland Priest did not come. After consultation among the party, all agreed it would be best to remain in their present quarters until morning, and make a fresh start for Lawrence on the following day.

Posting two pickets on each side of the creek, the little party went to rest at an early hour, after many hearty laughs at the individual and collective experiences of the day. Clayton retired late, after waiting in vain for the return of Roland Priest, till, from utter exhaustion, he fell into a profound sleep.

With the morning came the hurry and preparation for the day's march to Lawrence, and careful inquiry was made, whenever opportunity offered, as to where Roland Priest's mother lived.

At Grasshopper Falls Clayton learned from a citizen who knew Roland and his twin sister Isabel; one who had often seen them together out hunting, she being as fearless a rider as he. "He is called ' Rolla' by his family and ' Daredevil Roland' by others," said his informant.

And so the mystery was solved: Rolla and Roland Priest were one and the same person.

Clayton was silent during the long ride to Lawrence, recalling every word and look of the brave girl, and felt that he had "entertained an angel unawares."

CHAPTER XXXV.

Arrived in Lawrence, Clayton and his party dispersed, and but few citizens knew what had transpired in the rescue of Captain Brown.

Clayton wrote to his informant at Grasshopper Falls to make further inquiry in regard to the Priest family; and some time later thereafter, was in receipt of a short note, which ran as follows:

"House burned and family disappeared. If you are interested, come up and aid me in searching out the guilty parties."

Clayton resolved to go at once. On the evening before his departure, a letter was received from Captain Brown stating that he had gotten his party safely through to a land of freedom, and that Sam had been sent home, rejoicing; that among the greatest of his disappointments was strong opposition to his plans from friends upon whom he had so confidently relied for material, as well as moral, support.

"I am, however, resolved to make the grand effort, come what will," he wrote. "For yourself, I can hardly find words to express my thanks for your timely rescue."

"Now that I think of it, I beseech you to look up Roland Priest and the messenger who was so badly wounded, and insist on knowing both them and their needs. There is that about this affair which I am not at liberty to communicate to you, but which you can easily learn by seeing the parties.

"Roland delivered your message and your prisoner, Livingstone, whom I subsequently found to be a desperate man. We took him with four other prisoners several days on our journey, retaining their horses and arms, allowing them finally to go home on foot, wiser if not better men."

Soon after this, early in the month of May, Clayton

with his friend from Grasshopper Falls were crossing the ford of Danger Creek. Following the road that led to Mrs. Priest's cottage home, they soon arrived at the mound of ashes and the blackened beams that told the story of border ruffianism and the reign of terror in Kansas.

All that could be learned was, that Dr. Russell had taken the family to his own home, and they had now left the Territory.

Five miles up the stream in a beautiful grove of timber that skirted its banks, Dr. Russell's comfortable cottage was found. On introducing himself and his errand, Dr. Russell extended a hearty greeting as to an old friend, long expected.

"Mr. Clayton," said the doctor, "I have been hoping to see you for some time; but, for the object of your search, I fear you are too late. Mrs. Priest and her family have left the Territory, never to return."

"It is not too late, if I can learn whither they have gone."

"And that you can not have from me, Clayton, for I do not know exactly; and then I am forbidden to tell what I do know."

"Doctor," said Clayton, "I am in possession of a letter from Captain John Brown, an old friend of the family, and he urges me to deliver certain messages to them in person. You certainly have means by which you can communicate with them, and those means you can furnish me."

"Mr. Clayton, to be quite frank with you, for some reason Miss Belle does not wish to have you know their present abode. Under no circumstances, am I to be compromised in the matter."

"Doctor, you are safe with me and you ought to know that."

"Well, Mr. Clayton, then I will tell you this much. I am instructed to communicate through the post-office at Sacramento, California, whither the family have gone. They left some weeks since with a large train of emigrants, and I think will abide in the mountains on Roland's account."

"Are his wounds serious, Doctor?"

"Very, very serious; and he will never recover, in my judgment. The ball could not be extracted, and is lodged either in or near the left lung, and the injury is likely to involve the other at no distant day. I advised the change to California for his benefit."

"May I be allowed to ask, Doctor," said Frank, flushing, "what are their circumstances?"

"They have enough for present needs; and with the indomitable courage, energy, and resources of Isabel, any family would be assured against want. Why, sir, she is a mine of wealth in herself; she rises equal to any emergency, however great."

Dr. Russell then gave Clayton an account of the raid upon Mrs. Priest's cottage, which occurred the night after Isabel's departure with the despatch. The picket who shot Roland had also been wounded, and a party of ruffians, thirsting for revenge, ordered the family out of the house; after which they fired the cabin, and from the stables the family saw their home reduced to ashes. Dr. Russell had them removed to his own house, and from there they had started on their long journey to California.

Isabel, who returned so full of hope to their home that winter morning, had found it desolate and in ruins; but Dr. Russell had a messenger watching for her arrival, who conducted her to his own house, where the little family were gathered.

After the tears and excitement of the first meeting were over, Isabel was again brave and strong; so, when Roland was convalescing, by the doctor's advice, they decided to seek a new home in California.

CHAPTER XXXVI.

We invite the reader to turn back with us to a period just prior to the Kansas difficulties, and enter a stately mansion built upon the border of one of the small lakes of western New York, in a thriving manufacturing town.

Seated in the library is a woman of forty, whose clear-cut features, dark intelligent eyes, indicate a rare combination of refinement and good sense. A son and daughter, in whom the mother's features seemed reproduced in a higher type of beauty, were seated at the table, and all were attired in mourning.

At the opposite side of the library table sat a grave, determined-looking man, with a face combining great firmness with greater kindness.

"I am going," said he, "to make a new home and to lend my aid in making Kansas a Free State, to erect a wall of adamant to the north and westward beyond which slavery shall not go; and if you will allow Roland to go with me, I promise a father's protecting care."

And so it was arranged, after further conversation, that Roland should join John Brown's party of emigrants for the territory of Kansas, while the widowed mother and Isabel should remain for the present at the old home.

Roland Priest senior, had been partner in a large manufacturing concern in western New York, as well as director in a railroad company in which he had invested. Of this large corporation, Colonel Vandergrip was president and was known far and wide as a shrewd business man, immensely wealthy, and almost as unscrupulous as he was rich. His eldest son, Henry W., had been taken into the firm, also into the devious paths of his father in making money. Colonel Vandergrip declared that if Henry proved an adept he would make him sole heir to millions.

The son did not disappoint the father, for he inherited his love of money; but this did not prevent his falling a victim to the charms of the beautiful and accomplished Isabel Priest.

As the young lady did not reciprocate his feelings, he pressed his suit to the extent of appealing to her father, who declined to coerce or unduly influence his daughter in a matter so delicate; and this course offended both father and son.

"They're too proud of their learning and of their ancestry," said the colonel in a talk with his son. "Poverty humbles people wonderfully, and I will give the Priests a taste of that."

In the course of a few months, the wages of the operatives were reduced in the factories, and the employes of the railroad were put on starvation wages, until finally, there was a general strike. The corporation held out, as did the laborers. No revenues were received by the stockholders, and the shares began to droop in the market, lower and lower. Then certain overdue mortgages held by the colonel were foreclosed, and thousands of stockholders were, as the colonel expressed it, "neatly frozen out." Among those who had fallen under the blow, ruined and heart-broken, was Roland Priest the elder, whose funeral had just preceded the opening of this chapter. Colonel Vandergrip succeeded in all his plans for amassing wealth, but the idol he worshipped could not save him from the keen dart of death, which struck suddenly without warning, and in a few weeks after mourning friends had followed Roland Priest to the cemetery, there was another grave near it, and before long a tall marble shaft recorded the name and virtues of Colonel Vandergrip.

Thus, Henry Vandergrip the son and heir, found himself the head and chief owner of one of the largest fortunes in the country. Months after Roland had gone to Kansas, Isabel received a call from the rejected lover, renewing his suit for her hand, and offering to lay millions at her feet in her own right and name.

Isabel looked proudly at her suitor as she replied: "My father went to his grave a victim of your father's greed for money. Do not ask me to share this ill-gotten wealth. I wish none of it. Your victim would haunt me by night and pursue me by day.

"Are you aware, Miss Isabel, that I own the roof that protects you and yours?"

"I did not know it, Mr. Vandergrip, or I would not have been so long thus protected. I would far rather have the open air, the sheltering arch of heaven, above me. At this time to-morrow you shall not have occasion to reproach me."

"Take time, Miss Isabel. You may change your mind. I am in no hurry for your answer."

"You have my answer, sir; and I bid you good-morning," and with a wave of the hand he was dismissed.

On the following day, true to her word, Isabel Priest and her mother quitted the house in which the children were born. Hastily disposing of their household goods, they took the western-bound train, and three weeks later were domiciled in the log cabin in Kansas wherein Roland Priest took refuge, fainting from the wound of a border ruffian's bullet.

CHAPTER XXXVII.

FRANK CLAYTON felt there could be no rest for him till he beheld once more the face which had shone by the red light of the camp-fire that night in the wintry storm. It haunted him, coming between him and everything he attempted.

About the last of May he started with a party of emigrants, in canvas-covered wagons, drawn by horses and mules. Some of his fellow-travellers were in search of California gold, others of adventure, while he was in quest of what might prove an *ignis fatuus*, but which none the less lured him irresistibly and steadily on.

The first few days were without special adventures, when there came one which was indeed crowded with perils and excitement.

One morning when they had been moving for ten days westward, Clayton mounted his horse and rode rapidly ahead of the train as was his custom, to hunt game, which abounded along the Republican Fork, up the course of which they were now making head.

The sun was shining brightly on the green carpet of the plains intervening between the ridge on which he rode and the Republican River, some five miles away, though it seemed not half as far. Great patches of wild flowers here and there seemed like bouquets woven cunningly in the texture to brighten and beautify the emerald covering in this seeming fairyland, to which the dark line of timber skirting the river made a fitting border.

While contemplating this beautiful panorama, every moment changing, under the swaying breeze and the shadows of fleecy clouds that sailed over the sun, he heard a sharp whistle or hiss, like escaping steam under great pressure. His horse wheeled quickly round, and there standing but a hundred yards away was one of the most beautiful animals he had ever beheld. A large elk with full antlers had come up out of the valley and, seeing an intruder, had given this signal to warn him off the monarch's domain. His head erect, his muzzle protruding, his large eyes gazing scornfully, filled with wonder at such audacity, his form the very embodiment of grace, his chestnut coat of velvet with the sheen of satin in the morning sun, gave him the pose and almost the semblance of an imperious and queenly woman.

Ever and anon, one of the front feet was brought down on the earth with lightning rapidity and force which, with the slight movements of the ears, was the only evidence of life.

The horse, his rider, and elk, stood thus for a few moments, seemingly lost in admiration, each of the other.

Finally, Clayton raised his rifle, and in taking aim at the beautiful beast, thought what a pity to mar such a picture and to betray the confidence of such a noble creature! Evidently this monarch of the plains was only acquainted with the Indians' rude bow and spear, and felt secure in being out of range of either.

Lowering his rifle, Clayton surveyed, with increasing delight, the beautiful head crowned with branching antlers.

"Falcon," said he, patting the horse's neck, "he looks like you;—the same color, not quite so large, his coat not so glossy, eyes much the same, nostrils red and wide, and in the place of your flowing mane, he wears the horns —and for that, we will bring him down."

He raised his rifle the second time, resolved to secure the prize dead since he could not have it alive.

The elk, as if at last scenting danger, made one great bound and cleared the ledge upon which he stood, then disappeared under cover of the bluff for some distance, and emerged in the plain below, accompanied by several others, none of whom had antlers.

Half-amused and half-chagrined, Clayton rode on towards the west, thinking what an unsportsmanlike event it was. "Many a man would have given a kingdom for such an opportunity and I have let it slip, purely from love of the beautiful."

Thus he thought as his agile horse bounded over the plain below. Before reaching the wood skirting the river, he slackened his pace and listened. He heard a low rumbling sound which he detected as that of a herd of buffalo running. He had, not long to wait,

for the vast plain was soon covered with a cloud
of dusky forms, crowded together in masses, pushing and being pushed, grunting and laboring on toward the river, pursued by a party of Indians who
were striving to run the herd over the precipitous bank
of the river further down.

Clayton saw he was directly in the line of march of
these frightened beasts and knew the danger, but relied on his skill and the fleetness of his horse to carry
him through any emergency. He only strove to get as
near the outskirts of the herd as possible, and in doing
so, espied a beautiful cow, dark and sleek as a mole.

Still suffering a little from mortification at the loss of
the elk, he resolved to have this prize in revenge. By
degrees, he came alongside, raised his rifle and fired.
The cow fell dead on the spot and Clayton sought to
check his horse and get out of the rush of the black,
woolly and irresistible torrent, but the report of his gun
had alarmed them more than the Indians, who were still
crowding them from the other side. The herd seemed
to know where the crossing was, and the danger of the
precipitous bank below, and they kept their course, bearing Clayton on like a feather in the torrent.

On reaching the low shelving bank of the river, the
horse and its rider had no choice but to plunge in and
swim across with the wild and frightened beasts. In the
middle of the stream, he nearly lost his life in a jam of
the buffalos who were borne down the stream with eyes
and nostrils red and distended, the body submerged and
only head and horns above the muddy eddying tide.

As far as the eye could reach, there was but a struggling mass of black heads and horns, dotting the water
thickly, while upon either shore the great black hulks
were emerging, or plunging in. It required all Clayton's
presence of mind and energy to keep above the water
and out of the crowd.

After crossing the river, he found himself still borne on
yet by skilful movements he worked his way to the outer
edge of the herd and at the end of another hour's ride
was freed from his boisterous companions. He turned
his horse's head to retrace his steps, both feeling and
looking the worse for wear. Still he was determined not
to lose his dead buffalo,

It was late in the afternoon, after recrossing the river, that he found his prize. He removed the hide, cut a nice roast from the hump, strapped them on behind his saddle, and struck out to overtake the train by bearing up the river and striking the road some miles ahead.

It was nearly dark when he reached the trail, but he pressed onward with good heart. The sun had set in a dark bank of cloud which, borne on the wings of the wind, had soon overspread the heavens. Lightning flashed from the black masses, making the darkness more dismal, and he had to give Falcon the rein as he could no longer see the trail.

Soon there arose in the distance, a blood-curdling cry above the low rumbling of the approaching storm, which caused horse and rider to shudder as it was followed in quick succession by a similar cry in another quarter, only nearer at hand.

" Steady, steady, Falcon. Those are only wolves that scent our beautiful robe and fresh meat. We can out run them, old boy. You hold to the path, and I'll hold to the rein and revolver," as he suited the action to the word. A few seconds elapsed and the cry was repeated and answered, like signals from two attacking armies. Again, at short intervals, was this fiendish and unearthly "Yi, yi, yi" hissing and cutting through the air, and finally bursting in one grand demoniacal howling chorus.

Falcon seemed literally to fly, while the flashes of lightning revealed the way, as the fiends hung threateningly near on either flank, keeping pace with what they deemed their prey.

Suddenly the gallant steed threw himself back upon his haunches and gave a loud snort. The darkness shrouded from the rider what the cause could be, and he spoke again to the now thoroughly frightened steed :

" What's the matter, old boy ? "

At that instant, the heavens flashed on her electric light, and lo ! a thousand hungry chops armed with ivory spears, surmounted by twice as many phosphorescent lamps, looked hungrily toward their victim. To make the peril worse, Clayton observed he had lost the trail in trying to avoid the pack that had finally intercepted further progress.

He levelled his revolver and fired six shots in quick succession as the lightning aided his aim.

At several shots, there was a sharp cry of pain, ending in a loud wail of distress as the wounded beast was torn into fragments and borne away by his hungry companions.

Falcon stood back upon his haunches with distended eyes and nostrils, awaiting results. When the pack gave way in the scramble for the blood of their kin, the horse rallied and started forward.

Clayton checked him, and said :

"No, no, old fellow, we'll remain here; they have brought us to bay where we are protected upon two sides at least by this ledge of rock and the steep river bank."

Clayton feared to go forward, lest he lose the trail entirely and the wolves, he knew, would soon renew the attack.

Reloading his pistol, he dismounted and set fire to some driftwood from the river at the foot of the ledge of rocks, and by the light of the blaze, the eyes of his enemies were easily sighted, and shot, only to be replaced by others.

As he suspected, the pack soon returned and kept up the siege until dawn, with an occasional charge more desperate than before, when they would venture closer, to yell and snarl louder and snap their teeth.

At each of these attacks, some one or more were sent by Clayton's revolver howling away to the rear, borne not in the *arms* but in the *teeth* of their comrades.

During the night of horror, the flickering fire and flashes of lightning followed by deafening thunder, revealed the besieging force, some sitting upon their haunches, some prowling round, but all fearfully near and on the watch. Falcon stood by the side of his master, often pawing the ground fiercely, and snorting defiance at the hungry brutes as they came too near.

With the dawn of morning, the disappointed pack slunk away to their dens, and Clayton, mounting his faithful steed, was soon riding rapidly on the trail, to be met by his companions, some of whom had started back to find their lost comrade, and listened enviously to the story of his thrilling adventures.

CHAPTER XXXVIII.

At Independence Rock, on the banks of the Sweet Water River, the train went into camp for general preparations before departure from the old trail via Salt Lake and entering the new one with General Lander, who commanded the expedition, through the South Pass, at this time an untried path.

General Lander's party of United States troops and quite a number of civilians had joined the emigrant train only a few days previously, among them being the distinguished artist Albert Bierstadt.

It was high noon when the train after several days' rest moved out and crossed the Sweet Water River, a sparkling mountain stream running through what is called the "Devil's Gate," whose scenery combines the awfully grand with the beautiful and picturesque.

The Sweet Water River, ages or cycles of centuries ago, followed for a long way the jagged and eccentric base of a spur of the Wind River Mountains as it tapers to the plain on both sides. Here, the spirit of liberty must have welled up in her bosom, and she made a heroic dash against the narrow line of granite, cleaving two perpendicular walls several hundred feet in height, and when she debouched into the valley on the opposite side, she celebrated the victory in one of Nature's most perfect bowers, arched and crowned with wild roses and all manner of climbing vines and flowers.

Clayton explored this spot, riding Falcon over broken stones and jagged rocks, along the banks of the murmuring stream, to where the angry waters were lashed to fury and foam by huge fallen boulders. But the Sweet Water that had cleft her way through such solid granite, was not to be impeded by the débris; and with a bound, her laughing waters descend in a cascade of hundreds of feet, waving in madcap style her white feathery mist and spray that, like the white plume of Henry of Navarre, is the signal of victory.

Reaching the impassable barrier, the horse who had been given the rein as he entered this wonderful fairy-land, now stopped, gazing at the beautiful spectacle in wonder, his ears moving backward and forward as if trying to measure the distance he would have to leap to clear the noisy cataract. He finally lowered his head, sniffed the ground and began to paw it lustily; then, raising his head and gazing intently at the threatening barriers to further progress, he snorted as if in defiance, and turning his head to look at his master, he began to nibble at the grass, as though to say, "We can go no farther."

Clayton sat upon the horse, wrapped in wonder and admiration. As Falcon turned and retraced his steps, his rider looked up through those great lips of granite that seemed about to close and shut out the narrow line of bright light,—the only evidence of their not being swallowed up by some great Ogre.

Just before emerging from this weird cañon, Clayton observed a large birch-tree, overhung with masses of vines and wild roses, a perfect bower, and he uncovered his head as he entered. The sunlight glancing through the branches, gave glimpses of the outer world with its music of bird and bee, and he exclaimed:

"Thank God for life and light in this beautiful world of ours."

Throwing himself upon the mossy carpet, he allowed Falcon to nibble at the grass walls of his bower until his daydream more than an hour later was disturbed by a crash, and a mass of birch bark with clinging vines came down near his head, and he remounted his horse, then emerged from this enchanted grotto as the rays of the setting sun were gilding in a glory of light the lofty summit of Independence Rock.

From the drapery of vines, he ascended a green knoll, when suddenly a sharp whistle sounded off to the right. Turning his head in that direction, he observed Bierstadt the artist making a sketch while his assistant was taking a photographic view of the Devil's Gate which, in that glorious sunset, was a thing of beauty.

Bierstadt waved his hand in sign that he was to stand still—and Clayton drew rein just at the crest of the hill, —Falcon standing with curved neck and proud mien, tail and mane waving in the wind.

" There," said Bierstadt, holding up his sketch, after he found him " you make quite a respectable gatekeeper for the ' Devil.' "

Clayton knew that in going through the South Pass, he was leaving the route taken by Roland Priest's family and that he should next touch it at the crossing of Snake River beyond old Fort Hall; but there was no remedy, as he could not go alone, and to wait for another train was uncertain and hazardous. So he impatiently trod the new and untried route, which in itself was full of interesting adventure, through wild mountain scenery.

Climbing to almost unattainable heights to plant his feet where no white man had stood before, was a stimulant and a source of pleasurable excitement to a man of his temperament.

On a hot July day, he stood near the top of Fremont Peak. Here, with the eye of an artist, he beheld the panorama of cloud and snow-capped mountains and green valleys below as the threatening black clouds were tipped with gold and reflected the glory of the summer's sun, giving an unearthly beauty and grandeur to the magnificent scene.

He uncovered his head as though in divine presence, when he was saluted by the screaming of a flock of ravens and a great vulture flapped his sable wings in close proximity to his head, with loud croaking, as if to frighten the intruder.

Here he lingered, despite the warnings received from the dusky winged messengers of this throne of snow and the lengthening shadows of the lofty peaks, feeling the charm which every lover of nature realizes when alone in the great and awful presence of the Creator and His wonderful works. Here, thought he, the worst infidel or atheist would be forced to acknowledge the existence of a God with powers surpassing the grandest conceptions of the wisest and greatest of His creatures.

CHAPTER XXXIX.

Leaving Fort Hall, the train of emigrants moved down
to Snake River Crossing, at which point, the old Salt
Lake trail was intersected, and where a portion of the
train diverged, *en route* to Oregon.

Here, Clayton found that a cut which Falcon had received in his foot from a sharp rock upon the mountain
road, lamed him so as to make further travel impossible
for some days or perhaps weeks. The animal received
every attention from his master with human intelligence
and more than human appreciation. After several days'
tarry, Clayton resolved to push forward on foot, leaving
the horse in the care of a veterinary surgeon attached to
the train for Oregon, with special instructions to attend
him carefully, and that he be sent to him in California
when recovered. He dreaded the separation from the
noble steed, whose good qualities were legion and whose
fleetness almost equalled that of the royal swift-winged
bird for whom he was named.

The horse neighed in a coaxing way as his master approached, and, lifting his lame foot, held it from the
ground as if to attract attention.

Clayton stroked his mane, unfastened the bandages
about his foot, rebound them, gave the usual lumps of
sugar, and starting to go, with a heavy heart, was recalled
by a neigh in a kind of undertone that went to his heart.
Retracing his steps, he put his arms about the horse's
neck as he said:

"Good-bye, old boy. It's hard to part from you in
distress. Your sore foot does not limp worse than my
heart that goes halting away. God bless you. Yes,
Falcon, I see no reason why I might not ask His bless-
ing on one of His noblest creatures."

Harry Burke, the companion and guide, whom Clayton
had employed to accompany him, was impatiently awaiting the leave-taking, and the two men slung their blank-

ets, buckled on their revolvers—their only baggage—
and strode away.

Clayton turned and waved his hand to Falcon, who
stood looking intently as though he were trying to have
a last glimpse of his departing master.

After some days' travel, the pedestrians met a party of
miners, who warned them that only a few days before, an
emigrant train had been surprised at a point called Chimney or Cathedral Rock, fifteen miles farther on, and a
number of men, women and children murdered by the
Indians.

With an anxious heart, Clayton continued his journey,
until they came in sight of this one of Nature's greatest
curiosities.

These rocks are of a grayish sand formation, and rise
above the surrounding plain from one to three hundred
feet in height, tapering in all fantastic circular shapes
from a base of thirty to one hundred feet in diameter,
and terminating in a perfect cone; and of these chimneys
or spires, there were more than a hundred in regular irregularity, of from fifty to one hundred feet apart. Evidently, when hoary old Time was a mere boy, these
cathedral towers were part and parcel of a spur or mountain of sandstone, and Nature had been at work with her
levelling processes, leaving here and there a pile, a shaft,
or monument, to her once lofty greatness. And through
this wonderful group, the road wound its serpentine
course.

A few ravens were perched here and there on the
high pinnacles, like specks of crape as tokens of mourning for the unfortunate women and children who had so
recently perished near by. Just as they were emerging
from this city of the dead, Clayton observed some remains of a wagon and fragments of garments near the
base of one of these monuments, and he turned aside to
examine them with a heart full of apprehension lest some
chance proof should reveal the identity of the unfortu-
nates with the object of his great love and long search.
Blood-stains were found here and there upon stones and
bits of clothing, revealing nothing beyond the heroic but
fruitless struggle of the victims and the fiendish brutality of the savages. A woman's slipper and a long tress
of dark hair were among the *débris*, and Clayton stood

horror-stricken at the picture this called up of the unfortunate travellers and their possible identity with those for whom he was searching.

"Come," said Harry, "let us go forward; for I see far up the trail what seems to be a party of Indians coming this way.

"Where? Let me see them?" anxiously inquired Clayton, putting his hand on his revolver. "I could slay a race of savages for such an outrage as has been perpetrated here."

The approaching party of six or seven Indians came leisurely on foot.

"It is madness to attack them," exclaimed Harry Burke, "and we cannot retreat."

"No," said Clayton, "we must go forward and meet them ;—put on a bold front as though a large train were at hand."

Acting on the suggestion, the two men moved on.

Seeing a large rabbit, Clayton drew his revolver and shot it ; then hastily reloading, he picked up the dead hare and walked on ;—both men with revolver in hand.

Soon, the Indians came up and saluted them :

"How, how; me want caps ? "

" No," replied Clayton, unmoved, as both men walked on. " Go back,"—and he pointed over his shoulder; "big train ; heap caps," and the two men turned round, walking backward, on their way talking to the Indians about the approaching train that was more than a dozen miles away. As soon as they were out of sight of the Indians, Clayton and Burke took up a pace that put many miles between them and the savages before the *ruse* was discovered.

After ten days of weary marching, they reached the banks of the Humboldt River, down which their course now lay to where it sinks from human sight, and the great desert begins. The waters of this wonderful river were quite brackish, as the thirsty travellers found on reaching the banks, and they looked longingly for a spring from which to drink.

At intervals of eight or ten miles, a cool rippling stream found its way into the sluggish river from the range of mountains that hung like a dark curtain eastward, while in the west was an endless plain of sand and sagebrush, reminding one that this vast expanse might at one time have been the bed of a great ocean, with its mountain coast toward the east. Many a night these two men pillowed their weary heads upon a mound of sand and made their beds of the same accommodating material, literally covered with a blanket to keep off the myriads of mosquitos of fabulous size that infest the region, protected only by the sagebrush, the darkness, and the over-arching heavens. They durst not make a fire, to smoke and keep off the vermin and wolves, lest its light should direct and tempt some roving savages to steal upon them and commit murder. The blankets defied the mosquitos, and the Indians were left to take chances with their more wolfish neighbors in finding the prey.

At a point near the sink of the Humboldt, where its waters were thick with alkali, at noontide when the sun's power was at its zenith, Clayton and his companion were delighted to discover a sparkling stream that ran laugh-ingly across the road, to be swallowed up in the Naseus River near by. Foot-sore and weary, Burke threw aside his Indian moccasins and waded joyfully into the stream, but with a bound and yell, rushed out on the other side and falling upon his back with his feet aloft, looking like two cooked lobsters, he cried lustily for help.

"Is it a snake bite?" asked Clayton.

"Snake bite," exclaimed his suffering companion, "I am scalded, terribly."

The spring was of volcanic origin, and the beautifully clear waters came boiling and bubbling up from subterra-nean fires only a few rods from the trail.

Clayton remembered the practice of his mother, to apply a strong solution of soda to a burn : so he led, or rather half carried his friend to the brink of the Hum-boldt River, reeking with alkali, where the unfortunate guide plunged his feet into its waters, and soon the lines of pain left his face. In twenty minutes the skin was restored to its normal condition, and the two pedestrians resumed their journey an hour or so afterward. At ten o'clock on the following morning, they arrived where the great river sinks out of sight, and, like the stream of life, ended, swallowed up by mother earth, leaving a whitened line—a spectre finger, pointing the way to the great here-after that, to the materialist, lies like the desert, only dead matter, the future stretching out.beyond the ken of man.

At this point there was a small trading-station, and the old man who kept it, advised the two travellers to rest during the day and make the entrance on the desert in the cool of the evening, and thus make most of the journey by night.

The old pioneer's advice was taken, and the day spent in rest and preparation for the march over the desert. Clayton inquired of the men for information concerning the massacred family and the one for which he was in search, but could get no tidings.

The sun set in a kind of smoky cloudless sky like a ball of fire, and the full moon rose in the east, equally as large and only a little less lurid, as the two men paid the host for the meagre fare and set out on their desolate journey.

The road in the desert was smooth and hard, unlike the dust and sand encountered up to this point, and the men walked briskly along, unmindful of what was curtained from them in front by night and distance. Two hours passed; conversation flagged and whistling took its place, but the notes died away in the great expanse that was spread out before them like a silver carpet, as the alkali sparkled in the moonlight, covering everything like frost. After a long silence, Burke, broke out, with:

"I'll be d——d, Clayton, if I don't wish I could hear an owl hoot;—one of those regular old Indian backwoods owls that can just everlastingly make the welkin ring. It would be real cheerful music in this great grave-yard. Now, let us stop and see if we can hear anything." And the two men stood silent for a moment. "Oh, confound it, Clayton, go further away; that old watch of yours makes as much noise as a train of empty freight cars on a down grade. There, that will do," added Burke, as his companion had gone forward some twenty paces.

After a short silence, the profane Hoosier said in awe-inspiring tones:

"My heart keeps such an everlasting thumping and bumping, I can't hear anything else. Why, I hear the blood circulating in my veins like mountain streams. My very joints creak on their hinges, and the sands of time rattle into the past like clods on a coffin. What in thunder is that, Clayton ?" pointing with his finger to an object that sparkled in the moon's rays like frost on a snow bank. "As I am a sinner, that is a spectre ship. See its great white sails, bare masts, and its freight of skeletons with eyes that give a phosphorescent glare. Look ! the light of the moon shines through her hull, and her huge ribs form great shadows on the molten sea of silver. Hold, Clayton ! Don't go near it," continued the terror-stricken man, as his companion walked forward to the object of horror.

"There," said Clayton, "come here, Burke, and man this phantom ship," and he kicked over with his foot the bleached bones of some huge ox that had perished and whose skeleton had been left by the wayside intact.

On through the silent night, the weary travellers plodded, and the "spectre ships" grew more and more frequent and the broken fragments of wagons and all manner of travelling paraphernalia literally lined the road side, but all alike shimmering with the frosted alkali.

Among the *débris*, a human skull was seen, its silvery coat making it more ghastly.

" If we don't leave our own skeletons here to bleach in this alkali, we shall be fortunate," remarked Harry Burke gloomily, turning from the skull with a shudder.

Pointing to the thousands of wagon tires that lined the road for miles, where they were left in '49 and '50 by the gold-hunters, Clayton said with a laugh :

"This looks like a tired world, Burke, and if you are not afraid of her ' phantom ships ' here, seat yourself upon the great hub and let the weary orb roll on."

"Clayton, you were born to *punish* mankind and you will die to afflict his satanic majesty," responded Burke, seating himself upon the old wagon hub beside the skeleton of a great ox. After resting themselves, the men set out again on their desolate tramp, as the evidence of former dissolution grew thicker and more awful.

It was early on an August morning, 1859, when the two men emerged from the desert, foot-sore, thirsty, weary, and feeling ten years older than when they began the forty mile march through the great American desert. They seated themselves upon the porch of what was called an " hotel," but looked like a cross between an ark and an ambulance, constructed as it was of every conceivable material of travelling vehicle, that had been brought together from the odds and ends of the earth. Some vines were growing over, and a few stunted trees shadowed it. The rippling waters of a stream gave a freshness to the spot, and it seemed a haven of rest, an oasis in the desert, to the tired and wayworn travellers after the journey through the alkali sands.

Arriving at Sacramento, California, after a weary march over the Sierra Nevada mountains, Clayton rested from his long journey, and finally learned that a note had been received by the postmaster requesting mail matter for the Priest family to be forwarded to Coultersville, a mining camp far up in the foot-hills of the Sierras.

To this point, Clayton betook himself, and, in response to his inquiries, was informed that no letters had been received or inquired for by any one named Priest. Feeling assured that Coultersville was the place for him to wait and watch, there he remained.

CHAPTER XL.

Isabel Priest sat gazing alternately at the glorious panorama before her and at her sketch-book, where she was striving to imprison some of the majestic lines which made the view from the Giant's Elbow so glorious.

It was growing rapidly dark from an approaching thunder-storm, bringing out a stronger and more sombre beauty in the scene. She longed to stay and finish her sketch, but large drops of rain warned her. that she must return. So, gathering her drawing materials together, she turned toward the path, and was startled to see a man obstructing her way in the narrow pass between two rocks. She saw no way of making a detour, so said:

"Pardon me, sir; I shall have to trouble you to allow me to pass."

He turned. It was Henry Vandergrip.

"So you are the mountain nymph who guards this sylvan spot?"

"Will you allow me to pass, sir? You forget that we are strangers—here and elsewhere."

"Oh, now, Miss Belle, don't be so severe on a poor fellow who has come so far——"

"Why did you come?" said she, turning upon him eyes which made him shrink and quail. "I thought I had found a spot where I should be in peace and never endure your persecution more."

"Take care, my fine young lady!" he answered, with an ugly scowl. "Take care! You had better measure your words rather more carefully, or by Heaven! I will not be answerable for what I do." And, brave though she was, the girl felt her heart stand still as she saw the demon which had come to the surface and was looking out of his bloodshot eyes.

"Please allow me to pass, Mr. Vandergrip," she said, quietly. "Roland is waiting for me just below there."

She knew well he was at home, poor girl; but the end justified the means.

"No, by the Eternal, I will not let you go! And this has got to be settled here and now forever. I have been tormented by your d—d handsome face long enough, and I'm not going to stand it any longer; and if you will not be my wife, why, d—n it, I don't care so much for this infernal existence, and I shall die and take you with me. Do you hear?" And before she could evade his grasp, his arms held her in his desperate embrace.

Seeing her peril, she had given one wild cry for "Roland! Help!" A moment later a heavy hand fell upon Vandergrip's shoulder, and sent him reeling twenty paces away, while a rough voice seemed attempting to modulate its tones in reassuring the terrified girl; then the rescuer turned to the slender youth who was picking himself up, and brushing off the leaves and dirt.

"Cur! Coward!" he exclaimed, in wrathful contempt.

"How dare you!" said Vandergrip, stung by the insult in Belle's presence.

"How dare I? I think, young man, you have done enough harm in this world for a fellow of your size. Now," with a fierce grip on his shoulder, "down on your knees, and ask the forgiveness of this lady, or by all that's sacred, I'll throw you over the cliff. I will, by Heaven!"

"Release me first, and I will do it," said the fellow, humbly.

The iron muscles relaxed, and Vandergrip was free. He sprang to his feet, instead of kneeling, gave one bound to the ledge of rock above them, and was almost out of sight in a moment.

Like a lion deprived of its prey, the wrathful giant disappeared through the brushwood, and the horror-stricken girl saw him, in another instant, emerge with the cringing form of Vandergrip held high over his head. He strode to the very brink of the awful abyss, then, poising him in the air, he hurled him straight out with the force and momentum of an engine. Like an arrow shot from the bow the doomed man went out, out, over the yawning chasm until the propelling force waned, then down, down, to the fathomless bottom of rocks below, and on the evening air was heard a wail like that of a lost spirit as he disappeared through the branches of the lofty pines beneath.

The young girl and her rescuer stood like statues on

the cliff above as they heard that blood-curdling cry, he with arms upraised and still extended, just as he had let go the form of Henry Vandergrip, every muscle drawn to its utmost tension, his form strained to its greatest height. He then stooped, as if gathering all his energies for one last and mighty leap, his face convulsed with desperate resolve, nostrils distended, eyes wild with a fixed stare, as though already peering into the eternity beyond.

Isabel divined his intention, and, with her nerves wrought up to meet the awful emergency, seized his arm, saying: "Stop! For God's sake, do not leave me alone in this horrible place! I need your aid, my kind friend. Do not be cruel!" She kept her eyes fixed upon his and her hand upon his arm.

After a few moments the expanded chest relaxed, with a long sigh; the arm, the muscles of which had retained their iron tension, sank gradually to his side, as he permitted himself to be led step by step backwards to a place of safety.

"What will you have me do?" said the man hoarsely, his herculean chest heaving like the bosom of old ocean even after the storm had subsided. "You have saved me from going out of the world in bad company, perhaps to be launched into eternity at the rope's end. No matter; I am here. Do with me as you like."

He was saved, thank God! Then, the tension being removed, all the horrible scene came before her, and she felt the world growing black and sense benumbed. For many moments Ben was trying to revive the unconscious girl with water from a spring near them; and, at last the quivering eyelids showed returning life, and, pale as ashes, she tried to stand and to regain control of her suspended powers.

"My God, this is horrible, horrible!" she said, shuddering as she looked at the brow of the cliff. "How did it all happen? How did he"—and she looked shudderingly toward the fatal spot—"how did he know I was here? And you—how did it happen that you came?"

"Miss Isabel, do you not know me? I am Ben Hoadly. I laid in the grave my father, broken like your's in body and mind under the grinding greed of the Vandergrips. In my first lonely hours, I resolved to *kill* Henry Vandergrip, in such manner as would be a warning to others engaged as he and his father had been before him. Since then I have been his shadow. Thank God, I was here to-day to save you from a brute who richly deserved his terrible fate ! "

" You must go away from here. This dreadful tragedy will become known and suspicion will attach to you. Come this evening to our cottage at ' The Eagle's Nest.' "

Her courage returned as she saw this man's peril, and she was strong again.

Ben Hoadly arose and, lifting the fringed corner of a long scarf that hung loosely about Isabel's neck, he kissed it reverently. Then, bowing low, he said: " I obey," and departed under the edge of the cliff where Clayton had seen him disappear in the morning.

CHAPTER LI.

When Henry Vandergrip was struggling in the iron grasp of Ben Hoadly, a party of miners were prospecting on the banks of the Merced River with pan, pick, and rocker, when there suddenly came from the cliffs above and the cloud-capped peaks of the Giant's Elbow, a shower of blood, fragments of flesh, and shreds of clothing, spattering through the lofty pines, filling even those rough miners with horror.

A wailing sound had preceded the horrible shower, and one of the men declared that the day of judgment had come and a rain of fire would succeed that of flesh and blood.

In the breast pocket of the coat were found letters addressed:

" Henry W. Vandergrip,
Coultersville, Cal."

Inquiry at the hotel in Coultersville disclosed the name of "Henry W. Vandergrip, New York." He had been stopping there several days, but had not been seen for twenty-four hours. He was accustomed to ramble in the mountains, the clerk said, and had been heard to speak of the beautiful view from Giant's Elbow.

One of the miners had seen Mr. Vandergrip frequently, and had done some little business in the matter of finding for him the residence of a family named Priest, and had only that evening seen him talking and walking near the extreme point of the Giant's Elbow with the beautiful young lady who lives at "The Eagle's Nest"; and who, he believed, was Miss Priest.

An informal inquest was held next day. Among the witnesses summoned was Miss Priest, who was the last person seen with the deceased.

When the facts as stated had been proven, "Miss Isabel Priest will now be sworn!" said the pompous little man who had been chosen to conduct the examination because he had a little smattering of the law and was therefore called "Judge" at the camp.

Frank Clayton, drawn simply by curiosity, had entered the crowded improvised court-room just as the above words were uttered. Hearing that name, so sacred to him, spoken there in such a place and amid such a scene —good God! What did it mean? His heart beat so violently he could hear nothing but its pulsations. In another moment he had realized that no one had responded to the strange summons; and after a pause, which seemed to him an age, the constable said:

"Miss Priest refuses to testify, your Honor."

"That is contempt of court," said the little man in the seat of judgment; "and you will arrest her, Mr. Officer, for that offense, and also as a suspected party to the murder, as she was the last person seen with the deceased."

In another instant Frank, self-possessed and pale, was on his feet.

"May it please your Honor, I would like to speak with this lady."

"Who are you?" inquired the pompous judge.

"My name is Clayton, an attorney-at-law; and I wish to advise with the defendant."

"No tricks of the law here, Jedge?" shouted two or three voices. "We can deal out justice without law or lawyers."

"Silence in the court!" again vociferated the little man, on his mettle that he should be dictated to by the mob that had made him. "The prisoner is entitled to a fair trial and also to counsel. Mr. Officer, bring the prisoner here, or conduct the gentleman to the prisoner."

Was it possible he was about to see her? How he had looked forward to and longed for that moment! And why was she here? These were the questions that sped like lightning flashes through Frank's mind, as he followed the officer to a remote corner of the room; and soon, he found himself standing before a lady dressed in black and thickly veiled.

Was it his imagination, or did the hand he took in his own tremble as she said, very simply:

"I have heard my brother speak of you often, Mr. Clayton."

With what a thrill of delight Clayton recognized the voice which had been ringing in his ear every step of the way across the continent, luring him on with its strange sweetness!

But she was in peril; she needed his help; that thought was uppermost now.

"Miss Priest, will you entrust yourself to me in this matter? I presume there is some mistake—some misapprehension here. You will have to give me some idea of the position you wish to take."

She spoke very calmly as she answered: "I am not guilty, Mr. Clayton; I know the man who threw Henry Vandergrip over the precipice, but I would suffer for the deed myself rather than reveal his name. The rest I leave to you."

With what a jealous pang he heard this avowal! She seemed slipping away from him just as he believed he had found her. But, setting aside every thought in his determination to screen her from this horrible charge, he approached the judge, saying :

"May it please the Court, we recognize the fact, that though this trial is wholly without form of law, yet there is great necessity for prompt and speedy justice. That we shall have patient hearing and a verdict in accordance with the facts and the evidence we see plainly in the countenances of the twelve honest men to whom, though convened as a coroner's jury, we most willingly submit our case and the evidence that has been adduced."

"That's fair and a square hand ; no bluff or call for a new deal in that, pard !" shouted one of the crowd.

"Silence in court !" again called the judge. "No interrupting the gentleman when he is speaking."

"Your Honor, and you, gentlemen of the jury, will please remember that one of the witnesses testified to seeing the accused talking with Mr. Vandergrip only a little while before the time when the miners were overwhelmed with the shower of human fragments, and upon that slender thread hangs this horrible charge.

"If the court please, the witnesses who have examined the edge of the cliff from whence the deed was committed, testify to foot-prints, and evidences of a fearful struggle; but, in what manner, I would ask, could the accused attack or struggle upon the brink of that fearful precipice with a powerful man in full health, as the deceased was in life ?

"Again, one or more of the miners who have examined the spot from above and below, testify that he must have been propelled by a power almost superhuman, before he began that fearful descent.   No one of you, gentlemen of the jury, can have any idea that this feeble girl could have accomplished this horrible deed in the manner shown."

"That's so, that's so," shouted a voice in the crowd. "She never done it."

"Order in court.   We can't proceed without order," vociferated the judge.

"May it please your Honor," continued Clayton, "and you, gentlemen of the jury, there must have been some mysterious force to have accomplished this terrible result, entirely independent of, and beyond the power of the accused.   And let me beg of you, one and all, not to construe the silence of this timid girl into an admission of guilt, for there is none of you here who is without sisters, mother, or some one dear to you, at your homes toward the rising sun, and does not the remembrance of them excite your pity and enlist your sympathies for the orphan girl, thrown by rough fortune here among you brave men on the western wilds of the Sierras?   The only woman among you here, is it strange that she should tremble and be voiceless ?

"Determined, brave men, clamoring for justice, would not knowingly injure the innocent, and especially an unprotected woman."

"We will protect her.   It would be a sorry day for any chap in this here ranch, what 'd tech a har of her head," said the leader of the band of miners, who had brought the remains of Henry Vandergrip in the rocker, and now sat listening to the lawyer's statement.

"That's so, that's so," joined in the crowd.

"And now, may it please your Honor, and you, gentlemen of the jury," continued the advocate with deep emotion, "into your hands I commit the cause of this innocent girl, and ask you to do by her as you would have other brave men do by your daughters, wives or sweethearts, under like circumstances, feeling assured that you will permit no harm or injustice to come near her sacred person."

"We'll see to that, stranger, you can bet your bottom dollar on that hand," said an old miner, who found a hundred echoes—"That's so, that's so."

The Court shouted "Silence!" and called on the officer to enforce order.

Clayton returned to his client amid an ovation of hearty hand-shakes from the rough but honest miners, and the defendant gave him cordial thanks for the dexterous manner in which he had won over the crowd.

After order had been restored, the judge asked if "Colonel Simms" was in court, as he desired the prosecution properly conducted.

Colonel Simms responded, and took his place before the jury. He opened by saying that he was loth to be placed in so ungallant a position as to prosecute a lady.

"Then, yer'd better not," exclaimed an old miner, who had been silent up to this time.

"That's so; yer better pass out on that hand, Colonel," echoed another voice.

"But," continued the colonel, not noticing the remarks of the crowd, "I am called upon on behalf of the court and the people whom it represents, to see that the guilty shall not go unpunished.

"The eloquent gentleman who has just taken his seat, was very shrewd in covering up one of the gravest charges against his client: that of contempt of court, under the cloak of timidity on the part of the then witness, now prisoner at the bar.

"It is fair to presume the witness refuses to testify, lest she may criminate herself as a party to this atrocious murder.

"Of course, all the circumstances point to an accomplice, and we are not called upon to show the motive or object that the fair prisoner had in committing or abetting the murder."

"That's false as hell!" thundered a voice from the crowd and Ben Hoadly, seemingly with one great stride, brought his giant form beside the speaker, hatless, with tattered garments, dishevelled hair, and eyes ablaze with indignation.

One heavy hand he laid upon the shoulder of Colonel Simms with the iron grasp of a Hercules, while with the other clenched fist, he literally split into fragments the pine table the colonel had been pounding, as he repeated his assertion :

"It's false as hell! and if the base insinuation is repeated, I'll tear that sacrilegious tongue out by the roots."

Isabel Priest grasped the arm of Clayton at the sound of Ben Hoadly's voice, saying :

"Oh, there he is! Quick, Mr. Clayton, don't let him speak!" But Ben Hoadly brushed Clayton and all else aside.

"I am responsible "—and then he stopped, as Isabel Priest, who had eluded Clayton and struggled through the crowd, reached his side, saying in anguish :

"Hush, Ben Hoadly! Do, for my sake, be silent!"

"No, Miss Belle ; for your sake I have spoken ; and I have already gone too far to retrace. Let me now tell the whole story and abide the consequences."

"That's so, Miss ; let him make a clean breast of it now," exclaimed the old miner at the post of chief mourner. "You needn't fear for yourself ; no, nor for him nuther," he added, soothingly ; "he's a brave one an' is gwinter tell ther truth."

"Let the giant tell the story ; let him talk!" said the crowd.

"Yes," remarked Colonel Simms ; "but first let go my shoulder," which had been held firmly during the interruption.

Without seeming to notice anything further than to relax his hold on the silenced and frightened colonel, Ben Hoadly gazed at the retreating form of Isabel Priest as she was led to her seat by Frank Clayton ; then, drawing himself up to his full height, nearly seven feet, he continued the incomplete sentence.

"I am responsible for the death of that man and I stand here to answer to the honorable court and this jury, as well as to my God, for this deed ; and I ask your patience while I relate the moving cause of this act upon which it is your duty to pass sentence, acquittal or condemnation ; and, whatever it shall be, I promise to abide by it, without murmur."

"That's fair."

"Nuthin sneakin 'bout that."

"Go ahead, stranger. He's a big one, ain't he?" shouted the crowd.

"Gentlemen of the jury, my home was in the western part of York State, and my father and I were in the employ of the firm of Vandergrip & Priest, wealthy manufacturers. The senior partner was father of that—dead man.

"There was a deliberate plan to break down and ruin financially, the junior member of the concern, Mr. Priest, because his daughter, there," (pointing to Isabel) "refused the hand of young Vandergrip. In order to accomplish this unworthy object, there was a reduction of wages to starvation prices, followed by a strike of the workmen in self-defence ; closing of the mills, followed by months of idleness and distress.

"Broken in fortune and in health, Mr. Priest died, leaving a desolate family.

"In this wreck perished also my own father, mother and sister. This young lady was still persecuted by Vandergrip and, as all their property had passed into his hands, her family left for the Territory of Kansas and subsequently made California their home. Here they were tracked by young Vandergrip ; and, my own family being ruined and dead, I followed him. I did not know why, but God perhaps sent me to protect that young girl." Then, turning to the rough miners, he continued in a lower voice : "You all have mothers, some of you sisters in the States, whose memory is dear to you ; and I take it every man here would do as I did to save from such a ruffian a frail girl, helpless, and struggling for life. Yes, you would have killed him, as I did."

"That's so, that's so, pardner ! stake yer bottom dust on that, old fel !" shouted the crowd, as the Court commanded silence again and again.

"This is true to you, men who are strangers to her and her cause ; but for my part, who know her well, and all that she has suffered from him, the man who lays violent hands on her, or wags his tongue in disparagement of her good name, I'd pulverize him if he were the last man on earth, and the Creator had forgotten how to make any more."

"Served him right ! Served him right !" shouted the miners ; and the Court let them have their say.

"My own family are gone—starved, murdered—and by that man. And then for him to look roughly or to lay violent hands on her! Do you wonder I killed him!"

"No, no!" shouted the crowd.

"No, I know you don't; and you wouldn't have had me stop short of a hundred lives, if he had possessed so many. And now, good friends, I thank you for your attention, and I leave my case in your hands." Then, sinking in a seat, he bowed his head.

The noisy demonstration of the miners had ceased, and a deeper feeling of sympathy had sway, as this large-hearted and unfortunate man, with great emotion, told the simple story of his life.

Frank Clayton was the first to break the silence when Ben Hoadly had taken his seat.

"May it please the Court, and you, gentlemen of the jury, this is a novel but necessary proceeding in these troublous times, when the slow processes of the law work injustice to the innocent and ofttimes allow the guilty to escape just punishment. Here we have a court and jury organized by a people accustomed to self-government, for the purpose of an inquest. Then, trying the accused and seemingly guilty party, you are now to pass judgment on the self-confessed and real perpetrator of the deed,— the same court, the same jury, the same witnesses, and with the same audience. And allow me to say just here that if the people could always manifest on such occasions the moderation and patient spirit of justice we have had here displayed, much of the tedious circumlocution of law could be done away with. I stand here to say, in behalf of the young lady, my client, that you, gentlemen of the jury, must, according to the established rules of evidence and justice, acquit her of any part in the killing of the deceased, Henry Vandergrip, and recognize in the person here before you the real actor in the tragedy. But how far he is criminally responsible for his act, you must determine. By his permission, I wish to call to your attention some of the leading features of this case and the causes leading to this dreadful deed. His temperament, mental and physical organization, you have seen, and can judge something of, and also of the effect on such a nature of the treatment he and his family received at the hands of the deceased. Let the court and this intelligent jury place themselves in his circumstances, then go deep down in the recesses of the heart, the sacred closet where you commune with your God, and there put the question in the presence of your Maker: What would I have done to the author of all my distress under like circumstances? Ben Hoadly appeared on the cliff at the Giant's Elbow just in time to rescue this lady from the hands of a ruffian. It was the same mailed hand which had oppressed, even unto death, those who were nearest and dearest to him. Can you blame him, that, in a moment of desperation, he hurled the body of the miscreant into the gulf below?" (Cries of "No! No! Served him right!") And now, gentlemen of the jury, I commit into your keeping the future welfare of our unfortunate brother; and, with your higher natures fully aroused, may God give you courage to 'do unto others as ye would they should do unto you.'"

Clayton resumed his seat amid thunders of applause. Isabel Priest rose on his approach, and placed both her hands in his own, and diamond drops of gratitude stood in her dark eyes.

Ben Hoadly still sat bent over, with his face hidden in his hands.

When the silence had become so protracted as to seem awkward, one of the jurors rose and said:

"I vote, Not Guilty."

"And I," "And I," responded the twelve.

"I chip in a half-ounce of dust to buy the big un a coat and hat and ter kinder care for him till he can git a stake," one old miner rose and said.

"I raise yer one," exclaimed another.

"That's the size of my pile," said a third; and one after another of the crowd came forward, and the jury and the judge joined in the general contribution to Ben Hoadly.

When the contributions had ceased, "the big un" was carried away in the hearts and sympathies of the miners, and, literally in a triumphal procession, he left the court-room to sup with the admiring crowd at the miners' camp.

As Isabel Priest left the building, the rough crowd opened respectfully, every head uncovered as she passed. And she acknowledged the rough homage with gratitude.

CHAPTER XLII

For the second time this fair girl acted as a guide to Frank Clayton, as she led him through the mountain paths towards her home at " Eagle's Nest."

Was it the ozone of the air that made him feel he had quaffed a new elixir of life, as he walked by her side? The veil was withdrawn, and he could gaze now into that pure, beautiful face; pale from the dreadful agitations of the recent scenes, it looked to him like an angel's. He could have walked on forever; but they were soon at their destination; and, amid tears and embraces, the wonderful experience was related. Roland, wan and emaciated, lay upon the lounge, which he seldom quitted now, close clasping his sister's hand, as she recited the strange events; she gently stroking his hair, and pausing when he seemed too much moved. Clayton's opportune arrival seemed to them all little short of a miracle; and Mrs. Priest embraced him as if he were another son, saying :

" How can I ever repay you? God only knows what might have happened but for your providential arrival ! "

" And to think, Isabel, of your going *alone* to meet such a monstrous charge ! " and Roland shuddered with horror. " Only to think, Mr. Clayton, of her keeping this awful secret from us and bearing it alone ! Isn't she a heroine ! " and he looked with admiration at the brave girl. " By Heaven," he added, flushing, " I would have gotten up from this couch and gone myself had I known it, if it had killed me ! "

" Yes, my darling," said she, kissing him fondly, " I know that, and that is just the reason why I kept my secret so well. And now," she added, with a look of resolution and authority, " now listen : not one word more, from any one, upon this horrible subject ; we will bury it out of sight *forever*." And, kissing Roland once more, she arose, saying, " Come, Mr. Clayton, and I will show you the garden and my beautiful flowers and vines."

Need it be said that Frank found them beautiful indeed!

And the dainty cottage, with its simple decorations, its magnificent views, seemed to him nearer like Paradise than anything his eye had ever beheld.

Day after day found him there, after a climb up the steep mountain side, walking and riding with Isabel, devising new ways for Roland to enjoy the outer air. The poor boy drank eagerly the fresh life and magnetism which Clayton's strong, invigorating presence brought him, and clung to him as a new hold upon life.

CHAPTER XLIII.

The Summer had passed and the Autumnal foliage was at the height of its glory at " Eagle's Nest," when news came of John Brown's attempt and capture at Harper's Ferry.

It was the first moment of pain Frank had experienced in that life of enchantment. He was deeply moved and shocked. He had talked with Isabel of her old friend's visionary and dangerous schemes, and had imparted to her their divergence of views over his wild enterprise. Now his fears were confirmed—and what would they hear next?

The post of that day answered this conjecture by the following letter from John Brown himself to Clayton:

" Harper's Ferry Nov. 20, 1859.

" My Dear Friend :

"You were partly right—I have failed in my attempt. But an over-ruling God is working this out in His own way. There will be a colossal conflict between the North and the South, and freedom to the slaves will be the *result*, though not the object.

> " ' The sunset of life lends a mystical lore,
> And coming events cast their shadow before.'

"My sun is setting, and I see the breaking of another and a brighter dawn.

"Yes, the slaves have not as yet sufficient intelligence to know that ' he who would be free, *himself* must strike the blow ! ' They will not respond to the opportunity I gave them. But I have no repinings, no reproaches. I have often felt that, as there was no remission of sins without the shedding of blood, so there could be no complete freedom to the Southern slave without the crimson seal—little thinking that it would be my own life's current that should first, and at least, in part, fulfil the awful revelation.

"Yes, my friend, God has not forsaken me in this hour of trial, but leads me safely above the thorns that hedge about the closing hours of life. Were I ruler of the earth, I would not change in one jot or tittle my situation. I am decreed to die on the gallows on the second of December, and I pray the day shall be as bright and joyous as my spirit on that occasion. You may think of me as going forth to meet my fate with a fortitude that is no stranger to your own heart.

"May God, the Father of us all, watch over, protect and care for you and for the dear friends whom I commit to your charge, through all the changes of an earthly life.

"And now I bid you adieu here below, to extend in the future a Heavenly welcome above.

"Believe me, more than ever,
"Your devoted friend,
"JOHN BROWN."

There was weeping and bitter lamentation at the cottage on the mountain side when Frank, with broken voice, read this letter aloud.

Isabel was too much moved to remain in the room, and, after an hour of solitude, returned calm but with traces of deep suffering on her face.

Roland was lying on the sofa, his eyes wearily closed, as if he wished never to open them again upon a world which could be so cruel. Isabel looked at his wan face anxiously for a moment, then went up to him with an inexpressible brightness in her face.

"Come, my darling; we must go outside, where the air is so fresh and sweet. We are all going to take our tea out there under the great oak. No, Mamma dear, don't go; Jenny knows about it and is laying the table there now." She busied herself gathering the shawls and cushions as she spoke.

"Now, Mr. Clayton, your arm, please, for Rolla!"

Oh, what brightness she infused! How her clear vibrating voice dispelled the gloom! How her strong presence filled them all with gladness! And how beautiful she was as she poured the tea under the glancing shadows of the oak leaves!

Clayton looked at her spellbound. How dear she was growing to him! And now this common grief seemed to bring them nearer than ever before. They sat long and gazed at the marvelous sunset and its wonderful after-glories ; the landscape below hazy and indefinite, and the sky a mass of molten splendor.

Isabel had looked in silence for a few moments, then said as if to herself, "It hath not entered into the heart of man to conceive of the things which God hath prepared for those who love him." Then, looking at them all, "Think of the glories that await our dear, kind friend!"

"How I envy you your beautiful faith!" Clayton said, wistfully.

She turned her eyes full upon him, with an expression of surprise : "Envy me? Why, do you not believe a glorious future awaits him?"

He felt the reproof of those clear eyes, and said, quite humbly, "I'm sure, I hope you are right and I am wrong. God knows I hope it is as you suppose ; but for myself I can only say, I do not know. It is all a mystery ; life and death are mysteries to me, and one can only hope for that which he can, at least, in part believe."

No one spoke. Isabel very gravely began to make preparations for their return to the house, as she thought deep, unutterable things in pity for a doubting heart.

"Come, Rolla, dear," she said gently. "It grows a little cool."

The light had faded out of the sky, and a cool shadow had crept into two hearts as Clayton helped the invalid indoors, touching the cold hands of Isabel and indefinably chilled by her manner and the atmosphere about her.

CHAPTER XLIV.

ALL through the ensuing week Isabel fought bravely with the gloom which oppressed every heart in that circle. For the sake of Rolla, there *must* be nothing but sunshine. When the dreaded second of December came, not one word did anyone utter upon the subject uppermost in each heart.

The following letter was received by Clayton **a few** weeks later. It was from Claude Duvall.

"HARPER'S FERRY, DEC. 2, 1859, MIDNIGHT.
"MY DEAR FRIEND:

"How shall I tell you what I have come to see this day! I will try, for there can be no sleep this night.

"When I heard there was no hope of pardon for our poor old friend, you may think I lost no time to come from St. Louis, all the time thinking, in the cars, if there was perhaps some way I can help him to escape. But, my God! when I get here this morning and see all the crowds on the streets—the whole town like one of our *fêtes* at home—and soldiers, soldiers everywhere—then I know how such thoughts are vain; and I only think to see him, to speak with him once more. But when I ask at the jail, *that* hope, too, seems vain. Still, I wait; and as a guard goes on, I slip a gold piece in his hand, and pass in, and behold our old friend. Oh, if you could see the light in his eyes when he came to see me!

"'*You* here? Is Clayton with you?' And he looked so eagerly behind me. I only shake my head for answer. I could not speak; I was weeping, my friend.

"Then he says: 'Tell him he knew better than I; but tell him I have no regrets—I see a glorious——'

"Then another guard roughly pushed me outside the door, and I heard no more.

"I go out in the street, and wait to see what may come. Such crowds! People, people; in windows, on tops of houses; and soldiers here and everywhere!

"At last, there is a roll of drums, and I see an escort of cavalry, like for a king to be crowned, with plumes all dancing and shining in the sunlight. On they come, nearer, nearer; and then, oh, *Mon Dieu!*—there, in a car, drawn by two white horses—there he is—sitting on his coffin—yes, my friend, my eyes have seen that cruel sight —*sitting on his coffin!* But with such a majesty, like it was a throne! his white hair shining like a crown in the sunlight.

"I keep close as I may by the car, and try to make him see me, but cannot tell if he does. The drums always beat, so he cannot hear. At last, when the car stops at that dreadful spot, I feel ill, and cannot look; I think of Savonarola, of Bruno, of Christ, of all who have come to die for their glorious idea! And I hear always still those drums, those dreadful drums; so I know that voice will not be heard more.

"At last—oh, *Mon Dieu!* how long it seems! when the drums no more beat; in all that thousands there is not one sound! Then I know the awful moment is arrive; that a great soul is going out to meet its God! and, I can only—pray.

"What would I do now, if like you, my friend, I cannot pray?

"I know not then what I do for hours. I go—it matters not where. Crowds everywhere, so gay; buying fruit, and eating something in great baskets. I can only think of that line by your English poet:

"'Butchered to make a Roman holiday!'

"And all day and all this night that is in my mind, and I am saying:

"'Butchered to make a Roman holiday!'

"I know well your eyes will weep on this page when you read it, as do mine who write it.

"For this once I must subscribe me, not Claude, but, in very truth, as in deep dejection,

"CLAUDIUS."

Many times did Frank peruse this sad letter before he

determined to show it to Isabel, who was terribly moved
by the details of the scene; and together they decided
not to read it, at least for the present, to her mother nor
to Roland, who was now making such visible progress
toward health they feared to put one sorrowful thought in
his ardent and sympathetic heart.

CHAPTER XLV.

More and more closely were the threads of their lives becoming entwined by these mutual confidences. Isabel believed she was grateful for his kindness to herself, and, still more, for his marvellous effect upon Rolla; for the boy's recovery had certainly dated from the moment of Frank's arrival. So she treated him with a frank cordiality, never for a moment concealing the great pleasure it was to have him among them.

Vanity was a stranger to her heart; hence she thought it quite natural that his stay was prolonged by "investments which made his presence necessary on the Pacific Coast." And so the weeks and months sped on, binding secretly two hearts more and more closely.

With infinite delicacy, Frank had refrained from any allusion to their experience on the prairie and the night by the camp-fire.

"Does he know?" she would sometimes ask herself; and a crimson flush would sweep over her at the thought.

They were walking alone one day, when he said, rather irrelevantly:

"Do you know, I think of all Shakespeare's heroines, Rosalind has for me the greatest charm."

Swift as lightning, her thought divined his own; and she sent back the color which was mounting to her cheek, saying coldly:

"I cannot agree with you; I think nothing but a matter of life and death could excuse a woman for assuming masculine dress."

Then, quickly changing the subject, each knew that the other had understood; and Frank felt that he had been ordered by this determined young goddess not to venture again on that dangerous ground.

The doctor ordered a trip, a change for Roland; so preparations were made to visit the Yosemite. Mr. Bayard Taylor, whom Clayton had recently met, promised to join their party; and a few days later found them in that region of marvellous beauty and sublimity.

When that first morning dawned in the "Yosemite Valley," the mist and spray of the many waterfalls rising like incense to greet the sunlight, it seemed the opening of a festal day to our travellers. The mountain breeze came in the tent doors ladened with fragrance and the melody of forest birds, accompanied by a deep monotone as of the rushing of mighty waters.

While breakfast was preparing, an excursion was made to the nearest and most beautiful waterfall, the Bridal Veil. It hung in vapory folds from the rocks above in an arch of exquisite beauty; the filmy lace now and then lifted or turned back by the wind or some unknown power, disclosing a broad ledge of rocks; and back of it, a cavern of unknown depth. To a mountain climber and an adventurous spirit, the temptation was irresistible to step behind the veil that was raised. Just as the party was leaving the spot, Isabel Priest, yielding to a sudden impulse, darted forward, and in an instant, was lost to view behind the veil.

Bayard Taylor and Clayton watched for a rift in the waters to follow. It came in a few minutes, which seemed an age, and Clayton sprang into the opening to join the young girl. The capricious waters seemed disposed to punish the daring mortals who invaded their domain. For several long minutes, the cascade was an unbroken sheet; then it was again put aside a shower of diamonds and pearls falling upon the water nymph. As she emerged with her companion from their crystal prison, there was a brighter radiance in her face. Perhaps she had wondered who would follow her if she disappeared in that realm of mystery, and now, she was glad that the question was answered.

Roland, who had come to meet the party, scolded his sister for her temerity, but Isabel had often visited Niagara, which was near their early home, and had gone with others behind the sheet of water—one of the feats daily performed there, which is almost sublime from its foolhardiness. Instead of the green wall of liquid emerald of Niagara, this Bridal Veil was like foam and mist when it reached the rocks below and it seemed an easy matter to step behind it.

"Such an enchanted place to play 'hide and go seek,'" said Isabel with a bright laugh.

But she was silent and penitent too, perhaps, for she took her brother's arm and walked back to the encampment, where breakfast was waiting for the party.

Appetite was not wanting after such a morning excursion. Fresh brook trout, coffee, mountain quail and Yosemite grapes were part of the bill of fare, with the "feast of reason and flow of soul" that inspired the table talk of Bayard Taylor and his companions.

At the foot of the falls, were discovered several round smooth stones like billiard balls. Some thought they were Indian implements for a game, or that they belonged to the "Stone Age." On ascending the top of the cliff, they found the roaring waters of the river took a step, as it were, on the granite table before making the dizzy leap; and at this spot, numerous perfect holes were formed, resembling in size and shape the interior of a druggist's mortar. So much symmetry indicated design and skill in the construction.

After further search, one of these holes was discovered without water, and in it a perfectly round ball similar to those below.

"*Eureka!*" exclaimed Mr. Taylor, holding it aloft, and then explained :

"A small pocket or irregularity catches a pebble, the surging waters keep it revolving, wearing the pocket larger and the pebble smaller, but both rounder, for months and years, till, by some freak of the current, a sudden lurch, and out of the pocket it is thrown, carried over the falls, and deposited where the traveller and scientist may speculate upon its origin."

Above the falls, they came to what they called the "Spouting Cave,"—a deep cleft in the rocks in which was a rapid current of water that, without any apparent cause, would occasionally stop in its onward course, and roll back for a time, when a hugh volume of water and spray would rise in the air, followed by a puff of wind like the breath of some great monster with cavernous lungs, then, the pent up waters overcame all resistance, and, with a noise of thunder and gurgling sound, the conduit was filled and the stream flowed on its downward course.

All stood gazing in wonder at this phenomenon of nature.

"It may be," said Mr. Taylor, "that this fissure connects with the grotto under the falls, and has something to do with the lifting of the veil, for which I can see no sufficient explanation down there in the currents of air getting behind it, as we were speculating this morning, Mr. Clayton."

All the secluded haunts of nature in this wonderful valley were explored by the travellers, and the purity of the atmosphere seemed like a draught of inspiration to the health and spirits of the party. Upon no one was its effect more apparent than Roland Priest. His vigorous youth was asserting itself with a rapidity which filled Isabel and Frank with happiness and astonishment. He found no end of amusement in drawing out the guide upon scientific and other subjects.

"Look!" exclaimed Clayton, pointing to the crystal stream. "Do you observe the fairies have paved the bed of the river with gold?" And, as a large brook trout swam leisurely by, he said, "See, they have flecked even the fish with the same precious and shining metal!"

"They call that 'fool's gold,'" said Mr. Taylor.

Roland saw his opportunity; so, turning to the guide, he said:

"What do you think of it, Bob?"

"Wall, stranger," said Bob: "you see, when the gold fever struck the States, nigh every kind o' stories was told of the big strikes and finds in the mines; so a party of prospectors started out from 'Frisco with all these big notions, each feller tryin ter git ahead and ketch the golden worm. One day one of them came to a creek not fur from Mariposa, where this truck was a layin thick on the bottom, jis like tis here, only with ther sun shining on it the stuff looked twice as bright and big as 'twas in natur. Then, his eyes commenced to grow bigger an bigger tryin' ter take all in, an he got kinder excited, and throwed off his close an jumped inter the creek with a shovel; an when t'others kum up, there he was a ravin idiot, tryin ter scoop it up an throw it out on the bank an tellin all on em to stan back, this was his claim as he had discivered it. Since then, old ones calls it 'fool's gold.'"

"Where does it come from?" asked Mr. Taylor.

"Wall, sir, there's several ways 'countin' for it, an' I'll give yer the one what suits my idees best, an' that is its miky (mica) from the rocks which gets heated in mountain fires in the dry season, an' when the rainy season comes on, the rocks kinder slack like lime, and the miky turns gold color an' floats away in the creeks to fool people and turn their heads."

"That is good reasoning," said Mr. Taylor, a sly twinkle in his eye, as it caught Roland's.

What a happy, joyous time it was! And with what delight was it all recounted to the dear mother awaiting them at "Eagle's Nest"! And how they enjoyed her happiness in her boy's returning health and bouyancy! And how enchanting it was to hear that there was not enough food in all Coultersville to satisfy the demands of his appetite!

CHAPTER XLVI.

It was now the second Summer of Clayton's sojourn near his friends. Letters from the East brought good news from the Colony, Petrel was happy with the good Sisters. So it needed only to make peace with his consceince by making business which should detain him, which he did by investing quite largely. Then, too, he found the quiet of the mountain side favorable for literary pursuits, to which he was addicted. So his conscience was appeased.

Isabel was a superb horsewoman, and as she rode Tempest, with Frank at her side upon Falcon, who had now been returned safe and sound from Oregon, there was abundant time for confidences; and there were few subjects they had not discussed in this way *al fresco*.

"Your riding is characteristic," he said to her one day.

" How is that ? "

" Well, you are so supple, and yet so immovable ; your touch is so tender, yet so firm."

" There, that'll do," said she, waving her whip with an air of authority. " Now, sir, we'll talk about *yourself*, if you please. Tell me some more about Uncle Ned and your pony and Aunt Eliza and Uncle Stanley and Petrel. Why, do you know, those people are all as *real* to me as if I had seen them. I can see your pretty cousin, too, with her deep blue eyes."

" They are not blue, if you please."

" Oh, yes ; grey, I mean," and she laughed. " Well, why didn't you marry her yourself, sir, and save her from that dreadful Mr. Fletcher? Of course you fell in love with her."

" Never," said Frank, emphatically. " Kate and I were like brother and sister."

" Why, I thought boys always fell in love with their cousins," said she, laughing. " I had always supposed that was part of the discipline of life."

"Well, it was not a part of the discipline of mine," answered Frank. "We were too good friends to be lovers.—You laugh," said he; "but I tell you there is philosophy in that."

"So you think lovers must not be good friends?"

"Well, no; not quite that; but love in the earlier stages is fed by mystery; and with a person you have known from the cradle there is no place to begin. Do you see?"

"I see that you have studied the subject very carefully," and Isabel laughed again. "I know nothing about such things, so I presume you are right."

"But I will be frank with you," said he, looking very steadily at her as he spoke; "I *have* had my little romance, which if you would care to hear I should like to tell you some time."

He spoke very seriously now and Isabel had a disturbed consciousness that the blood was dyeing her cheek to the temples for a moment, and then returning and leaving it very pale. But she managed to say, very quietly, that she should be pleased by the confidence; and, a few weeks later, one quiet evening, he told her the following story:

"After leaving college, I went to Louisville and studied law in the office of Mr. Wyckliffe, who stands at the head of his profession and is one of the noblest and best of men. He lived in a fine old mansion just out of the city, and I was occasionally invited there to dine. His only daughter presided at the table, and the guests were usually much older men than myself. Mr. Wyckliffe was a student of German philosophy, ancient history, and delighted in the society of a few chosen friends of similar tastes. One was Mr. Ernest Bausen from Heidelberg, an Oreintal scholar, who afterwards introduced Dr. Simonides, a Greek physician.

"The conversation of these men was both interesting and improving to a young fellow of my age, and gave a new turn to my reading and studies. It was an added charm to these discussions that Alice Wyckliffe also delighted in the stories of Greek life and art told by the doctor.

"One day, he dwelt with poetic effect upon the cremation of the dead, and preserving the sacred ashes in urns of beautiful and artistic workmanship, which he compared to the disadvantage of the modern idea of Christain burial.

"'The body,' he said, "which we have cared for through life and is endeared to us by such ties, becomes food for worms and is a source of disease and death to those left behind.'

"Once, Doctor Simonides invited us to his house and displayed his collection of urns, or treasures as he called them. One in particular, attracted Alice's attention as being a rare work of art, and she inquired if it had a history.

"'Yes,' said the doctor, embracing it reverently, 'this contains the ashes of my darling, my first and only love. She died on the day set for our marriage. In accordance with our custom, I have preserved her memory thus, and while I do not believe that my beloved Ursula dwells in this urn, yet it is of all things on earth to me, the most sacred. I have seen but one Ursula and this rare pattern of Greek vase serves as a telescope through which I behold anew each day, in the world of spirits, my angel bride.'

"Alice was profoundly impressed by this, and we talked much together of the habits of the ancients, of poetry, of philosophy—of which she was quite a student. We read German together—and—well, naturally enough, we drifted from philosophy into sentiment and from sentiment into love—as we thought.

"One day, while riding, Alice's horse took fright and threw her. She was carried home insensible; and when I saw her pale face that evening, the pang it gave me was deeper than that felt by any brother; and now, Isabel, my story is nearly ended. The injury to her spine proved fatal, and this blooming young creature knew that her days were numbered.

"Her father and I watched over her for two months. Day by day, little by little, the light burned lower in the socket until the oil of life was consumed. Soon, the lids closed, and the light of heaven went out from those soft blue eyes; the pulsations of the heart grew fainter and fainter. 'She sleeps,' said her father. 'Yes,' said the doctor, taking the hand of his patient, 'but when she awakens, it will be in heaven. Like the swinging pendulum of a clock when the spring is broken, each vibration is shorter and you can hardly perceive when it ceases to keep time, or passes into eternity.' Mr. Wyckliffe was overcome with grief when the last sad moment came ; and her dear body, attired for death, was left alone with the faithful servants and attendants.

"I was permitted to watch by the mortal remains of Alice that night. Robed in white, she lay like a pale, broken lily. So pure, so beautiful ; her face almost radiant with a sweet smile as though beholding a heavenly vision.

"'There is no indication of life,' said the doctor on the next morning, 'except an external appearance, and that sometimes continues for several days.'

"Still, I could not feel that she was dead, and after my night's vigil, I gave place to her father with the promise that he would not leave her alone.

"Toward evening, I resumed my watch and opened the blinds of the window overlooking the garden. The golden rays of the setting sun illumined the room, casting a rosy tint upon the face of Alice.

"I knelt by her side, and untying the white satin ribbon that bound the waxen hands together,—they seemed like snowflakes as they fell apart,—I reverently took them in my own, saying 'Dear, dear Alice, speak to me ! Tell me what you see behind that mysterious veil !'

"Gradually there came a rose-tint into her cheek, a trembling of the long lashes, and the blue eyes slowly opened. I was not astonished, but kissed her again and again, saying, 'Be quiet, my love. You have been sleeping nicely. Close your eyes again. You must have some nourishment.'

"'Dear Frank,' she whispered, as I put some wine to her lips, and then called her nurse from the adjoining room. Soon her father was bending over his child. The doctor came, and pronounced it one of the rare cases of abnormal suspension of vitality, or trance.

"Dr. Simonides had been absent from the city. He was now called in, and found the patient again in what seemed a natural sleep. He told Dr. Wyckliffe that the lamp of life was flickering in its socket, and would soon be extinguished forever ; and so it proved.

"Breathless with hope, we watched for her awakening again. Her eyes opened, and such a smile illumined her face as she said :

" ' Papa,—Frank, I have seen wonderful things. I cannot tell you, for you would not understand. But you must
rejoice when I am gone.'

" Presently the face became more radiant, the voice sank
to a whisper ; and in perfect peace the spirit took its everlasting flight. There was no mistake this time. Death
had surely claimed his victim and affixed his seal on the
rigid and icy form.

"After this wonderful experience Mr. Wyckliffe would
not consent to having his daughter put under the sod.
The urn containing the ashes of Ursula had interested
Alice and a similar vase, which she herself had decorated,
was now ready to receive her earthly and sublimated
remains.

" Again the body was robed in white. It was placed in
a casket and surrounded by flowers, the natural emblems
of frail mortality. After the funeral services at the house,
the casket was followed by the loved ones to a building
erected by Dr. Simonides at his home. Here the body
of Alice was removed from its rosewood casket and placed
in a similar one made of clay. The doctor then placed
around the body, a white powdered incense, which, he said,
had the double effect of causing it to consume like tinder
and at the same time, emitting an agreeable resinous
odor.

" ' We will now,' said he solemnly, ' give back to mother
earth the mortal portion of her child.'

" Placing the casket upon a sliding frame, it entered the
glowing furnace, and the door was closed.

" ' It is thus,' said the doctor, ' that pure gold is separated
from the dross.'

" Soon, there was perceived a pleasing odor from the
incense pervading the room, and in a short time, by a
simple mechanism, the crucible was removed to the cool-
ing chamber, Demetrius the faithful Greek servant, having
charge of all the details.

" Mr. Wyckliffe and I followed the doctor to his labora-
tory where, upon a marble slab, rested the crucible. The
lid was lifted by the doctor and Demetrius, revealing to
the sight a mound of white ashes.

" ' The Greeks observed a religious ceremony in depositing the ashes in the urn,' said the doctor, ' and the wing
of a white dove was used, together with a unique silver

ladle like these, fashioned after two human hands joined together."

"The urn brought by Mr. Wyckliff was placed in the centre of the crucible and the ashes, carefully and reverently collected by the dove's wing and the silver ladle, were placed in the beautiful receptacle. Then,. hermetically sealing the inner metal lining of the urn, it was placed upon a small pedestal, and thus presented by the doctor to Mr. Wyckliffe and the bereaved friends, saying:

"'Here are the sacred ashes of your child, which once enclosed her beautiful spirit. Cherish them for her sake.'

"And we turned away feeling that we left her at the gate of Paradise, and not in a dreary cemetery."

As Isabel listened to this narrative the nature of the feeling she entertained for Frank became clearly revealed to herself. She could no longer delude herself by calling it gratitude or friendship. She loved him, and she could not help a pang of something like jealousy at even the sublimated image of this young girl, who might now have been his wife with a claim upon his supreme devotion.

She spent that night in deep and solemn communings with her own heart. She did not know that he loved her; perhaps his tender care was simply the ordinary expression of a sympathetic nature. But if he did—what then? Was there not an impassable gulf between them? Her religion, which was interwoven with her life, was to him a delusion and a superstition. No happiness would be possible in a marriage built over this chasm—her world not his world; their souls would be perpetually divided, and such a union a mockery.

Such were the conclusions at which she arrived after a sleepless night; but she had fought her fight and had vanquished, and came down to breakfast very pale, though in other respects much as usual.

She was not sorry to find a note from Frank saying that unexpected and urgent business would take him to Sacramento for a few weeks.

Instead of galloping over the hills with Falcon and his master at her side, she now rode alone, excepting such days as Roland could accompany her. How the glory had faded out of the sunsets, the landscape, and the joy out of everything, since she had sternly faced the fact that this had only been an episode, and that she must live on her life alone, without that one presence which gave it its chief charm! But she was strong and brave, and never wavered in her resolve. "And yet I am glad to have known him. I am richer for having loved him," she said again and again to herself in solitude. And, recalling his unflinching adherence to what he thought right and just as applied to every-day life and duty, then his perfect consistency as applying the same rule to all he held sacred in religion, in the face of all opposition or influence, she wondered if God would or could leave such an earnest soul long in the dark and doubt. Can it be possible in the providence of a kind and loving Father, for such a spirit to be eternally lost?

CHAPTER XLVII.

It was a bright, crisp morning in the early winter, when Isabel heard once more the welcome sound of Falcon's hoofs upon the steep mountain road. What glad music there was in the resonant voice she heard extending words of gay greeting to Roland and her mother! She trembled to think the joy that presence brought to her heart.

"Are you well? he said, looking at her anxiously, his quick glance at once detecting a little less color, something gone from her contagious buoyancy.

But Isabel was an adept in diverting attention from herself, and had soon drawn him to tell of the things and people he had seen. Then he must ride with Rolla, as she had pressing duties at home; and after the ride and early dinner, she had an important letter to write; and so the delightful hour when he could be with her alone seemed to be eluding him.

Frank had been thinking for many days of this interview, for he had determined at last to ask that question upon which hung his hope of happiness in life. If she did not love him—he dared not think how it would empty life of hope and aim! And just because the question involved so much, he had waited all these months, not daring to ask it; but now, it could no longer be delayed. His presence was required at home, and he must know his fate, and perhaps—oh, what joy! Perhaps she would go with him! And with pride and rapture he thought of introducing to Kate this glorious woman as his wife!

"Am I never to see you alone?" he asked in a low tone, as they came out from the tea-table.

The color rose swiftly to her face as she hesitated a moment, then said:

"Shall we walk to the great oak and see the sunset?"

He gave her a grateful pressure of the hand in reply. Her heart was beating very rebelliously as he wrapped the soft folds of the cloak tenderly about her; and they walked on in silence, thinking unutterable things.

"I believe I like this crisp air even better than those soft, languorous summer evenings." Isabel said this with a feeling that *something* must be said.

"Isabel," said he, "I am going to make a confession. I am a pretender, a dissembler, and, more than that, I am a coward. I have framed all sorts of pretexts for staying here—pretended there was business requiring it. There was none, except such as I made to suit my purpose. It was all an insincere sham. It is because I love you, Isabel—because I could not tear myself from the enchantment of your presence—that I almost forgot the calls of duty. *You* were in the sunsets, in the landscape ; it was *your* presence that made these mountain wilds a Paradise. And I dared not tell you, Isabel, because I feared I should then lose you utterly."

Her hand was trembling in the strong grasp of his now.

"I dared not tell you," he went on, "because I dared not hope. You seemed sometimes so remote and so unattainable ; and sleepless nights have I spent in trying to nerve myself for what might come. But now, oh my darling one ! you do not turn from me ; now I begin to hope that your heart beats responsive to my own !"

Isabel was pale and trembling and unresistingly allowed the strong arms to enfold her. Then, disengaging herself, she looked with a pathetic earnestness into his eyes and said:

"Yes, Frank, I love you."

Again she was held close to his heart, while he, in passionate joy, murmured, "Thank God !" and again and again kissed her.

She closed her eyes and rested like a tired child, while Frank's words rushed on in a torrent.

"And now, there need be no cruel separation. I must go away, but you will go with me."

The eyelids opened reluctantly, and she said, "No—that cannot be. God knows I long for it, but Frank, it cannot be."

"Why, Isabel," said he, "there will be no separation from your mother and Rolla ; they shall go with us."

"No ; you do not understand me," she said painfully, and freeing herself entirely from his embrace. "Listen, I will try to tell you what I mean—but oh, it costs me so much !"

"My dear one, you tremble. I have agitated you. Here, let me put this cloak about you. There,—now, don't try to speak yet. We have plenty of time to talk over everything now; and all shall be just as you wish, dear. Perhaps it may be better to wait if you prefer it; I can arrange to come back for you in a few weeks."

"Oh, you do not understand yet, and I must give you such pain. I cannot—marry you, Frank. It would not be right."

"My God, what do you mean? Not right?"

"No, Frank; not right, and not wise; we should not be happy."

"What in God's name do you mean?" said he.

"We should not be happy," she repeated, now more firmly. "We hold opposite views upon a vital subject. What is to me the most sacred of all beliefs is to you nothing, or less than nothing; and we should lead sundered lives, however we might strive to cover it up."

Frank had been looking at her in speechless amazement, utterly incredulous of the power of such an obstacle to separate them. He took both her hands in his and looked steadfastly into her troubled eyes.

"I would not for all this world disturb your faith. I could not love you nearly so well if you hadn't it. I shall always treat it as sacred, for it is yours; and if God or a generous heaven should ever grant us children, I should wish them to receive it as a precious inheritance and to cling to it; for I tell you, Isabel, it is miserable to be compelled to doubt and grope in the darkness after the truth."

He had never seemed to her so deserving of all the best that anyone could bestow as at that moment; and the miserable girl burst into a flood of tears, which she was utterly unable to control.

Again Frank folded her closely in his arms and soothingly stroked her hair.

"Now, dearest," he said, "we will not talk any more; you are tired. It is enough to be together in silence. Now my heart is laid bare to you, and I have the joy of knowing that you love me—a little. So what is there to arrange? There is time enough to harmonize all these smaller points. And if the kind and loving Father is as you believe, then He knows how much I love His laws and how earnestly I am striving to seek them out."

"You are quite right," she said ; "we had better say no more to-night. To-morrow I shall be better able to tell you what I mean and to make you understand why I feel this sacrifice imposed upon me."

"Dearest," said Frank, as they approached the now lighted house, "may I tell your mother and Rolla?"

"No,—no,—no!" said she ; "not for the world. Leave that to me."

Those two people, however, had their own conjectures about this prolonged view of the sunset, and were not a little mystified in observing its effect upon Frank and Isabel, who scarcely spoke after returning. Mrs. Priest watched him very closely, for that gentle lady had her own unspoken hopes, and she said to herself : "Assuredly no unhappy man ever looked like that. Why, his face seemed transfigured! And how he watched her! But something has happened. What is it?" And she lingered about her daughter's room when she retired, in hope of a confidence, which, however, was not bestowed.

CHAPTER XLVIII.

Isabel made a pretext of retiring while her mother was there ; but soon as she was alone and the house quiet for the night, she arose, put on a warm dressing-gown and sat down to her desk, and wrote as follows :

My dear Frank :

"In the solitude of this hour and place, I will try to say what I could not this evening ; and if it pains you to read, know that my own heart is torn in writing it.

"Need I tell you again that I love you! Yes, I love you, and can think of no greater joy than to spend my life under the protecting care of your tender and generous heart ; and yet, I cannot accept this happiness, which would, as I told you to-day, be built over a chasm—and an ever-widening chasm. At first we might not be so conscious of it, but we should soon realize that we lived apart ; that we were not in sympathy upon the most vital of all subjects ; and this would inevitably react upon our feelings.

"Terrible as it is to part now, it is better than drifting gradually asunder after marriage—seeing love fade into indifference, and possibly the chain which bound us becoming a wearisome burden.

"Oh, why need it be so? Why can you not, in childlike simplicity, accept this beautiful and sustaining faith ? But I know your convictions are as deeply rooted as my own. So I see no hope, and will try to take up my life, shorn of its beauty and its joy, and for the sake of others, live it cheerfully as I can. But, I am now, and shall always remain,

" Yours, and only yours,

" Isabel."

It was not until near morning that the tired eyes closed in sleep. Her mother, finding her still sleeping when breakfast was ready, kept the house quiet, wondering, as she softly moved about, what it all meant.

The sound of Falcon's hoofs speeding up the road to the cottage dissipated the dreams of the sleeping girl, and she arose and called her mother.

"Mamma, dear," she said, "I did not sleep very well, and I have a headache. Will you please give this note to Mr. Clayton and tell him I will see him later in the day."

With eager, trembling hand, Frank seized the note, and went out into the fresh air and sunshine to read his fate.

During the long hours of the day he could not have told whether he was most happy or miserable. Assuredly he could not be very wretched with those words she had uttered last night still ringing in his ears, and repeated again in her note. And he felt confident of being able to persuade her of the folly of her decision. Still, as he read again the words so resolutely penned, he was anxious.

She heard his horse coming up the path on his return at the hour appointed, and, throwing a wrap about her, walked down to meet him.

He sprang to the ground, and was at her side in another instant, leading Falcon by the bridle.

"Let us walk," said she; "we are more undisturbed than in the house."

With trembling hand he tied Falcon in a sheltered spot, and they turned down a secluded path toward the glen.

"Dear one, you are pale," said he, anxiously. "Now, we must sweep away all those miserable obstacles, and then we shall both be happier."

"Ah, if they could be swept away!" she said, with a wistful look at him.

"But you know, dear, I must be honest. I cannot make myself hold beliefs—I——"

"Yes, I know," she said, sighing, "that is it, and that is just why it is so hopeless."

"But you would not for such a cause condemn us both to wretchedness; you cannot mean that!"

"Oh, Frank, don't break my heart! Help me to bear this bravely. Do you not see what it is to me?" And she buried her face in her hands.

"Isabel, listen," said Frank, taking both of those

hands into his own; "listen! Do you know what it would mean for me if you persisted in this cruel course? It would destroy me. My life would be ruined. Think —think what you are doing before it is too late." And he looked into her eyes with an intensity which frightened the girl. "Think of your realizing when it is past recall that you have destroyed the happiness of two lives, and for—what shall I call it?—for a mistaken idea, a fantasy, a whim! For I tell you, Isabel, there is no foundation in this structure of the imagination. We would *not* be sundered. We would *not* grow apart. God and nature intended our souls to be united as one. You are *mine*, whether you give yourself to me or not. Have confidence in our ability to help each other to a right understanding of the matter."

Isabel trembled at his vehemence, and his eyes fairly burnt her own with their intensity. She felt her courage wavering. At that moment a step was heard approaching. Fate did not intend she should reply in a moment of weakness.

"A dispatch, sir, for Mr. Clayton," said the messenger. "They told me to look for you here."

Frank tore open the envelope. It ran thus:

> "It will be well to come at once; important.
>
> "CLAUDE DUVALL."

"Very well," he said, dismissing the messenger.

"Isabel, my fate cannot be delayed; read this. I shall sail to-morrow, unless—" and he looked with an eagerness almost pathetic into her eyes for a ray of hope.

Her hands trembled as she took the paper, and her lips were very white when she said, "Well, it is better so. You had better go, dear Frank," laying her hand with sad tenderness on his shoulder.

"Go, I implore you!" she repeated, seeing he hesitated. "It sounds cruel, but I must say it."

"Yes, it is cruel," he said, in a choking voice. And they walked back in silence to the house.

Isabel could never remember how it was when they returned, and Mrs. Priest and Roland were told of Frank's unexpected and immediate departure owing to the receipt of an urgent message. In the midst of all the regrets and leave-taking, she sat as as one benumbed. She heard something said of a possible war between North and South, and heard Roland say :

"Of course you will fight, Clayton, in that case?"

"Oh, yes ; you know I have no one to live for,—and such men make brave soldiers," he added, with a grim laugh.

She could not stay longer in the room, and disappeared for some minutes.

When she returned Clayton was about leaving. He hesitated a moment, and then said, turning to Mrs. Priest :

"May I see your daughter alone for a few moments before I leave?"

They passed into the little library, and closed the door. Ten minutes later the door again opened, and both came out, pale and silent.

Frank did not glance at her again, but silently pressed the hands of Roland and his mother, and in another moment was gone.

CHAPTER XLIX.

The war-cloud not larger than a man's hand had gradually darkened the whole sky, and in April, 1861, the first lurid flash at Fort Sumter was followed by a thunder peal which shook the land. The country was in arms. John Brown's prediction was in process of fulfilment. The pent up fires North and South had found vent, and the awful conflagration must now run its course. Few there were who could foresee the extent—the length, nor the end—of that fiery track. But with what splendid, unflinching bravery did men throw themselves into it !

How well this opportunity for action suited Frank Clayton need not be said. He knew not the meaning of fear; and now, under the stress of his great disappointment, he could think of no fate more to be desired than to lay down his life for his country. He was too brave to commit suicide; but this other he might do, and so end it honorably and for a purpose.

The colonelcy of a regiment in Kentucky was offered him ; but with a characteristic steadfastness and tenacity of purpose he preferred the lieutenant's commission in a cavalry regiment from Kansas, which seemed to offer an opportunity of serving his old ends near and about this field of action in days gone by.

One warm afternoon in September of 1861, a troop of cavalry rode in hot haste into Fort Scott. The young officer at their head dismounted and hastily presented himself before the commanding officer, saying as he saluted him :

"General, I have just captured a Confederate messenger. He is just outside. Would you like to see him? He was the bearer of these dispatches from General Price, at Drywood Creek."

General Lane seized the paper eagerly, smiling as his eye hastily ran through them.

"Lieutenant Clayton," said he, "send me this fellow at once. This *is* a piece of good fortune ! You look tired !

Go and get something to eat, order a fresh horse. Rest for two hours, and then report to me. We must hit General Price in the face to-morrow morning before he gets it washed."

"Are we to be reinforced to-night?" asked Clayton, in surprise.

"Oh no, we must gain time by our audacity, which is often equal in results to real power and skill. Our eight hundred men and the little mountain howitzer will make a deeper impression if hurled in the face of the sleeping lion, than ten times the number coming up in regular battle array at the usual fighting hours."

Very little rest was there for man or beast in Fort Scott on that September night. The few families of soldiers and sutlers which had not been removed during the day were busy all night. The coming and going of messengers, orderlies, teamsters and soldiers bivouaced anywhere and everywhere, in houses, on porches, verandas and yards, all so recently occupied, and now deserted by the owners, who had fled toward Lawrence and the interior of Kansas.

Lieutenant Clayton returned from the second scouting expedition on which General Lane had despatched him at ten in the evening, and reported the enemy quietly encamped, with but small. picket force out, and that so posted as to make surprise and capture easy.

"Lieutenant," said the general, as Clayton was about departing after making his second report, "we shall move by three in the morning. You had better get some sleep if you can. There is a mattress in the parlor thrown on the piano—take these blankets, go in there and lie down. I'd rather have you near in the event I should need you. We are likely to have a lively time in the morning, and your bed there may enable you to get keyed up to concert pitch."

"And that we may all pitch in concert," added Clayton, as he took the blankets from General Lane's hand and adopted his suggestion.

Just before daylight on the following morning Clayton with a small detachment of cavalry might have been seen carefully moving along the timber that skirted Drywood Creek and near its crossing on the road to Fort Scott, then halting till a messenger came from the same direction with the command from General Lane to move at once as his force was in position to strike.

The light was just sufficient to reveal the enemy's pickets. Then as quietly as possible he got between them and their camp. Coming leisurely up behind, he was halted by the picket, who cried:

"Who comes there?"

"Relief," responded Clayton.

"Advance, relief, and give the countersign."

Clayton rode up, and the first thing the picket knew he felt the muzzle of a revolver thrust in his face, with the stern command, "Surrender without a word, or you die!"

"I will, sir, you bet," said the picket, coolly. "Don't you shoot, and I won't, either."

After disarming him, Clayton said: "Now, if your life is worth the pains, go along with me and aid by directions the capture of the other pickets. We want to give General Price a surprise-party."

"I'll do it, Mr. Clayton."

"How, do you know my name?" said Clayton.

"Well, you see, Lieutenant, I was with Tom Livingstone once when he tried to give you a surprise-party in your cabin near Lawrence, and you and that devil, Claude Duvall, got the drop on us, and we just lit out, and Duvall he's now in prison at Independence."

"There, never mind," interposed the lieutenant, "I know all the rest, and you are talking too loud now for your own good or ours, for remember your life depends on our success. If you betray us you'll be shot then and there, and court-martialed afterward."

"You don't need to swear to that, Lieutenant. I believe you're telling the truth, and I intend to act on your gentle hint, for you know a wink's as good as a nod to a blind hoss."

"How far are we from the next picket?"

"Only round the point there. See, Lieutenant, he's comin' this way thinkin' we're the relief. You've struck it rich, seein' it's the very time for relieving guard."

At this moment a horseman was seen approaching, and the picket rode straight into the trap.

"That was neatly done," said Clayton, laughing, as the fellow, before he could recover his senses, found himself relieved of his arms and accoutrements.

Thus one after another of the outposts were taken, until the main crossing was reached. By this time it was getting light enough to disclose the color of the clothing of the men approaching, and the sentinel made a bold dash for the crossing in the direction of the camp, when an exciting race ensued.

Seeing the picket was gaining on them, and observing General Lane's force coming up at double-quick, Lieutenant Clayton ordered a corporal whom he knew to have a cool head and a steady aim, to halt and shoot.

The order was instantly obeyed. A sharp report of a rifle rang out on the morning air, and horse and rider rolled in the long grass. Upon reaching him, Clayton found the man lying stunned by the fall, and the horse dead by his side.

He then joined his command in the advancing column, and was first in position in front of the enemy's confused and excited force.

General Price had barely time to throw forward his infantry into a valley, where they lay low in the long grass, back of which on a ridge were posted six pieces of artillery, while resting back on the timber to his right was his cavalry.

Clayton seeing a gleaming line of bayonets of the infantry sinking out of sight in the long grass, wisely determined not to charge the artillery as he had been ordered by General Lane to do, if success seemed at all likely.

The firing was opened by the cavalry with carbines, and mounted as they were on green horses, the aim was wild as that of the enemy's cannon, which alone replied. Clayton seeing his men exposed to a severe fire, with untrained horses in the face of such noise—shouting men —rumbling wheels—cracking of rifles and booming of cannon—realized they had all they could do to control the maddened steeds. Hastily wheeling them into column Clayton resolved to march them to the rear, dismount them and try on foot, with greater hope of success. Just at this point, under cover of the ridge on which they had first formed, the adjutant with more foreign airs than military skill rode up. Observing Clayton, he exclaimed:

"Retreating?—For shame. Why the devil don't you halt your command and fight?"

"By the Eternal, Adjutant, if you don't stand out of my way, I'll strike you with my sword!" said he, raising it as he spoke high above his head. "I know my duty, and I dare do it, too. Don't you see those men can't fight mounted?"

The adjutant stood aside and soon saw the dismounted cavalrymen return under their commander, the only mounted man in sight of the enemy's artillery, which was at once trained on the horseman. Fortunately, however, all save one piece was too far removed to endanger him. But this piece sent at last a shot so close as to make the position anything but pleasant. Directing the aim of his men toward it, a number of rounds were fired without effect.

"By Jove! that was a close shave," said Sergeant Jack, as a shot carried away Clayton's overcoat, which was rolled and strapped to his saddle.

"Yes," answered Clayton, coolly, "it was pretty close. I don't think the horse likes it much," and he tried to soothe the terrified animal. Then riding up to the officer in charge of the firing-party, he said:

"What's the matter? Your shots don't seem to take effect."

"No, confound it," he answered angrily. "It's those long blades of grass, they interfere with our aim."

Just then another solid shot went by, humming a requiem of death so near as to make both start.

Sergeant Jack was at Clayton's side in a moment. "For God's sake, get off that horse," he said. "Don't you see you are just a target for that piece?"

"Sergeant," said Clayton, not seeming to hear, "bring me your rifle. Now hold my horse by the bits, two of you, and let me try my hand on those gunners." The first shot told on one of the number, and he was carried to the rear, so one after another the men at this piece were picked off by his steady aim, they responding the while with shot and shell, grape and canister. Finally the piece was hauled off by hand, and the duel with the cannon ended in victory for the lieutenant.

By this time General Lane had come up with infantry and one mountain howitzer under immediate command of Colonel Montgomery. The battle continued at long range for several hours, only the Springfield rifles of a portion of the infantry and the Sharps carbines of the dismounted cavalry being able to reach the enemy or do any execution.

Observing that the cavalry posted to his left was moving rapidly in the direction of the crossing with evident intention of cutting off the retreat, Clayton called Colonel Montgomery's attention to the fact.

"He has discovered our strength," said the colonel, "and is going to try a flank movement on us."

"It looks as though it was our *weakness* he had discovered," Clayton was saying to himself.

"We must retreat quietly without his knowledge," continued the colonel. "Lieutenant, mount your men and cover our retreat."

The order to fall back was passed down the line and the whole force retreated in order, leaving only the cavalry detachment under Lieutenant Clayton in sight of the enemy. Watching their movements Clayton fell back just in time to make the crossing before the enemy's cavalry could reach him. But despite his efforts several unfortunate fellows were cut off and killed at the very banks of the stream. After crossing over Clayton threw his men in line of battle, and held the ford against more than ten times his number, which came up to the timber's edge and opened fire, but dared not venture to charge the strong position.

The retreat back to Fort Scott was made in such good order that it was not until next morning that General Price learned it was only a small picket force holding the crossing of the Drywood.

The audacity of the movement had resulted as General Lane thought. Everything valuable had been removed from Fort Scott. Fort Lincoln had been strengthened in men and munitions of war, and the little army was in light fighting trim. Price hovered near the spot where he had been out-generaled for two days, by which time the little army was reinforced by several militia companies, and two or three regiments of volunteers. General Price saw the force accumulating, and then commenced a retrograde movement back to Missouri. The enemy out of the way, a portion of the cavalry was sent to reconnoitre and harass his rear. Lieutenant Clayton was of this command, and so closely did they follow that several skirmishes ensued between it and the enemy's rear-guard.

Then the enemy broke up into detachments and took different routes; the main body going south under General Price.   At Ball's Mills, near the border, quite a large force of graycoats had made a stand at the bridge across the creek, and thrown up temporary breastworks along its banks ; a strong force defending the cornfield, which flanked the only road or lane leading to the bridge.

Again the mountain howitzer which accompanied the command was brought into requisition, to shell the timber and sweep the field with grape and canister.   This had the effect of driving the enemy from his position, when a charge was sounded and away went the cavalry with a shout, and gleaming steel flashed brightly in the sunlight, as over ditch and fence, through hedge of thorns, across the field, amid the corn, here a friend and there a foe, they stop to shoot and away they go.   The shells went screaming overhead like destroying angels from Hades loosed, bursting mid-air with hideous cry, then crashing through bridge, horse, rider, or falling spent to the ground.   On rushed maddened, frighted steeds, riderless, bent on escaping destruction.   It was a scene of wild horror.

Clayton's detachment was first to cross the bridge in hot pursuit of the enemy's fleeing rear-guard, who having fired it, didn't wait to see destruction complete, but fled after their retreating comrades.   After detailing men to extinguish the flames, Clayton rushed on in pursuit of the fleeing remnants.

Only a short distance away, he saw two men running for the shelter of the wood on the left.

"After them!" he cried, pointing toward the field where they were.

The officer stopped to take down the fence, when Clayton, foreseeing the men would escape such deliberate pursuit, put spurs to his horse, and ordering a file of men to follow he cleared the fence, and gave chase, shouting "Halt! halt!"   Then sheathing his sabre and drawing his revolver, he fired a shot which brought the men to a stand within twenty paces of the wood, where pursuit would have been almost fruitless.   The man in the rear cried :

"I'se shot, I gibs up, Mars Yankee, I gibs up."

"Hands up and surrender," shouted Clayton, as the first man, in full Confederate colonel's uniform, turned with blanched cheek, and in a faltering voice, said :

"I surrender, sir, don't fire."

"Yes, sah, we gwinter gib up dis heah race."

The man who spoke last was getting up from the ground as he uttered the words, a look of smiling satisfaction on his face.

"I done tole Mars Henry way back yander dat it was mighty more skerry to run dan to stop and gib it up."

"Yes, you d—d black rascal, if you hadn't been so infernally slow, and had run as glibly as you talk, we could have escaped," said his companion, scowling fiercely. "Your smiling face shows how much you are afraid of the Yankees."

"Now, Mars Henry, you knows how much I wanted to go long wid de wagons, only a little way roun de bluff road dah, wid de odder niggers an de mules, an de hosses, an yer wouldn't lem me. but made dis nigger stay wid you and tote dese yere tings," holding up as he did so the colonel's sword and belt, and other impedimenta of which he had relieved himself in the race.

Quickly relieving the negro of his valuables and his master of his revolver, then turning the latter over to a file of soldiers, Clayton ordered the negro to guide him to the wagons, and to show the route the fleeing rebels had taken.

After a short, sharp ride the fleeing party were brought to a halt by the firing of the advance. Only a short skirmish ensued, when the guard of the enemy fled, and in a thick wood in an angle of the creek was found the train of over a hundred and fifty negroes, men, women and children, gathered from the neighborhood to be taken further south with the army, all huddled together with the horses, mules and provisions for a long journey. After a brief pursuit of the fleeing and discouraged enemy the spoils of war and freedom were sent back to Ball's Mills, where late in the evening the Union forces went into camp for the night.

CHAPTER L.

On the following morning Clayton obtained permission of General Lane to send the colony of negroes into Kansas, with all the stock, wagons, etc., etc.

"General Lane," said Clayton, " I want to keep trace of these fugitives so that at the proper time when the Government will permit, they may be armed, equipped and made soldiers of. There is splendid fighting material here," said he.

The general shook his head.

" I believe you are right," said he, after a pause, " but, our Government is not ready for such a radical innovation, and would suffer the rebellion to succeed rather than allow these sable sons to aid in its suppression. However, it can do no harm for you to carry out your idea of massing them together in Kansas. Indeed, it must do good, inasmuch as laborers are greatly needed, and these men will take the places of white men who would readily enlist if a substitute on the farm could be had."

And so it turned out that the colony went to Kansas and Gilbert returned as a body-servant to Lieutenant Clayton.

Shortly after this, information was received that the enemy were establishing a depot of supplies at Osceola, in Missouri, and from that point large quantities had already been distributed to other points.

General Lane decided to attack and destroy this depot. He moved quickly by night, and with break of dawn splinters of shot and shell rained on the unsuspecting citizens and garrison.

Fortunately the Confederate forces were so posted that neither the offensive nor defensive part of war put in jeopardy the lives of the innocent women and children. But the babble of voices, conflicting commands, swearing of men, blowing of trumpets, clash of arms, the cries and groans of frightened and dying men ; above which broke at short intervals the booming cannon and bursting shells, casting their lurid glare high in the heavens, made a terrifying combination, to which was soon added flames from the temporary barracks; so that a novice might have concluded that the crack of doom had indeed come.

Thus the battle raged for some hours, when the Confederates precipitately fled, leaving the town and such of its inhabitants as had not followed or preceded their defenders an easy and unresisting prey. At the close of the day, when the Union army was preparing to retreat, General Lane despatched an orderly to command the immediate presence of Lieutenant Clayton.

As he presented himself with the usual military salute, General Lane looked intently in the frank open face of the young officer, and said:

"You were up all last night, Lieutenant, and have slept none to-day."

"Yes, and 'no, General. Under the circumstances, I could not sleep if I would, and would not if I could."

"Good, I like that. Now tell me, are you fond of war, —bloodshed and carnage—shrieking women and children—burning homes and all the miseries attendant thereon?"

A shadow fell upon the young officer's face and he answered vehemently:

"No sir, I abhor it. The whole front and circumstance of war is harrowing to my soul, and nothing but the highest sense of duty could induce me to inflict such horror upon a fellow-man. I could have an arm taken off in the line of duty with a better grace."

"Give me your hand, Lieutenant," said the grizzled old general. "Now, Lieutenant, it is a military necessity that this town shall be burned, *utterly destroyed*, do you hear?—and I want it done as speedily and humanely as possible. Mingle no unkindness with the flame of your torch, but spare *nothing* which will afford protection, food or comfort to the enemy. That large storehouse of salt—I am at a loss how to dispose of it."

"You may leave that to me, General," answered Clayton, with a smile. "I'll see that it loses its savor. There is room on the top for a lot of whiskey, turpentine, coal-oil, tar and rosin lying now in the warehouse, which when fired will saturate the mass. Do you not think it will make a good combination? But, General,"—and the smile died out of his face, deep lines furrowing his forehead between the eyes—"there is a harder problem for me to solve ; how shall I resist the appeals of the poor women and children, who, having confidence in the honor, integrity and humanity of the old flag, and the brave officers and men who bear it aloft, have remained at home? In God's name, tell me that. How can I resist their pleadings that their homes be spared ?"

"Yes, it's hard, but, that is WAR," said the general, grimly. "Wrap about them the stars and stripes; help them to remove their household goods ; weep with them in kindly sympathy; but—destroy the houses, it must be so."

By the time the sun had set and the victorious army was well moved out of Osceola, Lieutenant Clayton, with his detachment of men, was busily engaged in piling high on the huge mass of salt all the combustibles at hand, which completed, he set about removing the goods from the various houses of such of the poor as would not believe destruction was imminent.

The piteous and heartrending appeals for home and shelter, the hardening of a heart naturally tender to such appeals, must be passed over in silence. It was too terrible. The memory is too harrowing.

And now the hour has come, as the shades of night draw nigh, for the lighting of the candles. And such huge tapers as Clayton and his little band did light! casting long spectral shadows as the men under his almost omnipresent and personal supervision helped the weeping women to take to places of safety such things as could be removed before the torch was applied.

Late at night, when the work of destruction had wellnigh subsided, then Clayton and his party, after knocking in the heads of barrels of whiskey, oil and tar resting on the mass of salt, touched a match and in an instant the whole roof of the huge structure seemed to lift high into the heavens, a living sheet of blood-red flame ; and the burning stream ran like fiery serpents in every direction. The very heavens were ablaze.

A few hours later, the conflagration having partly spent its fury, Clayton stood on an eminence overlooking not Osceola, but where that rebellious town was only yesternight in all her vaunted security and pride, where now shone only a vast assemblage of fire-flies, small luminaries winking 'neath their ashen brows at the colossal jack-o-lantern, or great central sun, seemingly destined to set the world on fire.

"Thus it was," soliloquized he, "that Sodom burned, and I wonder if the pillar of salt into which Lot's wife was turned could have been half as bright and beautiful as the many-colored columns of fire and smoke that shoot heavenward," as ever and anon a loud report of a bursting barrel of some combustible would send burning staves and cinders like meteors high above the blazing column, to be lost finally in outer darkness.

Turning his back on the sickening sight, where shelterless women and children hover around these smouldering mounds, Clayton sought General Lane's tent, where the army had gone into camp five miles from the city of ashes.

"General, your orders are obeyed," said he.

"You are pale, sir," said the commanding officer, looking at him intently for a moment.

"Yes, it is horrible work. I feel ten years older for those five hours of cruel destruction."

"Clayton, give me your hand," said the elder man. "I wanted that work done thoroughly as a man who loved such destruction would do it, and yet I wanted it divested of all unnecessary brutality, with one eye to obedience and the other eye on humanity's claims: I thank you. I think the order has been faithfully executed in spirit and in letter. Go get your breakfast, dinner and supper, and after that two nights' rest in one."

On the following morning, while the soldiers were busy with breakfast around their camp fires, Dick and Gilbert were seen standing apart in earnest conversation with a tall colored man dressed in homespun. He wore also a well-worn, high silk hat, his hands resting on a long, old-fashioned Kentucky rifle, as he talked, and by his side the faithful coon-dog which seemed to be an attentive auditor as he looked up in the faces of those men. After a time Dick approached Lieutenant Clayton and informed him there was a man who wanted to see him on important business.

"Lieutenant, 'dis yeres an ole feller-serbant of mine, whats jis left a big lot of darkies bout five or six miles from heah."

"Oh, Gilbert," interposed the other, "it's more'n dat, it's wellnigh on to eight miles eben if they stayed whar I lef em las night."

"What is your name," asked the lieutenant.

"My name, sah's, John Murray," and he took off the old hat which in size, color and length resembled a joint of stovepipe, at the same time bowing low and bringing the right foot backward with a long scrape as a mark of respect and submission. "An I come, Mars Lieutenant, to de Yankee army to see if enybody as wud like ter take in a big party of niggers what's all tucked in wagons wid mules and hosses, an dars precious few sogers wid em either, and deys skeered bad nuff to run away if a chestnut pop right loud at dey heels."

"In which direction from here, John, is this train?" asked the lieutenant.

"Oh, sah, it's jis off heah to de sunrise, and we kin trot dat mighty quick. Yes, sah, dey'll stay dah till de Yankee dun clean gone. Deys afeared to move les dey get kotcht by the Yankee cabalry. You see, Mars Lieutenant, deys tryin to get us niggers fudder souf and we don't keer to go; we's too far dat way now, bless yer."

When the march was resumed Lieutenant Clayton obtained permission of General Lane to make a detour from the direct line with his troop of cavalry, and under John Murray's skilful guidance the whole train of over a hundred negroes, thirty odd wagons and teams, were captured without any bloodshed. The few stragglers from the defeated army at Osceola, who were making a pretence of guarding the train, fled precipitately on the firing of the first gun.

Not a white man could be found in camp. "Every one on em gon'd, all dun run away, Mars Yankee," said an old white-headed man, who took the lead in emerging from a corral of negroes.

John Murray was soon espied, and a shout went up from the throng, and they literally lifted him off his horse and carried him to the wagons, singing and shouting "Hallelujah. Dis de Moses what com'd for the children ob Israel."

One of the old men who was next in importance to John Murray on this plantation, rode up by the side of Clayton on the march, and said:

"Mars Lieutenant, I'se got a ole oman an seven mighty likely boys an gals down heah on the plantation by de creek at Mars Lindsay's, I'd like monstrous well to tuck em along wid us ter freedom."

"Well, old man, what is your name," said Clayton.

"My name, sah, is Sam, an dey some times call me Uncle Sam, at you sarvice, Mars Lieutenant."

"Indeed, no, Uncle Sam, I am at your service, now more than before I knew you personally, and when I only served 'Uncle Sam's' cause."

Then drawing his sword Clayton with utmost formality saluted Uncle Sam, and bade him lead the way to where his wife and the seven boys could be found.

The white-haired old darkey looked in astonishment as he rode bare-headed by the officer's side, who finally explained that all the Yankee army served the United States, which was called Uncle Sam, which he enjoyed very much.

John Murray rode up and verified Uncle Sam's account of his family, adding that there were a number of other colored people on the same plantation who would like to go along "wid de army ob de Lord."

Crossing the creek at a ford near by, and after a sharp march of an hour or so, Clayton, with his detachment and colored guides, came to Colonel Lindsay's farm, and to their utter astonishment saw quite a body of cavalry in the barn-yard.

Skirmishers were deployed, who soon discovered the troops wore Uncle Sam's blue livery, and a shout of joy went up from both sides, who had been taken by surprise.

Lieutenant Clayton rode into the yard, where were standing several United States officers of a Wisconsin regiment, earnestly talking to a crowd of negroes of all ages. In the midst of the group stood old Colonel Lindsay, with his white hair flowing down on his shoulders, a kind and benevolent face, with a long staff for a cane in his hand. He was speaking earnestly to the slaves, who stood around listening attentively.

"You all know I have ever treated you kindly, and you have fared about as well as your master ; you have never been required to work when you were not able and were well fed and clad. If any of you are anxious to leave me you have the opportunity, for you can readily understand I cannot resist this armed force."

"Yes," said a large officer, wearing a captain's straps and uniform, " now is your time if you want your freedom ; pack up your traps and come right along. I am d—d if I leave a mother's son of you that don't want to stay. What say you, old man ? " he continued, as he approached a group of the negroes, who stood near where Clayton sat on his horse, a silent spectator.

"Mars Lindsay allus been kine to us, sah, and we doesn't want to leab him, sah."

"There, I told you so," chimed in the colonel. "All of these people prefer to stay with me rather than go with you."

"All right," said the captain. "I have offered you freedom and you choose to remain in slavery ; mount your men, Sergeant, and let us go on."

Clayton rode up and saluting, said :

"Captain, will you permit me to manage this affair ? "

"Certainly you may, Lieutenant. I have done with it, and you may take charge."

"Thanks, I'll see what I can do.—Colonel Lindsay, I believe," lifting his hat, as he dismounted and stood by the old patriarch. "My name is Clayton, and I have to ask that you'll step into the house. I want to talk to these negroes away from the presence of their master."

"No, Mr. Clayton, this is my yard, and these are my negroes, who have already decided to remain with me."

"All right, Colonel, I simply wanted to spare you the painful sight of their being forced to leave you, and take all the available horses, teams and provisions on the plantation."

"My God! you are not going to rob me, are you? Here's my purse, sir, but spare these people."

"Keep your purse, Colonel Lindsay, that's trash; we want negroes and horses for Uncle Sam," and without waiting for further reply he mounted; then drawing his sword he rode among the negroes, commanding with a threatening attitude :

"Each and every one of you pack up in a hurry whatever of clothing and other effects you have, and leave here in half an hour. Some of you hitch up those horses, mules and wagons; get together provisions to last a month now, and don't be long about it. Come now, quick, we have only a few moments."

Then such bustling around, with faces intended to be long and sad, but shining through the very thin mist was the silent joy that like a deep stream ever runs quietly to the haven of repose.

Colonel Lindsay stood mute with astonishment, and the tears ran down his cheeks as he saw evidences of gladness, not grief, in the faces of those people who were now under the sword compelled to do that which they had refused when invited. The women in the house pleaded with those to remain who had grown up under their charge in vain.

"Bless yer life, missus, ef dat man whats got dat knife whats longer dan a fence-rail, will only lem me stay den I will. But you des see him out dar like a wild sabbage, jis swarin' all ob us got to go, and I'se afeard, I is."

To all appeals Clayton was deaf, and the uniform answer was : "No, ladies, these people must go to Kansas and taste the sweets of freedom; then if they want to come back they will be privileged to do so, but go they must, and that now,"

Captain Sampson stood amazed at the alacrity with which the negroes obeyed the command to march to freedom, and when the caravan was under way, he asked old Uncle Pete who rode along with a smiling face through which shone a deep joy:

"How is it, Uncle, that you refused my entreatry and obeyed so willingly the lieutenant's command?"

"Well, yer see, sah, de old mars he stays dar looking on, an he see de nigger ob his own will gwine away, an ef he eber kotch him agin it go jes' as hard on the bare back wid de cat es ef he run away in de night on de undergroun road. An ef yer come at a nigger wid freedom, stickin' on de pint ob a sword, like dat mad lieutenant jis now, and say, 'Heah, nigger, open yer mouf an tuck dis, or I cut yer head off,' den ole mars feel sorry for us, an ef he kotched me agin he knowed de nigger could not help hesef."

"Dat's a fac," put in Uncle Sam, who had been listening to the conversation; "an den again I'se offen heard de ole missus say t'want good manners to say to de gess what at de table: 'Won't yer like some ob de nice presarbs what I'se got in de pantry?—mighty nice jelly an jam and pound-cake, too, ef yer'd like some.' No, sah, jis plump de good tings down on de plate right afore you an say, 'Take dis, now; it's good for you, an don't make fuss 'bout it needer. Now, dat's de way de mars lieutenant whats comin yonder does wid freedom; he got de bes kind er manners. He gibs you taste ob it first, an den ax yer how yer like him, eh, Uncle Pete?"

"Dat's a fac, Uncle Sam," responded the old man.

Clayton rode up, and Captain Sampson went forward with him, leaving the two old darkies to talk over the prospects of freedom, that now seemed assured after so many years of slavery, with scarcely a spark of hope to break the thick cloud that had hedged them about from birth and promised them a winding-sheet in death.

CHAPTER LII.

THE news of Claude's arrest, which Clayton had learned from his prisoner the morning of the battle at Drywood, was true. Confirmation of the story soon reached him. Duvall had been aiding the escape of a slave woman, it was said, near Independence, Missouri, and was now kept there awaiting safe conduct to the penitentiary at Jefferson City.

On the arrival of the command at Kansas City, Clayton obtained permission from General Lane to attempt his rescue, and with a detachment of cavalry, made a night march, reaching Independence at daylight. In a few minutes he had surrounded the town, the jailer was a prisoner, and Duvall found himself in the arms of his friend and deliverer.

"My God! you are like to an angel from heaven to deliver me from this place!" exclaimed he, gratefully embracing Clayton.

"Why, old fellow, you are a skeleton! How long have you been in this foul den?" he asked, looking around with a shudder. "Come out into the sunlight and let me get you something to eat. You look as if you were starved."

Claude was so utterly broken down by many months of suffering in mind and body, that he could not stand the sudden revulsion of feeling in finding himself a free man, and safe with the friend he adored. He covered his face and sobbed like a child.

Leaving the jailer and citizens to wonder as to where the force came from or whither it tended, the pickets and sentinels posted were called in, and the line of march for Kansas City resumed by a different route than the one by which they came.

They had not ridden very far when a messenger on horseback met them and inquired for Lieutenant Clayton.

"I am Lieutenant Clayton," was the answer, extending his hand for the dispatch in the hand of the orderly, and quickly tearing open the paper. His face changed as he read. With a deep frown and compressed lips, he handed the paper to his companion, saying, "Duvall, read that."

"An officer from General Sturgis is on his way to meet you with orders to return all slaves and other property to their rightful owners; Kansas is a safer place than Missouri for these people. See that you have none of them in your command when this order is received.

"L."

"What are you going to do?" asked Claude.

Not seeming to hear the question Clayton ordered the train to be turned off from the main road into one less frequented. Then he said :

"Claude you must take care of these people; I will give you a small detachment of soldiers. Get them safely into Kansas—to Lawrence, if possible."

Hastily saying farewell, he pressed on with his column of cavalry.

About a half hour later the staff officer bearing General Sturgis' order came in sight. He was a lieutenant of the Regular Army, and in parade uniform. He was accompanied in great state by a guard of troopers, and at their heels were a half-dozen or more aggrieved slave-owners, who had come to claim their property.

Clayton properly measured the swelling importance of the young officer, and was saying inwardly, "I'll make short work of this young 'fuss and feathers.'"

Bowing courteously, he said, after reading the order :

"Certainly, if these gentlemen will point out what property here belongs to them, I shall assuredly return it. Look for yourselves, gentlemen."

It is needless to say, they did *not* find what they sought.

Disappointed and angry, one of them said with an insolent defiance :

"Were you at Independence this morning?"

Clayton said very gravely : "I must decline, sir, to answer any questions concerning my duty here."

"Oh, you may answer the gentleman's question," interposed the pompous little second-lieutenant, "it is a perfectly proper one."

Clayton turned and looked at him for a moment in silence, then said :

"Of course I understand that I *may* do so, but I do not choose to comply."

The young lieutenant looked as if he were about to burst with rage and astonishment.

"The devil you don't," he blurted out. "Well, I am a member of General Sturgis' staff, and I *command* you to answer."

"And I decline," said Clayton, "to receive orders from a subordinate," and as he said this he threw back the corner of his military cape, revealing one bar too many for the young braggart. "Besides," continued Clayton, eyeing him as if not yet through with him, "besides, I hold my commission direct from the President of the United States."

Then turning to the men who looked as crestfallen as their leader, he said :

"Since we have nothing here belonging to you, gentlemen, I shall go on at once," and instantly the bugle sounded "Forward," and the interview was ended.

But there was to be a sequel to the episode.

Soon after arriving in camp and whilst Clayton was reporting to General Lane the result of his expedition, an officer came in with an order from General Sturgis placing Lieutenant Clayton under arrest for disobedience of orders.

"This is the officer you seek," said General Lane, turning to Lieutenant Clayton, who was sitting near by and handing him the order to read.

When he had finished General Lane said quietly, "Lieutenant Clayton, you will give me your sword and consider yourself under arrest with the liberty of the camp, which includes the city."

Clayton unbuckled his belt and handed his sword to General Lane, who smiling said :

"We will have a court-martial to-morrow and the matter inquired into."

Then turning to the aid in attendance, he said, with mock solemnity and military air :

"Captain, you will report to General Sturgis that his order has been executed and that I will communicate further with him in writing."

Then with a formal salute the captain took his leave.

On the following day a court-martial was convened and Lieutenant Clayton duly arraigned and pleaded not guilty. The Judge Advocate proceeded to read General Sturgis' order, and put on the witness-stand the pompous second-lieutenant, who when cross-questioned by Clayton, who conducted his own defence aided by Colonel Anthony, admitted that every facility was afforded him and the aggrieved slave-holders to find their property and that none such could be found in the command. Witnesses were introduced to prove that Lieutenant Clayton had, on that morning, broken open the jail at Independence, Missouri, and taken therefrom a prisoner convicted of a heinous crime and also robbed the plantations of several citizens of Missouri of fifteen or twenty valuable negroes, several teams, horses, mules, provisions, etc., which were a part of his command in the morning.

"I protest, may it please the Court," said Clayton, "against the introduction of this testimony before this Court, as not being pertinent to the charge of disobedience of General Sturgis' order which has been read to this honorable Court. As you are aware, neither the charge nor any of the several specifications allude to the subject on which this testimony is sought to be introduced. If I am guilty of disobedience or transcending orders on this expedition, I am accountable to General Lane, under whose orders I was acting up to the moment I received the order from General Sturgis, which forms the basis of the charges preferred against me. I ask this honorable Court to rule out this testimony and consider only such as will tend to show whether or not the property alluded to in General Sturgis' order was under my control or in my custody at the time when this order reached me; and whether or not I showed a disposition to respect and execute that order as coming from my superior officer in the military service. If other testimony than the prosecuting witness be needed to prove that the order was complied with to the letter, I have it at hand. You will see that I am required to turn over to these aggrieved parties such slaves and other property as may be with or attached to my command. If it is not shown that I refused compliance, then I ask acquittal at your hands, and on that I rest my case."

The court was cleared for consideration of the protest, which resulted speedily in ruling out the testimony offered, and the Judge Advocate having no other testimony, Lieutenant Clayton was acquitted without further formality, and by General Lane placed on duty with his command.

CHAPTER LIII.

CLAUDE returned in a few days and reported his mission safely accomplished. The negroes were now on free soil in Kansas.

Now that the two friends were united once more, it was Clayton's determination to keep Claude as near him as possible.

"How would you like a lieutenancy in my company?" asked he.

Duvall's face beamed.

"There is a vacancy. Wilcox has been obliged to resign on account of ill-health."

And so it came about that Claude found himself in the uniform of an officer of the Army of the United States, and threw himself, with all the ardor of his temperament, into the conflict.

"Ah! You all seem like Italians," he said to Clayton; "it makes me to love your countrymen, to see such a splendid courage, such bravery. *Mon Dieu*, it is a country worth sacrifice! But then, my friend, one need not be reckless; it is enough to be brave, but why shall one go always into the place most dangerous? You do not right, my dear Clayton; you ask always for this post of danger or that—you make nothing of your life—and you have no right to do this."

As Clayton was leaving General Lane's quarters in the afternoon of his acquittal by the court-martial, he met Dick, accompanied by a man too near white to be called a negro, and yet so dark as to be a questionable white man. He was one of those squarely-built, heavy-set men, reminding one of the cube. No matter what happens he is always the same height, same proportion, indeed come good or ill he is always right side up. His face, like his form, was square, with deep-set eyes which beamed with intense brightness like great lamps in a cavern, overhung with great shaggy brows; and a chin and mouth in perfect keeping with his entire make up. With broad-brimmed

black hat, his huge form loosely draped in a suit of butternut jeans, he moved with the easy strength of a colossal
engine.

"Why, Dick," exclaimed Clayton—"You here? I
thought you were in Lawrence."

"Well, yer see, Mars Frank," explained Dick; "this
here man's name is Dan Dickson, an so he tole me he's
got a wife an three children jis across the river here an he
has rund over to see if he can find anybody what 'll dar
go an bring um to Kansas an not let em go back 'cept
they take all hands dead. An I tole him what you'd
done for me, an that you kinder use to help Captain
Brown an sometimes the captain had ter help you in this
business, an he said at once I mus cum rite along an
help him plead wid you to get his folks away.—An now
Dan," said Dick, turning to this man, who stood the while
with uncovered head, looking intently at the lieutenant
who, though listening to Dick in his earnest appeal, was
none the less studying the strange-looking man before
him. He was wondering how such a combination of
physical and mental force could be kept in slavery for a
day; to say nothing of the nearly half century this man
had evidently passed under the yoke.

"It is like seeing a lion held in leading-strings by
children," mused he, "unconscious that one stroke of his
mighty paw would annihilate the beings who hold him."

There was a native strength and dignity about the man,
which impressed Clayton powerfully.

"Put on your hat, Dan," said he, unwilling to receive
the homage of this Titan. "What's your other name,
Dan?"

"Well, sah," said Dan, speaking for the first time, and
his voice like the rest of him had the characteristics of the
cube. "My ole mars' name was Lucas an lived in Washington, District of Columbia, where I were born, sah, but
dey allus call me Dan Webster, sah. Caws he, dat mighty
man, sah, used to kinder take some notice ob me, when he
come to see Mars Lucas, and he make me bring him drink
of water, say he's goin to buy me some ob dese days, an
have a plantation of his own. An they call me Dan
Webster an so it stuck to me ever sence. Then Mars
Lucas he died, and Miss Mary she married Mr. Dickson
of Missouri, jis across the river heah, an so we moved to

the ole plantation, where my wife an the childern are
now, waitin an spectin me jis any night to drop down,
pick em up and fly away wid em."

As he ran on with this family recital Clayton was watching the man's face.

"Extraordinary!" he exclaimed. "Positively extraordinary—Dan, you are well named. Do you know you are
the living image of that great statesman?"

But Dan was thinking about the dusky family across
the river and ingeniously showing "Mars Clayton how
very easy it would be to get a small boat—then on the
other side turn to your left till you cum to the branch——"

"Well," said Clayton, good-naturedly, "Come along—
we'll see what can be done. I'm going to take you in to
see General Lane. But, listen to me. I have a particular reason for wishing you to keep on your hat for a
moment after we enter."

"But, Mars Clayton," gasped Dan, in horror. "Whar'll
he think my manners is gon ter."

"No matter, do as I tell you," laughed Clayton.

On entering, Lieutenant Clayton said:

"General Lane, allow me to introduce Daniel Webster,
who comes on an important mission in which your good
offices are solicited."

The general turned his eyes in the direction indicated,
and Clayton amused himself by watching the look of
amazement which spread over his face. Then turning to
Clayton, he said:

"Who is this? What does it mean?"

"Take off your hat, Dan," said Clayton, and there he
stood the absolute double, or *alter ego* of the man for whom
he was named.

"Well," said the general, "that is the most extraordinary resemblance I ever beheld. Why, positively, the fellow frightened me. Who is he? and what does he want?"

"Just what we all want in this world, General, to have
those he loves near to him. His family are just across
the river yonder, and I think I might——"

"That'll do," said the general, with a warning gesture.
"That'll do. No matter about the details. Remember, I
know nothing about it. Do you hear? Nothing whatever.
You see your friend Sturgis might want to know something
about it, too," added he, a humorous twinkle in his eye. "I

leave Daniel Webster in your hands, Lieutenant, and—oh, by the way, you needn't report to me before nine o'clock to-morrow morning."

About ten o'clock that night four men in citizens' clothes passed through the lines, and went rapidly down the river-bank where were moored two old-fashioned dugouts or canoes. They paddled across the river, and quietly made their way up the bank for some distance, then turning to the left, struck off across the country for a mile or so. A turn in the road brought them directly in front of a large house, the black outline of which was all that could be discerned in the darkness.

"That's Mars Dickson's house," whispered Dan. "An you see that clump of trees over yonder, that's where I lives. I'll jist slip round to the back an git inter the winder—cause Mars Dickson, he keeps his shot-gun loaded an it's mity close to my front door, too."

"Where are the horses?" said Clayton, prudently whispering as Dan had done.

"They's in the barn over there," said Dan, pointing, "an it'll be mity ticklish bizness gittin em out, too."

"The boys will look after that," said Clayton, reassuringly. "You go in the cabin and get your family safely out. We'll see to the rest."

Going back to where the other two men stood, there was a short whispered conference; then Clayton followed the path he had seen Dan take toward the group of trees indicated by him.

A faint light glimmered somewhere within. The window was open, and it was evident Dan had mounted a chicken-coop beneath it and thus gotten inside of his own domicile.

Clayton stood waiting silently and breathlessly, dreading lest some sounds should come from the barn, from which the men were removing the horses preparatory to the flight. But he was satisfied they were moving skilfully, as not a sound broke the stillness. Presently a head cautiously appeared at the window.

"You there, Mars Lieutenant?"

"All right," whispered Clayton.

Dan lowered first a bundle, cautiously, then one child, then the mother with still another in her arms climbed down upon the chicken-coop, Clayton speeding her movements from below and Dan helping her as he followed behind. Just as it was all accomplished, an unluckly touch from Dan turned the button, and down came the sash with a crash.

All stood perfectly still for a minute, then hearing nothing, started fast as feet could carry them toward the barn.

At the distance of a hundred yards they were compelled to emerge from cover, and as they came in sight there was a flash and a loud report from the house, followed closely by another, and the buckshot went whistling through the air all around them. The babe in the mother's arms gave one terrified scream, but was soon quieted by her soothing voice. Clayton drew his revolver and fired several shots at three men, whom he could distinguish at the door; then Dick and the other two men fired also.

Dan mounted a horse, and with his wife behind him and a child clasped by one arm, dashed swiftly away, saying, "Follow me, Mars Clayton. Mars Dickson he'll go cross the hill on foot soon's he finds the horses done gone, and try to git to the crossing fust. You'll have to be mity spry." And on he rushed, with his family clinging to him on all sides. It was a desperate dash for freedom.

Once out of range of the shot-guns, they took it more easily, knowing there were no more horses with which to pursue them, and that they were safe until they met at the ferry, where as Dan said, Dickson would certainly try to head them off.

It was just before dawn that they came in sight of the river. The boats were waiting for them. Daniel placed his wife in the bow of the canoe, she still holding the sleeping child in her arms. He then passed the rope halter of the horse he had ridden to the men, with instructions to hold on and let the horse swim by the boat. Then jumping in the stern, he pushed off, and Daniel led the horse he had ridden. The other members of the party took the other canoe. Clayton plunging his horse in rode over on his back, whilst the other horses were led alongside. They had only gotten well into the rapid current when the loud report of a gun was heard, and the buckshot splashed ominously in the water around the boat. Clayton drew his revolver and responded to the fire, as did the other members of the party. The horse led by the boy plunged, and came near upsetting the boat as he strained on the rope by which he was led, and which had served as a bridle also.

"We done git away from dose shot-guns, and now it seems like we's goin ter be drownded," said Dan's wife, whose courage was wellnigh exhausted. "Why didn't you leab tings alone? We wuz cumftable enuff," said she.

"Now, Molly," said Dan, "don't you go and lose your sperrit. We've got through the wust of it. We're safe as if we wuz home in our own cabin now. Dose shot-guns may fire away, but dey can't reach you now, honey."

And sure enough, the shot were falling far short of the fast receding boats.

Dan's words had the desired effect. Molly began to watch the proceedings with interest.

"Take care dar, Charley," said she. "Doan pull so hard on de rope; yers chokin ole Balley—kotch him by de mane—dare now!"

Dan was delighted at the proof of reviving spirits.

"He can help to row us across," said he, his white teeth glistening in the dim light, and the old horse literally served as more than one horse-power to carry the boat across.

At last the opposite shore was reached. Again the party was mounted somewhat as before, and proceeded toward camp.

At daylight they came in sight of a little structure. Scarcely a house—but a shelter occupied temporarily by some Indians, on Kansas soil, and Dan was informed that he and his were now free and beyond the reach of slavery.

"I think we had better stop here," said Clayton. "We can get some coffee, perhaps, and, at all events, can rest for a couple of hours."

"'Clare to goodness," said Molly, "ef I ain't so stiff I can't hardly move. You take baby, Dan. She's done been mity quiet."

"Yes," said Dan, beaming with satisfaction; "and it's

mighty fortunate, Molly, for she mighter given a sight er trubble by makin a fuss."

The father took the sleeping child and laid it down carefully, then coming back for the rest.

"For goodness' sake! Whar dis yere blood come from?" said he, looking in puzzled wonder at his hands and then at his clothes.

"Must er come from some whar," said Molly, looking about. All joined in the search but found nothing and she stooped and picked up the baby.

"Now I tink yer don sleep enuf, honey, and you bes have some brekfus."

She saw something on the wraps about the child which hushed her crooning speech. She uncovered the liule face; then giving a wild shriek, she let the baby fall from her arms. The child was dead with a bullet hole through the heart.

A little grave was dug in a sheltered corner, and as the sun mounted up toward the zenith a band of sympathizers stood about it.

"Radder all ub us died in slabery wid Mars Dickson dan to hab dis lamb murdered," moaned the mother.

Dan's eyes were moist with tears, too; but he said: "No, Molly; don't say dat. How kin we tell what might er come to dis chile ef she'd bin took off Souf long wid Mars Dickson. De Lord he led us dis way, an we mussen be ongrateful an grudge him dis lamb."

Dick's heart was much touched by the incident, and to comfort Dan he told him during the afternoon on their march to Lawrence about his own troubles—how wife and child, too, were taken away, and how much easier it would have been to have laid them both in the quiet earth than to have suffered these years of uncertainty about their fate.

"*What* you say her name is? Martha?"

"Yes; Martha Stanley. Why, Dan, what makes you look so?"

"Well, I clare to goodness!" said Dan. "I knows her. Yes, sah. I knows her—an—I seen her, nigh about six weeks ago."

Dick seized his friend by the shoulder. "Dan, for de Lord's sake, you know where my wife is—tell me. Oh, has the good Lord——"

" Why, don go on like dat, man," said Dan. " Jess be still, an I'll tell yer. Yer see it's jess dis way," and he crossed his legs and settled into a comfortable attitude. " *Her* missus"—marking off on his fingers with deliberation—" is sister to *my* missus, Mars Dickson's wife, an last month—was it ? No, I reckon 'twas month afore lass, Miss Hall, she come up to see her sister, up to our place, an brung along Martha for lady's maid, coz Martha she mighty nice bout doin up hair an all dat ; so *she* cum along too—an——"

" Dan, for God's sake tell me, where is she ? "

" Lor, how can *I* tell whar she is in *dese* times ! Dey been fightin rite on her Missus' plantation nigh to Independence an I spec thur ain't much fixin hair an sech fine doins *now*, for Miss Hall, she done clare out may be."

"Well, where do you suppose Martha is ? "

" *I* dunno," said Dan. She mout be took off down Souf, an den agin she mouten."

There was not much comfort in all this, and yet Dick felt that he had been nearer to her than at all ; in fact, six weeks ago, she had been within ten miles of him. He carried his strange news and his rekindled hopes to his new master, Duvall, and, of course, to Lieutenant Clayton.

" Keep up your courage, Dick," said the latter. " We'll find your wife and child ; keep a sharp lookout among the refugees, and some day you'll see them safe and happy."

Lieutenant Duvall, however, had his own plans about the matter, but kept quiet as to the time and manner of putting them into execution.

CHAPTER LIV.

General Lane had received information at headquarters in Fort Scott, Kansas, of the presence of a detachment of Price's army in Bates County, Missouri, engaged in recruiting and harassing the people. Colonels Montgomery and Johnson were ordered, each with a detachment of cavalry, to make a night march and surprise this camp at early dawn on the following day.

At three A. M., on a cool, starlight night, the column halted, and a group of officers held a consultation as to the best mode of attack. It was decided to make this simultaneously, at the faintest dawn of day, from two opposite points, each under the command of its colonel.

As the men were separating, Colonel Johnson took Clayton by the hand and said:

"I am sorry, Lieutenant Clayton, you are not going with me, for old Kentucky's sake; I would have been glad of your support."

"Thanks, Colonel Johnson," answered Clayton; "I should have been glad to go with you, but you saw Colonel Montgomery made it a point to have my command with him."

"All right, Lieutenant, see that you do not arrive a day after the feast and find the banquet-hall deserted."

"No fear of that," said Clayton. "I'm not apt to be late in keeping such engagements."

He did not sleep at all that night but, with his command mounted, was waiting impatiently for the first gray streaks of coming day, when there rung out on the still morning air the report of a rifle, from the direction of the enemy's camp. Then, another—and another—in quick succession, until volley succeeded volley; and Clayton dashed forward with his company, under the spur, followed by Colonel Montgomery and the rest of the command.

"By Heavens!" said Clayton, "he has commenced the attack before the dawn! What does that mean?"

Then, as he divined the ungenerous purpose to deprive Colonel Montgomery's command from participation in the engagement, he had a key to Colonel Johnson's parting injunction to be "not a day after the feast," and he said to himself, with a bitter smile, "Ah, Colonel, your towering ambition to do alone, and claim for yourself the honors intended for two, may prove a dangerous experiment sooner or later."

When the first streaks of day shone on the eastern horizon Clayton's troops went dashing down a ravine leading to heavy timber to the southward, the point where Colonel Montgomery's command was to have been when the attack opened, and just in time to intercept the enemy's rear guard, or retreating rear of the enemy. A brief skirmish—the capture of a few prisoners—and a short pursuit of the main force into the timber, and Colonel Montgomery's force returned to the enemy's abandoned camp, held by Colonel Johnson's command. One of the first objects Colonel Montgomery and Clayton saw, as they rode side by side, was the dead body of Colonel Johnson lying where it fell, pierced by the enemy's bullets, as he led the charge into the very heart of the enemy's camp.

"He was brave," said the colonel, looking at his dead comrade, "brave, but rash."

"And ungenerous," was Clayton's unspoken thought.

Late in the afternoon of this same day Clayton entered his tent. Duvall was there awaiting him, having been on the sick list and unable to accompany the expedition.

"*Mon Dieu!* what is happen to you? You look like you are ill."

"Duvall, get me some brandy, please," said Clayton, falling, rather than sitting, on the chair near him.

His friend hastened to pour out a wineglass of spirits, which Clayton drank without opening his eyes.

"Now, some color come in your face," said Duvall, watching him.

Clayton opened his eyes and looked at his friend.

"Duvall, I have had a horrible duty to perform, and have just come from reporting to General Lane. I should resign,—yes, I know I should resign—if I thought I should ever again have to do such a thing. Sit down, and I will try to tell you. As we were coming home— and, by the way, you know Colonel Johnson was shot?"

Duvall nodded, and Clayton went on. "Well, just as we started to return to Fort Scott our scouts brought in nine prisoners.

"'Clayton,' said Colonel Montgomery, turning to me, 'I think these men will come under Fremont's order.'

"'How is that, sir?' I answered.

"'Why, his order to try guerrillas by drum-head court martial, if found carrying arms.'

"'But, Colonel, these men declare that they are on detached service from Price's command and are not guerrillas at all.'

"He turned upon me evidently annoyed, and said:

"'*That*, sir, will be determined at the court martial I shall convene at once.'

"Which was done, and held, then and there, as we sat in our saddles. I was terribly excited, I confess, and perhaps spoke more warmly than was my right. But, my God! there stood those nine men imploring—pleading—declaring by all they held sacred that they were Confederate soldiers. And, would you believe it, I was the only one who befriended them. The decision was announced and sentence passed in less time than I am taking to tell you—to be executed as soon as the soldiers could dig a trench to put the poor wretches in. My dear fellow," turning to Claude, "I shall have to ask you to give me some more brandy." After a moment he went on.

"Thinking I was their friend and their only hope, in desperation they clung around me, with such harrowing appeals—such faces—my God, shall I ever forget!" and he covered his face as if to shut it out.

"The colonel saw this, and turning to me, he said coolly:

"'Lieutenant Clayton, you will detail the firing party, and see that the order of the court is executed at once.'

"Think of the malignancy of selecting *me* to execute this order! And I believe he hoped I would disobey him—and you know what that means in these times and in the enemy's country. I have long felt that man's secret hostility to me. My God! I believe I would have sacrificed all hope of meeting the woman I love, in this world or the next, to have saved those men who were clinging in despair to my stirrups and bridle. But I tried to remember I was a soldier, and not a man with a heart.

"I said : 'Men, there is no hope. The order must be carried out. Prepare yourselves to die bravely as you can, like soldiers.'

"Then I rode away while the horrible preparations were being made.

"When I returned, a half-hour later, they were calm. Some had written words of farewell to their loved ones; and I received tokens and keepsakes from their cold trembling hands, with piteous appeals that they be sent, and so they were, a few hours later, by a prisoner who luckily escaped when no one was looking.

"At the command, all kneeled on the brink of that long grave, and the fatal order was given by the sergeant in charge of the firing party. All were shot, some dead ; but not without a second volley, and with the use of the sabre were the nine hearts stilled. I know not how, for my eyes refused their office, and I only seemed to see a great blank spread out before me.

"In less than two hours from the capture, nine men, still warm in death, lay under the cold clods of earth on the prairie, and the accursed work was done. And this is the nineteenth century," added Clayton with bitterness.

"And I, with instincts of humanity almost morbidly developed,—I have been the instrument of this horror. My God! War is more cruel to the living than to the dead."

CHAPTER LV

THE next morning as the two friends were at breakfast the orderly brought the mail. There were two letters for Clayton; one from his cousin Kate, and another from Petrel. The one from Kate was as follows:

" MY DEAR FRANK :

"Your letter is most welcome. I am glad that this wretched war has served some good purpose and that you are happier than when you visited us last year, upon your return from California. My heart sometimes rebelliously asks: Why are these sufferings laid upon us? Why is life made so hard when it might be so beautiful? But you are brave and strong, and I am confident, however thwarted in your wishes, will be able to make it rich and abundant in fulfilment.

" I did not intend to speak of these things, having, in fact, sat down to write you upon another and most agreeable subject—that is, your little ward Petrel. I want your consent to have her visit us during the coming holidays. My little Katrine and she are, as you know, frequent correspondents, and I am in love with the child without having seen her. Her letters are enchanting—so brimming with humor and delicate sense of everything her pen touches. How did such a flower blossom within the walls of a convent? And how does she know so much, having seen so little? Katrine was inconsolable that she could not make us the pormised visit last year; so now, I want you to promise that she shall come to us when the roses bloom.

" We are not a very gay household, with Bernard in the army and all the terrors and uncertainties of this horrible war. But Petrel will not miss the gayeties and I am sure will be happy with us. She writes that she is engaged in hospital work much of the time, with the good Sisters. What an experience for such a child! It has fired Katrine with a desire to do something in that way herself; but she has to be content to make bandages and scrape lint at home, which we all do, as you may imagine, to dress the wounds made by your dreadful Federal bullets! Ah, my dear Frank,—to fight with natural enemies is bad enough, but to have them of your own household! Well, you and I could not be arrayed against each other whatever happens, and you know how *I* felt about that wicked secession!

"Let me hear from you very soon that the dear child may come to

"Your ever-loving cousin,

"KATE. "

"Incomparable, steadfast Kate!" said Frank to himself as he folded the letter. "Yes, Petrel shall go to her."

Then he broke the other seal, and read this:

"MY DEAR UNCLE FRANK:

"I have had such a sweet letter from Katie's mamma. How lovely she must be! And why did *I* not have such a mamma? What it must be—but—no matter—no repinings. Have I not the dearest of uncles? And are not the Sisters good as angels? Well, to return, Mrs. Fletcher urges me to make the visit which my stupid illness cheated me out of last year; and if you say I may go— why—I think I shall be happier—well—happier than anyone has a right to be, with such a dreadful war going on, and with pain and suffering and death all about us. But, then, you know, dear Uncle, I have seen so little, and am wondering,—wondering,—all the time about that bright, strange world beyond these walls. And now, if you are *very* good, and say I may go, I shall see—and I shall see my friend Katrine, to whom I have been writing all these years.

"Alas! I *have* seen something beyond these walls. But, oh, it is so sad! But do not object, dear Uncle, to my going to the hospital with the Sisters; it does me good, I know it does, to realize what others suffer; then my own little pains and repinings seem so foolish, I am ashamed of them.

"I enclose a little sketch which I hope may please you. I enjoyed doing it; but not so much, I think, as my music.

Ah, that is my chief joy! And perhaps when I get out into that distant world I may hear some of those wonderful things played and sung that I sometimes read about in the papers you send.

"Your fond and loving
"Petrel."

"What a child she is!" said Clayton, laying down the letter and taking the water-color sketch to examine.

"Duvall," said he, "what do you think of that?"

Claude took it and looked critically at the paper.

"What do I think?" he said. "Why, I think that is the work of a true artist. Look at that distance—at that sky."

"Well, that is the work of Petrel, my ward," said Clayton with pride.

"Eempossible! Eempossible!" said the enthusiastic Claude. "Ah! no! You mistake—that ees *not* the work of a child."

Clayton, smiled sadly. "She is getting beyond childhood, Duvall. I was astonished when I saw her last. She is a woman,—a beautiful woman; she is not more than fifteen, but she looks two years older. It does not seem possible," he said, musing, "that she is the little creature I held in my arms fourteen, yes, nearly fifteen, years ago."

"Well, I am surprised, much surprised," said Claude, still gazing at the sketch. "I have thought always about this being a leettle child—*comme ça*, like zat"—and he held up his hand to show how tall he had fancied her.

"And so she was when you and I first met; but, my dear fellow, as we have been knocking about the world she has been growing—behind those convent walls. And she is so clever in everything, so gifted," said Clayton, as he strode to and fro in the tent, "that, I tell you, Duvall, I feel the weight of the responsibility in guiding this young creature."

"It was well you place her in that convent—so safe. 'Tis dreadful to see the young girls in this countree—such freedom—such dangers! Ah, you did well."

At that moment Dick, the most respectful and punctilious of servants, burst into the tent without knocking, and out of breath with excitement.

" Excuse me, Mars Frank and Mars Duvall, but she's foun—Martha's foun. Dan, he's foun where Miss Hall is livin—not more an about ten miles from here."

"Well, my good fellow, I am rejoiced. I'll arrange to make a call upon that good lady and you may depend upon our bringing your wife safely away."

The next morning an early start was made for the plantation, with a force large enough to overcome any resistance from Livingstone's Guerrillas, whom they learned were in the vicinity of Independence, Missouri. Dan acted as guide, and presently pointed out a large white farmhouse as the object of their search.

Lieutenant Duvall was in charge of the expedition, and, in the midst of the curiosity and excitement caused by the arrival of the troops, ascended the steps of the porch, and quietly asked to see " Mees Hall," his orderly standing respectfully near him as he awaited the coming of the lady.

Presently Miss Hall appeared, flushed and with ill-concealed nervousness. She did not ask him to enter, but said, with an attempt at frigid composure :

" To what am I indebted for this visit ? "

Lieutenant Duvall, in his most deferential manner, told her in his broken English that they had come to find a colored woman named Martha Fletcher ; that they understood that she was there, and he desired to restore her to her husband, from whom she had been stolen many years before.

The shapely face, which would, under some circumstances, have been wreathed with smiles of welcome for this interesting foreigner, grew more and more frigid in its lines as he went on.

"Then I am to understand you wish to purchase my maid," she said, at last, " and that you have come with all this military display to make me an offer for her."

" *Certainement*," said Claude, with a twinkle of amusement in his eyes, as he drew a Confederate note out of his pocket, " if you will do me ze honor to accept a note which I will copy after zat," pointing to the words, " to be paid one year after the establishment of the Southern Confederacy."

She turned scarlet, and then white with anger. " I do not wish to part with my servants upon any terms," she said, " and now, if you'll excuse me, I will——"

"Pardon, mademoiselle, I have a duty to perform, and I hope I shall not be compelled to use ze force you see here. But your servants have ze right now to go or to stay. Eef Martha prefer to stay with you, madame, certainement she shall do so. I wish to see her, and we will ask her what she will do."

"Your insolence is as great as your cruelty," said the exasperated woman. "How dare you come into my house and demand my servants? Have I not suffered enough already from—" And here she broke down with hysterical weeping.

Of course, there had been plenty of witnesses of this scene, all the servants hovering curiously and furtively about the porch.

Dick, according to the lieutenant's instructions, was just outside the grounds with the soldiers. Suddenly there was a cry and a wild rush from the house. A woman was seen flying, with the speed of a bird, toward Dick, and in another moment they were locked in each other's arms.

Miss Hall's sobs were arrested, and she sprang to her feet as she saw the flying woman, crying, "Come back, come back, Martha, this instant!"

"I tink, madame, my question ees answered. Ze maid will go back wiz her husband." Then turning to his orderly, he said: "Tell the men to bring over the trunk that you report found in the barn."

With an hysterical scream, Miss Hall came rapidly toward him. "Would you rob me before my face?"

In the blandest way Duvall explained that her silver would not feed or clothe his soldiers, and instead of aiding would demoralize their cause; and, advising her not to risk such valuables by keeping them hidden in the barn, had the trunk safely deposited in the house, and then, with respectful courtesy, withdrew, and, a few hours later, was giving Clayton a humorous account of his interview with "Mees" Hall.

The grave, olive-skinned woman, with sad, serious eyes, Dick led in by the hand, was not the Martha he remembered; still, there was enough remaining of the old look to assure him it was indeed she,—the poor girl, who, like Hagar, went off with her child, and then disappeared as utterly as if the earth had swallowed her.

"And your baby, Martha?" said Clayton. "Where is she? Is she living?"

"Oh, Mars Frank, I don't know, but my belief is she was drowned in the river of ice by that cruel man who got us away from Mars Harry Barnes."

Frank's face turned ashy pale as she said these few words, which connected the two mysteries by this missing link—Martha's disappearance and the finding of Petrel. So simple, and yet he had never thought of it before! But what a solution! My God, what is to be done? These were the thoughts that sped swiftly through Clayton's mind.

He soon kindly dismissed Dick and Martha on the plea of urgent business, telling her he wished to see her again in the morning. Then he took counsel with himself, as he paced the floor. What must he do? Go to that sensitive child and tell her she was the daughter of a slave? Tell her that the mother for whom she had so longed had been found, and she is none other than this humble, faithful daughter of a despised race? He could not do it. And yet what right had he to deprive this mother of her child? For hours he thought, and at last came to this determination: He would tell Martha all, and let *her* decide.

His eye fell upon Kate's letter, still lying on his desk. "Of course, she must not go there; that is out of the question now. Well," he thought, "it need not be answered at once, and, in the meantime, I can frame excuses for not allowing the child to make the proposed visit."

CHAPTER LVI

It was with a heavy heart that he sent for Martha the next day. He had a strange and delicate task before him, and how should he perform it?

"Now, Martha," he said, when she came, "I want you to sit down there and tell me just how you lost your little girl; I hadn't time yesterday to ask all I wanted to know about it."

She sat down obediently on a camp stool he pointed to, and began, in a soft, musical, contralto voice.

Clayton sat, his eyes fixed immovably upon her face, as she told the story. Every incident of the scene was precisely as he witnessed it that winter morning fifteen years ago. There was no room for doubt; she was the mother of his ward.

"Martha," he said, "you must prepare yourself for a surprise. Your little girl was not drowned; she came safe into my arms when that brute tossed her away."

Martha was at his feet, the tears streaming down her face. "Oh, my God! At last! At last!"

Clayton took away the hand she was kissing and raised her.

"Sit there," he said, "and when you are ready I will tell you the rest; there is much more to be said when you can hear it."

She did as she was told, and fixed her eyes eagerly upon him as he went on.

"She has been, since she was six years old, in a convent in Kansas, where she has received an education; has studied music and painting; so she is now no longer a child, but a beautiful and accomplished young girl, fitted for the highest station in life."

A pained, bewildered expression began to mingle with the joy which had a moment ago illumined the melancholy face.

"Of course she will cling to you and love you for, her heart is of gold; but, I tell you frankly, Martha, it will make a great change in her future when she learns that the blood of a slave is in her veins."

Martha gazed now with a pitiful intensity at the speaker; tears unwiped rolling down her face.

"Now, my poor girl," he went on, "I have told you the truth. I place your child in your hands to do with her as you think best ; I have no right to influence or to advise."

"Mars Frank," said she, in a low voice, "she *never* must know it. Why should *I* come into her life to spoil it, after the Lord has done so much for her—and for me ? If I can *see* her sometimes," she said, looking at him timidly, as if, perhaps, she were asking too much, "if I might *see* her ! "

Clayton felt touched by the divine patience of this woman and grasped her by the hand.

"You are an heroic woman, Martha. *See* her? Yes, you shall see her, and you shall *live* with her. Now, I will tell you what I have been thinking. Petrel needs a maid, and will always need one, being so alone ; you shall occupy that position. Would you like that ? "

"Oh, Mars Frank, how can you ask me ? Wouldn't it be like Heaven to me ? "

And so it was arranged that he would at once write Petrel that Martha, Dick's wife, had been found, and was going to be in the future her maid, or, if need be, nurse. "And then next week I will take you there myself," he said.

Dick was not forgotten in this arrangement. Clayton promised that some occupation should be found for him too in the vicinity of his wife.

Frank Clayton procured the necessary leave of absence, and arrived, with Martha, late one evening at the Mission.

He thought it best to see Petrel at first alone and prepare the way for the meeting between the two. She received him with the usual enthusiastic greeting.

"What a dear, darling uncle you are, to think of giving me a maid ! Do you know, I think I must be a wonderfully good person not to be spoiled by so much petting," and she gave him the prettiest little mouth to kiss ; and then when he answered "And so you are," such a gay little laugh rang through the room, and she said : "That shows how little you know about me. Why, I suppose I'm the naughtiest—you ought to see me one of those days when I have what Sister Agatha calls my '*tantrums.*' Oh, by the way, of course I am going to Lucaston—though you did not say so, you bad uncle!"

"Time enough, my dear child; we cannot settle *everything* in one half-hour."

"Uncle," said she, confidentially, "I want to tell you something, of an experience in dreams. Do you know there is a very strange dream which comes to me at intervals, and always just before *something* happens."

"Naturally," said Clayton, "as something happens about every——"

"Now, don't be scornful and unbelieving, or I'll not tell you; and it's *very* interesting."

"Well, go on," said he, with an amused laugh.

"The dream is always the same. There is a river full great cakes of ice—and noise and confusion—and I'm afraid—I do not know of what—and a face so loving and tender looks into mine, and I feel safe in a moment."

Frank listened speechless with surprise.

"Well," said he, "what do you think of it?"

"I think—it is very strange," said he, "but—now, don't you want to see your new maid?"

"Oh, yes, indeed I do."

A moment later he returned with Martha.

Petrel uttered a little scream.

"Why, Uncle," said she, trembling, and holding tightly his hand, "it is the face in my dream?"

"Nonsense, child," said he, drawing her toward the woman, who was standing as if petrified, gazing at the beautiful young girl.

"Martha," said he, "this is the young lady you are going to take care of; see that you keep her safe and happy."

Petrel took her hand kindly in her own, as she said shyly, "I am so glad you have come, Martha, and *so* glad they have found you after all these years. And you never found your little girl?"

Martha could only shake her head in reply.

"Well, no matter," said Petrel soothingly, stroking her hair; "you mustn't feel unhappy any more, for *I* am your little girl now."

"Oh! thank you thank you, for saying those words!" said Martha, and she clasped lovingly the hand she passionately kissed.

CHAPTER LVII.

The following morning Petrel went with her uncle to the hospital. "I spend two hours there every morning," she said, as they were on the way. "Sister Agatha goes with me, and I have learned to do *so* many things; I assure you, Uncle, I am quite a good nurse. I do not go into the *very* sick wards, you know; Sister Agatha will not permit that."

"Well, how do you like your new maid?" asked Clayton.

"Uncle, she is perfectly lovely. This morning when she came in to awaken me, she opened the blinds and the sun streamed in upon her, and she looked so happy, why she was really beautiful. And do you know what I did? I jumped out of bed and ran and put my arms about her and kissed her. I couldn't help it.

"You know," she went on, "her little girl would have been just my age, and I suppose that is why she felt so yesterday when she saw me; but I am going to make her so contented she will forget all her sorrows. You don't know how startled I was by her resemblance to the face in my dream. Of course, as you say, it was only a fancy.

"Here we are," concluded she. "How short the walk has been!"

One of the surgeons was coming out of the gate. Clayton stopped and introduced himself, asking him about the patients, to which commands they belonged, etc.

"Most of them are doing very well," said he, "but a Confederate officer was brought in last evening, very badly wounded, and he died in the night. He was brought with other wounded soldiers from the battle near St. Joe two days ago."

"Do you know who it was?" asked Clayton.

"No," answered the doctor; "I did not learn his name.

They passed in, Petrel with a feeling of awe at being so close to death, never having been in that awful presence,

"You stay here, my dear," said he, placing her with one of the Sisters, "and I'll go and inquire about this Confederate officer."

The sheet was withdrawn to show him the dead man's face, when he uttered an exclamation of horror.

"My God! It's Bernard Fletcher!"

After some time he returned to Petrel.

"Uncle, what has happened? You are pale."

"Yes, my darling, I have had a shock. Petrel, the officer who died last night is Colonel Fletcher—your little friend Katrine's papa."

Petrel burst into sobs and tears, exclaiming:

"Oh, my poor Katie! What *will* she do! and how will dear Mrs. Fletcher ever bear it!"

"Uncle," said she, after she grew calmer, "may I not see him? Please let me?"

Frank Clayton looked at the child strangely as she asked this question; he seemed to be debating with himself what he should do. At last he said:

"Yes, you may see him: come with me."

Petrel trembled as the handsome, stern face was uncovered, and her eyes were held with a mysterious fascination. She was thinking unutterable things—of Katrine's grief when she should look upon that man who looked so like a dead prince; she was thinking how *she* should feel if she were looking upon *her* dead father!

"Come away," said Clayton, taking her hand.

"One moment," said the girl, and loosening a white rosebud from her breast, she placed it in the dead hand, and turned away weeping.

"My dear child," he said, "we must go right back to the Mission. Of course I must go with the remains of Colonel Fletcher to Lucaston and break the news to his family." And they returned in silence.

Clayton asked to see Martha alone, to give her some parting instructions about her duties.

"Martha," he said, closing the door, "a very strange thing has happened. Colonel Bernard Fletcher died last night at the hospital. We have just seen him."

"My God!" said the woman, clasping her hands, as a deadly pallor spread over her face, but with a strange, hard look in those dry eyes. "Did *she* see him, sir?" asked she, in a low voice, significantly.

"Yes," answered Clayton; "he did not deserve it, but I thought perhaps it was as well; and she placed a white rosebud in his hand. Now, I must go with the remains to Lucaston; and, Martha, take care of—your charge. She is much overcome by what she has seen and by her sympathy for her friends; so watch her carefully."

"Ah! Mars Frank, the Lord seemed so cruel for so long—and now, how good, how *just* He is!"

Frank's unspoken answer was, "Yes; 'the mills of the gods grind slowly, but grind *exceeding* fine.'"

CHAPTER LVIII.

Throughout all the exciting incidents just related, Frank Clayton never for one moment forgot his own deep unhealed wound. As he consoled Kate and her daughter over the open grave of Bernard Fletcher, he saw always before him that grave wherein he had buried the dearest hope in his own life. " Flowers will blossom upon this," he said to himself, as he looked at the fresh clods of earth, "but upon that other—never." He should never love again, nor ever cease to love Isabel Priest.

His gentle cousin Kate had her own unhealed wound, as he well knew; she had buried her ideal fifteen years ago, and had ever since been trying to adapt herself to the *real*. She had never loved her husband as much since that fatal discovery as now, when she looked upon him as Petrel had seen him at the hospital, clothed in the silent beauty and majesty of death; and for the first time from her heart gave him a kiss of forgiveness and peace.

When this sad task was over, Frank returned to his duties. He dreaded the opportunity to think—to dream over the letters which came from Roland, trying to read between the lines more than was said of his beloved. Ah! how many times in the silent night did he live over those last interviews—recall the sound of her voice when she uttered the words for which his soul had been thirsting! And when he realized it was to be nevermore, he would dress, go out under the stars and strive to become patient and calm.

He often thought how easy it would have been to say the words which would have removed all obstacles. They were simple to utter; thousands repeated them every day and Sunday too without thinking, or much caring, what they mean. Why should he be so scrupulous? But that was a price he could not pay, even to win her. He could not perjure himself by seeming to acquiesce in humanly constructed dogmas. Not even for the bliss of possessing the woman he adored could he pretend to comprehend the mysteries of the Great Creator, The One First Cause, nor yet the full measure of the Law of Laws. How could he claim to know the plans and designs of the Supreme Being regarding the human race? He, a mere atom in an ocean of mist and mystery—should he say what are the attributes of the Mighty Unknown? Should he attempt to define its limits and its nature, whether it be three in one, or one in three, or in fact say whether it exist separate and apart from its work at all? Others might do this if they could; but for him, he must, at any cost, be faithful to his own convictions—be they beliefs, or unbeliefs.

He longed for action, something more stirring than being upon the outskirts of a great conflict; and a few months later received the orders for which he had asked and hoped. An active campaign was laid out for the army corps to which he was attached, and he was transferred to the command of a regiment of colored troops which he had been chiefly instrumental in creating, the Government having at last seen the wisdom of this once unpopular measure. This separated him from Duvall, which was a source of regret to both.

In that last private interview with Isabel, just before leaving "Eagle's Nest," Frank had received from her a little packet, covered with chamois-leather, and attached to a fine gold chain. This she placed about his neck, exacting from him a solemn promise never to remove nor to open it. "It is an amulet," she had said, smiling through her tears, "and its charm will be lost if you understand it." Much as he longed to know its contents, Frank would not for the world have broken his pledge to keep it inviolate. He would have ample need of its protecting power now; and it was with a feeling of exultation that he found himself in one of the fiercest centres of the desperate conflict.

"Now," he said, "now I have an opportunity to do, and, perhaps, to die!"

Kissing the amulet, he added:

"You can do nothing better for me than that, my little friend; only let my life accomplish something for my country first—then—adieu, green fields and sunshine and elusive joys, forever!"

The fact that the Confederates showed no mercy to the negro soldiers or their officers, made this arm of the service a desperate one ; and this had strongly influenced Clayton in attaching himself to it. There were no branching roads ahead, leading to prison or hospital— only one highway, which led to *Victory*—or *Death.*

CHAPTER LIX

"Fort Leavenworth Hospital, Dec. 20, 186–.

"My Dear Uncle:—

"Your letter, with kind permission for me to come here with Sister Agatha, was received, and so—here I am—in the dress of a novitiate, with partial charge of a ward. I like it so much better than the desultory work I did at home, although the experience obtained there is most valuable now.

"Who do you think was brought here this morning? Your friend, Lieutenant Duvall; and, strangely enough, he was placed in our ward. He is seriously, though not dangerously, wounded, and was in a half-unconscious state all day. You may imagine with what interest I regarded him, knowing how great was your friendship for him. I will keep this letter open and add anything which there may be to tell you concerning him.

"My dear, faithful Martha has rooms near the hospital, and watches me as if *I* were a patient, doing a thousand things for my comfort. She is certainly an angel! She brings a basket of flowers every morning, which I place where they will gladden the eyes of my poor patients. But do not suppose this is all I do; I really, in my poor way, am useful. Oh! my dear Uncle, it is solemn and awful to be near so much suffering. I know it makes my soul grow and expand, and I thank God for giving me this experience. I might not in years have learned, as I now have, all the bitterness and sorrow which life holds for some.

"There is a Confederate officer here, who, I think, will die, and he will scarcely let me be out of his sight. He is a foreigner—a Captain De Montholon—and he says I remind him of his daughter Flora. He has had some terrible trouble in his life, and when he fixes his great sad eyes upon me it fills me with such pity and such longing to comfort him; and yet I know not what to do, and can only make his pillow easier and brighten him with flowers and sunshine. But what is that to a sick soul? I think if he could talk of his trouble and of those he loves, that would be better than all the doctor's medicines. I shall try to lead him to do this.

"Dec. 22nd—Lieutenant Duvall is better, but extremely weak; his right arm is broken and he is otherwise severely injured, but is very patient, and the doctor thinks will do well unless fever sets in. He *will* talk, and that is bad for him. When he found out my name—well, you should have seen him! He knew at once I must be *your* little girl, of whom he had heard so much, and would have asked fifty questions if I had let him; but I am *very* strict, and as he cannot help himself, he has to be good.

"Captain De Montholon is very, very ill; he is delirious at night and talks of Italy—of Flora—and of Claudius, his son—and of some one he calls Orsyna, or something like that; he speaks in half-Italian and half-English, so I cannot make out anything connected; but I know it is grief—terrible regret at something in his past which is eating away his life more than his wounds. Whether he has suffered wrong, or, what is worse yet, committed it, God only knows.

"I will send this without anything further now, but will write in a day or two again, knowing how anxious you will be about your friend, Lieutenant Duvall.

"Most lovingly,

"PETREL."

The second day after Claude was admitted to the hospital he awoke from a long, refreshing sleep, just as the sun was setting, and its slanting rays gilded in burnished gold every article in his room; the plain pine table, with cups and spoons, the chair, the hospital cot on which he lay, with its coarse, strong and white covering, all swam in the liquid golden light that literally flooded the room, which by some mysterious process seemed to multiply and beautify all things as he, with only partially opened eyes, looked down the long row of cots with their burdens of patient sufferers. In this almost ecstatic state, he let his mind drift backward, to a point sufficiently distinct and tangible on memory's tablet to form a starting-place from

which he could take reckoning and determine his present whereabouts—whether in the body or out of the body,
he could not tell.   Certainly nothing in the flesh had ever
seemed to him as lovely as that fair creature who softly
passed and repassed before his bewildered vision.   Sometimes it seemed as if she were Flora, his sister, and
again some fairy, he knew not who.   Then his mind
drifted back to his home ; he saw his mother, as she took
him in her arms that morning long ago and told him that
his father had gone ; that in a quarrel with his best friend
he had been dashed by a storm of passion upon the fatal
reefs of what he believed to be a deadly duel, and had fled
to America, taking with him money which he held in trust
for another.   He saw his mother's uplifted eyes as she declared before God she believed his father was innocent of
intended wrong in betraying the trust ; he heard her voice
trembling with feeling as she said :   " You must find your
father, my boy.   God knows I can ill spare you now, but
you must go and bring him back to us ; tell him my own
fortune shall go to pay the money.   I give it willingly.
What is that to give if it will bring him back !   Tell him
all will be forgotten, if he will only *come !* "   Then swiftly
his mind sped upon the long search.   From New York to
San Francisco, thence to St. Paul and back to St. Louis,
where he met Clayton ; and, almost despairing of success, how he lingered for months enjoying this friendship
with the man he came to love as a brother.   Their experience in Kansas drifted before him ; their acquaintance
with Brown, and finally that awful day at Harper's Ferry !
Then he saw the old man's prophecy fulfilled ; the
country in arms, his own enrollment, and, at last, the
fight with the guerillas at Baxter's Springs, led by that
ill-omened Livingstone ; he saw the ghastly forms of
dusky men falling thick and fast about him, towering
above which was Daniel Dickson, as he last beheld him,
with the barrel of his broken musket in the left hand,
and the right clutching a great gleaming sabre bayonet,
as he cut right and left, front and rear ; and then saw
him, with an awful lunge, bury it to the hilt in the chest
of his adversary, and the world seemed to fade and fall
on him, bringing with it Dan and his victim.

Then, as in a dream, his mind took hold of the slender
thread of events that brought partial recovery at Baxter's

Springs, the rough ride to Fort Scott, and the almost blank journey to Fort Leavenworth.

This strange, kaleidoscopic or panoramic glance backward brought a sigh, as he turned to look for a presence which he felt, more than heard, near him. His eyes opened wide to take in the lovely face that bent over his pillow with an anxious, inquiring gaze. Looking into the soft, amber eyes filled with tender solicitude, he tried to speak, and his tongue refused its office, as he wondered if she were angel or mortal. Then he reached out to touch or test this phantom, and the effort cost a twinge of pain, as the right arm fell back helpless by his side ; and Petrel said gently, placing her hand on the disabled one of her patient :

"You must be very quiet; such are the surgeon's instructions."

"Then you are mortal, like myself?"

"Oh, yes," said she, smiling; "we are all mortals here."

"I thought perhaps I was in Paradise, and that you—"

Two fingers of a fair, soft hand were placed on his lips, and an effort at a frown failed on the face, as the snowy folds of the Sister's bonnet fringing it shook menacingly—commanding silence.

The patient submitted to the gentle authority and waited and watched, with a faint smile, as, without speaking, she brought him his medicine and gently raised his pillow. His eyes followed her as she set down the glass and spoon and arranged the little tray on the table, then quietly sat down by his cot.

"May I ask just *one* question—who it is who takes such care of me?"

A shake of the white crest and a threatening finger raised was the only response.

Claude felt powerless before this lovely impersonation of tyranny, and was content quietly to watch and return to the occupation of arranging his confused thoughts; and as he was striving to separate the real from the fantastic, fell asleep.

Upon awakening an hour later, he looked about for the fair face, and it was gone. Another, in the same garb, was there.

"Where is she?" he said, impulsively.

"Who?" asked the good Sister.

Then, realizing his maladroitness, he said, in some confusion :

"Oh, it is nothing ; I have been dreaming."

And so he had.

He had not long to wait ; he saw the dream face coming toward him through the long avenue of cots, and half-closed his eyes, feigning sleep. She poured out his medicine and approached him, then paused. He opened his eyes.

"Oh," said she, "I am afraid I awoke you. Sister Agatha said you were already awake."

"And so I was," said he, and obediently took the medicine.

"Thanks, Ganymede," said he, smiling. "If you will not tell me your real name, I must invent one."

The prettiest rose-tint crept up into the olive, under her white hood, as she said :

"And if I should tell my name you will ask other questions and make yourself worse, and I shall be scolded by the surgeon."

"No, on my honor," said he. "I will ask no more questions."

"Why can't you call me 'Sister'? That is quite enough I——"

"But there are so many Sisters," interposed the patient.

"Well, then, call me Sister Petrel," she said, smiling.

A look of utter amazement swept over the sick man's face, as he repeated after her :

"Petrel ! *Ciel !* Then you are—— "

"Ah ! take care—your word of honor ! "

"Well, it is not a question ; I said I would ask no questions. There is no need ; you are my friend's ward and niece ! *Mon Dieu*, may I tell you——? "

"Nothing," said the little nurse ; "absolutely you shall tell me nothing ; you have said quite too much now." And, indeed, there were two ominously bright spots in the patient's cheeks as, with eyes wide open with wonder, he watched her profile intently ; then closing them almost wearily, thought " How beautiful ! How beautiful she is ! " and thinking thus, fell asleep again.

It was not until the next morning was well advanced that he saw her graceful, lithe form coming down the vista of little beds. His face and eyes must have given sign of the gladness of heart he felt.

"How much better you are!" she said, looking at him brightly.

"Oh, yes," he said, with a show of determination; "the doctor say I may talk some now."

Petrel laughed at the little foreign-English speech with which he asserted his independence.

"Do you know what I was thinking as you came to me in the sunshine just now? Well, I was thinking many things, but one is that you look just like my sister, my dear sister."

"Well, how many people do I look like, I wonder?" said she, with a blush and a merry laugh. "Poor Captain De Montholon says I am just like his daughter."

As she said this Duvall's face suddenly changed and became very pale.

"Who did you say?" asked he, trembling in strange agitation.

"Captain De Montholon; that poor Confederate officer who is so ill," answered Petrel. "Oh, I am doing *very* wrong," said she, clasping her hands in real distress; "you must *not* talk any more. Here, let me give you a sip of this water; it has just a spoonful of brandy in it, and you look *so* tired."

And he was very tired, as he closed his eyes and sank back on his pillow; it seemed that earth with all its hopes and its joys receded. He felt as if he were near the goal toward which he had been long and wearily pressing—could almost touch it—and yet now had not the strength to grasp it. His thoughts grew confused again, and it was some time before he could arrange them and remember when and how that long-silent name had come to him. Had he dreamed it, or did some one say he was here? At last the mists cleared away; he was in the hospital. Petrel, Clayton's lovely niece, was his angel ministrant. She had said that Captain De Montholon was a wounded Confederate officer in the same ward with himself; he had it all firm and sure now.

De Montholon was his father's mother's name and one it was often his fancy to assume in the gay, careless, old life at home. A deep conviction grew in Claude's mind that his search was to come to an end here; and he waited feverishly for the dawn.

CHAPTER LX.

"Fort Leavenworth Hospital, Dec. 28, 186–.

"My Dear Uncle :—

"How can I tell you the strange things that have happened since I wrote you last? Where shall I begin? You know I told you there was a Confederate officer here who seemed very fond of me because I looked like his little daughter at home. Well, when Lieutenant Duvall began to get better so that he could talk a little, I spoke about this Captain De Montholon one day, and when he heard the name I thought he was going to faint away, and I laid awake all night, fearing my imprudence would bring on fever. And as I lay thinking, my mind began to piece together little stray bits here and there. I wondered why Lieutenant Duvall was so moved; then I thought of their both being from Italy, and I remembered that Captain De Montholon's son was called Claudius, and something seemed to whisper to me 'You can serve him; don't delay or it will be too late.' Over and over again those words sounded in my ear, so that I could scarcely wait for the morning: and my dear Martha thought I must be ill because I got up and sat by the window watching the east. She said : 'My dear child, you will kill yourself with this work; it is too much for a delicate girl.' I could not tell her why I was restless nor why I was so impatient for the day, for I had not made up my mind what I should do when it came. I fell asleep just before day, and it was nine o'clock when I was awakened by Martha, bringing me a cup of coffee. You may think how sorry I was to find I had lost two precious hours; and as soon as I could I hastened to the hospital.

"I found Captain De Montholon had been given up by the surgeons, and Father Walter had already been there to administer the Holy Sacrament. He had told the surgeon he wanted to see me; so I went to him at once,

my heart beating and praying the dear Virgin to help me
to do what was wise and right.

"He looked, oh! so ill.

"'My child,' he said, 'it is most over. You are not
afraid, are you, to sit down by a dying man?'

"'Oh, do not say that,' I said. 'You will not die.'

"'Yes,' he answered; 'they have told me, and I am
not sorry; I am a desolate old man, and it is better so.
Life can hold nothing more for me; but I want you to do
me one more service, and this is the last I shall ask.
Get pen and paper. Can you write Italian? No, I suppose not. Well,' with a sigh, 'then it must be in English.' And at his dictation I wrote the following:

"'My Adored Wife:

"'I am about to die, and at such times men speak the
truth. I did not intend any wrong in bringing away those
securities. In the horror and despair at finding I had
slain my friend, Count Orsyni, I fled. When far out at
sea, I discovered that I had brought the papers away
with me, and I realized that I would rest under the awful
suspicion of having betrayed this trust. Oh, the horror
of that voyage! My hand red with the blood of my
friend! My name tarnished with the suspicion of dishonor! I thought of you, my adored wife—of my children,
my son—and I would have killed myself.but for my desire to reach land and send back those accursed papers.

"'This, as you know, I did, through my solicitor at Na-
ples, with full explanation. Then I waited. I thought
you would write; but you did not—communicating with
me only through my solicitor. Perhaps you were right—
but, ah! it was bitter—to know that I was not forgiven
for the stain I had brought upon our untarnished name!

"'Then the years of torment which followed, thinking of
the ruin I had wrought, not only in my own home, but
that of my murdered friend; that *I*, the petted child of
fortune, was an outcast, a price upon my head if I returned, and my son ashamed of the name he bears! Do
you wonder that I grew old before my time? that my
hair whitened? But I toiled, and was not unsuccessful.
I leave an ample fortune, which is to be divided between
you and my children. Mr. Wickliffe, of Louisville, Kentucky, is my solicitor and has all the needful papers.

Communicate with him. I have suffered enough to expiate the wrong I have done. Think of me kindly, if you can, my adored Giuletta, and try to make my children feel I was not entirely bad, though the most unfortunate of men.

" 'Adieu, my beloved. It is hard to die solitary and unwept. But God wills it; so it is right.'

" When I had finished this he asked me to read it to him. I do not know how I did it, my eyes so filled with tears and my voice choked with sobs; but when I had finished, he said: 'Now, put that pen in my hand,' and I did as he bid me, placing the letter on a book directly under the pen. Then he wrote quite distinctly,

" 'COUNT CLAUDIUS DAVILA.'

" The surgeon came in then, and seeing he was sinking very fast, gave him some stimulant and motioned me to leave him.

" I folded the letter I had written and put it under the girdle of my dress, then made a sign to the surgeon that I wished to speak with him alone.

" I told him I had a very important communication to make to Lieutenant Duvall. 'In fact,' I said, 'Doctor, I think this gentleman is Lieutenant Duvall's father. Will it do him harm to tell him of his presence here?'

" The doctor looked startled and puzzled. He said he would go and examine the lieutenant's condition carefully and let me know. But before he went he made me take a glass of wine and lie down, because, he said, I looked so white.

" Presently he came back and said: 'He is fairly well this morning, just a little feverish, but I fancy his mind is disturbed about something, and we had better let things have their natural way; sometimes it is better to be led by circumstances, and if this is as you say, we have no right to keep the knowledge from him.'

" So I went to his bedside, with the letter held firmly under the girdle of my black dress.

" His face was feverish, but his eyes lit up when he saw me, as if he had been waiting.

" 'Oh, at last you are come!' You know his little foreign way. 'I could not sleep last night,' he went on, 'because I am so impatient to learn more about that Confederate officer,' and he fixed his eyes on me with such a strange eager light in them. 'Who is Captain De Montholon? If you know anything about him, for God's sake tell me.'

" I do not know what I said or how I tried to prepare him for it, but, at last, I drew out the letter, and showing him the signature, said:

" ' There is the answer to your question.'

" Then I called the surgeon and went away, for I needed to be calm myself. In a half hour I returned. He was very pale, the color all gone now out of his face. He held out his hand to me and said:

" ' Petrel, you have brought me blessed news; my father, for whom I have sought for years, is here, and I am to see him in a few moments. I have read this letter to my mother. He has been the victim of a cruel conspiracy, and I hope I may live to bring vengeance upon that cold-blooded villain, Valerias, who has betrayed and killed him. His friend did *not* die from the wound. His solicitor, Valerias, *never* sent my mother those papers, nor one single letter from my father, and made us believe, poor dupes and fools that we were, that he was leading a life of shame and dishonor away from his family.'

" The surgeon now came in, and said : ' I think Captain De Montholon should be in some way prepared for what he is to hear.'

" Of course I knew this meant that I was to go to him, which I did. I knelt down by his bedside and covered his poor, thin hand with tears, as I told him, I know not how, of what was in store for him. But, never, never can I forget the look of joy in that dying face. He said: ' Am I dreaming? I have often dreamed this. No, it cannot be——'

" ' Yes, yes,' I said, ' it is true ; he is here ; he has been years looking for you ; he loves you.'

" ' Oh, my God !' he cried, ' let me live another hour ! Only that—one hour to look into the face of my son !'

" ' Doctor,' he said, turning toward the surgeon, who had come in, ' do not let me die quite yet ; can you not give me something to prolong——'

" ' My dear friend,' said the surgeon, kindly, ' drink

this; and do not waste your strength; say not another word.'

"At a sign from the doctor, two strong attendants quietly took up Lieutenant Duvall's cot and placed it close beside that of the dying officer, so that they were directly face to face, and near enough for the eager hands to clasp; and we all withdrew—only the surgeon and I remaining near enough to be called if needed.

"We could hear the heartrending tones of that strange interview—but it was all veiled in the mystery of a foreign speech.

"Now that there was nothing more to be done I found I was thoroughly exhausted, and I think I fainted; I am not sure, but I found myself in my own room and Martha leaning over me, and have no idea how I got there. They will not let me talk, or tell me anything about what I so long to know. They think by making me quiet they can stop thought. Ah, well! I will wait and be patient. But I did have my own way about writing you this letter, and now I will try to sleep.

"Fondly,
"PETREL.

"December 29.

"Captain De Montholon died last night at midnight, in his son's arms. "PETREL."

CHAPTER LXI.

Frank Clayton read this letter way to its close. Of the conflicting emotions which agitated him, astonishment seemed the strongest. "De Montholon Claude Duvall's father!" he exclaimed, at last. "Impossible! And I have known him all these years, and met him again and again! How well I remember his air of foreign distinction and the surprise with which I often listened to his perfect English. I can see now his fine, European courtliness of manner, the sad, aristocratic face, with white moustache and imperial. And *that* was Claude's father! Good God, why did I not then know it? How much suffering might have been saved! If Claude had only confided in me! But, even then, I should never have suspected, for the name was French. And now to think that she, Petrel—that child, with her inspired sympathy and insight—has unravelled this mystery and brought them together at last! What a strange story! and who shall say that truth is not stranger than fiction!"

It was far in the night, and there were stirring events on the morrow; but he sat down in his tent and wrote two letters—first, to Petrel, and then to Duvall. The latter was as follows:

"My Dear, Dear Friend:—

"You will know why my hand trembles and why my heart throbs with deep emotion when I tell you that Petrel has written me of the joy and the sorrow which have in the same moment come to you. How deeply I sympathize in both, need I say? And now, a new surprise awaits you. I knew your father well—have had intimate personal and professional association with him for years, through Mr. Wickliffe, my former partner, whose client he was. I knew him as Colonel De Montholon, and had the greatest admiration for his character and abilities, although there was an impenetrable reserve about him which always prevented me from coming near

to him as I desired. On one occasion when you and
I were at the St. Charles in New Orleans, I invited him
to dine with us. He pleaded an engagement, and when
I repeated the invitation, said—I remember so well how
he looked, with his melancholy and distinguished air—
'You are kind, but you will have to excuse me; I am
such a recluse; I rarely accept invitations.' Had he
come—oh, think of it! You would have met, and how
much been saved! But you must often have been near
to each other, and, perhaps, even under the same
roof.   *

"Whether this will comfort or sadden you I do not
know, my dear Claude; but I shall have much more to
tell you of your father which you will be so glad to hear.

"I hope to hear that these agitating events have not re-
tarded your recovery, and also that the time is not far distant when we may meet once more.

"Faithfully yours,
"FRANK CLAYTON."

"An engagement is imminent—probably will take place
to-morrow. If anything should happen to me, I will take
comfort in knowing my ward will find a friend in you.
She will be amply provided for in my will, of course.

"F. C."

A week later, Frank was not at all surprised to learn
from his friend, Doctor Magruder, at Leavenworth Hospital, that Petrel was suffering from nervous exhaustion.
"She is not ill," he wrote, "but there is a reaction from
the tremendous strain of those two days in the hospital,
when she played such an heroic part, and I have ordered
that she be kept absolutely free from excitement."

Clayton sent peremptory orders that she was on no
account to engage again in any hospital work, and that as
soon as she was able she should return to the convent
with Martha.

Rest and quiet brought back health to the young girl;
but in vain she tried to return to her former occupations.
Nothing brought the old feeling of enjoyment; her painting—music—books—all wearied her; and Martha saw
with grief and anxiety a settled look of melancholy upon

the face she so loved. Her old friend, Tom, the gardener, shook his head, and said : "It was a bad day when they let that tender young thing go to nuss in that hospital; she ain't no more fit for it than nuthin, and she ain't bin the same sence. Why, she don't care no more for these flowers than if they wuz dirt." And he wiped his sleeve across his eyes to brush away a tear of disappointment. "I tole Martha jest how 'twould be. I sez, 'Martha, some things is right, and some things izn't.'"

One sunny morning, in the early spring, a gentleman called at the convent and asked permission to see Miss Petrel.

She dressed and came down-stairs, perfectly calm and self-possessed, although she knew well whom she should see. But, was that tall, pale, distinguished-looking man her patient? Yes; there were the great luminous eyes, there was the same smile of welcome, and there the poor right arm in a sling. He too had his feeling of strangeness and surprise. He had only seen her in the black gown and white head-dress of the Sisterhood; and this graceful creature in flowing draperies was a new revelation to him. Was this young goddess ever his nurse? Ah! how lovely she was, with her quickly changing color, as he talked to her of his father, of his gratitude for the joy and the comfort she had brought to him. How deftly she parried his praise of her heroism and her kindness to his poor father!

He told her he was going home to Italy, and as her color faded until she looked like marble, an expression of joy came into his own pale face.

"Petrella," he said, very softly.

She gave him a quick, startled look.

"Why do you call me that? There is only one other who ever called me by that name."

"Yes; I know," he said. "I have come to learn that pretty name from my father. We had eight hours—eight blessed hours together, Petrella, and we talked of much things. He told me how you were an angel to him—how you solace and make lighter his poor heart. And now, Petrella, I go away, but I hope—not for always. I come back some day—do you know why? Because I cannot stay away. Because—I love you, Petrella."

Ah! was this the same poor, grey, sickly sunlight that shone this morning? Were these flowers poor old Tom was bringing her the same dull things she had seen only a few hours ago? Claude had gone, an ocean would soon roll between them—but he had said those four words, " Petrella, I love you," and is it strange she had no regrets for that one kiss which lingered in her memory?

CHAPTER LXII.

FRANK CLAYTON's mail had brought him many surprises
of late, but no letter had given him food for so much
anxious deliberation as the one he received from his old
friend, written just on the eve of sailing for Europe.
After telling him of the circumstances which rendered it
necessary for him to resign his commission in the Federal
Army, consequent upon the new duties in assuming his
father's title and settling up his estate, he went on to say
—what we already know—that he loved Clayton's niece ;
and he formally asked permission of his friend to offer
her his hand in marriage.

Clayton was profoundly perplexed and distressed. He
had never told Claude of the discovery of Petrel's mother
and the clearing away of the mystery of her birth and
origin ; that was a secret known only to Martha and himself ; now he must divulge it. She had seemed to him
such a child, he had never thought of a strange complication such as this ; and yet what more natural than that she
should fall in love with Claude, who was beyond compare
the most fascinating man he had ever known ! But—it
could never be. Had his friend remained obscure, it
would have been different ; but now that he bore a distinguished name and title and was allied to some of the
proudest families in Italy, it would be a misalliance and
would bring only misery in the end to both.

All this he embodied in a carefully written letter—the
most difficult he ever penned—and a few weeks later
received the following reply :

"SORRENTO, June 12, 186–.

" MY DEAR FRIEND :—

"For the first time, I am angry, yes, angry, with you.
I have suffered much, God knows ; and now you would
take away my great joy. I have read with deepest interest all you write about Petrella, because all that touches
her is to me so sacred ; but what care I who was her

ancestor, or what color the blood in her veins ! It is *she*, *Petrella*, whom I love, and for that—we Italians think not so much disgrace in that race as do you Americans. And if they did, what should I care? Where is there such another? Such a soul? such a heart? Ah ! *Mon Dieu !* Have I not reason to know what she is? Did not my dying father say : ' Petrella has consoled me like an angel; I should die happier, my son, if I thought she would some day be your wife'? And did I not tell him : ' Father, I love her !'?

"No ; you say wrong, my friend ; it is *not* gratitude ; for I love her before she make me that great service. And now—I am not angry—no, I unsay that, but you make me suffer with this delay. No one will ever know the secret you tell me in this letter, *no one*. We will bury it, and go on as if it did not live.

" My mother and sister talk of Petrella, only Petrella, the good angel which restored to us our father and make us know how honorable and how injured he is ; and think you not I will feel pride to bring her here—to say to my friends ' This is my wife'?

"Write on the moment you receive this letter, and address me Sorrento, Italy.

" Faithfully yours,
"CLAUDIUS DAVILA."

The same mail which brought this to Clayton had brought to Petrel in her quiet retreat two letters : one in a foreign handwriting, evidently from a lady, and accompanying it a mysterious packet. She examined the postmark, " Sorrento," with anxious eyes, and her fingers trembled not a little as she broke the crested seal. This was what she read :

"SORRENTO, June 10, 186-.

" MIA CARRISSIMA PETRELLA :—

" My heart is so full that my poor English cannot contain its thought. My son has told us how heroique, how beautiful, was your devotion to my poor husband, and you are enshrined like a saint in our house. My beautiful child, we shall never cease to thank you for the joy you have brought back to our unhappy, darkened hearts. So many years ! And all for naught ! Such wickedness and such misconception, and, alas! such suffering! But, through you, we have his dear ashes now safe with us, and are happier than in eight long years.

"Will you have the goodness to accept this *souvenir* from your grateful and loving friend,

"CONTESSA GIULETTA DAVILA.

"Pardon me my poor English, *Mademoiselle*."

The mysterious wrappings one after another were removed from the package, and at last revealed a red Morocco box, with a gold monogram and a crest on the cover. Petrel scarcely dared press upon the little spring —it was all so impossible, so dazzling an experience to come to her, in her hitherto quiet and uneventful life. When she opened it, there lay, softly cushioned in satin, a gold locket and chain, and upon the locket was traced in diamonds one single word:

"PETRELLA."

The eyes which looked within the locket were too blinded with tears to see, at first, the miniature faces which looked out upon her—the Count and Countess Davila, taken at the time of their marriage—so a little, brief letter from Claude told her. And when she had taken these treasures to her own room and locked the door, she looked longest and most earnestly—at the beautiful gift? Ah, no! At a little letter, containing not more than four lines; not one word in it that all the world might not have seen! And this exacting young lady was more sad than glad, and came down-stairs later with eyes that looked as if they had wept.

CHAPTER LXIII.

OF course Clayton's opposition gave way before Claude's invincible temper; and he was glad indeed not to be the instrument in making two people miserable, as he himself was. He wrote at once to Martha a confidential letter, telling her of Count Claudius Davila's proposal. He then said:

"As her mother, it is your privilege to decide what shall be done in this matter; and I shall delay my reply to his letter until I hear from you."

A few weeks later, another letter and another little packet sped across the sea and half across the continent, to the little Convent of "Sacre-Cœur," in Kansas; but *this* letter might *not* have been seen by all the world! It was read behind locked doors, and the reading seemed to occupy fully two hours; after which a young lady emerged with a shining radiance in her face.

Martha's quick eye detected the look, and, at the same moment, the jewelled ring on her hand.

Petrel laid her head on the faithful woman's bosom and said in a low voice:

"Martha, dear, I am going to be the wife of Count Claudius Davila; he has asked me to marry him. Only think," said she, raising her head and looking into the kind eyes, "only think of his choosing *me*, poor little me, out of all this world! Isn't it like a fairy-tale?"

The kind Sisters treated the little maid as a person of great distinction when they heard what was to happen; and her old school-fellows were not a little awed by her brilliant romance. But Martha was her only confidante.

"Martha, dear," she said, "I must study; I ought to know *so* much. First, I must learn Italian; and then— why, there is so much about Italy that I don't know *at all*. Oh, dear," she said, sighing, "*now* I want a mother. And how proud and happy she would be! Do you know, I see her often, and I know *just* how she would look," and she threw her head back with half-closed lids, as if painting a picture in space. "She has soft brown hair, with only a few silver threads—and a fair sweet face—with just a faint little color; and she wears soft, shining, gray silks, and creamy lace at her throat; and she has lovely, gracious manners," and her color kindling as she gave the reins to her imagination, "and when she rides in her daughter's carriage the great ladies in Sorrento look after her and say: 'That is the beautiful American lady, the Countess Petrella's mother!'" And with a laugh, hiding her head on her maid's shoulder, she said: "No one but you, dear, knows how silly I can be." Then, starting up quickly, "Why, you are crying— you are crying! What is it?"

"Oh, nothing, nothing," said the poor woman, struggling to check her sobs. "Only I am thinking I may lose you—that you will go away."

"Why, you dear, foolish, old Martha; if *that* is all, do not cry any more, for you shall *never* leave me; when I am married, I shall take you with me—to Italy or to the ends of the earth."

CHAPTER LXIV.

" BEECHWOOD, July 3, 186–.

" MY DEAR FRANK :—

"I have heard through Doctor Magruder of Petrel's strange and romantic experience at the hospital; and now comes the rumor of her engagement to Count Davila. I am a little—just a little—hurt to learn this first from strangers; but Katrine and I can talk and think of little else. Do write me at once, and confirm or deny the story. We were sorely disappointed that you would not let her come to us after her illness in May, and I cannot understand, my dear Frank, why you deny me the privilege of acting in the place of a mother to this dear child, whom, not having seen, I still love as my own.

"Still I am, always affectionately yours,
"KATE FLETCHER."

Concealments were of all things in the world most distasteful to Clayton; and yet he was all the time entangled in a mesh of subterfuges and evasions. He wrote Kate, parrying as well as he could her reproaches for keeping Petrel away from her, and told her that the engagement to Count Davila was indeed a fact, but that he should urge that the marriage be delayed until she was nineteen.

Then he wrote to Roland Priest announcing the event, with a brief account of the circumstances which had led to it. This letter was read with a twinge of disappointment by that young man, who had had romantic visions of his own regarding Clayton's beautiful ward, of whom they had heard so much but never seen.

But Isabel listened to the recital with very different emotions. In her sleepless nights, her long rides over the mountains, she had made many forecasts of her lost lover's future, and had a jealous suspicion that he would, at last, console himself by marrying this lovely girl; and she felt an indescribable peace in seeing this phantom laid low.

Like most people with strong natures, she was reserved and reticent. Her mother and Roland knew that she had suffered, but had never fathomed the depth of her sorrow, nor suspected the desperate resolve which sometimes seized her to go to him. She read with sickening horror of battles and slaughter. He was now where the conflict was the hottest, and her nerves were strained almost past endurance by the rumors of fresh engagements, or by delay in the arrival of his letters to Roland. In the night, while others slept, she said bitter things to herself—arraigned her own soul for arrogance and pride and conceit. She had closed the door upon this angel visitant—this beautiful, transfiguring love—and for what? Because she was better than he? Because she knew more than he about the great problems of infinity? Better than he about the nature of that inscrutable Being whom man clothes with his own attributes? In the awful crucible of suffering her soul had grown beyond the limits of human creeds; and had he been here now, how different had been her answer! "Too late! Too late!" was her piteous cry.

One night in the late autumn she had slept better than usual, but just before the dawn was awakened by something touching her hair lightly. She started, fully awake in a moment, and saw two outstretched arms, and a face radiant in the moonlight, which streamed in from the window—the rest of the form indistinct in the darkness—the arms stretched appealingly, as a voice said:

"Come to me, my beloved, come to me!"

Then the vision faded, and she heard only the clock ticking on the shelf. The face, the voice, were Clayton's. With solemn intensity, Isabel stretched out her own arms toward the darkness where she had seen the vision, and said:

"Yes, dearest, I will go to you."

Her nerves were firm and strong; she was not fanciful nor superstitious. What was this summons? Her resolve was taken. She went to the breakfast-table very pale and calm, and when it was over she put her arm around her mother's neck and kissed her.

"Mamma, dear," she said, "you know if Roland had

been well we could not have kept him with us. He would have been in this cruel war, and then my duty would have been here; but now I think you ought to spare me. Don't, don't," she said, putting her finger on her mother's lips, "wait; I am not happy, my darling mother. I think you know it. I will be better where I can do some good—where I can do my part in this time of sorrow and trial. Now, do not oppose me, dear mamma," and she kissed the sad, patient face. "It will be better for us all to let me go. I will nurse the wounded—and—perhaps—perhaps—*he* may need me."

Opposition to the plan was useless, so Mrs. Priest and Roland acquiesced, and preparations were made for Isabel's departure by the next steamer for Panama. Her first destination would be Washington city, to which place letters would follow her.

The parting at the steamer was a trying one for all, but borne bravely; and the mother and brother, as they watched the loved form upon the deck of the receding vessel, never suspected that she was going in answer to a summons from a phantom.

CHAPTER LXV.

THE voyage seemed interminable, and was, indeed, greatly prolonged by storms and head-winds after leaving Aspinwall : but New York was reached at last ; and Isabel and her small luggage were soon speeding by cars to Washington. She found protection in a kind lady, who was on a similar errand—that is, who was going to give her services to the care of the wounded wherever she found them most needed ; and Isabel gladly accepted the invitation to join her, for their mutual benefit.

Where she should go from Washington, she did not know ; that must be determined by what she could learn there, her idea being to find some field of usefulness as near as possible to Frank's vicinity.

Soon the dome of the Capitol appeared in dazzling white on a field of azure—and in a few moments more they bowled into the station and then took a carriage for Willard's Hotel. As she had hoped, letters from home awaited her, having come by the quicker route of the "Pony Express." Two letters—one from Roland and another from her mother—then a long envelope, addressed in an unfamiliar hand, to "Miss Isabel Priest, Coultersville, California," which had been readdressed by Roland to Washington. What could it be ? She opened it, and from within the letter dropped a folded piece of paper. Marble is not whiter than was her face as she opened it and discovered, in her own handwriting, these words :

"Any one finding this upon Mr. Frank Clayton will please at once communicate with Miss Isabel Priest, Coultersville, California, informing her of his precise condition."

It was the "amulet" she had placed about his neck in parting !

The paper dropped from her nerveless grasp, and she

sat like a statue for many moments, not daring to read the letter, which was as follows:

"NEAR CHATTANOOGA, TENN., Nov. 12, 186–.
"DEAR MADAM :—
"Mr. Clayton was found on the battlefield, badly wounded in the leg, and with a severe cut over the left eye, from a bursting shell. He has remained unconscious from the latter wound, which I fear is a serious fracture of the skull. Our hospital accommodations are meagre for our own sick and wounded, but such as they are, rest assured we will share with your friend.
"Respectfully,
"EDWARD EVE,
"ASSISTANT SURGEON C. S. A."

November 12! It was the night of November 11, or the morning of the 12th, that she had seen those outstretched arms and heard that voice supplicating her to "come!" And at that moment he was lying wounded on the battlefield! Now her way was clear, and her nerves felt firm as steel, as she rose with a solemn conviction that she should find him and that it would *not* be too late.

After consultation with her friend, Miss Anna Plant, it was decided to go at once to Secretary Stanton, to try and secure the necessary pass within the Confederate lines.

The great war secretary was too busy to give time to such small matters, and quickly disposed of it by a peremptory refusal.

What was to be done next? Go to the President? Isabel thought of a letter to Mr. Lincoln which her old friend, Captain John Brown, had long ago given to Roland, and which he had never presented. To this she added these words:

"Roland Priest's sister desires to see the President upon a matter of life and death."

It was an inspiration. Doors opened like magic before the two ladies who waited below, and who found themselves a few moments later in the presence of the President.

So absorbed was the brave girl in the object of her

coming she was utterly unconscious of the sensation she made in the glittering array of uniformed and distinguished men, who respectfully fell back to make way for her in the Audience Chamber. She thought of nothing but of Frank—wounded—and waiting for her—and threw back her veil, that she could look more closely into the kind face of the President, as he said :

"What can I do for you, Miss Priest?"

"Mr. President, I have a friend, a brave officer, who is wounded and a prisoner in a Confederate hospital, in Tennessee. I have been sent for, and his life may depend upon my going to him. Secretary Stanton has refused the pass; can *you* give it to me?"

Whether it was the pathos of the story or the beauty of the girl, none can tell; but the President was captured, and he reached his hand for the paper on which Secretary Stanton had endorsed his "No," saying :

"Let me see your application," and quickly wrote on a separate sheet :

"If not very detrimental to the public service, grant Miss Priest's request.

"A. L."

Then writing a few lines, which he folded and placed in the same envelope, he said very kindly :

"There, Miss Priest, give this to Secretary Stanton, and I think you will have no further difficulty. Now, God bless you, my child, in your brave undertaking," and, leaning toward her with a significant smile, he added in a low tone: "I think your heart will lead you right— and I think—Colonel Clayton ought to be a very happy man."

Isabel was too glad at her success to mind the blush she knew was dyeing her cheeks way up to the temples, and with just a murmured word of gratitude, presssd his hand and was gone.

He was right ; Secretary Stanton sent back the paper reinforced with still another—an order to "Commanders of the United States forces wherever stationed, to give to the bearer, Isabel Priest, any aid or information that she may ask not absolutely detrimental to the Government service." Then signed, "EDWARD M. STANTON, Secretary of War."

The messenger who gave this to Isabel and her friend said :

"The Secretary will see you for one moment if you will come this way."

They followed him, and were soon in the august presence. Continuing his writing for a while, as if unaware of their presence, he then looked up and motioned for them to approach.

"Which is Miss Priest ?" said he ; and then bowed slightly when Isabel answered that she was the lady.

"Miss Priest, what is the name of the officer you seek ? We may be able to aid you in finding him."

"It is Colonel Clayton, of the First —— Regiment," said she, coloring deeply.

"Clayton ?" he answered abruptly. "I know him— why, he's dead."

"Dead !" said Isabel, sinking into a chair with a look of despair.

"Yes ; the records of this office show that he was killed. Several of his officers saw him and his horse blown to pieces by an exploding shell at the very moment when he was leading a charge on a Confederate battery."

Isabel rallied in an instant.

"I think," she said, "if you will read this you will see that he was alive after the battle to which you allude," and she handed to him Dr. Edward Eve's letter.

The secretary read it carefully.

"Yes," he said, nodding his head ; "I see ; it may be as you say. Of course, I hope so," handing it back to her ; "but officially he is dead. My advice to you, Miss Priest, is to find this Doctor Eve ; that is your surest way."

A nod indicated that the interview was ended ; and in a few hours the two ladies were on their way south, the powerful open sesame ready to remove obstacles by the way.

CHAPTER LXVI.

" Near Richmond, January 6, 186–.

" My Dear Mother:

"Since my last letter, written at Knoxville, we have passed through experiences strange and terrible. No words can ever fitly describe what I have beheld! Think of our spending one whole day in the cars at Chattanooga while the fiercest battle of the war was raging so near us that we heard every detonation, every explosion of shell—saw the smoke, behind which was so much human agony, rolling in billowy masses up the mountain side. Oh, the rush and the roar and the wild tumult of that day! Troops endlessly coming, disembarking and marching to cries of 'Column Left!' 'Forward!' 'Double-quick!' and a thousand other unintelligible commands, all mingled so that we wondered any human being could understand. And then, above all else, the whizzing, hissing cry of the shells, as if a legion of fiends were rushing and shrieking in mid-air. It was hideous! And to know that every separate detonation and volley meant slaughter, or even worse, suffering—awful human suffering! To be in it, it seems to me, would have been less terrible than to sit, as we did, in those motionless cars, and only think and *feel*.

"Toward sunset the sounds grew less frequent, dying gradually with the day, until when the stars came out they shone on a scene of absolute stillness ; and we had been told there was a great victory for our side. Alas! my patriotism seemed dead. How could I rejoice at anything so awful! Was *anything* worth such human sacrifice? This is the question I asked myself as Anna and I went with others, carrying lanterns, to the battle-field, to see if there might not be some living among the dead.

"I cannot dwell upon this now—perhaps some day I may tell you, but not now. Enough to say we rescued a Confederate officer, a Captain Arnold, who is now at the hospital tenderly cared for, instead of being stark and dead, as he would have been before morning if Anna and I had not discovered faint signs of life when others insisted that he was dead.

"And now I come to a strange part of my story. We found by letters about Captain Arnold's person that he was an intimate friend of Dr. Edward Eve, the Confederate surgeon for whom I am looking, who alone can give news of Mr. Clayton.

"We staid a week at the hospital at Chattanooga, and in that time came to know well this Captain Arnold whom we had the happiness of rescuing. His recovery is doubtful, and he made me his confidante, giving me letters and remembrances for the young lady to whom he is engaged, knowing that I was going to Richmond, where Dr. Eve now is, and that I would be able to see her, as she lives just outside the city. My acquaintance with this brave Confederate officer has done much to widen my charity and to enlarge my point of view. Ah! Mother, dear, tell Roland, the valor, the courage, the splendid devotion to a principle, is not all on our side. None could exceed this Southern hero in these qualities; and I have come to understand that his cause is as sacred to him as is ours to us!

"To-morrow we are to see General Grant and try in some way to communicate with Dr. Edward Eve, who is within the city, and perhaps—our friend—our dear friend—is also there, in Libby Prison. All is vague until I see Dr. Eve—which God grant may be soon!

"Kiss my Roland, and tell him to embrace you for
"Your dearly loving daughter,
"ISABEL."

"January 8, 186–.

"MY DEAR MOTHER:

"I write this from a haven of peace! We had no difficulty in finding Miss Henry, Captain Arnold's *fiancée;* and you may imagine our interview, in which she learned of her lover's narrow escape from death! The gratitude of the family knows no bounds, and they insisted that Anna and I should come to their beautiful, stately old home, where we now are, and where we are treated like princesses. Mrs. Henry is a majestic old lady, with a soft white lace cap resting on her snowy hair; and Miss Virginia—well, she is all that she should be, to be the heroine of this romance. If these are typical Southerners, I am afraid I should love them and feel little like killing their sons, and carrying the torch into their households!

"Virginia's story is indeed romantic. Colonel Tucker, Captain Arnold's superior officer, was madly in love with her and insanely jealous of him, and there is little doubt he tried to sacrifice him in the hope of winning her. But he is foiled; for Captain Arnold will not die, and she will yet be his wife.

"I have not seen General Grant, but Colonel Babcock, one of his staff, has promised me that I shall do so to-morrow. There is an occasional interchange, by flag of truce, between the beleaguered city and the army outside, and I can by this means get a letter to Doctor Eve. You may think how terrible it is when I tell you that I long to hear that he whom I seek is in that dreadful prison.

"I will leave this open, and add more to-morrow.

"January 9, 11 P.M.

"Mother darling, this has been a weary and alas! an unfruitful day—a day of strange experiences, of which some time I will tell you and Roland. Fancy my going in an ambulance to a place where there was to be a con-ference by flag of truce, in order to meet General Grant, and there having a glimpse of war behind the scenes, as it were.

"It was a smiling, peaceful landscape, with nothing to indicate the presence of an army; but here and there, from behind fresh mounds of earth, would now and then come a puff of white smoke, soon followed by a loud report.

"I was told we were on the picket-line, and behind these mounds were keen, watchful eyes, losing no chance to lay low an enemy who should carelessly expose him-self—taking deliberate aim, and with no more compunc-tion than if it were a wild bird at which they were firing! Only think how horrible! And then, at a signal which both sides understood, the firing ceases, and there is an interval of amity, when they meet half-way, exchange gos-sip and tobacco for coffee, sugar, flour, etc.; and then, at a signal, each party betakes himself to his post, and war begins again. The eye that smiled and the hands which clasped in friendly recognition, deal out death on the first opportunity.

"We saw a man waving a red flag from a great high tower, up and down, right and left, then fast and slow. 'Why does he expose himself?' I exclaimed. 'He will be shot.' And sure enough, shells began to explode all about the tower where he stood. 'Why does he not come away?' I cried. The officer laughed, and explained to me that he was signalling some movements of troops, and would not think of deserting his post until his message was given. Then, taking his glass, he said, 'I'll tell you what he is saying: 'A small body of men approaching from the direction of Petersburg bearing white flag.' Good! That's our conferees coming to arrange for the exchange of prisoners.'

"Before the Confederate officers arrived I saw General Grant. When, in reply to his questions as to how he might serve me, I said, 'General, I want to go to Richmond,' you should have seen the humorous twinkle with which he said, 'And so do I. So *you* expect to do what I have tried in vain to accomplish with a hundred thousand men, eh? Thus far we have only come within *hailing* distance.'

"But he was kind; and, to make a long story short, Dr. Edward Eve had received my letter, and when the officers came, under escort of the flag of truce, for conference, he was with them. Only think of it! There I stood face to face with him. The eyes which looked into mine had seen *him*. Do you wonder I trembled, and that I cannot now tell you connectedly what he said? But this is what it all meant. Colonel Clayton was *not* in Libby Prison, nor did Dr. Eve know where he was. He had been badly injured by a shell, and was found at the dawn of day by the Confederates apparently dead.

"Then he went on to say: 'His wounds healed like magic, but the shock to his mind was too great for medical skill. I have thought that there was fracture of the skull,' he said, 'but other surgeons examined the wound, and disagreed with me; so no operation was attempted. When we retreated Colonel Clayton was in the hospital, though not strictly a patient or a prisoner. In the hurry and disorder he was missed, and no one could give any account of him beyond the fact that he started with the hospital wagons ; but how far he came, or where he went, no one knows. I have made diligent inquiry so far as I could inside our lines, but without avail.' In answer to my question, he said, ' I think the best place to look for him, Miss Priest, is where he was last seen, Camp Hood, not far from Chattanooga.'

" So, mother dear, we leave our kind, kind friends in the morning, and go back to Chattanooga ; and beyond that, I cannot say.

"Yours, with an aching heart,
" ISABEL."

CHAPTER LXVII.

Once more the two brave women found themselves under the shadow of Lookout Mountain, which rising sheer 2,000 feet, stands like a sugar-loaf amid the billowy hills of " Missionary Ridge," while Chattanooga crouches at its feet.

How Isabel would have loved to take a mad scamper on Tempest up that steep road which climbed the mountain-side! But she felt as if such pleasures were for her nevermore, as they sadly returned to the hospital.

The surgeon, Dr. Crosby, met them kindly, but had no news to tell of Colonel Clayton, whom he had been instructed by them to make inquiries for from all probable sources.

He talked with Anna of his patients. " I am glad you are with us again ; we need your steady hand and cool head, and I do hope you will stay. There is a poor fellow who is to be trepanned this afternoon, who, I think, I shall put in your charge. It is a strange case. He says he is a Confederate officer, but we cannot make out who or what he is. He is mad as a March hare—sometimes thinks he is Raphael. There is a scar which leads me to the suspicion that a violent blow has caused a slight fracture or depression of the skull, which presses on the brain ; at any rate, we are going to work on that theory ; for if he doesn't get relief soon he will die in the mad-house. Now, will you and Miss Priest walk through the wards ? "

Anna called her friend, who was wistfully looking out of the window at a cloud-wreath, which encircled the head of Lookout Mountain. Sighing wearily, she turned and listlessly followed them into the other parts of the building.

Doctor Crosby explained the different cases as they passed along the double row of white cots—but Isabel heard only words—words—words. She felt as if her sympathies were becoming benumbed, under the tension of her overstrained nerves. Finally he paused at a door and said: "Now I will show you the patient I told you of, Miss Plant," and turning the key he opened the door. Alone in the room, there stood a tall, haggard-looking man in Confederate uniform—pencil in hand, with rapt expression, wholly unconscious of their presence.

With a wild cry and a swift movement, Isabel was at his side.

"My beloved!" she said, seizing his hand. "My beloved, it is I—Isabel—look at me!"

The wild eyes turned upon her without a ray of recognition.

"Frank," she went on, in heart-rending tone, "don't you know me? I am your Belle—your 'Belle, with the silver tongue'—your 'Priestess!'—Look at me—you called me to come to you, dear, and I am here; try to remember!"

"I ought to know you," he answered, with a troubled look; "I ought to know you. But, oh!" and the blood surged into his face and throat, "oh! this Vesuvius in my brain!" and loosening his hand from her grasp, he put both his own despairingly on his head.

Isabel slipped down upon the floor at his feet in a dead swoon, and was carried away unconscious and laid upon her own bed, where her friend tenderly tried to restore her.

It seemed as if the effort at recognition had been too much for the unfortunate man, and he was raving like a maniac and imploring to have the volcano opened that the hot lava surging in his brain might escape.

Doctor Crosby made immediate preparations for the operation, Miss Plant in the meantime watching by the still unconscious Isabel. After a long time, the eyelids trembled and the breath began to come softly; then the eyes opened and she realized what had happened.

"Now lie perfectly quiet, dear," said Anna, putting a hand firmly upon her arm.

"I must go to him," said Isabel, feebly. Then realizing the detaining hand of her friend, she said: "Anna, let me go to him; I can bear it; I will be perfectly calm —but I *must* see him."

"Listen," said her friend, very quietly, "you *cannot* go now, dear; by and by you shall; but he must be quiet now, and for *his* sake you must stay here.   Now take this valerian."

Isabel no longer resisted; she took the draught, then fell back on the pillow, white and still as if she were dead.

After some time, Miss Plant softly arose and left her alone, going to seek information of Colonel Clayton's condition, thinking the operation must by this time be over. The doctor smiled reassuringly when he saw her.

"Yes," he said, "it was just as I thought; there was a pressure on the brain ; and, do you know, the instant that was relieved he took up his life precisely at the moment he was injured, and sprang to his feet grasping a long knife from the table and wildly waving it above his head, cried ' Charge ! I say, charge ! and give them a taste of cold steel !' Then he fell back as if he were dead. Now he is asleep, and I think he will awake as sane as you or I."

"Oh, how wonderful it is !" exclaimed Anna. "To think she has found him at last, Doctor ! It was all I could do," she went on, "to keep her quiet after she came to herself. She said she *must* see him."

"Well, I think there will be no harm in her seeing him when he awakens; you may tell her so, and then she will be more contented. But I want *you* to take entire charge of his case. You understand, Miss Plant? My impression is he will have no fever and will come right up ; but she is in no condition just now to nurse any one, poor child ! "

Anna returned with a look of joy on her sympathetic face and told Isabel the good news, who, after the strange fashion of her sex, threw herself into her friend's arms and burst into a fit of hysterical weeping. It seemed as if her very heart were dissolving in tears—the long tension was over—nature found this mode of relief —and now a heavenly calm pervaded her being, and she lay with closed eyes on the bed.

Again she was left alone, as Anna went to inquire about the condition of the patient. When she returned a half-hour later, Isabel had arisen and was coiling her long hair about her shapely head. She looked quickly into Anna's eyes to read the news they bore, and smiled serenely at what she saw there.

"He is sleeping quietly as a child," said Anna, "and

the doctor says, dear, you may go and sit in the room if you will keep out of his sight should he awaken, and on no account speak to him until the doctor gives you permission."

CHAPTER LXVIII.

For hours he slept on, all unconscious who was watching him. And she—of what did she think, as she sat with hands tightly clasped, lips parted, her eyes fixed upon the face she had so longed to see? She had time to recall it all, in those silent hours—the meeting on the prairie—the night by the camp-fire—then his sudden apparition at Coultersville; the rides—the walks—on the mountain-side; the sure growth of that love, which had now usurped supreme control in her life—the rapture of hearing and knowing that he loved her—her own cruel folly in throwing away the happiness—the long days and nights and months of repinings and regrets—the torture of apprehension lest he be killed. Then—that summons in the darkness—that supplicating voice—the outstretched arms—at the very moment he was lying almost in death agony, alone under the stars—and now—he was there! "Oh, God! how merciful!" she murmered again and again.

The softly-shaded lamp was lighted—and still he slept on, the doctor looking in at intervals to see if all was well. A little after eight o'clock he stirred as if about to awaken. Isabel's heart stood still—and then beat so she feared he would hear it. His eyes opened, and he lay calmly looking into space. The doctor entered, quietly felt his pulse and temperature, and said nothing.

Clayton looked at him a moment in silence, and then said:

"Where am I?"

"At the hospital."

"I thought so." Then a pause. "How did the battle go to-day?"

"They beat us," answered the doctor, knowing what that "to-day" meant.

Clayton sighed and said nothing. After another pause:

"Am I badly hurt?"

"No; stunned by a shell."

"Then I must go on with the old round, eh? I must live on?

"Yes."

Clayton again sighed deeply, and was silent.

"I am glad I didn't fall into the hands of the enemy," said he, after a long pause. "I suppose my boys took care of me?"

The doctor nodded, and there was another silence, as he dropped out medicines and arranged powders.

"Doctor," said the patient at last, with sudden impulsiveness, "some of those rascally rebels have taken away a small packet, an amulet, which I wore always suspended about my neck. The chain is here all right," said he, putting his hand to his neck, "but the amulet is gone—and I would rather they had taken my life."

"I'm sorry for that," said the doctor, dropping the white liquid very steadily into a tumbler. "Now, Miss Plant, some water, please."

Frank watched him. "I suppose people usually are glad when you bring them to life, eh, Doctor?"

"Why, yes, they are," said the doctor. "Miss Plant, give this one first, then the other, every half-hour, until he sleeps; but don't awaken him on any account."

Frank's eyes were still fixed upon him.

"I wonder if you have any medicine which can give a man interest in life—which can create a desire to live."

The doctor's eyes rested upon his with a strange look of amusement, as he said: "Why, yes; I think I have precisely that medicine," and with a look of invitation to the waiting girl, he and Miss Plant quickly left the room, closing the door after them—and—Isabel—stood before Frank's bewildered eyes.

He gazed at her as one paralyzed—motion and speech impossible—then putting his hand to his head, he said:

"Am I mad?"

"No, no," she said, sinking upon her knees and laying her head upon his breast; "you are not mad. It is I— it is Isabel. Don't speak—not a word," and she lifted her face, placing her finger on his lips, "because you are ill, dear;" and then, with a divinely lovely smile shining through her tears, "and unless you do just as I say I shall go away. Now, listen—I've come thousands of miles to tell you something—and I have been thinking all the way—what I should say. So now keep perfectly still and listen."

Again she laid her head on his breast, where she heard his heart beating so wildly; then in the same low voice went on:

"I was very cruel that day when I let you go away alone—very cruel to you, and to myself. I repented when it was too late—and I have been *so* unhappy—oh! *so* miserable, dear—and now—I have come to you—and if you will let me stay—I will never—never—leave you any more."

"If I will *let* you stay? *let* you stay?" said he, in a voice suffocating with joy. His arms folded her closer, closer to his heart. "Oh, my dear one, it seems as if I must die with this happiness!"

Many times Doctor Crosby and Miss Plant paused outside that door and listened to the murmur of voices within. At last, as the clock struck ten, the doctor was remorseless and went in quite as he would make his final evening call upon any other of his patients.

"Well," he said, brightly smiling at the transformed look in the sick man's face, "I think my prescription has worked pretty well—you don't look as if you wanted to die just this moment."

"Ah, Doctor," said Clayton, "it was *earth* I was tired of, and *this*," turning with a look of unutterable joy toward Isabel, "*this* is Heaven!"

The doctor's glasses needed wiping for some reason, and at the same moment he looked about for some one to scold.

"I suppose, Miss Priest—you—you have not forgotten to give the medicine—one teaspoonful every half-hour?"

Isabel gave a little cry of alarm as she guiltily sprang to her feet. "What had she done?"

"No?" said the doctor. "Humph—well, I suppose not. I see we shall have to depose you. Now, Miss Plant," turning to that young lady, "I place *you* in charge, and I want this young man to have at least eight or nine solid hours of sleep to-night—do you hear?"

"O Doctor," said Clayton, clinging to Isabel's hand, "don't send her away!"

Isabel rose resolutely, saying: "You are right, quite right, Doctor." Then stooping, she whispered, "It is better so. Good-night, dear love." And Clayton's eyes hungrily followed her till she had vanished.

Clayton could hardly realize, when told by the surgeon, that he had been for months unconscious, and that many battles had been fought and won since the engagement of "yesterday" when he fell in the face of the enemy, and passed through their hands to the hospital where then he rested.

There was a feeling of vague curiosity in the hospital the afternoon of the next day at mysterious preparations which were going on in the room of Colonel Clayton. A large basket of flowers and trailing vines was seen to go in there; and when the chaplain accompanied by the doctor disappeared within, followed soon after by Miss Plant accompanied by Miss Priest, with a cluster of great white roses at her waist and another lying in her beautiful dark hair, the closed door was watched by curious and wondering eyes.

It was even as they suspected, and as Doctor Crosby looked at the girl who sat at the bedside clasping his patient's hand, he thought he had never seen a lovelier bride.

CHAPTER LXIX.

"CAMP NEAR KNOXVILLE, Feb. 8, 186–.

"MY DARLING MOTHER :—

"Here we are at last, at the headquarters of Frank's regiment, where he has come to establish the fact that he is alive.

"Such a strange complication has grown out of his reported death, and it was like surviving himself to come here and see the vacancy filled—a new officer in command of his regiment, and a long list of promotions which would be made void by his unlooked-for return.

"There was such a strange scene when he met his friend, Captain Jack—a glorious fellow, with such a brave great honest heart shining out of his deep-blue eyes. Of course he had mourned Frank as dead, and if you could have seen his expression when he beheld him! and how they embraced like two girls! And then how that great, manly fellow struggled to control his voice, which would break in spite of his efforts, as he said, 'I am rejoiced to see you, but some of the others will not be so glad, I'm afraid.'

"The rapidity of Frank's recovery has been almost miraculous. But you may imagine my joy in the near approach of peace, which will make it unnecessary for him to be exposed again to such perils.

"I can scarcely wait for your letter in reply to mine announcing our marriage. But I know perfectly, dearest mother, that you and Roland will approve, and that you will acquiesce in Frank's new plan that you should join us at The Glen, which he has repurchased. Frank's cousin Kate is having the dear old place renovated, under his directions, and we will live in the house so sacred to him, so associated with the mother he adored and the grandfather he so venerated.

"Only think, we were married with his mother's wedding-ring, which Frank has always worn. Everything was so sudden ; no one had thought of the ring until just at the last moment. Then Frank took this from his finger, and found it fitted me precisely. Oh! it was all so strange and so beautiful ! And, mother, we are so happy !

"Your more than ever fond daughter,

"ISABEL. CLAYTON."

"WILLARD'S HOTEL, WASHINGTON, April 14, 1865.
" MY DEAR MOTHER :—

"We have been here three days, still arranging the tiresome matter about Frank's reported death. Of course he wants his papers certifying to an 'honorable discharge,' dated from the close of the war, while they are, in fact, dated by mistake from the time of his injury or supposed death. It is all such a stupid piece of circumlocution, but will be made right in a day or two, and then we go to New York and await the arrival of Frank's friend Claude ; and after that immediately West. Petrel is with friends of Frank's in St. Louis. Her marriage is, after all, to take place immediately upon Count Davila's arrival, in May. Frank thought they had better wait until she is nineteen, but this impetuous fellow sweeps all obstacles away. I am sure he must be interesting and that we shall be the best of friends. And as for his Petrella —why, I adore her already.

"We go to the theatre to-night. I hear the President is to be there, and to tell the truth, it is more to see him than the play that I am going.

"Your fond daughter,

"ISABEL CLAYTON.

"April 15—I have opened this to add such terrible words ! You will have heard before this reaches you of the awful deed committed last night, and which we witnessed ! Oh! what a moment it was ! We sat where we could look directly into the President's box. He leaned forward to speak to the young lady sitting in the front of the box. I said, ' Frank, look at him now ; that is just the way he looked that day when he whispered " Tell Colonel Clayton I think he ought to be " '—Before I had uttered the words, there was a flash and a report ; a man leaped wildly from the box to the stage ; and they were holding up the President's apparently lifeless form. Then a cry and a tumult :

"'He's shot! The President is shot!'"

"Oh, my God, what a scene! Frank placed me in a carriage and sent me here, while he waited to learn the end. It was one o'clock when he came in with the solemn, awful words :

"'Isabel, the President is dead!'"

CHAPTER LXX.

PETREL'S marriage was fixed for the last day in May. Count Davila was expected to arrive in New York by the steamer from Havre about the 5th; so there Frank and Isabel awaited him, that they might all go West together. It was long since the friends had met, and how much had happened to both since they last looked in each other's eyes! With what pride and happiness Frank presented his beautiful wife need not be told, nor how her sweet, gracious tact soon captured the enthusiastic Claude, who said :

"Ah, my friend, it is no wonder you were miserable when you think you have lost this lovely, this glorious woman ! She is *magnifique !* You must bring her to Italy to see us, my Petrella and me ; and I will astonish, yes, surprise, those people, when I show them these beautiful *Americaines.*"

The wheels could not turn fast enough to suit the mood of this returning lover; and had Frank not been so fond of her himself, the name of Petrella might have become a weariness before they reached St. Louis, where they were to meet her. But while Claude went immediately on, Frank and Isabel determined to carry out a long-anticipated plan of stopping, and visiting the old colony of freedmen at what was now known as Claytonville.

John Stanley and Sam met them at the landing, and there was much to hear and to tell as they drove out to the settlement, which was in a tremendous excitement over the event of the arrival, and no royal visitors could have been treated with more demonstrations of loyalty. Frank was received as a reigning prince and worshipped as a saviour. A holiday was proclaimed, the town dressed with wreaths and triumphal arches, while Uncle Ned headed a procession which met them, and made a speech of welcome ; and Aunt Eliza clasped Frank's knees and wept, and kissed the beautiful wife's hands again and again. Never had Isabel imagined such an experience ;

and looking into her husband's eyes that night she said, with an expression of profound humility :

"How honored I feel by your love. Your life is devoted to making others happy—and *I* thought you were not good enough for me ! What contempt you must have felt for me !"

Petrel was waiting for them at the station, and, of course, Claude with her. One carriage seldom holds four people so completely happy as the one which conveyed them to the hotel that lovely afternoon.

Frank looked at his ward, actually dazzled by her brilliant loveliness.

"Why, Petrel," he said, holding both her hands and looking into her face as they rolled along, " I cannot believe it is you."

Claude had had a similar surprise on his own arrival, and watched with delight Frank's looks of admiration.

"It's all because I'm so happy, Uncle Frank," the young girl whispered in his ear; and neither of the others were jealous when he put his arm around her and kissed her on one rosy cheek.

Petrel and Isabel were close friends in an instant.

"What am I to call you ? " said Petrel, shyly. "Aunt Isabel would be so absurd : you look like my older sister. And," she said, with a pretty blush, as they stood together in Isabel's room, before dinner, " how beautiful you are ! " Then, with her arms encircling her waist, "No wonder Uncle Frank was unhappy ! Why, do you know, dear, it used to break my heart to look into his sad face, and—may I tell you ? And—I did not like you at all—because you had made him suffer so."

" You dear, frank child," said the young wife, laughing such a gay, happy laugh ; " you could not have thought as bad things of me as I did of myself. But I shall tell you all about it. Ah, there is *so* much to tell and to hear—and only two short weeks ! "

" Yes, but you know, Claude will bring me home again next summer, and then, he says, you are coming to visit us next winter. Oh, how beautiful it all is ! " and she clasped her hands in a kind of rapture, at the excess of joy which had come into her life.

CHAPTER LXXI.

But, alas! these were halcyon hours. That very evening Martha, Petrel's faithful maid, was taken ill with a cold. Fever set in; the doctor came, and pronounced it pneumonia of the most fatal type; and two days later she breathed her last in Petrel's arms.

The poor girl was overwhelmed with grief, which even Claude could not console. She reproached herself, thinking in the preoccupation of her own happiness she had not realized the severity of the cold, and said again and again: "I was selfish! and perhaps I neglected her."

With a premonition of her approaching death, Martha had indicated where she wished to be buried; and there, with many tears, they laid her, with the solemn rites of the Catholic Church.

The day succeeding the funeral, Petrel busied herself sadly, collecting all her dear nurse's clothing and little treasures, packing them safely away as something sacred. She stopped to read now and then some letters of her own or her Uncle Frank's, recalling the time and circumstances with sad retrospection.

One letter of her uncle's she was about to destroy with others when a line, which she idly read, turned her to stone. It was this:

"It is but right that you, as her mother, should decide whether this marriage shall take place; and I shall delay my reply to Count Davila until I hear from you. God forgive me! but when I saw her place that rosebud in the hand of her dead father, I had bitter thoughts of that cruel man which even death could not efface."

Petrel could not move, but sat with her eyes fixed upon those cruel words, going over them again and again until they seemed burned into her very brain.

Then she tried to stand, and supporting herself by the furniture, reached the door and locked and bolted it; then fell prone upon the floor in a paroxysm of despair. She knew not how long she laid there. After a time some one knocked, then tried the door ; and she kept perfectly still. Again she heard a light step outside and Isabel's voice said :

"Petrel ! Petrel, dear !"

But all was still as the grave. It was growing dark, and now there were two persons outside, and her Uncle Frank's voice said :

"Are you there, Petrel ?"

What should she do? She gathered all her forces, arose, and went to the door.

"Please, Uncle Frank, do not ask to come in ; I cannot see any one now."

"Are you ill ? "

"No ; but I want to be alone. Please go away."

"But, my child, we are anxious about you."

"I am not ill ; don't be anxious ; only please let me be alone for a while."

Her voice sounded so strange to herself ! Later, Isabel's again said :

"Dearest, I have brought you a cup of tea and some toast. I will not come in if you do not want me, but you must take this—for *our* sakes, dear."

The door was opened, and a cold little hand received the tray, and drawing it into the room again locked the door.

But the hardest trial was when she heard the step of her lover. How well she knew it !

"Petrella, may I not speak with you ? For just one moment ? You will not deny me that."

The distracted girl went to the door and said, so that he could just hear it :

"Claude, if you love me, you will not ask me to see any one to-night."

She groped her way in the darkness to where the matches were kept, and lighted the gas ; then picked up the letter which lay on the floor, and read again the words which had destroyed her happiness forever. What ravages those ten hours of suffering had made already ! She smiled bitterly as she saw her reflection in the glass.

"Countess, indeed !" she said, with scornful emphasis. "*I*—child of a slave—and then—oh ! the shame of it ! "

said she, shuddering, as she covered her face with her hands. "The shame of it! Worse than nameless! *I*, to be the daughter of the Countess Giuletta! And some day—when he—when Claude knows—see his cheek crimson with mortification at his wife's disgrace! O God, there's no place for me here. I am a blot upon existence. Where shall I go? What *must* I do?—I must think."

And alone she tried, poor child, to arrange the cruel problem of her existence—sitting, for she knew not how long, motionless—her eyes fixed on space.

Sometimes in the stillness which now wrapped the hotel she heard a soft footstep outside. Was it the porter—the night watchman—or was it Claude—or Isabel—watching the light streaming through the cracks of her door?

At last she got up—opened her desk. "It is the only way," she said; "the only way," and her trembling hand wrote, folded and directed three letters. One was addressed to Frank Clayton, the other to Claude, and another to

"JOHN WILSON,
    "Superintendent of Riverview Cemetery,
          "St. Louis, Mo."

She opened her check-book, and filling out a check put it into the last-named letter. Then, selecting a few things from her wardrobe, packed a small handbag.

With a trembling hand she unlocked a trunk and took out a red Morocco case, with crest and monogram on the cover—she could not resist the temptation—opened it once more and gazed at the two beautiful faces; then closed it, as if it were a coffin closing upon the dead.

Another miniature she gazed at with despair and love in her eyes.

"Why should I not keep that? Oh, my beloved," she said, bursting into an agony of weeping, "my beloved; you will suffer too—but it is better so!"

The eyes looked out at her so kindly, that a wild hope came into her heart. She imagined herself telling him, and his saying: "What do I care for that? Do you not know that nothing could make me give you up?" She almost felt as if she heard him say these blessed words;

but no, he was so noble, so honorable ; he might refuse to release her, but none the less he would feel humiliated. No—no—no ; it must all go. Her ring—ah ! that was the hardest—all together, in one package—and then addressed to

"COUNT CLAUDIUS DAVILLA."

CHAPTER LXXII.

THE gray dawn was creeping into the window, making
the gas look sickly and pale. She put it out, and threw
herself down upon the bed in utter exhaustion, just as
she was, in her dressing-gown. She was awakened by
hearing a voice at her door. The room was flooded
with brilliant sunlight. It was Isabel.

"Petrella, darling, I have brought a cup of coffee.
Will you let me give it to you?"

She rose, and took the tray as before. A dozen rose-
buds, fresh, cool, and dewy, lay beside her coffee-cup.
Their fragrance smote her with such strange anguish!

"May I not come in, dear?"

Petrel was about to yield, when she saw the letters and
package on her desk.

"Dear Isabel," she said gently, "please do not think
badly of me—but—I cannot let you come in now. Come
back in about two hours, and I will see you."

"Very well, dear. I need not tell you who the flowers
are from. Poor fellow! He was out hours ago, before
the shops were open, to get them for you."

Isabel reported to Claude and Frank the promise Petrel
had given.

"And now you must take some breakfast, too," she
playfully said to Claude. "I declare, I believe you
spent the whole night in that hall, and you look ill yourself this morning. There, drink this coffee. I assure
you, it is just as we told you; she is simply nervous, and
overcome by the shock of Martha's death, and then arranging her things yesterday, revived recollections. She
is a tender, sensitive child, and you will have to take
good care of her, Claude. You must cherish her carefully."

"Ah! will I not?" said he, smiling rapturously.

At precisely the time appointed, Isabel returned. She
found the door unlocked, and Petrel sitting in an easy-
chair, carefully dressed and perfectly calm.

"Why, my darling girl," she said, embracing her. Then looking at her pallid face, her strange, haggard expression, she added, anxiously: "You are making yourself ill, dear; it is wrong to grieve so; of course it is natural that you should feel sorrow, but not to give way to it in such excess. Why, my child, your hands are like ice. Let me warm them. Did you drink your coffee? Yes? Well, now, for the sake of others, you must be brave; you must think of Claude's happiness."

"I am thinking of nothing else," said the miserable girl, hopeless tears coursing down her cheeks.

"Well, he has been like one distracted, dear; he has consented at last to drive with us; we thought it would divert him—and he has ordered some flowers, which we are to place on dear Martha's grave," and she stroked the little hand soothingly. "He thought perhaps you would go too?—No?—Well, perhaps it is better not. Now, when we come home," she added, brightly, "you will not shut yourself up here any more, dear?"

Petrel shook her head.

"That's a good child," kissing her. "Remember, one week from to-day is your wedding-day. Why, Petrel—Petrel, what is it, dear?" Then, with troubled, questioning eyes, she added softly, "You are *sure*, dear, that you love Claude?"

"Love him! More than my own life!"

"Well then, dear, there is no reason why all should not be beautiful as a dream; no reason why you should not be as happy as—as we are. What can I say more than that?" And such a radiant smile shone out upon the hopeless face before her.

"And now—now—I must go—they are waiting for me," and she kissed the young girl, who clung to her with a strange intensity. As she reached the door she looked back with another bright smile:

"Remember, no more locking of doors."

"No."

"You promise?"

"Yes, I promise."

CHAPTER LXXIII.

THE day was beautiful beyond description, and the breath of flowers and the promise of near joys of summer dissipated all thoughts of sadness, as they drove back in the open landau. The river flowed majestically in its turbid splendor, and as they watched the out-going steamer, with its freight, Claude thought with supreme gladness that after one more week he and Petrella would be on board of that same vessel, on their way to St. Paul!

Arriving at the hotel, Isabel said :

"Now, Frank, you go, and bring Petrel to our room, and Claude and I will wait for her there."

Frank Clayton went with glad step to the door, tapped lightly, and without waiting, entered. It was empty. He looked about, with a feeling of bewilderment, and conspicuously placed on the desk, saw two letters, addressed, as we already know, to himself and Claude.

His hand could scarcely break the seal. An awful prescience of calamity paralyzed him. From the opened letter dropped another—a folded piece of paper; he saw his own handwriting. "Good God!" he uttered, as with horror he read the words he had written to Martha—then the following :

"MY DEAR, DEAR, GOOD GUARDIAN AND FRIEND :—

"My dream of happiness is over. You have been like an angel to me—you and your beautiful wife. But I must go; there is no other way. I have thought and thought, and I can see no escape but in effacing my wretched existence. It would be easy to end it all—but—I cannot do that—God save me from that sin! I love Claude too much to bring this shame upon him. So, farewell! Try to think kindly of

"Your unhappy

"PETREL."

Claude and Isabel waited ; and when Clayton returned

with that terrible look in his face they were smitten with vague terror.

"She's not there—read those," he gasped ; and thrusting the letters into Claude's hand, he seized his hat and ran in wild haste down-stairs.

Claude was too bewildered at first to understand fully—then uttered a cry of pain, as if mortally wounded, and rushed like a madman after Clayton, whom he met returning.

"Where is she?" said he, seizing his arm.

"Just as I supposed ; she was on that steamer. Come, we can overtake her."

In another moment the two men were driving furiously toward the river. A small steamboat had just landed her passengers; and five minutes later they were on the bosom of the great stream they had idly watched a half-hour ago—in pursuit of the out-going steamer. More and more steam was put on, in answer to their entreaties; and in an hour they could see the vessel ahead of them. Nearer, nearer, they came, until they could distinguish people moving about her deck. On, on, they went, silent, and intent only upon the looming object in front of them. The sun was sinking in dying splendor, when suddenly there seemed an excitement upon the deck of the steamer, and oh, horror ! there was smoke rising out of the hatchway. A moment later her head was turned toward the shore. The increasing volume of dense smoke, with red tongues of flame, shot forth, showing the conflagration must have been well under way before discovered.

The pursuing vessel was now near enough to distinguish individuals amid the wild confusion which prevailed upon the upper-deck of the doomed steamer.

"There she is ! There she is !" cried Claude, wildly ; and, stretching out his arms, called, " Petrella ! O my Petrella !"

Yes, it was she, standing by the rail, her long gray veil floating in the wind, her eyes fastened upon the little boat, and her face fixed and white as if frozen.

"We come for you, my Petrella. You are safe !" said Claude, wildly waving to her. "Do not flee from me ! Come, come !" and he held out his arms.

They could not hear the cry of recognition, but as she extended her arms, as if in supplication, the look of despair melted into an expression of hope and almost of rapture ; and as she folded her hands tightly across her heart, she eagerly bent forward, as if to read what was in those two faces she had never hoped to see again. So intent was this gaze, she seemed not to heed the flames, whose breath she must have felt now.

"Stay where you are !" shouted the men. "We will save you !"

At that moment a gust of wind caught up a billowy mass of smoke and flame, and swept it right across the spot where she stood. Through it they saw something which looked like a bird with outstretched wings descending into the water.

The black, lurid waves rolled slowly away, but they seemed to have swallowed up Petrella. She was gone. When she felt the fiery breath of that sheet of smoke and flame, she had sought refuge in the water. Swift as thought the small boat was lowered, and three men were in it, silent, horror-stricken, as, with oars bending under the strain, they shot toward the spot which had engulfed her. Once she had risen to the surface, and now a second time they saw her come up from the cruel depths into the fading sunlight.

Strong arms caught her and drew her into the boat. There was no sign of life in the form Claude clasped in almost delirious joy. Back they went to the waiting steamboat, carrying tenderly their precious burden.

Restoratives were applied. "'Tain't no use," the captain said, pointing to a slight contusion on the temple. "That's what done it. She hit somethin' floatin' in the water."

He was right : there was no use. The poor, tired heart made one or two faint attempts to take up its work, then stopped. Petrella was dead !

Again the great hotel was enshrouded in darkness, excepting only the long, dimly-lighted halls. Again the young girl was back in her own room, not wringing her hands and uttering piteous ejaculations, but lying upon her bed, and oh, so white and still ! That soft, lace-trimmed gown was made by Martha's loving hands, and many visions of her darling's happiness were wrought into its snowy folds ; and now she lies within it cold and still.

There was no more to be done. Isabel had dismissed her attendants, and sank, exhausted with weeping, into a chair—the same in which she had seen the poor child, a few hours ago. The door opened, and the two men entered, Clayton half-supporting his friend, who, with a wild, heart-rending cry, sank down by the side of the bed.

Appalled by his frenzied grief, Isabel clung affrighted to her husband.

"Dearest," he whispered, "you must not witness this. It is too terrible," and placing his arm about her, drew her tenderly out of the room, softly closing the door upon Claude and his dead bride.

CHAPTER LXXIV.

A great eclipse had fallen upon their joy. Still the roses bloomed brightly at The Glen that summer; the trees waved their pliant branches in languorous rapture in the breeze; and the sun shone just as gladly as if its rays did not fall on that freshly-sodded mound.

There were glad hearts when the gentle mother and Roland came from the Pacific Coast.

Kate Fletcher, who now occupied Beechwood, her old home, and Isabel became the dearest of friends, and the attachment which swiftly ripened between Roland and the fair young Katrine knit their hearts together by a new bond under the genial rays of a Kentucky sun.

At last Kate knew why Frank Clayton had so persistently defeated her desire to meet Petrel: the tragic fate of the poor child was so intertwined with all the threads of her sad story, he could no longer conceal it. But time had softened early resentments and grief, and none mourned the loss of the beautiful Petrella more than Bernard Fletcher's widow.

Letters, heart-rending letters, came from Claude, from Sorrento. His grief was beyond earthly consolation.

"Do you know, Frank," Isabel said, "I should not be at all surprised if dear Claude should take orders in a monastery. He is devout, and he is hopelessly wretched; so what is more natural?"

It seemed like old times to have Ned and Eliza there; for, much as they loved Claytonville, those two devoted people would come back to the old place when they found "Mars Frank" was going to make it his home.

As Clayton sat dreaming upon the piazza, he heard Eliza say, "Miss Belle, you see dat big apple-tree over yonder? Well, dat's just whar Mars Frank stood on his pony, all mixed up wid de blossoms dat day, when I called Miss Fanny to come and look at him."

Her young mistress was always a willing listener to such reminiscences, especially when they were about "Miss Fanny" and "Mars Frank"; and, as their voices were lost in the distance, Frank thought of his mother, and then of the present; and a great peace settled upon his heart.

He recalled his childhood, his grief at his mother's death, the dawning sense of the injustice of slavery as he grew older, the atrocities committed upon Ned, the struggles with his uncle and Bernard, and finally the manumission and colonization of his negroes.

Then recollections both bright and sad crowded upon him, as he saw Isabel, Petrel, Duvall, John Brown—the struggle in Kansas—the four years of horrible fratricidal strife—drifted past his mental vision. How much suffering there had been! What hours terrible to endure, what moments which were burnt into his brain! And then, what joy, what peace! And as he looked up, and saw his wife coming through the trees, beautiful, fresh, and lovelier than the flowers on her breast, a great wave of gladness swept over him.

She was holding in her hand a long envelope which she gave to her husband, saying: "Kate's maid has just brought this from her mistress at Beechwood. I told her to wait, as it might need a reply."

Frank opened the package which contained some folded sheets of foolscap, and a half sheet of note-paper.

Was that Kate's writing? He examined its broken, tremulous lines in surprise and wonder.

"Read this. It has just come addressed to papa, evidently sent by some one unaware of his death. My God! what does it all mean? Unhappy girl! And I—I brought much added suffering into her life! God forgive me, and all of us! Too late—too late for reparation now!

"KATE."

Amazed and bewildered by these incoherent words, Frank opened the long, soiled sheets covered with strange scrawling characters, and read as follows:

"The following is the sworn statement of Ben Baugh made in view of his approaching death."

"I swear to God, that the story i am goin ter tell is trew.

"In the year 184– Thomas Hawks cum to me one day and sed he had a job that wud pay him a big pile er money, but he must have sumbody to help him, an if i cud keep a silent tung in my head, he'd go snacks with me. Well, the long and short of it wuz, i sed i wud ; then he tole me how a great swell over in Italy wanted ter git rid of a kid, that there was a big fortune which wud cum to him, if she wuz out er ther way, caus he wuz next er Kin, i never knowd jest how much Swag Hawks was to git, but he promised me 5000 dollars if i helped him threw and got ther gurl in New Orleans all rite, where i cud sell her easy, and the money fur the sale was throwd in for my shair, caus he didn't want ter have nothink ter do with it on this side ther water, so i went into ther cussed biz-ness. It took a mity deal of plannin and waitin and a deal of money, too, but the swell over in Italy he fixed that all rite.

"I went over there and wuz nigh onto a year hangin round and waitin, fust in Rome then in Sorento, where they had a house big as the City Hall, with grounds like a park and fountens and white statures and windin walks and fellers with red coats trimmed with gold lace, a hangin round the big portico all the time, and when the kid cum out to play ther wuz nurses with caps and ribunds runnin after her every minnit. So agin and agin we slipt up, till it looked like we never wud git a chants at hur, but wun day, she cum dartin down the side of the hege aloan, and quickern a flash, i clapt my big coat over hur, and stopt hur mouth with my hand so she cudnt screem, and in 2 seconds we wuz in a carriage an in 2 minnits more we wuz outer site. It makes me kinder sick to think about that baby how she took on that day, it seem'd like shed go inter fits, then she got wore out, and laid kinder stupid like, we had her safe on board ship that nite. An italyan woman with a red hankerchuft tide round hur hed and big gold hoops in hur eers took her on bord and made out like it wuz hur own baby. Nobody suspected, cause all hur fine close wuz took off and hur long curls cut short. I uset to feel sorry for the pore little thing, she moaned and moaned fit to brake yur hart, and wud call *Madray, Madray*, and then the woman wud giv her suth-

ing outen a bottle an shed quiut down agin and go off
sorter stoopid like, she got so thin her own muther wodnt
er knowd hur, and i thout shed dye, i wish now i had tole
the hole cussed story wen we got to New Orleans and let
Hawks do his wust—dam him—wen we got to New
Orleans i put her on a plantation whair a frend of mine
wuz overseer, so shed play with the little niggers and git
to be jest like them in hur ways, but she never did a mite.
She wuz only 3 years old but she knowd hur own name,
and wen ennybody called her Martha she wud stamp hur
little foot and say no, no, Cecilia, til she foun she got a
beatin evry time she dun it, and at last she giv up and
dursnt say Cecilia no more, but that wuz hur name, and
the name of the cove that got rid of hur and got her fortune is—*I forgit it now*, but i think it is Valerias and he
lived near Sorento. And all i hope iz that this iznt
too late to have hur rites given to hur, and that blak
harted villin punisht for what he dun to hur, and fur git-
ten me into a scrape witch has ruind mi life fur i aint had
a minnits peace sence i dun it. Wunst in New Orleans,
nigh onto 10 years after i went to the theatur and seen
jest sutch a grate White Cassle and grouns and flunkies
standin round drest in red coats and silk stockins, and i
bolted outer that theatur zif i wuz shot. Well to continue
mi story—i took her up to the slave market at New
Orleans long with a likely wench pritty nye white who
wuz goin ter be sold. An she vowed to Mr. Stanly who
took a grate fancy to the child that twas hur gurl but she
sed, she hopd hed buy hur caus he lookt like hed be kind
to hur, the minnit he clapt eyes on her he sed, thats jest
wot i want fur a present fur mi Kate, i tole him the price
an he pade it rite down and went off with ther gurl pleased
as ennything, i knowd the woman was savin up money to
by hur freedom to jine hur husband whod run away
north, so I tole hur if she helpt me this way and made out
the girl wus hurs, i wud give hur a 20 dollar gold peace,
an i dun it too, hur name is Ofelia Jonson, and if you cood
find her shed tell yer this is God's truth that i'm tellin,
hur husband wuz coachmen to a rich swell in the north
somewhar, an i guess she jined him thair if she didnt die,
fur she was mity determind and wuz sot on goin so that
wuz all i knowd about the gurl til more an 15 years after,
wen i met Hawks on a steamer comin down the river and

he was in mity high sperrits about a gurl hed jist bought. Somehow i found out she uset to belong to Jedge Stanly of Kentucky—and i jumpt 6 feet—"by God," I sed, "Hawks, do you know who she is?"—"No," he sed—"what do you mean?"—"Take a good look at hur," sez i, "does she look much like a nigger!—do you know who i sold that italian kid to 15 years ago? to Jedge Stanly of Kentucky." Hawks turned wite as a sheet. "You don't say so," he sez, kinder scart, then he watched her, and walked roun her a good menny times eyeing hur, an i saw him go up and talk to hur in a soft kinder coaxin way an i knowd what he was plannin, the scoundril, an i sed, sez i, "Tom Hawks, if you harm that gurl or her baby i'll tell the hole damd story, cuss me if i don't," an he sed, "Don't you try ter bluster round me, Ben, your deeper in it than i am." Well i lost site of hur after that, i wisht i hadnt, i wisht i had braved him, the bully, but i didn't, and after he wuz dead i dazn't tell mi part in it, but now its out, and may God have mercy on mi sole and forgive this wickid deed as i am expectin soon to die.

"BEN BAUGH.

"Witnessed
    "James Ferguson.
    "Sarah Miller."

Was it strange that Isabel and Kate wept, and that Clayton's heart was torn and wrung as he came to understand the cruel circumstances which had brought about such tragic results? What would he not have given to have brought back life to those two beings lying cold and still under the sod; to have been able to tell them the tidings contained in this dying confession; to have made late reparation to that gentle woman who had served them as a menial, while all the time there was patrician blood in her veins! Oh, it was cruel! And to have said to her daughter: "Lift up your head, my child. You do not belong to a despised race. Your blood is *not* tainted. Your husband's family, proud though they be, need not fear to have it mingle with their own."

But it was too late. The curtain had dropped on mother and child.

There was but one thing to be done now. Clayton sat down to the task with a heavy heart, and the outgoing mail carried to Claude the whole harrowing story. He knew well the wild yearnings and regrets it would awaken. But it must be done.

Then they waited for the wailing cry of anguish which was sure to come back from the Italian shores.

Grief, vain regrets and despair were poured out upon the closely-written pages which soon came as they expected. Then with beating hearts Clayton, Isabel, and Kate Fletcher read these words:

"You ask if I heard of this abduction years ago. Alas! Who did not hear of it? Was not all Italy talking about it? So my mother has often told me, and people are yet wondering and wondering; for they are a family *tres exaltée*, very distinguished, and the little girl had very large estates.

"And now it turns out that it was all the work of that monster, that assassin. He ruined my father's life, and broke his heart; and now it was *he* who planned this devilish, fiendish plot. He it was who employed those men to steal the child. Only think, if I have not reason to curse him! My Petrella! My Petrella! Think you I should not call him assassin?—Such grief, such shame— when there was no cause! Oh, my God! All my life I heard about this event. The disappearance of this child. Her mother became insane and died in one year. They thought the little girl must have strayed to the waters' edge and slipped in. No one suspected him, for was he not far away?—up the river Nile with some friends? The cunning monster! And, when they wrote him the intelligence, was he not so grieved they felt almost sorry for him when he came back all dressed in deep black, and took possession of her estates? Ah yes, he played his part well!

"And now, my dear, dear friends, I have only one thing to ask, and I ask it on my knees. It will be the only consolation which can come to me before I join her. Will you permit the dear remains of my beloved—my bride —to come here with her mother's and rest, as they should, in the tomb of their ancestors? It is a fair spot, looking out on the Mediterranean. Will this not be one act of justice to the mother who was cruelly torn from this same place? If you will grant my prayer, I will go once more to your land and I will bring home my bride.—But oh ! My God ! How different from my hopes ! How *can* I bear this ! Do you not pity my suffering, my despair ?"

"I think I should have killed myself in these last days but for one thing. My Church has saved me that, and will be my refuge when my darling's ashes are finally laid away."

Long and earnest were the conferences over this appeal. However painful to their own feelings, Kate and Isabel strongly advised that it be done.

"It is the only way now in which anything approaching restoration to their rights can be effected," urged Isabel. So it was decided.

A few weeks later Claude arrived.

What ravages those months had made ! Pale—haggard—a look of intense suffering in his eyes, they felt inexpressibly shocked at the change.

It was with many misgivings that they turned their faces toward St. Louis. How would he endure such cruel tearing open of his wound? But an awful calm seemed to have taken possession of him.

They went to the same hotel. With what terrible vividness the events leading to the tragedy arose before them ! Again they drove to the Cemetery, as on that fatal day, and in bewildered surprise beheld, at the head of the mother's grave a simple, white marble cross, on which was inscribed only:

MY MOTHER.
June 30th., 1865.

Had she come back to pay this last tribute to that mother? When was it done?

It was on a beautiful autumnal day that the ashes of the child who was stolen away years ago, touched once more the soil of her native home, and the promised bride of Claude reposed under the olive-trees, in the land of their happy dreams.

FINIS.